LORETTA CHASE

Lord of Scoundrels

AVON

An Imprint of HarperCollinsPublishers

This is a work of fiction. Names, characters, places, and incidents are products of the author's imagination or are used fictitiously and are not to be construed as real. Any resemblance to actual events, locales, organizations, or persons, living or dead, is entirely coincidental.

AVON BOOKS
An Imprint of HarperCollins*Publishers*
10 East 53rd Street
New York, New York 10022-5299

Copyright © 1995 by Loretta Chekani
Excerpts from *Love Letters From a Duke* copyright © 2007 by Elizabeth Boyle; *A Touch of Minx* copyright © 2007 by Suzanne Enoch; *Halfway to the Grave* copyright © 2007 by Jeaniene Frost; *Lord of Scoundrels* copyright © 1995 by Loretta Chekani
ISBN: 978-0-380-77616-0
ISBN-10: 0-380-77616-2
www.avonromance.com

First Avon Books paperback printing: January 1995

10   9   8

He *would* tame her...
and if that meant
marriage, then
so be it!

Dear Reader,

Lord of Scoundrels was and remains a special book for me. When Avon announced plans to reissue it in a splendid new package, I was thrilled.

As many of you know, we authors can be fragile creatures. Pale and wan, we toil in our garrets, talking to people who don't exist. Our tender egos hoard the snippets of praise that come our way from time to time, saving them to get us through a Really Bad Writing Day. Such praise is the main way we learn whether our efforts have been appreciated, or at least noticed.

This reissue represents a special kind of appreciation, reflecting the honor readers have done me, in their letters, in the many awards they've given this book, and in their voting *Lord of Scoundrels* an all-time favorite.

Some respond most strongly to Dain, the embodiment of "The Beast" as a hero—if that Beast hides a heart of mush deep inside a wicked exterior, a shell about as penetrable as a rhinoceros hide, as Dain himself admits. Others take to heart the indomitable Jessica, who'll do anything for her family (and who has far too much fun doing it, if you ask me).

I've been asked many times how these characters came to me. What were my inspirations, my models? As the fond parent, all I can say is, I don't know exactly where they got their genes or their manners, but I'm very, very proud of them. I truly hope you welcome them into your own bookshelf family, and that you enjoy their company as much as I (still) do!

Sincerely,

Loretta

By Loretta Chase

NOT QUITE A LADY
THE LAST HELLION
LORD OF SCOUNDRELS
CAPTIVES OF THE NIGHT

Coming Soon

YOUR SCANDALOUS WAYS

Thanks to: Sal Raciti, for the choice Italian phrases; Carol Proko Easton, for the loan of her splendid books on Russian icons; Cynthia Drelinger, for computer processing my pencil hieroglyphics; and my husband, Walter, and our friend, Owen Halpern, for an unforgettable journey through England's beautiful west country.

Prologue

In the spring of 1792, Dominick Edward Guy de Ath Ballister, third Marquess of Dain, Earl of Blackmoor, Viscount Launcells, Baron Ballister and Launcells, lost his wife and four children to typhus.

Though he'd married in obedience to his father's command, Lord Dain had developed a degree of regard for his wife, who had dutifully borne him three handsome boys and one pretty little girl. He'd loved them insofar as he was able. This was not, by average standards, very much. But then, it wasn't in Lord Dain's nature to love anybody at all. What heart he had was devoted to his lands, particularly Athcourt, the ancestral estate in Devon. His property was his mistress.

She was an expensive one, though, and he wasn't the wealthiest of men. Thus, at the advanced age of two and forty, Lord Dain was obliged to wed again and, to satisfy his mistress's demands, to marry pots of money.

Late in 1793, he met, wooed, and wed Lucia Usignuolo, the seventeen-year-old daughter of a wealthy Florentine nobleman.

Society was stunned. The Ballisters could trace their line back to Saxon times. Seven centuries earlier, one of them had wed a Norman lady and received a barony from William I in reward. Since then, no Ballister had ever married a foreigner. Society concluded that the Marquess of Dain's mind was disordered by grief.

Not many months later, His Lordship himself gloomily suspected that his mind had been disordered by something. He had married, he thought, a very beautiful raven-haired girl who gazed at him adoringly and smiled and agreed with every word he uttered. What he'd wed, he found out, was a dormant volcano. The ink was scarcely dry on the marriage lines before she began to erupt.

She was spoiled, proud, passionate, and quick-tempered. She was recklessly extravagant, talked too much and too loudly, and mocked his commands. Worst of all, her uninhibited behavior in bed appalled him.

Only the fear that the Ballister line would otherwise die out kept him returning to that bed. He gritted his teeth and did his duty. When at last she was breeding, he quitted the exercise and began praying fervently for a son, so he wouldn't have to do it again.

In May of 1795, Providence answered his prayers.

When he got his first look at the infant, though, Lord Dain suspected it was Satan who'd answered them.

His heir was a wizened olive thing with large black eyes, ill-proportioned limbs, and a grossly oversize nose. It howled incessantly.

If he could have denied the thing was his, he would have. But he couldn't, because upon its left buttock was the same tiny brown birthmark in the shape of a crossbow that adorned Lord Dain's own anatomy. Generations of Ballisters had borne this mark.

Unable to deny the monstrosity was his, the marquess decided it was the inevitable consequence of lewd and unnatural conjugal acts. In his darker moments, he believed his young wife was Satan's handmaiden and the boy the Devil's spawn.

Lord Dain never went to his wife's bed again.

The boy was christened Sebastian Leslie Guy de Ath Ballister and, according to the custom, took his father's second highest title, Earl of Blackmoor. The title was apt enough, the wags whispered behind the marquess's back, for the child had inherited the olive complexion, obsidian eyes, and crow black hair of his mother's family. He was also in full possession of the Usignuolo nose, a noble Florentine proboscis down which countless maternal ancestors had frowned upon their inferiors. The nose well became the average Usignuolo adult male, who was customarily built upon the monumental scale. Upon a very small, awkwardly proportioned little boy, it was a monstrous beak.

Unfortunately, he'd inherited the Usignuolos' acute sensitivity as well. Consequently, by the time he was seven years old, he was miserably aware that something was wrong with him.

His mother had bought him a number of handsome picture books. None of the people in the books looked anything like him—except for a hook-nosed, hump-backed devil's imp who perched on Little Tommy's shoulder and tricked him into doing wicked things.

Though he'd never discerned any imps upon his shoulder or heard any whisper, Sebastian knew he must be wicked, because he was always being scolded or whipped. He preferred the whippings his tutor gave him. His father's scolds made Sebastian feel hot and clammy cold at the same time, and then his stomach would feel as though it were filled with birds, all flapping their wings to get out, and then his legs would shake. But he dared not cry, because he was no longer a baby, and crying only made his father angrier. A look would come into his face that was worse even than the scolding words.

In the picture books, parents smiled at the children and cuddled and kissed them. His mama did that sometimes, when she was in a happy mood, but his papa never did. His father never talked and played with him. He'd never taken Sebastian for a ride on his shoulders or even up in front of him on a horse. Sebastian rode his own pony, and it was Phelps, one of the grooms, who taught him.

He knew he couldn't ask his mother what was wrong with him and how to fix it. Sebastian had learned not to say much of anything—except that he loved her and she was the prettiest mama in the world—because nearly everything else upset her.

Once, when she was going to Dartmouth, she'd asked what he'd like her to bring back. He'd asked for a little brother to play with. She had started crying, and then she'd grown angry and screamed bad words in Italian. Though Sebastian didn't know what all the words meant, he knew they were wicked, because when Papa heard them, he scolded her.

Then they would quarrel. And that was worse even than his mother's crying and his father's angriest look.

Sebastian didn't want to cause any horrible quarrels. He especially didn't want to provoke his mama into saying the wicked words, because God might get angry, and then she'd die and go to Hell. Then no one would cuddle and kiss him, ever.

And so there was no one Sebastian could ask what

was wrong and what to do, except his Heavenly Father. But He never answered.

Then, one day, when Sebastian was eight years old, his mother went out with her maid and didn't come back.

His father had gone to London, and the servants told Sebastian his mother had decided to go there, too.

But his father came back very soon, and Mama wasn't with him.

Sebastian was summoned to the dark study. His papa, looking very grim, sat at an immense desk, his Bible open before him. He ordered Sebastian to sit. Trembling, Sebastian obeyed. That was all he could do. He couldn't speak. The wings were flapping so hard in his stomach that it was all he could do *not* to throw up.

"You are to stop plaguing the servants about your mother," his father told him. "You are not to speak of her again. She is an evil, godless creature. Her name is Jezebel, and 'The dogs shall eat Jezebel by the wall of Jezreel.'"

Somebody was screaming very loud in Sebastian's head. So loudly that he could hardly hear his father. But his father didn't seem to hear the screaming. He was looking down at the Bible.

"'For the lips of a strange woman drop as an honeycomb, and her mouth is smoother than oil,'" he read. "'But her end is bitter as wormwood, sharp as a two-edged sword. Her feet go down to earth; her steps take hold on hell.'" He looked up. "I renounce her, and rejoice in my heart that the corruption has fled the house of my fathers. We will speak of it no more."

He rose and pulled the bell rope, and one of the footmen came and led Sebastian away. Still, even after the study door closed, even while they hurried down the stairs, the screaming in Sebastian's head wouldn't stop. He tried covering his ears, but it went on, and then all he could do was open his mouth and let it out in a long, terrible howl.

When the footman tried to quiet him, Sebastian kicked and bit him, and broke away. Then all the wicked words came out of his mouth. He couldn't stop them. There was a monster inside him and he couldn't stop it. The monster snatched a vase from a table and hurled it at a mirror. It grabbed a plaster statue and sent it crashing to the floor. It ran down the great hall, screaming, and breaking everything it could reach.

All the upper servants rushed toward the noise, but they shrank from touching the child, each and every one certain he was possessed by demons. They stood, frozen with horror, watching Lord Dain's heir apparent reduce the Great Hall to a shambles. No word of rebuke, no sound at all, came from the floor above. His Lordship's door remained shut—as though against the devil raging below.

At last the enormous cook lumbered in from the kitchen, picked the howling boy up, and, oblivious to his kicking and punching, hugged him. "There now, child," she murmured.

Fearing neither demons nor Lord Dain, she took Sebastian to the kitchen and, banishing all her helpers, sat down in her great chair before the fire and rocked the sobbing child until he was too exhausted to cry anymore.

Like the rest of the household, Cook was aware that Lady Dain had eloped with the son of a wealthy shipping merchant. She had not gone to London, but to Dartmouth, where she'd boarded one of her lover's ships and departed with him for the West Indies.

The boy's hysterical sobs about dogs eating his mother made the cook want very much to take a meat cleaver to her master. The young Earl of Blackmoor was the ugliest little boy anyone had ever seen in all of Devon—and possibly Cornwall and Dorset as well. He was also moody, quick-tempered, and generally unappealing. On the other hand, he was only a little boy, who deserved better, she thought, than what Fate had dealt out to him.

She told Sebastian that his mama and papa did not get along, and his mama had become so very unhappy that she ran away. Unfortunately, running away was an even worse mistake for a grown-up lady than it was for a little boy, Cook explained. It was such a bad mistake that it could never be fixed, and Lady Dain could never come back.

"Is she going to Hell?" the boy asked. "Papa s-said—" His voice wobbled.

"God will forgive her," Cook said firmly. "If He is just and merciful, He will."

Then she took him upstairs, chased his stern nursemaid away, and put him to bed.

After she had gone, Sebastian sat up and took from his bedstand the small picture of the Blessed Virgin and the Baby Jesus his mother had given him. Hugging it to his chest, he prayed.

He had been taught all the proper prayers of his father's faith, but this night he uttered the one he'd heard his mother say, holding the long strand of beads in her hand. He'd heard it so many times that he knew it by heart, though he hadn't yet learned enough Latin to understand all the words.

"*Ave Maria, gratia plena, Dominus tecum, benedicta tu in mulieribus,*" he began.

He did not know that his father stood outside the door listening.

He did not know that the popish prayer was, to Lord Dain, the very last straw.

A fortnight later, Sebastian was bundled into a carriage and taken to Eton.

After a brief interview with the headmaster, he was abandoned to the immense dormitory and the tender mercies of his schoolmates.

Lord Wardell, the oldest and largest in the immediate vicinity, stared at Sebastian for a very long time, then burst into laughter. The others promptly followed suit. Sebastian stood frozen listening to what seemed like thousands of howling hyenas.

"No wonder his mama ran away," Wardell told the company when he found his breath again. "Did she scream when you were born, Black-a-moor?" he asked Sebastian.

"It's *Blackmoor*," Sebastian said, clenching his fists.

"It's what I say it is, insect," Wardell informed him. "And I say your mama bolted because she couldn't stomach the sight of you another minute. Because you look precisely like a filthy little earwig." Clasping his hands behind his back, he slowly circled the bewildered Sebastian. "What do you say to that, Black-a-moor?"

Sebastian gazed at the faces sneering down at him. Phelps, the groom, had said he would find friends at school. Sebastian, who'd never had anyone to play with, had clung to that hope through the long, lonely journey.

He saw no friends now, only mocking faces—and all well above his head. Every single boy in the vast Long Chamber was older and bigger than he was.

"I asked a question, earwig," Wardell said. "When your betters ask a question, you'd best answer."

Sebastian stared hard into his tormentor's blue eyes. "*Stronzo*," he said.

Wardell lightly cuffed his head. "None of that macaroni gibberish, Black-a-moor."

"*Stronzo*," Sebastian repeated boldly. "Bumhole turd."

Wardell lifted his pale eyebrows and gazed at his assembled comrades. "Did you hear that?" he asked them. "It isn't enough he's ugly as Beelzebub, but he's got a filthy mouth besides. What's to be done, my lads?"

"Toss him," said one.

"Dunk him," said another.

"In the crapping case," another added. "Looking for turds, ain't he?"

This suggestion met with howling enthusiasm.

In an instant, they were upon him.

Several times en route to his doom, they gave Sebastian a chance to recant. He had only to lick Wardell's boots and beg forgiveness and he would be spared.

But the monster had taken hold of him, and Sebastian answered defiantly with a string of all the wicked English and Italian words he'd ever heard.

Defiance didn't help him much at the moment. What helped was certain laws of physics. Small as he was, he was awkwardly formed. His bony shoulders, for instance, were too wide to fit into the privy. All Wardell could do was stuff Sebastian's head into the hole and hold it there until he threw up.

The incident, to Wardell and his comrades' irritation, did not teach the earwig respect. Though they devoted the better part of their free time thereafter to educating him, Sebastian wouldn't learn. They mocked his looks and his mixed blood and made up filthy songs about his mother. They dangled him by his feet from windows, tossed him in blankets, and hid dead rodents in his bed. Privately—though there was precious little privacy at Eton—he wept with misery, rage, and loneliness. Publicly, he cursed and fought, though he always lost.

Between constant abuse outside of the classroom and regular floggings inside, it took Eton less than a year to thrash out of him every inclination toward affection and gentleness and trust. Etonian methods brought out the best in some boys. In him they awakened the worst.

When he was ten years old, the headmaster took him aside and told Sebastian his mother had died of a fever in the West Indies. Sebastian listened in stony silence, then went out and picked a fight with Wardell.

Wardell was two years older, twice his size and weight, and quick besides. But this time the monster inside Sebastian was cold, bitter fury, and he fought coldly, silently, and doggedly until he'd knocked his nemesis down and bloodied his nose.

Then, battered and bleeding himself, Sebastian swept a sneering gaze round the circle of onlookers.

"Anyone else?" he asked, though he could scarcely find breath for the words.

No one uttered a sound. When he turned to leave, they made way for him.

When Sebastian was halfway across the yard, Wardell's voice broke the strange silence.

"Well done, Blackmoor!" he shouted.

Sebastian stopped in his tracks and looked round. "Go to Hell!" he shouted back.

Then Wardell's cap flew into the air, accompanied by a cheer. In the next instant, scores of caps were flying, and everyone was cheering.

"Stupid sods," Sebastian muttered to himself. He doffed an imaginary hat—his own was trampled beyond redemption—and made a farcical, sweeping bow.

A moment later, he was surrounded by laughing boys, and in the next, he was hoisted onto Wardell's shoulders, and the more he verbally abused them, the better the idiots liked it.

He soon became Wardell's bosom bow. And then, of course, there was no hope for him.

Among all the hellions being thrashed and bullied toward manhood at Eton at the time, Wardell's circle was the worst. Along with the usual Etonian pranks and harassment of the hapless locals, they were gambling, smoking, and drinking themselves sick before they reached puberty. The wenching commenced promptly thereafter.

Sebastian was initiated into the erotic mysteries on his thirteenth birthday. Wardell and Mallory—the boy who'd advised privy dunking—primed Sebastian with gin, blindfolded him, dragged him hither and yon for an hour or more, then hauled him up a flight of stairs into a musty-smelling room. They stripped him naked and, after removing the blindfold, left, locking the door behind them.

The room contained one reeking oil lamp, a dirty straw mattress, and a very plump girl with golden ringlets, red cheeks, large blue eyes, and a nose no bigger than a button. She stared at Sebastian as though he were a dead rat.

He didn't have to guess why. Though he'd shot up two inches since his last birthday, he still looked like a hobgoblin.

"I won't do it," she said. Her mouth set mulishly. "Not for a hundred pounds."

Sebastian discovered that he did have some feelings left. If he hadn't, she couldn't have hurt them. His throat burned and he wanted to cry and he *hated* her for making him want to. She was a common, stupid little sow, and if she'd been a boy, he would have thrashed her to kingdom come.

But hiding his feelings had become a reflex by now.

"That's too bad," he said coolly. "It's my birthday, and I was feeling so good-humored that I was thinking of paying you ten shillings."

Sebastian knew Wardell had never paid a tart more than sixpence.

She gave Sebastian a sulky look which strayed down to his masculine article. And lingered there. That was enough to attract *its* attention. It promptly began to swell.

Her pouting lip quivered.

"I told you I was in a good humor," he said before she could laugh at him. "Ten and six, then. No more. If you don't like what I've got, I can always take it somewhere else."

"I 'spect I could close my eyes," she said.

He gave her a mocking smile. "Open or shut, it's all the same to me—but I'll 'spect my money's worth."

He got it, too, and she didn't shut her eyes, but made all the show of enthusiasm a fellow could wish.

There was a life lesson in it, Sebastian reflected later, and he grasped that lesson as quickly as he'd done every other.

Thenceforth, he decided, he must take his motto from Horace: "Make money, money by fair means if you can, if not, by any means money."

From the time he'd entered Eton, the only communications Sebastian received from home were single-sentence notes accompanying his quarterly allowance. His father's secretary wrote the notes.

When Sebastian was nearing the end of his time at

Eton, he received a two-paragraph letter outlining arrangements for his studies at Cambridge.

He knew that Cambridge was a fine university, which many considered more progressive than monkish Oxford.

He also knew that his father had not chosen Cambridge for this reason. The Ballisters had attended Eton and Oxford practically since the time those institutions were founded. To send his son anywhere else was the closest Lord Dain could come to disowning him. It announced to the world that Sebastian was a filthy stain on the ancestral escutcheon.

Which he most certainly was.

He not only behaved like a monster—albeit never quite badly enough before authority figures to be expelled—but had become one in physical fact: well over six feet tall and every inch dark and brutally hard.

He had spent the better part of his Eton career making sure he would be remembered as a monster. He was proud of the fact that decent people called him the Bane and Blight of the Ballisters.

Until now, Lord Dain had given no sign that he noticed or cared what his son did.

The terse letter proved otherwise. His Lordship meant to punish and humiliate his son by banishing him to a university no Ballister had ever set foot in.

The punishment came too late. Sebastian had learned several effective modes of responding to attempts to manage, punish, and shame him. He had found that money, in many cases, was far more effective than physical force.

Taking his motto from Horace, he had learned how to double, triple, and quadruple his allowance in games of chance and wagers. He spent half his winnings on women, diverse other vices, and private Italian lessons—the last because he wouldn't let anyone suspect he was at all sensitive about his mother.

He had planned to buy a racehorse with the other half of his winnings.

He wrote back, recommending that his parent use the allotted funds to send a *needy* boy to Cambridge, because the Earl of Blackmoor would attend Oxford and pay his own way.

Then he bet his racehorse savings on a wrestling match.

The winnings—and influence exerted by Wardell's uncle—got Sebastian to Oxford.

The next time he heard from home, Sebastian was four and twenty years old. The one-paragraph message announced his father's death.

Along with the title, the new Marquess of Dain inherited a great deal of land, several impressive houses—including Athcourt, the magnificent ancestral pile on the fringes of Dartmoor—and all their attendant mortgages and debts.

His father had left his affairs in an appalling state, and Sebastian hadn't the smallest doubt why. Unable to control his son, the dear departed had determined to ruin him.

But if the pious old bastard was smiling in the hereafter, waiting for the fourth Marquess of Dain to be hauled to the nearest sponging house, he was doomed to a very long wait.

Sebastian had by now discovered the world of commerce, and set his brains and daring to mastering it. He'd earned or won every farthing of his present comfortable income himself. In the process, he had turned more than one enterprise on the edge of bankruptcy into a profitable investment. Dealing with his father's paltry mess was child's play.

He sold everything that wasn't entailed, settled the debts, reorganized the backward financial system, dismissed the secretary, steward, and family solicitor, installed replacements with brains, and told them what was expected of them. Then he took one last ride through the moors he hadn't seen since his childhood, and departed for Paris.

One

Paris—March 1828

"No. It can't be," Sir Bertram Trent whispered, aghast. His round blue eyes bulging in horror, he pressed his forehead to the window overlooking the Rue de Provence.

"I believe it is, sir," said his manservant, Withers.

Sir Bertram dragged his hand through his tousled brown curls. It was two o'clock in the afternoon and he'd only just changed out of his dressing gown. "Genevieve," he said hollowly. "Oh, Lord, it is her."

"It is your grandmother, Lady Pembury, beyond doubt—and your sister, Miss Jessica, with her." Withers suppressed a smile. He was suppressing a great deal at the moment. The mad urge to dance about the room, shouting hallelujah, for instance.

They were saved, he thought. With Miss Jessica here, matters would soon be put right. He had taken a great risk in writing to her, but it had to be done, for the good of the family.

Sir Bertram had fallen among Evil Companions. The evilest of companions in all of Christendom, in Withers' opinion: a pack of wastrel degenerates led by that monster, the fourth Marquess of Dain.

But Miss Jessica would soon put a stop to it, the elderly manservant assured himself as he speedily knotted his master's neckcloth.

Sir Bertram's twenty-seven-year-old sister had inherited her widowed grandmother's alluring looks: the silken hair nearly blue-black in color, almond-shaped silver-grey eyes, alabaster complexion, and graceful figure—all of which, in Lady Pembury's case, had proved immune to the ravages of time.

More important, in the practical Withers' view, Miss Jessica had inherited her late father's brains, physical agility, and courage. She could ride, fence, and shoot with the best of them. Actually, when it came to pistols, she was the best of the whole family, and that was saying something. During two brief marriages, her grandmother had borne four sons by her first husband, Sir Edmund Trent, and two by her second, Viscount Pembury, and daughters and sons alike had bred males in abundance. Yet not a one of those fine fellows could outshoot Miss Jessica. She could pop the cork off a wine bottle at twenty paces—and Withers himself had seen her do it.

He wouldn't mind seeing her pop Lord Dain's cork for him. The great brute was an abomination, a disgrace to his country, an idle reprobate with no more conscience than a dung beetle. He had lured Sir Bertram—who, lamentably, was not the cleverest of gentlemen—into his nefarious circle and down the slippery slope to ruin. Another few months of Lord Dain's company and Sir Bertram would be bankrupt—if the endless round of debauchery didn't kill him first.

But there wouldn't be another few months, Withers reflected happily as he nudged his reluctant master to the door. Miss Jessica would fix everything. She always did.

Bertie had managed a show of surprised delight to see his sister and grandmother. The instant the latter had retired to her bedchamber to rest from the journey, however, he yanked Jessica into what seemed to be the drawing room of the narrow—and much too expensive, she reflected irritably—*appartement*.

"Devil take it, Jess, what's this about?" he demanded.

Jessica picked up the mass of sporting papers heaped upon an overstuffed chair by the fire, threw them onto the grate, and sank down with a sigh into the cushioned softness.

The carriage ride from Calais had been long, dusty, and bumpy. She had little doubt that, thanks to the abominable condition of French roads, her bottom was black and blue.

She would very much like to bruise her brother's bottom for him at present. Unfortunately, though two years younger, he was a head taller than she, and several stone heavier. The days of bringing him to his senses via a sturdy birch rod were long past.

"It's a birthday present," she said.

His unhealthily pale countenance brightened for a moment, and his familiar, amiably stupid grin appeared. "I say, Jess, that's awful sweet of—" Then the grin faded and his brow furrowed. "But my birthday ain't until July. You can't be meaning to stay until—"

"I meant Genevieve's birthday," she said.

One of Lady Pembury's several eccentricities was her insistence that her children and grandchildren address and refer to her by name. "I am a woman," she would say to those who protested that such terminology was disrespectful. "I have a name. Mama, Grandmama . . ." Here she would give a delicate shudder. "So *anonymous*."

Bertie's expression grew wary. "When's that?"

"Her birthday, as you ought to remember, is the day after tomorrow." Jessica pulled off her grey kid boots, drew the footstool closer, and put her feet up. "I wanted her to have a treat. She hasn't been to Paris in ages, and matters haven't been pleasant at home. Some of the aunts have been muttering about having her locked up in a lunatic asylum. Not that I'm surprised. They've never understood her. Did you know, she had three marriage offers last month alone? I believe Number Three was the straw that broke the camel's back. Lord Fangiers is four and thirty years old. The family says it's embarrassing."

"Well, it ain't exactly dignified, at her age."

"She's not dead, Bertie. I don't see why she should behave as though she were. If she wishes to wed a pot boy, that's her business." Jessica gave her brother a searching look. "Of course, it would mean that her new husband would have charge of her funds. I daresay that worries everybody."

Bertie flushed. "No need to look at me that way."

"Isn't there? You appear rather worried yourself. Maybe you had an idea she'd bail you out of your difficulties."

He tugged at his cravat. "Ain't in difficulties."

"Oh, then I must be the one. According to your man of business, paying your present debts will leave me with precisely forty-seven pounds, six shillings, threepence for the remainder of the year. Which means I must either move in with aunts and uncles again or work. I spent ten years as unpaid nanny to their brats.

I do not intend to spend another ten seconds. That leaves work."

His pale blue eyes widened. "Work? You mean, *earn wages?*"

She nodded. "I see no acceptable alternative."

"Have you gone loony, Jess? You're a *girl*. You get shackled. To a chap who's plump in the pocket. Like Genevieve done. Twice. You got her looks, you know. If you wasn't so confounded picky—"

"But I am," she said. "Fortunately, I can afford to be."

She and Bertie had been orphaned very young, and left to the care of aunts, uncles, and cousins barely able to support their own burgeoning broods. The family might have been comfortably well off if there hadn't been so very many of them. But Genevieve descended from a line of prolific breeders, especially of males, and her offspring had inherited the talent.

That was one of the reasons Jessica received so many marriage offers—an average of six per annum, even at present, when she ought to be on the shelf, wearing a spinster's cap. But she'd be hanged before she'd marry and play brood mare to a rich, titled oaf—or before she'd don dowdy caps, for that matter.

She had a talent for unearthing treasures at auctions and secondhand shops, and selling same at a tidy profit. Though she wasn't making a fortune, for the last five years she had been able to buy her own fashionable clothes and accessories, instead of wearing her relatives' castoffs. It was a modest form of independence. She wanted more. During the past year, she had been planning how to get more.

She had finally saved enough to lease and begin stocking a shop of her own. It would be elegant and very exclusive, catering to an elite clientele. In her many hours at Society affairs, she'd developed a keen understanding of the idle rich, not only of what they liked but also of the most effective methods of drawing them in.

She meant to start drawing them in once she'd hauled her brother out of the mess he'd got himself into. Then she'd see to it that his mistakes never again disrupted her well-ordered life. Bertie was an irresponsible, unreliable, rattlebrained ninny. She shuddered to imagine what the future held for her if she continued to depend upon him for anything.

"You know very well I don't need to marry for money," she told him now. "All I need do is open the shop. I've selected the place and I've saved enough to—"

"That cork-brained rag-and-bottle-shop scheme?" he cried.

"Not a rag and bottle shop," she said calmly. "As I've explained to you at least a dozen times—"

"I won't let you set up as a shopkeeper." Bertie drew himself up. "No sister of mine will go into trade."

"I should like to see you stop me," she said.

He screwed up his face into a threatening scowl.

She leaned back in the chair and gazed at him contemplatively. "Lud, Bertie, you look just like a pig, with your eyes all squeezed up like that. In fact, you've grown amazingly piglike since last I saw you. You've gained two stone at least. Maybe as much as three." Her gaze dropped. "And all in your belly, by the looks of it. You put me in mind of the king."

"That *whale?*" he shrieked. "I do not. Take it back, Jess."

"Or what? You'll sit on me?" She laughed.

He stalked away and flung himself onto the sofa.

"If I were you," she said, "I'd worry less about what my sister said and did, and more about my own future. I can take care of myself, Bertie. But you . . . Well, I believe you're the one who ought to be thinking about marrying somebody plump in the pocket."

"Marriage is for cowards, fools, and women," he said.

She smiled. "That sounds like the sort of thing some drunken jackass would announce—just before falling into the punch bowl—to a crowd of his fellow drunken jackasses, amid the usual masculine witticisms about fornication and excretory processes."

She didn't wait for Bertie to sort through his mind for definitions of the big words. "I know what men find hilarious," she said. "I've lived with you and reared ten male cousins. Drunk or sober, they like jokes about what they do—or want to do—with females, and they are endlessly fascinated with passing wind, water, and—"

"Women don't have a sense of humor," Bertie said. "They don't need one. The Almighty made them as a permanent joke on men. From which one may logically deduce that the Almighty is a female."

He uttered the words slowly and carefully, as though he'd taken considerable pains to memorize them.

"Whence arises this philosophical profundity, Bertie?" she asked.

"Say again?"

"Who told you that?"

"It wasn't a drunken jackass, Miss Sneering and Snide," he said smugly. "I may not have the biggest brain box in the world, but I guess I know a jackass when I see one, and Dain ain't."

"Indeed not. He sounds a clever fellow. What else does he have to say, dear?"

There was a long pause while Bertie tried to decide whether or not she was being sarcastic. As usual, he decided wrong.

"Well, he *is* clever, Jess. I should have realized you'd

recognize it. The things he says—why, that brain of his is always working, a mile a minute. Don't know what he fuels it with. Don't eat a lot of fish, you know, so it can't be that."

"I collect he fuels it with gin," Jessica muttered.

"Say again?"

"I said, 'I reckon his brain's like a steam engine.'"

"Must be," said Bertie. "And not just for talking, either. He's got the money sort of brains, too. Plays the 'Change like it was a fiddle, the fellows say. Only the music Dain makes come out is the 'chink, chink, chink' of sovereigns. And that's a lot of chinks, Jess."

She had no doubt of that. By all accounts, the Marquess of Dain was one of England's wealthiest men. He could well afford reckless extravagance. And poor Bertie, who couldn't afford even modest extravagance, was bent on imitating his idol.

For idolatry it surely was, as Withers had claimed in his barely coherent letter. That Bertie had exerted his limited faculties so far as to actually *memorize* what Dain said was incontrovertible proof that Withers hadn't exaggerated.

Lord Dain had become the lord of Bertie's universe . . . and he was leading him straight to Hell.

Lord Dain did not look up when the shop bell tinkled. He did not care who the new customer might be, and Champtois, purveyor of antiques and artistic curiosities, could not possibly care, because the most important customer in Paris had already entered his shop. Being the most important, Dain expected and received the shopkeeper's exclusive attention. Champtois not only did not glance toward the door, but gave no sign of seeing, hearing, or thinking anything unrelated to the Marquess of Dain.

Indifference, unfortunately, is not the same as deafness. The bell had no sooner ceased tinkling than Dain heard a familiar male voice muttering in English accents, and an unfamiliar, feminine one murmuring in response. He could not make out the words. For once, Bertie Trent managed to keep his voice below the alleged "whisper" that could be heard across a football field.

Still, it was Bertie Trent, the greatest nitwit in the Northern Hemisphere, which meant that Lord Dain must postpone his own transaction. He had no intention of conducting a bargaining session while Trent was by, saying, doing, and looking everything calculated to drive the price up while under the delirious delusion he was shrewdly helping to drive it down.

"I say," came the rugby-field voice. "Isn't that—Well, by Jupiter, it *is*."

Thud. Thud. Thud. Heavy approaching footsteps.

Lord Dain suppressed a sigh, turned, and directed a hard stare at his accoster.

Trent stopped short. "That is to say, don't mean to interrupt, I'm sure, especially when a chap's dickering with Champtois," he said, jerking his head in the proprietor's direction. "Like I was telling Jess a moment ago, a cove's got to keep his wits about him and mind he don't offer more than half what he's willing to pay. Not to mention keeping track of what's 'half' and what's 'twice' when it's all in confounded francs and sous and what you call 'em other gibberishy coins and multiplying and dividing again to tally it up in proper pounds, shillings, and pence—which I don't know why they don't do it proper in the first place except maybe to aggravate a fellow."

"I believe I've remarked before, Trent, that you might experience less aggravation if you did not upset the balance of your delicate constitution by attempting to *count*," said Dain.

He heard a rustle of movement and a muffled sound somewhere ahead and to his left. His gaze shifted thither. The female whose murmurs he'd heard was bent over a display case of jewelry. The shop was exceedingly ill lit—on purpose, to increase customers' difficulty in properly evaluating what they were looking at. All Dain could ascertain was that the female wore a blue overgarment of some sort and one of the hideously overdecorated bonnets currently in fashion.

"I particularly recommend," he went on, his eyes upon the female, "that you resist the temptation to count if you are contemplating a gift for your *chère amie*. Women deal in a higher mathematical realm than men, especially when it comes to gifts."

"That, Bertie, is a consequence of the feminine brain having reached a more advanced state of development," said the female without looking up. "She recognizes that the selection of a gift requires the balancing of a profoundly complicated moral, psychological, aesthetic, and sentimental equation. I should not recommend that a mere male attempt to involve himself in the delicate process of balancing it, especially by the primitive method of *counting*."

For one unsettling moment, it seemed to Lord Dain that someone had just shoved his head into a privy. His heart began to pound, and his skin broke out in clammy gooseflesh, much as it had on one unforgettable day at Eton five and twenty years ago.

He told himself that his breakfast had not agreed with him. The butter must have been rancid.

It was utterly unthinkable that the contemptuous

feminine retort had overset him. He could not possibly
be disconcerted by the discovery that this sharp-tongued
female was not, as he'd assumed, a trollop Bertie had
attached himself to the previous night.

Her accents proclaimed her a *lady*. Worse—if there
could be a worse species of humanity—she was, by the
sounds of it, a bluestocking. Lord Dain had never before in his life met a female who'd even heard of an
equation, let alone was aware that one balanced them.

Bertie approached, and in his playing-field confidential whisper asked, "Any idea what she said, Dain?"

"Yes."

"What was it?"

"Men are ignorant brutes."

"You sure?"

"Quite."

Bertie let out a sigh and turned to the female, who
still appeared fascinated with the contents of the
display case. "You promised you wouldn't insult my
friends, Jess."

"I don't see how I could, when I haven't met any."

She seemed to be fixed on something. The beribboned and beflowered bonnet tilted this way and that
as she studied the object of her interest from various
angles.

"Well, do you want to meet one?" Trent asked impatiently. "Or do you mean to stand there gaping at that
rubbish all day?"

She straightened, but did not turn around.

Bertie cleared his throat. "Jessica," he said determinedly, "Dain. Dain—Drat you, Jess, can't you take
your eyes off that trash for one minute?"

She turned.

"Dain—m'sister."

She looked up.

And a swift, fierce heat swept Lord Dain from the crown of his head to the toes in his champagne-buffed boots. The heat was immediately succeeded by a cold sweat.

"My lord," she said with a curt nod.

"Miss Trent," he said. Then he could not for the life of him produce another syllable.

Under the monstrous bonnet was a perfect oval of a porcelain white, flawless countenance. Thick, sooty lashes framed silver-grey eyes with an upward slant that neatly harmonized with the slant of her high cheekbones. Her nose was straight and delicately slender, her mouth soft and pink and just a fraction overfull.

She was not classic English perfection, but she was some sort of perfection and, being neither blind nor ignorant, Lord Dain generally recognized quality when he saw it.

If she had been a piece of Sevres china or an oil painting or a tapestry, he would have bought her on the spot and not quibbled about the price.

For one deranged instant, while he contemplated licking her from the top of her alabaster brow to the tips of her dainty toes, he wondered what her price was.

But out of the corner of his eye, he glimpsed his reflection in the glass.

His dark face was harsh and hard, the face of Beelzebub himself. In Dain's case, the book could be judged accurately by the cover, for he was dark and hard inside as well. His was a Dartmoor soul, where the wind blew fierce and the rain beat down upon grim, grey rocks, and where the pretty green patches of ground turned out to be mires that could suck down an ox.

Anyone with half a brain could see the signs posted: "ABANDON ALL HOPE, YE WHO ENTER HERE" or, more to the point, "DANGER. QUICKSAND."

Equally to the point, the creature before him was a lady, and no signs had to be posted about her to warn him off. Ladies, in his dictionary, were listed under Plague, Pestilence, and Famine.

With the return of reason, Dain discovered that he must have been staring coldly at her for rather a while, because Bertie—bored, evidently—had turned away to study a set of wooden soldiers.

Dain promptly collected his wits. "Was it not your turn to speak, Miss Trent?" he asked in mocking tones. "Were you not about to make a comment on the weather? I believe that's considered the proper—that is, *safe*—way to commence a conversation."

"Your eyes," she said, her gaze perfectly steady, "are very black. Intellect tells me they must be merely a very dark brown. Yet the illusion is . . . overpowering."

There was a quick, stabbing sensation in the environs of his diaphragm, or his belly, he couldn't tell.

His composure faltered not a whit. He had learned composure in hard school.

"The conversation has progressed with astonishing rapidity to the personal," he drawled. "You are fascinated by my eyes."

"I can't help it," she said. "They are extraordinary. So very *black*. But I do not wish to make you uncomfortable."

With a very faint smile, she turned back to the jewelry case.

Dain wasn't certain what exactly was wrong with her, but he had no doubt something was. He was Lord Beelzebub, wasn't he? She was supposed to faint, or recoil in horrified revulsion at the very least. Yet she had gazed at him as bold as brass, and it had seemed for a moment as though the creature were actually *flirting* with him.

He decided to leave. He could just as well wrestle with this incongruity out of doors. He was heading for the door when Bertie turned and hurried after him.

"You got off easy," Trent whispered, loud enough to be heard at Notre Dame. "I was sure she'd rip into you—and she will rip if she's a mind to, and don't care who it is, either. Not but what you could handle her, but she does give a fellow a headache, and if you was thinking of going for a drink—"

"Champtois has just come into possession of an automaton you will find intriguing," Dain told him. "Why don't you ask him to wind it up so that you can watch it perform?"

Bertie's square face lit with delight. "One of them what-you-call-'ems? Truly? What does it do?"

"Why don't you go look?" Dain suggested.

Bertie trotted off to the shopkeeper and promptly commenced babbling in accents any right-thinking Parisian would have considered grounds for homicide.

Having distracted Bertie from his apparent intention of following him, Lord Dain had only to take another few steps to be out the door. But his gaze drifted to Miss Trent, who was again entranced with something in the jewel case, and eaten by curiosity, he hesitated.

Two

*A*bove the whirring and clicking of the automaton, Jessica heard the marquess's hesitation as clearly as if it had been a trumpet's blare at the start of battle. Then he marched. Bold, arrogant strides. He'd made up his mind and he was coming in with heavy artillery.

Dain *was* heavy artillery, she thought. Nothing Bertie or anyone else could have told her could have prepared her. Coal black hair and bold, black eyes and a great, conquering Caesar of a nose and a sullen sensuality of a mouth—the face alone entitled him to direct lineage with Lucifer, as Withers had claimed.

As to the body . . .

Bertie had told her Dain was a very large man. She had half expected a hulking gorilla. She had not been prepared for a stallion: big and splendidly proportioned— and powerfully muscled, if what his snug trousers outlined was any indication. She should not have been looking *there*, even if it was only an instant's glance, but a physique like that demanded one's attention and drew it . . . everywhere. After that unladylike instant, it had taken every iota of her stubborn willpower to keep her gaze upon his face. Even then, she'd only managed the feat because she was afraid that otherwise she'd lose what little remained of her reason, and do something horribly shocking.

"Very well, Miss Trent," came his deep voice, from somewhere about a mile above her right shoulder. "You have piqued my curiosity. What the devil have you found there that's so mesmerizing?"

His head might be a mile above her, but the rest of his hard physique was improperly close. She could smell the cigar he had smoked a short time ago. And a subtle— and outrageously expensive—masculine cologne. Her body commenced a repeat of the slow simmer she had first experienced moments earlier and had not yet fully recovered from.

She would have to have a long talk with Genevieve, she told herself. These sensations could not possibly be what Jessica suspected they were.

"The watch," she said composedly. "The one with the picture of the woman in the pink gown."

He leaned closer to peer into the case. "She's standing under a tree? Is that the one?"

He set his expensively gloved left hand upon the case, and all the saliva evaporated from her mouth. It was a very large, powerful hand. She was rivetingly aware that one hand could lift her straight off the floor.

"Yes," she said, resisting the urge to lick her dry lips.

"You'll want to examine it more closely, I'm sure," he said.

He reached up, removed a key from a nail on the rafter, moved to the back of the case, unlocked it, and took out the watch.

Champtois could not have failed to notice this audacity. He uttered not a syllable. Jessica glanced back. He seemed to be deep in conversation with Bertie. "Seemed" was the significant word. What one generally meant by conversation was, with Bertie, barely within the realms of probability. *Deep* conversation—and in French—was out of the question.

"Perhaps I had better demonstrate how the thing operates," said Dain, yanking her attention back to him.

In his low voice, Jessica recognized the too innocent tones that inevitably preceded a male's typically idiotic idea of a joke. She could have explained that, not having been born yesterday, she knew very well how the timepiece operated. But the glint in his black eyes told her he was mightily amused, and she didn't want to spoil his fun. Yet.

"How kind," she murmured.

"When you turn this knob," he said, demonstrating, "as you see, her skirts divide and there, between her legs, is a—" He pretended to look more closely. "Good heavens, how shocking. I do believe that's a fellow kneeling there." He held the watch closer to her face.

"I'm not shortsighted, my lord," she said, taking the watch from him. "You are quite right. It is a fellow— her lover apparently, for he seems to be performing a lover's service for her."

She opened her reticule, took out a small magnifying glass, and subjected the watch to very narrow study, all the while aware that she was undergoing a similar scrutiny.

"A bit of the enamel has worn off the gentleman's wig and there is a minute scratch on the left side of the lady's skirt," she said. "Apart from that, I would say the watch is in excellent condition, considering its age, though I strongly doubt it will keep precise time. It is not a Breguet, after all."

She put away the magnifying glass and looked up to meet his heavy-lidded gaze. "What do you think Champtois will ask for it?"

"You want to buy it, Miss Trent?" he asked. "I strongly doubt your elders will approve of such a purchase. Or have English notions of propriety undergone a revolution while I've been away?"

"Oh, it isn't for me," she said. "It's for my grandmother."

She had to give him credit. He never turned a hair.

"Ah, well, then," he said. "That's different."

"For her birthday," Jessica explained. "Now, if you'll pardon me, I had better extract Bertie from his negotiations. The tone of his voice tells me he's trying to count and, as you so perceptively remarked, that isn't good for him."

He could pick her up with one hand, Dain thought as he watched her saunter across the shop. Her head scarcely reached his breastbone, and even with the overloaded bonnet, she couldn't weigh eight stone.

He was used to towering over women—over mostly everybody—and he had learned to feel comfortable in his oversize body. Sports—boxing and fencing, especially—had taught him to be light on his feet.

Next to her, he had felt like a great lummox. A great, ugly, *stupid* lummox. She had known perfectly well what sort of watch the curst thing was all along. The question was, What sort of curst thing was she? The chit had stared straight into his blackguard's face and not batted an eye. He had stood much too close to her and she had not budged.

Then she had taken out a magnifying glass, of all things, and evaluated the lewd timepiece as calmly as though it were a rare edition of Fox's *Book of Martyrs*.

He wished now he had paid more attention to Trent's references to his sister. The trouble was, if a man paid attention to anything Bertie Trent said, that man was certain to go howling mad.

Lord Dain had scarcely completed the thought when Bertie shouted, "No! Absolutely not! You just encourage her, Jess. I won't have it! You ain't to sell it to her, Champtois."

"Yes, you will, Champtois," Miss Trent said in very competent French. "There is no need to regard my little brother. He has no authority over me whatsoever." She obligingly translated for her brother, whose face turned a vivid red.

"I ain't *little*! And I'm head of the curst family. And I—"

"Go play with the drummer boy, Bertie," she said. "Or better yet, why don't you take your charming friend out for a drink?"

"Jess." Bertie's tones took on a pleading desperation. "You know she'll show it to people and—and I'll be *mortified*."

"Lud, what a prig you've got to be since you left England."

Bertie's eyes threatened to burst from their sockets. "A what?"

"A prig, dear. A prig and a prude. A regular Methodist."

Bertie uttered several inarticulate sounds, then turned to Dain, who had by this time given up all thoughts of leaving. He was leaning upon the jewel case, observing Bertie Trent's sister with a brooding fascination.

"Did you hear that, Dain?" Bertie demanded. "Did you hear what the beastly girl said?"

"I could not fail to hear," said Dain. "I was listening attentively."

"*Me!*" Bertie jammed his thumb into his chest. "A *prig.*"

"Indeed, it's thoroughly shocking. I shall be obliged to cut your acquaintance. I cannot allow myself to be corrupted by virtuous companions."

"But, Dain, I—"

"Your friend is right, dear," said Miss Trent. "If word of this gets out, he cannot risk being seen with you. His reputation will be ruined."

"Ah, you are familiar with my reputation, are you, Miss Trent?" Dain enquired.

"Oh, yes. You are the wickedest man who ever lived. And you eat small children for breakfast, their nannies tell them, if they are naughty."

"But you are not in the least alarmed."

"It is not breakfast time, and I am hardly a small child. Though I can see how, given your lofty vantage point, you might mistake me for one."

Lord Dain eyed her up and down. "No, I don't think I should make that mistake."

"I should say not, after listening to her scold and insult a chap," said Bertie.

"On the other hand, Miss Trent," Dain went on just as though Bertie did not exist—which, in a properly regulated world, he wouldn't—"if you *are* naughty, I might be tempted to—"

"*Qu'est-ce que c'est, Champtois?*" Miss Trent asked. She moved down the counter to the tray of goods Dain had been looking over when the pair had entered.

"*Rien, rien.*" Champtois set his hand protectively

over the tray. He glanced nervously at Dain. *"Pas inté-
ressante."*

She looked in the same direction. "Your purchase,
my lord?"

"Not a bit of it," said Dain. "I was, for a moment, in-
trigued by the silver inkstand, which, as you will ascertain, is about the only item there worth a second glance."

It was not the inkstand she took up and applied her
magnifying glass to, however, but the small dirt-
encrusted picture with the thick, mildewed frame.

"A portrait of a woman, it seems to be," she said.

Dain came away from the jewel case and joined her
at the counter. "Ah, yes, Champtois claimed it was human. You will soil your gloves, Miss Trent."

Bertie, too, approached, sulking. "Smells like I don't
know what." He made a face.

"Because it's rotting," said Dain.

"That's because it's rather old," said Miss Trent.

"Rather been lying in a gutter for about a decade,"
said Dain.

"She has an interesting expression," Miss Trent told
Champtois in French. "I cannot decide whether it's sad
or happy. What do you want for it?"

"Quarante sous."

She put it down.

"Trente-et-cinq," he said.

She laughed.

Champtois told her he'd paid thirty sous for it himself. He could not sell it for less.

She gave him a pitying look.

Tears filled his eyes. *"Trente, mademoiselle."*

In that case, she told him, she would have only the
watch.

In the end, she paid ten sous for the filthy, foul-smelling
thing, and if she'd dragged negotiations out much longer,

Dain thought, Champtois would have ended by paying her to take it.

Dain had never before seen the hard-nosed Champtois reduced to such agony, and he couldn't understand why. Certainly, when Miss Jessica Trent finally left the shop—taking her brother with her, thank heaven—the only agony Lord Dain experienced was a headache, which he ascribed to spending nearly an hour, sober, in Bertie Trent's company.

Later that evening, in a private chamber of his favorite den of iniquity, which went by the innocent name of *Vingt-Huit,* Lord Dain regaled his companions with a description of the farce, as he called it.

"Ten sous?" Roland Vawtry said, laughing. "Trent's sister talked Champtois down from forty to ten? By gad, I wish I'd been there."

"Well, it's plain now what happened, isn't it?" said Malcolm Goodridge. "She was born first. Since she got all the intelligence, there wasn't a crumb left for Trent."

"Did she get all the looks, too?" Francis Beaumont asked as he refilled Dain's wineglass.

"I could not detect the smallest resemblance in coloring, features, or physique." Dain sipped his wine.

"That's all?" Beaumont asked. "Are you going to leave us in suspense? What does she look like?"

Dain shrugged. "Black hair, grey eyes. Something near five and a half feet, and between seven and eight stone."

"Weighed her, did you?" Goodridge asked, grinning. "Would you say the seven to eight stone was well distributed?"

"How the devil should I know? How could anyone know, with all those corsets and bustles and whatever else females stuff and strap themselves into? It's all tricks and lies, isn't it, until they're naked." He smiled. "Then it's other kinds of lies."

"Women do not lie, my lord Dain," came a faintly accented voice from the door. "It merely seems so because they exist in another reality." The Comte d'Esmond entered, and gently closed the door behind him.

Though he acknowledged Esmond with a careless nod, Dain was very glad to see him. Beaumont had a sly way of getting out of people precisely what they least wished to reveal. Though Dain was up to his tricks, he resented the concentration needed to deflect the cur.

With Esmond present, Beaumont would not be able to attend to anyone else. Even Dain found the count distracting at times, albeit not for the same reasons. Esmond was about as beautiful as a man could be without looking remotely like a woman. He was slim, blond, and blue-eyed, with the face of an angel.

When he'd first introduced them a week earlier, Beaumont had laughingly suggested they ask his wife, who was an artist, to paint them together. "She could title it 'Heaven and Hell,'" he'd said.

Beaumont wanted Esmond very badly. Esmond wanted Beaumont's wife. And she didn't want anybody.

Dain found the situation deliciously amusing.

"You're just in time, Esmond," said Goodridge. "Dain had an adventure today. There is a young lady newly arrived in Paris—and of all things, it's Dain she runs into first. And he *talked* to her."

All the world knew Dain refused to have any dealings whatsoever with respectable women.

"Bertie Trent's sister," Beaumont explained. There was a vacant chair beside him, and everyone knew who it was intended for. But Esmond wandered to Dain's side and leaned on the back of his chair. To torment Beaumont, of course. Esmond only *looked* like an angel.

"Ah, yes," he said. "She does not at all resemble him. Obviously it is Genevieve she takes after."

"I might have known," Beaumont said, refilling his own glass. "Met her already, have you? And did she take after you, Esmond?"

"I encountered Trent and his kinswomen a short while ago at Tortoni's," Esmond said. "The restaurant was in an uproar. Genevieve—Lady Penbury, that is— has not been seen in Paris since the Peace of Amiens. It became very clear she had not been forgotten, although five and twenty years have passed."

"By Jupiter, *yes!*" Goodridge cried, slamming his hand upon the table. "That's it, of course. I was so stunned by Dain's astonishing behavior with the girl that I never made the connection. *Genevieve.* Well, that explains it, then."

"Explains what?" Vawtry asked.

Goodridge's gaze met Dain's. The former's expression grew uneasy.

"Well, naturally, you were a trifle . . . curious," Goodridge said. "Genevieve's a bit out of the common run, and if Miss Trent's the same sort of—of anomaly, well, then, she's rather like those things you buy from Champtois. And there she was, in the very man's shop. Like the Trojan horse medicine case you bought last month."

"An odd piece, you mean," said Dain. "Also, undoubtedly, an outrageously expensive one. Excellent analogy, Goodridge." He raised his glass. "I could not have put it better myself."

"All the same," said Beaumont, glancing from Goodridge to Dain, "I can't believe a Parisian restaurant was in an uproar over a pair of *odd* females."

"When you meet Genevieve, you will comprehend," said Esmond. "This is not merely a beauty, monsieur. This is *la femme fatale*. The men plagued them so, they could scarcely attend to their meal. Our friend, Trent, was much provoked. Fortunately for him, Mademoiselle Trent exercises great restraint upon her own charm. Otherwise, I think, there would have been bloodshed. Two such women . . ." He shook his head sadly. "It is too much for Frenchmen."

"Your countrymen have odd notions of charm," Dain said as he filled a glass for the count and handed it to him. "All I noted was a razor-tongued, supercilious bluestocking of a spinster."

"I like clever women," said Esmond. "So stimulating. *Mais chacun à son goût.* It delights me that you find her disagreeable, my lord Dain. Already there is too much competition."

Beaumont laughed. "Dain doesn't compete. He barters. And there's only one type he barters for, as we all know."

"I pay a whore a few coins," said Dain. "She gives me exactly what I require. And when it's done, it's done. Since the world seems to be in no danger of running out of whores, why should I go to what we all know is excessive bother for the other sort?"

"There is love," said Esmond.

His listeners broke into loud guffaws.

When the noise subsided, Dain said, "There seems to be a language gap, gentlemen. Wasn't love what I was talking about?"

"I thought you were speaking of fornication," Esmond said.

"Same thing, in Dain's Dictionary," said Beaumont. He rose. "I think I'll toddle downstairs to throw a few francs into that rathole called *Rouge et Noir.* Anyone else?"

Vawtry and Goodridge followed him to the door.

"Esmond?" Beaumont asked.

"Perhaps," said the count. "I will decide later, after I finish my wine." He took the seat beside Dain that Vawtry had vacated.

After the others were out of earshot, Dain said, "It's nothing to me either way, Esmond, but I am curious. Why don't you simply tell Beaumont he's barking up the wrong tree?"

Esmond smiled. "It would make no difference, I promise you. With me, he has the same problem, I think, he has with his wife."

Beaumont rutted with just about anything he could get his hands on. His disgusted wife had decided, some years ago, that he was to keep his hands off her. All the same, she still had her hooks in him. Beaumont was furiously possessive, and Esmond's interest in his wife was driving him demented with jealousy. It was pathetic, Dain thought. And ludicrous.

"One of these days, maybe I'll understand why you waste your time on her," Dain said. "You could have something very like Leila Beaumont, you know, for a few francs. And this is the right place to find precisely what one likes, isn't it?"

Esmond finished his wine. "I think, perhaps, I shall not come to this place again. It gives me . . . a bad feeling." He stood up. "I think, tonight, I prefer to visit the Boulevard des Italiens."

He invited Dain to join him, but Dain declined. It was nearly a quarter to one, and he had a one-o'clock appointment upstairs with an Amazonian blonde named Chloe.

Perhaps Esmond's "bad feeling" had put Dain's instincts on the alert, or perhaps he'd drunk less wine than usual. Whatever the reason, the marquess took careful note of his surroundings when Chloe welcomed him into the crimson-draped room.

He discerned the peephole as he was about to pull off his coat. It was several inches below his own eye level in the middle of the wall to the left of the bed.

He took Chloe's hand and led her to a spot directly in front of the peephole. He told her to strip, very slowly.

Then he moved, very quickly—out the door and into the hall, where he yanked open the door of what appeared to be a linen closet, and kicked open the door behind that. The chamber beyond was very dark, but it was also very small, and he hadn't far to reach when he heard the man move—toward another door, apparently. But not quickly enough.

Dain yanked him back, swung him round, and, grabbing the knot of his neckcloth, shoved him back against the wall.

"I don't need to see you," Dain said, his voice dangerously low. "I can smell you, Beaumont."

It was not hard to recognize Beaumont at close quarters. His clothes and breath usually reeked of spirits and stale opium.

"I'm thinking of taking up art," Dain went on while Beaumont gasped for breath. "I'm thinking of titling my first work 'Portrait of a Dead Man.'"

Beaumont made a choked sound.

Dain eased his grip a fraction. "There was a remark you wished to make, swine?"

"Can't . . . kill me . . . cold blood," Beaumont gasped. "Guillotine."

"Quite right. Don't want to lose my head on your filthy account, do I?"

Releasing the neckcloth, Dain drove his right fist

into Beaumont's face, then his left into his gut. Beaumont crumpled to the floor.

"Don't annoy me again," Dain said. And he left.

At the same moment, Jessica was sitting on her grandmother's bed. This was the first chance they'd had for an extended conversation, without Bertie fussing and fretting about. He'd departed about an hour ago for one pit of vice or another, at which point Jessica had ordered up some of his best cognac. She had just finished telling Genevieve about her encounter with Dain.

"An animal attraction, obviously," said Genevieve.

With that, Jessica's small, desperate hope—that her inner disturbances had been a feverish reaction to the effluvium emanating from the open gutter in front of Champtois' shop—died a quick, brutal death.

"Damn," she said, meeting her grandmother's twinkling silver gaze. "This is not only mortifying, but inconvenient. I am in lust with Dain. Of all times, now. Of all men, *him*."

"Not convenient, I agree. But an interesting challenge, don't you think?"

"The challenge is to pry Bertie loose from Dain and his circle of oafish degenerates," Jessica said severely.

"It would be far more profitable to pry Dain loose for yourself," said her grandmother. "He is very wealthy, his lineage is excellent, he is young, strong, and healthy, and you feel a powerful attraction."

"He isn't husband material."

"What I have described is perfect husband material," said her grandmother.

"I don't want a husband."

"Jessica, no woman does who can regard men objectively. And you have always been magnificently objective.

But we do not live in a utopia. If you open your shop, you will doubtless make money. Yet the family will turn their backs upon you, your social credit will sink, Society will pity you—even while they bankrupt themselves to buy your wares. And every coxcomb in London will be making indecent proposals. Yes, it shows courage to undertake such an endeavor when one is in desperate straits. But you are not desperate, my dear. I can support you well enough, if it comes to that."

"We've been over this ground time and again," Jessica said. "You're not Croesus, and we both have expensive tastes. Not to mention that you'll only create more ill will in the family—while I shall seem a great hypocrite, after insisting for years that you owe none of us a farthing, and we're not your responsibility."

"You are very proud and brave, which I respect and admire, my dear." Her grandmother leaned forward to pat Jessica's knee. "And assuredly, you are the only one who understands me. We have always been more like sisters or very best friends than grandmama and grandchild, have we not? It is as your sister and friend that I tell you Dain is a splendid catch. I advise you to set your hooks and reel him in."

Jessica took a long swallow of her cognac. "This is not a trout, Genevieve. This is a great, hungry *shark*."

"Then use a harpoon."

Jessica shook her head.

Genevieve sat back against the pillows and sighed. "Ah well, I shall not nag you. It is most unattractive. I shall simply hope his reaction to you was nothing like yours to him. That is a man who gets what he wants, Jessica, and if I were you, I should not want him to be the one reeling in the line."

Jessica suppressed a shudder. "No danger of that. He doesn't want anything to do with *ladies*. According to

Bertie, Dain views respectable women as a species of deadly fungus. The only reason he spoke to me was to amuse himself by trying to shock me out of my wits."

Genevieve chuckled. "The watch, you mean. That was a delicious birthday surprise. More delicious still was Bertie's expression when I opened the box. I have never seen his face turn quite that shade of crimson before."

"Probably because you chose to open the gift in the restaurant. With the Comte d'Esmond looking on."

And that was most exasperating of all, Jessica thought. Why in blazes couldn't she have fallen in lust with Esmond? He was very wealthy, too. And mind-numbingly handsome. And *civilized*.

"Esmond is *très amusante*," said Genevieve. "Too bad he is already taken. Something very interesting came into his beautiful eyes when he spoke of Mrs. Beaumont."

Genevieve had mentioned to Esmond the tensous picture and Jessica's belief that it was more than it seemed. Esmond had suggested asking Mrs. Beaumont for the names of experts to clean and appraise it. He'd offered to introduce Jessica to her. They'd made an appointment for the following afternoon, when Mrs. Beaumont would be assisting at a benefit for the widow of her former art master.

"Well, we'll get to see if anything interesting appears in her eyes tomorrow—or today, rather," said Jessica. She finished her cognac and slid down from the bed. "I wish we were there already. I feel strongly disinclined to sleep. I have the nasty feeling I'm going to dream about a *shark*."

Three

It would have eased Jessica's mind, could she but have known, that she gave Lord Dain nightmares.

That is to say, his dreams started out well enough, with thoroughly lewd and lascivious activities. Since he'd often dreamt of females he wouldn't, awake, have touched with the proverbial long pole, the marquess was not alarmed about dreaming of Bertie Trent's irritating sister. On the contrary, Dain thoroughly enjoyed putting the supercilious bluestocking in her place—on her back, on her knees, and, more than once, in positions he doubted were anatomically possible.

The trouble was, every time, just as he was on the brink of flooding her virginal womb with the hot seed of latent Ballisters, something ghastly happened. In the dream, he would wake up. Sometimes he found himself sinking in a mire. Sometimes he was chained in a foul black cell, with creatures he couldn't see tearing at his flesh. Sometimes he was lying on a slab in a morgue undergoing an autopsy.

Being a man of considerable intelligence, he had no trouble understanding the symbolism. Every nightmarish thing that had happened was, metaphorically speaking, exactly what did happen to a man when a female got her hooks into him. He did not understand, however, why, in his sleep, his brain had to make such a ghoulish bother about what he already knew.

For years he'd been dreaming about women he had no intention of becoming entangled with. Countless times, awake, he'd imagined that the whore he was with was a lady who'd caught his eye. Not very long ago, he'd pretended a voluptuous French tart was Leila Beaumont, and he'd come away quite as satisfied as if she had been that icy bitch. No, *more* satisfied, because the tart had made an excellent show of enthusiasm, whereas the real Leila Beaumont would have dashed out his brains with a blunt instrument.

Dain, in short, had no trouble distinguishing between fantasy and reality. He had met Jessica Trent and felt a perfectly normal lust. He lusted for virtually every attractive female he saw. He had a prodigious sexual appetite, inherited, he had no doubt, from his hot-blooded Italian whore of a mother and her family. If he lusted for a whore, he paid her and had her. If he lusted for a respectable female, he found a whore as a substitute, paid her, and had her.

That was what he'd done regarding Trent's sister. Or tried to do—because it still wasn't properly done.

The dreams weren't all that thwarted him. The incident at *Vingt-Huit* had not precisely killed his appetite for trollops, but it had left a sour taste in his mouth. He had not returned to Chloe to take up where he'd left off, and he hadn't taken up any other tart since. He told himself that Beaumont's voyeuristic tastes were hardly a reason for swearing off whores altogether.

Nonetheless, Dain felt extremely reluctant to enter any room with any *fille de joie*, which created a serious problem, since he was just fastidious enough to dislike having a female in a reeking Parisian alleyway.

Consequently, between uncooperative dreams and the foul taste in his mouth, he was unable to exorcise his lust for Miss Trent in the tried-and-true fashion. Which meant that, by the time a week had passed, Dain's temper was badly frayed.

Which was exactly the wrong time for Bertie Trent to tell him that the dirty, mildewed picture Miss Trent had bought for ten sous had turned out to be an extremely valuable Russian icon.

It was a few minutes past noon, and Lord Dain had moments earlier dodged the contents of a washtub, dumped from an upper-story window on the Rue de Provence. His attention on avoiding a drenching, he had failed to notice Trent trotting toward him. By the time the marquess did notice, the imbecile was already there, and well launched into his exciting revelations.

Dain's dark brow furrowed at the conclusion—or rather, when Bertie paused for breath. "A Russian *what?*" the marquess asked.

"Acorn. That is to say, not a nut sort of thing, but one of them heathenish pictures with a lot of gold paint and gold leaf."

"I believe you mean an *icon*," said Dain. "In which case, I fear your sister has been hoaxed. Who told her such rubbish?"

"Le Feuvre," said Bertie, pronouncing the name as "fooh-ver."

Lord Dain experienced a chill sensation in the environs of his stomach. Le Feuvre was the most reputable appraiser in Paris. Even Ackermann's and Christie's consulted him upon occasion. "There are countless icons in the world," said Dain. "Still, if it's a good one, she obviously got a bargain at ten sous."

"The frame's set with a lot of little gems—pearls and rubies and such."

"Paste, I collect."

Bertie grimaced, as he often did when toiling to produce a thought. "Well now, that would be an odd thing, wouldn't it? Sticking a lot of trumpery gewgaws onto a handsome bit of gold frame like that."

"The picture I saw was framed in wood." Dain's head was beginning to pound.

"But that's what's so clever, ain't it? The wood thing was part of the case they'd buried it in. Because it had been buried, you know. That's why it was so god-awful disgusting. Ain't it a laugh, though? That sly beggar, Champtois, hadn't the least idea. He'll be tearing his hair out when he hears."

Dain was considering tearing Bertie's head straight off his neck. Ten sous. And Dain had discarded it, had not given it more than a cursory glance, even while the dratted sister had pored over it with her curst magnifying glass. *She has an interesting expression*, she'd said. And Dain, distracted by the living female, had not suspected a thing.

Because there was nothing to suspect, he told himself. Bertie hadn't half the brain of a peahen. He'd obviously got everything wrong, as usual. The "acorn" was merely one of those cheap saintly pictures every religious fanatic in Russia had in a corner of a room, with a daub of shiny paint on the frame and some bits of colored glass stuck on.

"Course, I'm not to tell Champtois," Bertie went on in marginally lower tones. "I'm not to tell anybody—especially *you*, she said. But I ain't a dancing bear, like I told her, and there wasn't any ring in my nose that I could see, so I wouldn't be led about by it, now would I? So I hopped straight out to look for you—and found you in the nick, because she's going to the bank straight the minute Genevieve tucks away for her nap—and then it'll be locked up in a vault and you'll never get a proper look at it, will you?"

The Marquess of Dain, Jessica was well aware, was furious. He lounged back in his chair, his arms folded across his chest, his obsidian eyes half-closed while his glance moved slowly round the coffee shop. It closely resembled the species of sullenly sulphurous look she had always imagined Lucifer bestowing upon his surroundings when he first came to after the Fall.

She was much surprised the gaze didn't leave a trail of charred remains in its wake. But the patrons of the café simply looked away—only to look back again the instant Dain returned his brimstone displeasure to her.

Though she'd already made up her mind how to deal with the problem, Jessica was irritably aware that it would be easier if Bertie had been a trifle more discreet. She wished she hadn't taken him along yesterday when she'd gone to collect the picture from Le Feuvre. But then, how could she have known beforehand that it was more than simply the work of an unusually talented artist?

Even Le Feuvre had been astonished when he went to work on it, and found the bejeweled gold frame within the decayed wooden one.

And naturally, because the piece, when Le Feuvre had finished with it, was pretty and shiny and sparkling with gems, Bertie had become very excited. Too excited to listen to reason. Jessica had tried to explain that telling Dain would be like waving a red flag in front of a bull. Bertie had *pshish*ed and *pshaw*ed and told her Dain wasn't that sort of bad sport—not to mention he probably had a dozen such of his own and could buy another dozen if he liked.

Whatever the Marquess of Dain had, Jessica was certain it wasn't anything like her rare Madonna. And though he had looked bored when she showed it to him today, and congratulated her in the most patronizing manner, and laughingly insisted on accompanying Bertie and her to the bank to scare off any would-be robbers, she knew he wanted to kill her.

After the icon had been locked away in a bank vault, it was Dain who'd suggested they stop here for coffee.

They'd scarcely sat down before he'd sent Bertie out to find a type of cheroot that Jessica strongly suspected didn't exist. Bertie would probably not be back before midnight, if then. For all she knew, he'd hie to the West Indies in search of the fictitious cigar—precisely as though Dain truly were Beelzebub, and Bertie one of his devoted familiars.

The brother out of the way, Dain had just silently warned the café's patrons to mind their own business. If he took her by the throat and choked her to death then and there, Jessica doubted any one of them would leap to her rescue. She doubted, in fact, that any of them would dare utter a peep of protest.

"How much did Le Feuvre tell you the thing was worth?" he asked. It was the first word he'd uttered since giving the coffee shop owner their order. When Dain entered an establishment, the proprietor himself rushed out to attend him.

"He advised me not to sell it right away," she said evasively. "He wished to contact a Russian client first. There is a cousin or nephew or some such of the tsar's who—"

"Fifty pounds," said Lord Dain. "Unless this Russian

is one of the tsar's numerous mad relations, he won't give you a farthing more than that."

"Then he must be one of the mad ones," said Jessica. "Le Feuvre mentioned a figure well above that."

He gave her a hard stare. Gazing into his dark, harsh face, into those black, implacable eyes, Jessica had no trouble imagining him sitting upon an immense ebony throne at the very bottom of the pits of Hades. Had she looked down and discovered that the expensive polished boot a few inches from her own had turned into a cloven hoof, she would not have been in the least amazed.

Any woman with an ounce of common sense would have picked up her skirts and fled.

The trouble was, Jessica could not feel at all sensible. A magnetic current was racing along her nerve endings. It slithered and swirled through her system, to make an odd, tingling heat in the pit of her belly, and it melted her brain to soup.

She wanted to kick off her shoes and trail her stockinged toes up and down the black, costly boot. She wanted to slide her fingers under his starched shirt cuff and trace the veins and muscles of his wrist and feel his pulse beating under her thumb. Most of all, she wanted to press her lips to his hard, dissolute mouth and kiss him senseless.

Of course, all such a demented assault would get her would be a position flat on her back and the swift elimination of her maidenhead—very possibly in full view of the café's patrons. Then, if he was in a good humor, he might give her a friendly slap on the bottom as he told her to run along, she reflected gloomily.

"Miss Trent," he said, "I am sure all the other girls at school found your wit hilarious. Perhaps, however, if you would stop batting your eyelashes for a moment, your vision would clear and you would notice that I am not a little schoolgirl."

She hadn't been batting her eyelashes. When Jessica did play coquette, it was purposely and purposefully, and she was certainly not such a moron as to try that method with Beelzebub.

"Batting?" she repeated. "I never *bat*, my lord. This is what I do." She looked away toward an attractive Frenchman seated nearby, then shot Dain one swift, sidelong glance. "That isn't batting," she said, releasing the instantly bedazzled Frenchman and returning to full focus upon Dain.

Though one could hardly believe it possible, his expression became grimmer still.

"I am not a school*boy*, either," he said. "I recommend you save those slaying glances for the sorts of young sapskulls who respond to them."

The Frenchman was now gazing at her with besotted fascination. Dain turned and looked at him. The man instantly looked away and began talking animatedly with his companions.

She recollected Genevieve's warning. Jessica couldn't be certain Dain had any active thoughts of reeling her in. She could see, however, that he'd just posted a No Fishing sign.

A thrill coursed through her, but that was only to be expected. It was the primitive reaction of a female when an attractive male displayed the usual bad-natured signs of proprietorship. She was hammeringly aware that her feelings about him were decidedly primitive.

On the other hand, she was not completely out of her mind.

She could see Big Trouble brewing.

It was easy enough to see. Scandal followed wherever he went. Jessica had no intention of being caught in the midst of it.

"I was merely providing a demonstration of a subtle distinction which had apparently escaped you," she said. "Subtlety, I collect, is not your strong point."

"If this is a *subtle* way of reminding me that I overlooked what your gimlet eyes perceived in that dirt-encrusted picture—"

"You apparently did not look very closely even when it was clean," she said. "Because then you would have recognized the work of the Stroganov school—and would not have offered the insulting sum of fifty quid for it."

His lip curled. "I didn't offer anything. I expressed an opinion."

"To test me," she said. "However, I know as well as you do that the piece is not only Stroganov school, but an extremely rare form. Even the most elaborate of the miniatures were usually chased in silver. Not to mention that the Madonna—"

"Has grey eyes, not brown," Dain said in a very bored voice.

"And she's almost smiling. Usually they look exceedingly unhappy."

"Cross, Miss Trent. They look exceedingly ill tempered. I suppose it's on account of being *virgins*—of experiencing all the unpleasantness of breeding and birthing and none of the jolly parts."

"Speaking on behalf of virgins everywhere, my lord," she said, leaning toward him a bit, "I can tell you there are a host of jolly experiences. One of them is owning a rare work of religious art worth, at the very minimum, five hundred pounds."

He laughed. "There's no need to inform me you're a virgin," he said. "I can spot one at fifty paces."

"Fortunately, I'm not so inexperienced in other matters," she said, unruffled. "I have no doubt Le Feuvre's mad Russian will pay me five hundred. I'm also aware that the Russian must be a good client for whom he wishes to make a shrewd purchase. Which means I should do considerably better at auction." She smoothed her gloves. "I have observed many times how men's wits utterly desert them once auction fever takes hold. There's no telling what outrageous bids will result."

Dain's eyes narrowed.

At that moment, their host sallied forth with their refreshments. With him were four lesser minions who bustled about, arranging linens, silver, and crockery with painful precision. Not a stray crumb was allowed to mar a plate, not a trace of tarnish smudged the flawless sheen of the silver. Even the sugar had been sawed into perfect half-inch cubes—no small feat, when the average sugar loaf was somewhere between granite and diamonds on the hardness scale. Jessica had always wondered how the kitchen help managed to break it up without using explosives.

She accepted a small slice of yellow cake with frothy white icing.

Dain let the fawning proprietor adorn his plate with a large assortment of fruit tarts, artistically arranged in concentric circles.

They ate their sweets in silence until Dain, having decimated enough tarts to set every tooth in his mouth throbbing, set down his fork and frowned at her hands.

"Have *all* the rules changed since I've been away from England?" he asked. "I'm aware ladies do not carelessly expose their naked hands to public view. I did understand, though, that they were permitted to remove their gloves to eat."

"It is permitted," she said. "But it isn't possible."

She raised her hand to show him the long row of tiny pearl buttons. "I should be all afternoon undoing them without my maid's help."

"Why the devil wear such pestilentially bothersome things?" he demanded.

"Genevieve bought them especially for this pelisse," she said. "If I didn't wear them, she'd be dreadfully hurt."

He was still staring at the gloves.

"Genevieve is my grandmother," she explained. He hadn't met her. He'd arrived just as Genevieve had lain down for her nap—though Jessica had no doubt her grandmother had promptly risen and peeped through the door the moment she'd heard the deep, masculine voice.

The voice's owner now looked up, his black eyes glinting. "Ah, yes. The watch."

"That, too, was a wise choice," Jessica said, setting down her own fork and settling back into her business mode. "She was enchanted."

"I am not your little white-haired grandmother," he said, instantly taking her meaning. "I am not so enchanted with icons—even Stroganovs—to pay a farthing more than they're worth. To me, it's worth no more than a thousand. But if you'll promise not to bore me to distraction by haggling and trying to slay me with your eyes in between, I shall gladly pay fifteen hundred."

She had hoped to work him round by degrees. His tone told her he had no intention of being worked upon. Straight to the point, then—the point she'd decided upon hours ago, after catching the expression in his eyes when she'd let him examine her remarkable find.

"I shall gladly give it to you, my lord," she said.

"No one *gives* me anything," he said coldly. "Play

your game—whatever it is—with someone else. Fifteen hundred is my offer. My only offer."

"If you would send Bertie home, the icon is yours," she said. "If you will not, it goes to auction at Christie's."

If Jessica Trent had comprehended the state Dain was in, she would have stopped at the first sentence. No, if she had truly comprehended, she would have taken to her heels and run as fast and as far as she could. But she couldn't understand what Lord Dain barely understood himself. He wanted the gentle Russian Madonna, with her half-smiling, half-wistful face and the scowling Baby Jesus nestled to her bosom, as he had not wanted anything in all his life. He had wanted to weep when he saw it, and he didn't know why.

The work was exquisite—an art sublime and human at once—and he'd been moved, before, by artistry. What he felt at this moment wasn't remotely like those pleasant sensations. What he felt was the old monster howling within. He couldn't name the feelings any better than he could when he'd been eight years old. He'd never bothered to name them, simply shoved and beaten them out of his way, repeatedly, until, like his schoolmates of long ago, they'd stopped tormenting him.

Having never been allowed to mature, those feelings remained at the primitive childlike level. Now, caught unexpectedly in their grip, Lord Dain could not reason as an adult would. He could not tell himself Bertie Trent was an infernal nuisance whom Dain should have sent packing ages ago. It never occurred to the marquess to be delighted at present, when the nitwit's sister was prepared to pay—or bribe was more like it—him generously to do so.

All Dain could see was an exceedingly pretty girl teasing him with a toy he wanted very badly. He had offered her his biggest and very best toy in trade. And she had laughed and threatened to throw her toy into a privy, just to make him beg.

Much later, Lord Dain would understand that this— or something equally idiotic—had been raging through his brain.

But that would be much later, when it was far too late.

At this moment, he was about eight years old on the inside and nearly three and thirty on the outside, and thus, beside himself.

He leaned toward her. "Miss Trent, there are no other terms," he said, his voice dangerously low. "I pay you fifteen hundred quid and you say, 'Done,' and everyone goes away happy."

"No, they don't." Her chin jutted up stubbornly. "If you will not send Bertie home, there is no business on earth I would do with you. You are destroying his life. No amount of money in the world will compensate. I should not sell the icon to you if I were in the last stages of starvation."

"Easy enough to say when your stomach is full," he said. Then, in Latin, he mockingly quoted Publilius Syrus. "'Anyone can hold the helm when the sea is calm.'"

In the same language she quoted the same sage, "'You cannot put the same shoe on every foot.'"

His countenance betrayed nothing of his astonishment. "It would appear that you have dipped into Publilius," he said. "How very odd, then, that so clever a female cannot see what is before her eyes. I am not a dead language to play in, Miss Trent. You are treading perilously close to dangerous waters."

"Because my brother is drowning there," she said. "Because you are holding his head under. I am not large enough or powerful enough to pull your hand away. All I have is something you want, which even you cannot take away." Her silver eyes flashed. "There is only one way for you to get it, my lord Beelzebub. *You throw him back.*"

Had he been capable of reasoning in an adult fashion, Dain would have acknowledged that her reasoning was excellent—that, moreover, it was precisely as he would have done had he found himself in her predicament. He might even have appreciated the fact that she told him plainly and precisely what she was about, rather than using feminine guiles and wiles to manipulate.

He was not capable of adult reasoning.

The flash of temper in her eyes should have glanced harmlessly off him. Instead, it shot fast and deep and ignited an inner fuse. He thought the fuse was anger. He thought that if she had been a man, he would have thrown *her*—straight against the wall. He thought that, since she was a woman, he would have to find an equally effective way of teaching her a lesson.

He didn't know that throwing her was the exact opposite of what he wanted to do. He didn't know that the lessons he wanted to teach her were those of Venus, not Mars, Ovid's *Ars Armatoria*, not Caesar's *De Bello Gallico*.

Consequently, he made a mistake.

"No, you do not see clearly at all," he said. "There is always another way, Miss Trent. You think there isn't because you assume I will play by all the dear little rules Society dotes upon. You think, for instance, that because we're in a public place and you're a lady, I'll mind my manners. Perhaps you even think I have a regard for your reputation." He smiled evilly. "Miss Trent, perhaps you would like to take a moment to think again."

Her grey eyes narrowed. "I think you are threatening me," she said.

"Let me make it as clear as you did your own threat." He leaned toward her. "I can crack your reputation in under thirty seconds. In three minutes I can reduce it to dust. We both know, don't we, that being who I am, I need not exert myself overmuch to accomplish this. You have already become an object of speculation simply by being seen in my company." He paused briefly to let the words sink in.

She said nothing. Her slitted eyes were glinting furious sparks.

"Here is how it works," he went on. "If you accept my offer of fifteen hundred, I shall behave myself, escort you to a cabriolet, and see that you are taken safely home."

"And if I do not accept, you will attempt to destroy my reputation," she said.

"It will not be an *attempt*," he said.

She sat up very straight and folded her dainty gloved hands upon the table. "I should like to see you try," she said.

Four

Dain had given Miss Trent more than enough opportunity to see her error. His warnings could
not have been clearer.

In any case, to hesitate in such a situation was to in-
dicate doubt, or worse, weakness. To do so with a man
was dangerous. To do so with a woman was fatal.

And so Lord Dain smiled and leaned nearer yet, until
his great Usignuolo nose was but an inch from hers.
"Say your prayers, Miss Trent," he told her very softly.

Then he slid his hand—his big, dark, *bare* hand, for
he had removed his gloves to eat and hadn't put them
back on—down the sleeve of her pelisse until he came
to the first button of her frivolous pearl grey gloves.

He popped the tiny pearl from the buttonhole.

She glanced down at his hand, but didn't move a
muscle.

Then, aware that every eye in the place was fastened
upon them, and the noisy conversations had sunk to
whispers, he began to talk to her in Italian. In the tones
of a lover, he described the weather, a grey gelding he

was thinking of selling, and the condition of Parisian drains. Though he had never tried or needed to seduce a woman, he'd seen and heard other poor sods at that game, and he reproduced their ludicrous tones to a nicety. Everyone about them would think they were lovers. And all the while, he was working his way swiftly down toward her wrist.

She never made a murmur, only glanced now and then from his face to his hands with a frozen expression he interpreted as speechless horror.

He might have interpreted more accurately had he felt inwardly as self-possessed as he seemed outwardly. Outwardly, his expression remained sensuously intent, his voice low and seductive. Inwardly, he was disturbingly aware that his pulse had begun to accelerate at about Button Number Six. By Number Twelve, it was racing. By Number Fifteen, he had to concentrate hard to keep his breathing steady.

He had relieved whores beyond counting of frocks, stays, chemises, garters, and stockings. He'd never before in his life unbuttoned a gently bred maiden's glove. He had committed salacious acts beyond number. He'd never once felt so depraved as he did now, as the last pearl came free and he drew the soft kid down, baring her wrist, and his dark fingers grazed the delicate skin he'd exposed.

He was too busy searching Dain's Dictionary for a definition of his state—and too confused by what he read there—to realize that Miss Jessica Trent's grey eyes had taken on the drunkenly bewildered expression of a respectable spinster being seduced in spite of herself.

Even if he had comprehended her expression, he wouldn't have believed it, any more than he could believe his untoward state of excitement—over a damned glove and a bit of feminine flesh. Not even one of the good bits, either—the ones a man didn't have—but an inch or so of her *wrist*, plague take her.

The worst was that he couldn't stop. The worst was that his passionately intent expression had somehow become genuine, and he was no longer talking in Italian about drains, but about how he wanted to unbutton, unhook, untie every button, hook, and string . . . and slip off her garments, one by one, and drag his monstrous blackamoor's hands over her white virgin's flesh.

And while in Italian he detailed his heated fantasies, he was slowly peeling the glove back, exposing a delicately voluptuous palm. Then he gave one small tug toward her knuckles. And paused. Then another tug. And paused. Then another tug . . . and the glove was off. He let it fall to the table, and took her small, cool, white hand in his great, warm one. She gave a tiny gasp. That was all. No struggle. Not that it would have made the least difference to him.

He was overwarm and short of breath, and his heart pounded as though he'd been running very hard after something. And just as though he had done so and got it at last, he was not about to let it go. His fingers closed around her hand and he gave her a fierce look, daring her to try—just *try*—to get away.

He found she was still wearing the same wide-eyed expression. Then she blinked and, dropping her gaze to their joined hands, she said in a small, breathless voice, "I'm *very* sorry, my lord."

Though still not properly in control of his own respiration, Dain managed to get the words out. "I have no doubt you are. But it's too late, you see."

"I do." She shook her head sadly. "I fear your reputation will never recover."

He felt a prickle of uneasiness. He ignored it and,

with a laugh, glanced about him at their fascinated audience. "*Cara mia*, it is your own rep—"

"The Marquess of Dain has been seen in the company of a *lady*," she said. "He has been seen and heard wooing her." She looked up, her silver eyes gleaming. "It was lovely. I had no idea Italian was so . . . moving."

"I was talking about drains," he said tightly.

"I didn't know. Neither did anyone else, I'm sure. They all think you were making love." She smiled. "To nitwit Bertie Trent's spinster sister."

Then, too late, he saw the flaw in his reasoning. Then he recalled Esmond's remark about the legendary Genevieve. Everyone here would believe the chit followed in her grandmother's footsteps—a *femme fatale*—and the curst Parisians would believe he'd fallen under her spell.

"Dain," she said in a low, hard voice, "if you do not release my hand this instant, I shall kiss you. In front of everybody."

He had a ghastly suspicion he'd kiss her back—in front of witnesses—Dain, Beelzebub himself, kissing a lady—a *virgin*. He crushed his panic.

"Miss Trent," he said, his own tones equally low and hard, "I should like to see you try."

"By gad," came an obnoxiously familiar voice from behind Dain. "I had to go nearly to that blasted Bwy Bullion—and it ain't exactly what you wanted, I know, but I tried one myself first, and I daresay you won't be disappointed."

Oblivious to the tension throbbing about him, Bertie Trent set a small cigar box down upon the table one inch from Dain's hand. The hand still clasping Miss Trent's.

Bertie's gaze fell there and his blue eyes widened. "Deuce take you, Jess," he said crossly. "Can't a fellow trust you for a moment? How many times do I have to tell you to leave my friends alone?"

Miss Trent coolly withdrew her hand.

Trent gave Dain an apologetic look. "Don't pay it any mind, Dain. She does that to all the chaps. I don't know why she does it, when she don't want 'em. Just like them fool cats of Aunt Louisa's. Go to all the bother of catching a mouse, and then the confounded things won't eat 'em. Just leave the corpses lying about for someone else to pick up."

Miss Trent's lips quivered.

The hint of laughter was all that was needed to shrivel and crush and beat the tumultuous mixture inside Lord Dain into frigid fury.

He had commenced his formal education by having his head thrust into a privy. He had been mocked and tormented before. But not for long.

"Fortunately, Trent, you have the knack of arriving in the very nick of time," he said. "Since words cannot express my relief and gratitude, actions must speak louder. Why don't you toddle round to my place after you take your irresistible sister home? Vawtry and a few others are coming by for a bottle or two and a private game of hazard."

After enduring Trent's incoherent expressions of delight, Lord Dain took his cool leave of the pair and sauntered out of the shop, grimly determined to hold Bertie Trent's head under until he *drowned*.

Even before Lord Dain arrived home, the eyewitness reports of his tête-à-tête with Miss Trent were moving swiftly through the streets of Paris.

By the time, close to dawn, his private orgy of drinking and gambling had broken up—and Bertie, a few hundred pounds the poorer, was being carried by a brace of servants to his bed—wagers were being made regarding the Marquess of Dain's intentions toward Miss Trent.

At three o'clock in the afternoon, Francis Beaumont, encountering Roland Vawtry at Tortoni's, bet him one hundred fifty pounds that Dain would be shackled to Miss Trent before the King's Birthday in June.

"Dain?" Vawtry repeated, his hazel eyes widening. "*Wed?* To a gentry spinster? Trent's *sister?*"

Ten minutes later, when Vawtry had stopped laughing and was beginning to breathe normally again, Beaumont repeated his offer.

"It's too easy," said Vawtry. "I can't take your money. It wouldn't be fair. I've known Dain since we were at Oxford. That business in the coffee shop was one of his jokes. To get everyone in an uproar. This very minute, he's probably laughing himself sick about what a lot of fools he's made of everybody."

"Two hundred," said Beaumont. "Two hundred says he stops laughing inside a week."

"I see," said Vawtry. "You want to throw your money down another rathole. Very well, my lad. Define the terms."

"Inside a week, someone sees him go after her," said Beaumont. "He follows her out of a room. Down a street. Takes her hand. Gad, I don't care—grabs her by the hair—That's more in his style, isn't it?"

"Beaumont, going *after* women isn't in Dain's style," Vawtry said patiently. "Dain says, 'I'll take this one.' Then he lays down the money and the female goes."

"He goes after this one," said Beaumont. "Just as I said. Before reliable witnesses. Two hundred says he does it within seven days."

This would not be the first time Roland Vawtry's

profound understanding of Dain would make him money. Predicting Beelzebub's behavior, in fact, was how Vawtry made at least half his income. He thought that Beaumont ought to know better by now. But Beaumont didn't, and the smug, superior smile on his face was beginning to irritate Vawtry. Arranging his own fair features into an expression of profound pity—to irritate Beaumont—Vawtry accepted the bet.

Six days later, Jessica was standing at the window of her brother's *appartement*, scowling down at the street below.

"I shall *kill* you, Dain," she muttered. "I shall put a bullet precisely where that Italian nose of yours meets your black brows."

It was nearly six o'clock. Bertie had promised he would be home by half past four to bathe and dress, in order to escort his sister and grandmother to Madame Vraisses' party. Mrs. Beaumont's portrait of their hostess was to be unveiled at eight o'clock. Since Bertie needed at least two and a half hours to perform his toilette, and the evening traffic was bound to be heavy, they were going to miss the unveiling.

And it was all Dain's fault.

Since the encounter at the coffee shop, he could not bear to have Bertie out of his sight. Wherever Dain went, whatever he did, he could not enjoy himself unless Bertie was there.

Bertie, of course, believed he'd finally won Dain's undying friendship. Gullible baconbrain that he was, Bertie had no idea the alleged friendship was Dain's revenge on her.

Which only showed how despicable a villain Dain was. His quarrel was with Jessica, but no, he couldn't fight fair and square with someone capable of fighting back. He had to punish her via her poor, stupid brother, who hadn't the least idea how to defend himself.

Bertie didn't know how *not* to drink himself unconscious, or quit a card game, or resist a wager he was bound to lose, or protest when a tart cost thrice what she ought to. If Dain drank, Bertie must, though he hadn't the head for it. If Dain played or wagered or whored, Bertie must do exactly as he did.

Jessica did not, in principle, object to any of these practices. She had been tipsy more than once and, upon occasion, lost money on cards or a bet—but within discreet and reasonable bounds. As to the tarts, if she had been a man, she supposed she'd fancy one now and then, too—but she would certainly not pay a farthing above the going rate. She could scarcely believe Dain paid as much as Bertie claimed, but Bertie had sworn on his honor he'd seen the money change hands himself.

"If it's true," she'd told him exasperatedly, only last evening, "it can only be because his requirements are excessive—because the women have to work harder, don't you see?"

All Bertie saw was that she was implying he wasn't as lusty a stallion as his idol was. She had impugned her brother's masculinity, and so he had stomped out and not come—or been carried, rather—home until seven o'clock this morning.

Meanwhile, she'd lain awake until nearly then, wondering what exactly Dain required of a bed partner.

Thanks to Genevieve, Jessica did understand the basics of what normal men required—or provided, depending upon how one looked at it. She had known, for example, what the bewigged gentleman hiding under the lady's skirts had been doing, just as she'd known that such poses weren't common in naughty watches. That was why she'd bought it.

But since Dain wasn't normal, and he'd surely paid for a great deal more than mere basics, she had tossed feverishly in her bed in an agitated muddle of fear and curiosity and . . . well, if one was perfectly honest with oneself, which she generally was, there was some hankering, too, heaven help her.

She could not stop thinking about his hands. Which wasn't to say she hadn't contemplated every other part of him as well, but she'd had direct, simmering physical experience of those large, too adept hands.

At the mere thought of them, even now, furious as she was, she felt something hot and achy curl inside her, from her diaphragm to the pit of her belly.

Which only made her the more furious.

The mantel clock chimed the hour.

First she'd kill Dain, she told herself. Then she'd kill her brother.

Withers entered. "The porter has returned from the marquess's establishment," he said.

Bertie, following the custom of the Parisians, relied upon the building's porter to perform the tasks normally assigned at home to footmen, maids, and errand boys. Half an hour earlier, the porter, Tesson, had been dispatched to Lord Dain's.

"Obviously he hasn't brought Bertie back," she said, "or I would have heard my brother hallooing in the hall by now."

"Lord Dain's servant refused to respond to Tesson's enquiry," said Withers. "When Tesson loyally persisted, the insolent footman ejected him bodily from the front step. The servants, Miss Trent, are abominably well suited, in point of character, to the master."

It was one thing, Jessica thought angrily, for Dain to

exploit her brother's weaknesses. It was altogether another matter to allow his lackeys to abuse an overworked porter for trying to deliver a message.

"Pardon one offense," Publilius had said, "and you encourage the commission of many."

Jessica was not about to pardon this. Fists clenched, she marched to the door. "I do not care if the servant is Mephistopheles himself," she said. "I should like to see him try to eject *me.*"

A very short time later, while her terrified maid, Flora, cowered in a dirty Parisian hackney, Jessica was plying the knocker of Lord Dain's street door.

A liveried English footman opened it. He was close to six feet tall. As he insolently eyed her up and down, Jessica had no trouble deducing what was going through his mind. Any servant with a pennyweight of intelligence would see that she was a lady. On the other hand, no lady would ever come knocking on the door of an unwed gentleman. The trouble was, Dain wasn't a gentleman. She did not wait for the footman to work out the conundrum.

"The name is Trent," she said briskly. "And I am not accustomed to being kept standing on a doorstep while an idle lout of a lackey gawks at me. You have exactly three seconds to step out of the way. One. Two—"

He backed away and she strode past him into the vestibule.

"Get my brother," she said.

He was staring at her in numb disbelief. "Miss— Miss—"

"Trent," she said. "Sir Bertram's sister. I want to see him. *Now.*" She rapped the point of her umbrella upon the marble floor for emphasis.

Jessica had adopted the tone and manner she'd found effective in dealing with unruly boys bigger than she was and with those of her uncles' and aunts' servants who made nonsensical remarks such as "Master wouldn't like it" or "Missus says I may not." Hers was a tone and manner that assured the listener of only two choices: obedience or death. It proved as effective in this case as in most others.

The footman darted a panicked look toward the stairway at the end of the hall. "I—I can't, miss," he said in a frightened whisper. "He—he'll *kill* me. No interruptions. None, miss. Ever."

"I see," she said. "You're brave enough to throw a porter half your size into the street, but you—"

A shot rang out.

"Bertie!" she cried. Dropping her umbrella, Jessica ran toward the staircase.

Normally the sound of a pistol shot, even if followed, as this was, by feminine screams, would not have thrown Jessica into a panic. The trouble was, her brother was in the vicinity. If Bertie was in the vicinity of a ditch, he was sure to fall into it. If Bertie was in the vicinity of an open window, he was sure to tumble out of it.

Ergo, if Bertie was in the vicinity of a moving bullet, he may be counted upon to walk straight into it.

Jessica knew better than to hope he hadn't been hit. She only prayed she could stop the bleeding.

She raced up the long stairway and into the hall and headed unerringly toward the shrieks—feminine—and drunken shouts—masculine.

She flung open a door.

The first thing she saw was her brother lying faceup on the carpet.

For an instant, that was all she saw. She hurried to the body. Just as she was kneeling to examine it, Bertie's chest heaved jerkily and he let out a loud snore—a loud, wine-reeking snore that drove her instantly upright again.

Then she noticed that the room was as still as a tomb.

Jessica glanced about her.

Strewn about the chairs and sofas and sprawling over tables were, in various stages of dishabille, about a dozen men. Some she'd never seen before. Some—Vawtry, Sellowby, Goodridge—she recognized. With them were a number of women, all members of an ancient profession.

Then her gaze lit upon Dain. He sat in an immense chair, a pistol in his hand and two buxom trollops—one fair, the other dark—in his lap. They were staring at her and, like everyone else, seemed frozen in the same position they'd been in when she'd burst through the door. The darker female had apparently been in the act of tugging Dain's shirt from his waistband, while the other had evidently been assisting the process by unfastening his trouser buttons.

To be surrounded by a lot of half-dressed, drunken men and women in the early stages of an orgy did not distress Jessica in the least. She had seen little boys running about naked—on purpose to make the females of the household scream—and she had more than once been treated to the sight of a bare adolescent bottom, for this was often a male cousin's idea of witty repartee.

She was not in the least disconcerted or agitated by her present surroundings. Even the pistol in Dain's hand didn't alarm her, since it had already gone off and would need to be reloaded.

The only disturbing sensation she experienced was an altogether irrational urge to rip those two strumpets' hair out by the dyed roots and break all their fingers. She told herself this was silly. They were merely businesswomen, doing what they were paid for. She told herself she felt sorry for them, and this was why she felt so acutely unhappy.

She almost believed that. At any rate, whether she did or didn't, she was mistress of herself and, therefore, of any situation.

"I thought he was dead," Jessica said, nodding at her unconscious brother. "But he's only dead drunk. My mistake." She walked to the door. "Do carry on, *monsieurs*. And *mademoiselles*."

And out she went.

Up to a point, Lord Dain decided, all had gone swimmingly. He had finally worked out a solution to his temporary problem with trollops. If he couldn't tolerate having them in a brothel or in the streets, he would have them at home.

It would not be the first time.

Nine years ago, at his father's funeral, a round-heeled local girl named Charity Graves had taken his fancy, and he had taken her, a few hours later, in the great ancestral bed. She had been jolly enough company, but not nearly so jolly as the thought of his recently deceased sire spinning in the tomb of his noble ancestors—and most of the ancestors whirling along with him.

An annoyance had resulted nine months later, but that was easily enough dealt with. Dain's man of business had dealt with it to the tune of fifty pounds per annum.

Since then, Dain had confined himself to whores who plied their trade according to businesslike rules, and knew better than to produce—let alone attempt to manipulate and blackmail him with—squalling brats.

Denise and Marguerite understood the rules, and he

had every intention of getting properly down to business at last.

Just as soon as he dealt with Miss Trent.

Though Dain had felt certain she would accost him sooner or later, he had not expected her to explode into his drawing room. Still, that was, in a general way, in accordance with his plans. Her brother was falling to pieces with a gratifying rapidity, now that Dain had taken an active role in his disintegration.

Miss Trent would certainly know why. And being a clever female, she would soon be obliged to admit she'd made a grave error in trying to play the Marquess of Dain for a fool. He had decided she would be obliged to admit it upon her knees. Then she would have to beg for mercy.

That was where matters seemed to have gone awry.

All she had done was give her brother one bored look and the guests another, and dropped a faintly amused glance upon Dain himself. Then, cool as you please, the insufferable creature had turned her back and walked out.

For six days, Dain had spent nearly all his waking hours with her accursed brother, pretending to be that dithering imbecile's bosom bow. For six days, Trent had been yapping in Dain's ears, nipping at his heels, slavering and panting for attention, and tripping over his own feet and any hapless object or human in his way. After nearly a week of having his nerves scraped raw by her brainless puppy of a brother, all Dain had accomplished was to find himself the object of Miss Trent's *amusement*.

"*Allez-vous en*," he said in a very low voice. Denise and Marguerite instantly leapt up from his lap and darted to opposite corners of the room.

"I say, Dain," Vawtry began mollifyingly.

Dain shot him one incinerating glance. Vawtry reached for a wine bottle and hastily refilled his glass.

Dain set down the pistol, stalked to the door and through it, and slammed it behind him.

After that, he moved quickly. He reached the landing in time to see Trent's sister pause at the front door and look about for something.

"Miss Trent," he said. He didn't raise his voice. He didn't need to. The angry baritone reverberated through the hall like low thunder.

She jerked open the door and darted through it.

He watched the door close and told himself to return to shooting the noses off the plaster cherubs on the ceiling, because if he went after her, he'd kill her. Which was unacceptable, because Dain did not, under any circumstances, sink to allowing any member of the inferior sex to provoke him.

Even while he was counseling himself, he was running down the remaining stairs and down the long hall to the door. He wrenched it open and stormed out, the door crashing behind him.

Five

Then he nearly trampled her down because, for some insane reason, Miss Trent wasn't fleeing down the street, but marching back toward his house.

"Confound his insolence!" she cried, making for the door. "I shall break his nose. First the porter, now my maid—*and* the hackney. It is the outside of enough."

Dain stepped in her way, his massive body shielding the entrance. "Oh, no, you don't. I don't know or care what your game is—"

"*My* game?" She stepped back, planted her hands on her hips, and glared up at him. At least she seemed to be glaring. It was difficult to tell, given the large bonnet brim and the failing light.

The sun had not quite set, but massive grey clouds were submerging Paris in a heavy gloom. From a distance came the low boom of thunder.

"*My* game?" she repeated. "It's your bully of a footman, following his master's example, I collect—taking out his vexation on innocent parties. Doubtless he thought it a great joke to frighten away the hackney—with my maid inside the vehicle—and leave me stranded—*after* stealing my umbrella."

She turned on her heel and stalked off.

If Dain was interpreting this ranting correctly, Herbert had frightened away Miss Trent's maid as well as the hired vehicle that had brought her here.

A thunderstorm was rapidly approaching, Herbert had taken her umbrella, and the chances of locating an unoccupied hackney at this hour in bad weather were about nil.

Dain smiled. "Adieu, then, Miss Trent," he said. "Have a pleasant promenade home."

"Adieu, Lord Dain," she answered without turning her head. "Have a pleasant evening with your cows."

Cows?

She was merely trying to provoke him, Dain told himself. The remark was a pathetic attempt at a set-down. To take offense was to admit he'd felt the sting. He told himself to laugh and return to his . . . cows.

A few furious strides brought him to her side. "Is that prudery, I wonder, or envy?" he demanded. "Is it their trade which offends you—or merely their being more generously endowed?"

She kept on walking. "When Bertie told me how much you paid, I thought it was their services which were so horrifically expensive," she said. "Now, however, I comprehend my error. Obviously you pay by volume."

"Perhaps the price is exorbitant," he said, while his hands itched to shake her. "But then, I am not so shrewd at haggling as you. Perhaps, in future, you would like to conduct negotiations for me. In which case, I ought to describe my requirements. What I like—"

"You like them big, buxom, and stupid," she said.

"Intelligence is hardly relevant," he said, suppressing a ferocious urge to tear her bonnet from her head and stomp on it. "I do not hire them to debate metaphysics. But since you understand what I want them to look like, I should hasten to explain what I like them to do."

"I know you like to have them take off your clothes," she said. "Or perhaps put them on again. At the time, it was difficult to determine whether they were at the beginning or the end of the performance."

"I like *both*," he said, jaw clenched. "And in between, I like them to—"

"I recommend you try to fasten your buttons by yourself at present," she said. "Your trousers are beginning to bunch up in an unsightly way over the tops of your boots."

It was not until this moment that Dain recollected his state of dress—or undress, rather. He now discovered that his shirt cuffs were flapping at his wrists, while the body of the garment billowed in the gusting wind.

While the words "shy" and "modest" did appear in Dain's Dictionary, they had no connection with him. On the other hand, his attire, unlike his character, was always *comme il faut*. Not to mention that he was marching through the streets of the most sartorially critical city in the world.

Heat crawled up his neck. "Thank you, Miss Trent," he said coolly, "for calling the matter to my attention." Then, just as coolly, and walking at her side all the while, he unbuttoned all the trouser buttons, tucked the shirt inside, and leisurely buttoned up again.

Miss Trent made a small choked sound.

Dain gave her a sharp glance. He could not be sure, given the bonnet and the rapidly deepening darkness, but he thought her color had risen.

"Do you feel faint, Miss Trent?" he asked. "Is that why you have walked straight past what should have been your next turning?"

She stopped. "I walked past it," she said in a muffled voice, "because I didn't know that was it."

He smiled. "You don't know the way home."

She began moving again, toward the street he'd indicated. "I shall figure it out."

He followed her round the corner. "You were going to simply walk back, in the dead of night, to your brother's house—though you haven't the vaguest notion how to get there. You're rather a henwit, aren't you?"

"I agree that it's growing dark, though hardly the dead of night," she said. "In any case, I am certainly not alone, and it hardly seems henwitted to have the most terrifying man in Paris as my escort. It's very chivalrous of you, Dain. Rather sweet, actually." She paused at a narrow street. "Ah, I am getting my bearings. This leads to the Rue de Provence, does it not?"

"*What* did you say?" he asked in ominously low tones.

"I said, 'This leads—' "

"*Sweet*," he said, following her round the corner.

"Yes, there it is." She quickened her pace. "I recognize the lamppost."

If she'd been a man, he would have made sure her skull had an intimate acquaintance with that lamppost.

Dain realized he was clenching his fists. He slowed his steps and told himself to go home. Now. He had never in his life raised a hand against a female. That sort of behavior showed not only a contemptible lack of control, but cowardice as well. Only cowards used deadly weapons against the weaponless.

"There seems to be no imminent danger of your endlessly wandering the streets of Paris and agitating the populace into a riot," he said tightly. "I believe I might with clear conscience allow you to complete your journey solo."

She paused and turned and smiled. "I quite understand. The Rue de Provence is usually very crowded at this time, and one of your friends might see you. Best run along. I promise not to breathe a word about your gallantry."

He told himself to laugh and walk away. He'd done it a thousand times before, and knew it was one of the best exits. There was no way to stab and jab when Dain laughed in your face. He'd been more viciously stabbed and jabbed before. This was merely . . . irritation.

All the same, the laugh wouldn't come, and he couldn't turn his back on her.

She had already disappeared round the corner.

He stormed after her and grabbed her arm, stopping her in her tracks. "Now, you hold your busy tongue and *listen*," he said levelly. "I am not one of your Society fribbles to be twitted and mocked by a ha'pennyworth of a chit with an exalted opinion of her wit. I don't give a damn what anyone sees, thinks, or says. I am not chivalrous, Miss Trent, and I am not *sweet*, confound your impertinence!"

"And I am not one of your stupid cows!" she snapped. "I am not paid to do exactly as you like, and no law on earth obliges me to do so. I shall say whatever I please, and at this moment, it pleases me exceedingly to infuriate you. Because that is precisely how I feel. You have *ruined* my evening. I should like nothing better than to ruin yours, you spoiled, selfish, spiteful *brute!*"

She kicked him in the ankle.

He was so astonished that he let go of her arm.

He stared at her tiny, booted foot. "Good gad, did you actually think you could hurt me with *that?*" He laughed. "Are you mad, Jess?"

"You great drunken jackass!" she cried. "How dare

you?" She tore off her bonnet and whacked him in the chest with it.

"I did *not* give you leave to use my Christian name." She whacked him again. "And I am *not* a ha'pennyworth of a chit, you thickheaded ox!" Whack, whack, whack.

Dain gazed down in profound puzzlement. He saw a flimsy wisp of a female attempting, apparently, to do him an injury with a bit of millinery.

She seemed to be in a perfect fury. While tickling his chest with her ridiculous hat, she was ranting about some party and somebody's picture and Mrs. Beaumont and how he had spoiled everything and he would be very sorry, because she no longer gave a damn about Bertie, who was no use on earth to anybody, and she was going straight back to England and open a shop and auction the icon herself and get ten thousand for it, and she hoped Dain choked on it.

Dain was not certain what he was supposed to choke on, except perhaps laughter, because he was certain he'd never seen anything so vastly amusing in all his life as Miss Jessica Trent in a temper fit.

Her cheeks were pink, her eyes flashed silver sparks, and her sleek black hair was tumbling about her shoulders.

It was very black, the same pure jet as his own. But different. His was thick and coarse and curly. Hers was a rippling veil of silk.

A few tresses shaken loose from their pins dangled teasingly against her bodice.

And that was when he became distracted.

Her apple green pelisse fastened all the way to her white throat. It was fastened very snugly, outlining the curve of her breasts.

Measured against, say, Denise's generous endowments, Miss Trent's were negligible. In proportion to a slim, fine-boned frame and a whisper of a waist, however, the feminine curves abruptly became more than ample.

Lord Dain's fingers began to itch, and a snake of heat stirred and writhed in the pit of his belly.

The tickling bonnet became an irritation. He grabbed it and crushed it in his hand and threw it down. "That's enough," he said. "You're beginning to bother me."

"Bother you?" she cried. "*Bother?* I'll bother you, you conceited clodpole." Then she drew back, made a fist, and struck him square in the solar plexus.

It was a good, solid blow, and had she directed it at a man less formidably built, that man would have staggered.

Dain scarcely felt it. The lazy raindrops plopping on his head had about as much physical impact.

But he saw her wince as she jerked her hand away, and realized she'd hurt herself, and that made him want to howl. He grabbed her hand, then hastily dropped it, terrified he'd crush it by accident.

"Damn and blast and confound you to hell!" he roared. "Why won't you leave me in peace, you plague and pestilence of a female!"

A stray mongrel, sniffing at the lamppost, yelped and scurried away.

Miss Trent did not even blink. She only stood gazing with a sulkily obstinate expression at the place she'd hit, as though she were waiting for something.

He didn't know what it was. All he knew—and he didn't know how he knew, but it was a certainty as ineluctable as the storm swelling and roaring toward them—was that she hadn't got it yet and she would not go away until she did.

"What the devil do you want?" he shouted. "What in blazes is the matter with you?"

She didn't answer.

The desultory plops of rain were building to a steady patter upon the *trottoir*. Droplets glistened on her hair and shimmered on her pink-washed cheeks. One drop skittered along the side of her nose and down to the corner of her mouth.

"Damnation," he said.

And then he didn't care what he crushed or broke. He reached out and wrapped his monster hands about her waist and lifted her straight up until her wet, sulky face was even with his own.

And in the same heartbeat, before she could scream, he clamped his hard, dissolute mouth over hers.

The heavens opened up then, loosing a torrent.

Rain beat down upon his head, and a pair of small, gloved fists beat upon his shoulders and chest.

These matters troubled him not a whit. He was Dain, Lord Beelzebub himself.

He feared neither Nature's wrath nor that of civilized society. He most certainly was not troubled by Miss Trent's indignation.

Sweet, was he? He was a gross, disgusting pig of a debauchee, and if she thought she'd get off with merely one repellent peck of his polluted lips, she had another think coming.

There was nothing sweet or chivalrous about his kiss. It was a hard, brazen, take-no-prisoners assault that drove her head back.

For one terrifying moment, he wondered if he'd broken her neck.

But she couldn't be dead, because she was still flailing at him and squirming. He wrapped one arm tightly about her waist and brought the other hand up to hold her head firmly in place.

Instantly she stopped squirming and flailing. And in

that instant her tightly compressed lips yielded to his assault with a suddenness that made him stagger backward, into the lamppost.

Her arms lashed about his neck in a stranglehold.

Madonna in cielo.

Sweet mother of Jesus, the demented female was *kissing him back.*

Her mouth pressed eagerly against his, and that mouth was warm and soft and fresh as spring rain. She smelled of soap—chamomile soap—and wet wool and Woman.

His legs wobbled.

He leaned back against the lamppost and his crushing grasp loosened because his muscles were turning to rubber. Yet she clung to him, her slim, sweetly curved body sliding slowly down his length until her toes touched the pavement. And still she didn't let go of his neck. Still she didn't pull her mouth away from his. Her kiss was as sweet and innocently ardent as his had been bold and lustily demanding.

He melted under that maidenly ardor as though it were rain and he a pillar of salt.

In all the years since his father had packed him off to Eton, no woman had ever done anything to or for him until he'd put money in her hand. Or—as in the case of the one respectable female he'd been so misguided as to pursue nearly eight years ago—unless he signed papers putting his body, soul, and fortune into said hands.

Miss Jessica Trent was holding on to him as though her life depended upon it and kissing him as though the world would come to an end if she stopped, and there was no "unless" or "until" about it.

Bewildered and heated at once, he moved his big hands unsteadily over her back and shaped his trembling fingers to her deliciously dainty waist. He had never before held anything like her—so sweetly slim and supple and curved to delicate perfection. His chest tightened and ached and he wanted to weep.

Sognavo di te.

I've dreamed of you.

Ti desideravo nelle mia braccia dal primo momento che ti vedi.

I've wanted you in my arms since the moment I met you.

He stood, helpless in the driving rain, unable to rule his needy mouth, his restless hands, while, within, his heart beat out the mortifying truth.

Ho bisogno di te.

I need you.

As though that last were an outrage so monstrous that even the generally negligent Almighty could not let it pass, a blast of light rent the darkness, followed immediately by a violent crash that shook the pavement.

She jerked away and stumbled back, her hand clapped to her mouth.

"Jess," he said, reaching out to bring her back. "*Cara*, I—"

"No. Oh, God." She shoved her wet hair out of her face. "Damn you, Dain." Then she turned and fled.

Jessica Trent was a young woman who faced facts, and as she mounted, dripping, the stairs to her brother's *appartement*, she faced them.

First, she had leapt at the first excuse to hunt down Lord Dain.

Second, she had sunk into a profound depression, succeeded almost instantly by jealous rage, because she'd found two women sitting in his lap.

Third, she had very nearly wept when he'd spoken slightingly of her attractions and called her "a ha'penny-worth of a chit."

Fourth, she had *goaded* him into assaulting her.

Fifth, she had very nearly choked him to death, demanding the assault continue.

Sixth, it had taken a bolt of lightning to knock her loose.

By the time she came to the *appartement* door, she was strongly tempted to dash her brains out against it.

"Idiot, idiot, idiot," she muttered, pounding on the portal.

Withers opened it. His mouth fell open.

"Withers," she said, "I have failed you." She marched into the apartment. "Where is Flora?"

"Oh, dear." Withers looked helplessly about him.

"Ah, then she hasn't returned. Not that I am the least surprised." Jessica headed for her grandmother's room. "In fact, if my poor maid makes the driver take her direct to Calais and row her across the Channel, I should not blame her a whit." She rapped at Genevieve's door.

Her grandmother opened it, gazed at her for a long moment, then turned to Withers. "Miss Trent requires a hot bath," she said. "Have someone see to it—quickly—if you please."

Then she took Jessica's arm, tugged her inside, sat her down, and pulled off her sodden boots.

"I *will* go to that party," said Jessica, fumbling with her pelisse buckles. "Dain can make a fool of me if he likes, but he will not ruin my evening. I don't care if all of Paris saw. He's the one who ought to be embarrassed—running half-naked down the street. And when I reminded him that he was half-naked, what do you think he did?"

"My dear, I cannot imagine." Genevieve quickly worked the silk stockings off.

Jessica told her about the leisurely trouser unbuttoning.

Genevieve went into whoops of laughter.

Jessica frowned at her. "It was very difficult to keep a straight face—but that wasn't the hardest part. The hardest part was—" She let out a sigh. "Oh, Genevieve. He was so *adorable*. I wanted to kiss him. Right on his big, beautiful nose. And then everywhere else. It was so frustrating. I had made up my mind not to lose my temper, but I did. And so I beat him and beat him until he kissed me. And then I kept on beating him until he did it properly. And I had better tell you, mortifying as it is to admit, that if we had not been struck by lightning— or very nearly—I should be utterly ruined. Against a lamppost. On the Rue de Provence. And the horrible part is"—she groaned—"I wish I *had been*."

"I know," Genevieve said soothingly. "Believe me, dear, I know." She stripped off the rest of the garments— Jessica being incapable of doing much besides babbling and staring stupidly at the furniture—wrapped her in a dressing gown, planted her in a chair by the fire, and ordered brandy.

About half an hour after Jessica Trent had fled him, Lord Dain, drenched to the skin and clutching a mangled bonnet, stalked through the door a trembling Herbert opened for him. Ignoring the footman, the marquess marched down the hall and up the stairs and down another hall to his bedroom. He threw the bonnet onto a chair, stripped off his dripping garments, toweled himself dry, donned fresh attire, and rejoined his guests.

No one, including the tarts, was audacious or drunk enough to seek an accounting of his whereabouts and doings. Dain seldom troubled to explain his actions. He was accountable to nobody.

All he told them was that he was hungry and was going out to dinner, and they were at liberty to do as they pleased. All but Trent, who was incapable of any action beyond breathing—which he did with a great deal of noise—accompanied Dain to a restaurant at the Palais Royal. Thence they proceeded to *Vingt-Huit*, and discovered it had closed down that very day. Since no other establishment offered *Vingt-Huit*'s variety, the party broke up into smaller groups, each seeking its own choice of entertainment. Dain went to a gambling hell with his pair of . . . cows and Vawtry and his cow.

At three o'clock in the morning, Dain left, alone, and wandered the streets.

His wanderings took him to Madame Vraisses', just as the guests were beginning to leave.

He stood under a tree, well beyond the feeble glimmer of a lonely streetlamp, and watched.

He'd brooded there for nearly twenty minutes when he saw Esmond emerge, with Jessica Trent upon his arm. They were talking and laughing.

She was not wearing a ridiculous bonnet, but a lunatic hair arrangement even more ludicrous. Shiny knots and coils sprouted from the top of her head, and pearls and plumes waved from the knots and coils. The coiffure, in Dain's opinion, was silly.

That was why he wanted to rip out the pearls and plumes and pins . . . and watch the silky black veil ripple over her shoulders . . . white, gleaming in the lamplight.

There was too much gleaming white, he noted with a surge of irritation. The oversize ballooning sleeves of her silver-blue gown didn't even *have* shoulders. They started about halfway to her elbow, primly covering everything from there down—and leaving what should have been concealed brazenly exposed to the view of every slavering hound in Paris.

Every man at the party had examined, at leisure and close quarters, that curving whiteness.

While Dain, like the Prince of Darkness they all believed him to be, stood outside lurking in the shadows.

He did not feel very satanic at the moment. He felt, if the humiliating truth be told, like a starving beggar boy with his nose pressed to the window of a pastry shop.

He watched her climb into the carriage. The door closed and the vehicle lumbered away.

Though no one was by to see or hear, he laughed under his breath. He had laughed a great deal this night, but he couldn't laugh the truth away.

He'd known she was trouble—had to be, as every respectable female was.

"Wife or mistress, it's all the same," he'd told his friends often enough. "Once you let a lady—virtuous or not—fasten upon you, you become the owner of a piece of troublesome property, where the tenants are forever in revolt and into which you are endlessly pouring money and labor. All for the occasional privilege— at her whim—of getting what you could get from any streetwalker for a few shillings."

He'd wanted her, yes, but this was hardly the first time in his life the unacceptable sort of female had stirred his lust. He lusted, but he was always aware of the miry trap into which such women must—because they'd been born and bred for that purpose—lure him.

And the hateful truth was, he'd walked straight into it, and somehow deluded himself he hadn't—or if he had, it was nothing Dain need fear, because by now there was no pit deep enough, no mire thick enough, to hold him.

Then what holds you here? he asked himself. *What mighty force dragged you here, to gaze stupidly, like a moonstruck puppy, at a house, because she was in it?*

And what chains held you here, waiting for a glimpse of her?

A touch. A kiss.

That's revolting, he told himself.

So it was, but it was the truth, and he hated it and hated her for making it true.

He should have dragged her from the carriage, he thought, and pulled those ladylike fripperies from her hair, and taken what he wanted and walked away, laughing, like the conscienceless monster he was.

What or who was there to stop him? Before the Revolution, countless corrupt aristocrats had done the same. Even now, who would blame him? Everyone knew what he was. They would say it was her own fault for straying into his path. The law would not avenge her honor. It would be left to Bertie Trent . . . at pistol point at twenty paces.

With a grim smile, Dain left his gloomy post and sauntered down the street. Trapped he was, but he'd been trapped before, he reminded himself. He'd stood outside before, too, aching and lonely because he would not be let in. But always, in the end, Dain won. He had made his schoolboy tormentors respect and envy him. He had paid his father back tenfold for every humiliation and hurt. He'd become the old bastard's worst nightmare of hell in this life and, one hoped, his most bitter torment in the hereafter.

Even Susannah, who'd led him about by the nose for six wretched months, had spent every waking minute thereafter having her own pretty nose rubbed in the consequences.

True, Dain hadn't seen it that way at the time, but a man couldn't see anything properly while a woman was digging her claws into him and tearing him to pieces.

He could see now, clearly: a summer day in 1820, and another funeral, nearly a year after his father's.

This time it was Wardell inside the gleaming casket heaped with flowers. During a drunken fight over a whore in the stable yard of an inn, he had fallen onto the cobblestones and cracked his skull.

After the funeral, Susannah, the eldest of Wardell's five younger sisters, had drawn the Marquess of Dain aside and thanked him for coming all the way from Paris. Her poor brother—she'd bravely wiped away a tear—had thought the world of him. She'd laid her hand over his. Then, coloring, she'd snatched it away.

"Ah, yes, my blushing rosebud," Dain murmured cynically. "That was neatly done."

And it had been, for with that touch Susannah had drawn him in. She'd lured him into her world—polite Society—which he'd years earlier learned to shun, because there he had only to glance at a young lady to turn her complexion ashen and send her chaperons into hysterics. The only girls who'd ever danced with him were his friends' sisters, and that was a disagreeable duty they dispatched as quickly as possible.

But not Susannah. She couldn't dance because she was in mourning, but she could talk and did, and looked up at him as though he were a knight in shining armor, Sir Galahad himself.

After four months, he was permitted to hold her gloved hand for twenty seconds. It took him another two months to work up the courage to kiss her.

In her uncle's rose garden, the chivalrous knight had planted a chaste kiss upon his lady's cheek.

Almost in the same instant, as though on cue, a flock of shrieking women—mother, aunt, sisters—flew out of the bushes. The next he knew, he was closeted in the study with Susannah's uncle and sternly commanded to declare his intentions. Naive, besotted puppy that he'd been, Dain had declared them honorable.

In the next moment, he had a pen in his hand and an immense heap of documents before him, which he was commanded to sign.

Even now, Dain could not say where or how he'd found the presence of mind to read them first. Perhaps it had to do with hearing two commands in a row, and being unaccustomed to taking orders of any kind.

Whatever the reason, he'd set down the pen and read.

He'd discovered that in return for the privilege of marrying his blushing rosebud, he would be permitted to pay all of her late brother's debts, as well as her uncle's, aunt's, mother's, and her own, now and forever, 'til death do us part, amen.

Dain had decided it was a foolhardy investment and said so.

He was sternly reminded that he'd compromised an innocent girl of good family.

"Then shoot me," he'd replied. And walked out.

No one had tried to shoot him. Weeks later, back in Paris, he'd learned that Susannah had wed Lord Linglay.

Linglay was a sixty-five-year-old rouge-wearing roué who looked about ninety, collected obscene snuffboxes, and pinched and fondled every serving girl foolish enough to come within reach of his palsied hands. He had not been expected to survive the wedding night.

He had not only survived, but he'd managed to impregnate his young bride, and had continued to do so at a brisk pace. She'd scarcely get one brat out before the next one was planted.

Lord Dain was imagining in detail his former love in

the arms of her painted, palsied, sweating, and drooling spouse, and savoring those details, when the bells of Notre Dame clanged in the distance.

He realized they were rather more distant than they ought to be, if he was upon the Rue de Rivoli, where he lived and ought to be by now.

Then he saw he was in the wrong street, the wrong neighborhood altogether.

His baffled glance fell upon a familiar-looking lamp-post.

His spirits, lightened by images of Susannah's earthly purgatory, instantly sank again and dragged him, mind, body, and soul, into the mire.

Touch me. Hold me. Kiss me.

He turned the corner, into the dark, narrow street, where the blank, windowless walls could see and tell nothing. He pressed his forehead against the cold stone and endured, because he hadn't any choice. He couldn't stop what twisted and ached inside him.

I need you.

Her lips clinging to his . . . her hands, holding him fast. She was soft and warm and she tasted of rain, and it was sweet, unbearably sweet, to believe for a moment that she wanted to be in his arms.

He'd believed it for that moment, and wanted to believe still, and he hated himself for what he wanted, and hated her for making him want it.

And so, setting his jaw, Lord Dain straightened and went on his way, enduring, while he told himself she'd pay. In time.

Everyone did. In time.

Six

On the afternoon following Madame Vraisses' party, an unhappy Roland Vawtry paid Francis Beaumont two hundred pounds.

"I saw it myself," Vawtry said, shaking his head. "From the window. Even so, I shouldn't have believed it if everyone else hadn't seen it as well. He went right out the door and chased her down the street. To scare her off, I suppose. Daresay she's packing her bags this instant."

"She was at the unveiling celebration last night," Beaumont said, smiling. "Cool and collected and managing her swarm of panting admirers with smooth aplomb. When Miss Trent does decide to pack, it will be her trousseau. And the linens will be embellished with a *D* as in *Dain*."

Vawtry bridled. "It isn't at all like that. I know what happened. Dain doesn't like interruptions. He doesn't like uninvited guests. And when he doesn't like something, he makes it go away. Or he smashes it. If she'd been a man, he would have smashed her. Since she wasn't, he made her go away."

"Three hundred," said Beaumont. "Three hundred says she's his marchioness before the King's Birthday."

Vawtry suppressed his own smile. Whatever Dain did or didn't do with Miss Jessica Trent, he would not marry her.

Which wasn't to say that Dain would never wed. But that would be only to heap more shame, shock, and disgust upon his family, both the few living—a handful of distant cousins—and the legion dead. The bride, beyond doubt, would be the mistress, widow, or daughter of a notorious traitor or murderer. She would also be a famous whore. The ideal would be a half-Irish mulatto Jewess brothel keeper whose last lover had been hanged for sodomizing and strangling the Duke of Kent's only legitimate offspring, the nine-year-old Alexandrina Victoria. A Marchioness of Dain who was a gently bred virgin of respectable—if eccentric—family was out of the question.

Dain's being married—to anybody—in a mere two months or so was so far out of the question as to belong to another galaxy.

Vawtry accepted the wager.

This was not the only wager placed in Paris that week, and not the largest in which the names Dain and Trent figured.

The prostitutes who'd witnessed Miss Trent's entry into Dain's drawing room and his ensuing pursuit told all of their friends and customers about it. The male guests also related the tale, with the usual embellishments, to anyone who'd listen, and that was everyone.

And everyone, of course, had an opinion. Many put money behind their opinions. Within a week, Paris was seething and restless, rather like the Roman mob at the arena, impatiently awaiting the combat to death of its two mightiest gladiators.

The problem was getting the combatants into the same arena. Miss Trent traveled in respectable Society. Lord Dain prowled the demimonde. They were, most inconsiderately, avoiding each other. Neither could be persuaded or tricked into talking about the other.

Lady Wallingdon, who'd resided in Paris eighteen months and had spent most of that time striving, with mixed success, to become its premier hostess, saw a once-in-a-lifetime opportunity, and promptly snatched it.

She boldly scheduled a ball on the same day one of her rivals had scheduled a masquerade. It happened to be exactly a fortnight after the Chasing Miss Trent Down the Street Scene. Though Lady Pembury and her two grandchildren did not qualify as the *crème de la crème* of either Parisian or London society, and though Lady Wallingdon would not have bothered with them in other circumstances, she invited them to her ball.

She also invited Lord Dain.

Then she let everyone know what she'd done. Though she, like at least half of Paris, believed him to be enslaved by Miss Trent, Lady Wallingdon did not expect him to come. Everyone knew that the Marquess of Dain was about as likely to attend a respectable social affair as he was to invite the executioner to test the guillotine's blade upon his neck.

On the other hand, Dain had already behaved in an unlikely manner regarding Miss Trent, which meant there was a chance. And where there was a chance of something impossible happening, there would always be people wanting to be there in case it did.

In Lady Wallingdon's case, these turned out to be the very same people she'd invited. Not a single note of regrets arrived. Not even, to her disquiet, Lord Dain's.

But then, he hadn't sent an acceptance, either, so at

least she didn't have to pretend she didn't know whether he'd attend or not, and worry about being caught in a lie. She could keep her other invitees in suspense with a clear conscience. In the meantime, to be on the safe side, she hired a dozen burly French menials to augment her own staff.

Jessica, meanwhile, was acknowledging defeat. After a mere three encounters with Dain, a simple animal attraction had intensified to mindless infatuation. Her symptoms had not simply become virulent; they had become noticeable.

At Madame Vraisses' party, Mr. Beaumont had made a few sly remarks about Dain. Jessica, whose nerves were still vibrating with the aftershocks of one stormy embrace, had answered far too sharply. Beaumont's knowing smile had told her he'd guessed what her problem was, and she wouldn't have put it past him to tell Dain.

But the Beaumonts had abruptly left Paris a week after the party, and Dain hadn't come within a mile of her since the devastating kiss in the thunderstorm.

And so, if he *had* been told that Jessica Trent was besotted with him, he obviously didn't care. Which was just as she preferred it, Jessica assured herself.

Because there was only one way the Marquess of Dain could care about any woman, and that was for as long as it took to tumble her onto a bed—or a tavern table—unbutton his trousers, dispatch his business, and button up again.

Besotted or not, she knew better than to tempt Fate by risking another encounter with him, when he might see for himself her mortifying condition, and might take it into his head to treat her to his version of *caring*.

She had scarcely finished convincing herself that the

intelligent thing to do was to leave Paris immediately, when Lady Wallingdon's invitation arrived.

Within twenty-four hours, Jessica was aware—as all Paris was—that Dain, too, had been invited.

It did not take a genius to figure out why: She and Dain were expected to provide the main entertainment. She also understood that a great deal of money would change hands, based on her performance—or lack thereof—with His Lordship.

She decided she didn't want any part of it.

Genevieve decided otherwise. "If he goes, and you are not there, he will feel humiliated," she said. "Even if he merely wishes to go, for whatever reason, and learns you will not attend, he will feel the same. I know it is irrational and unfair, but men are often so, particularly in any matter they imagine concerns their pride. You had better attend, unless you prefer to risk his rampaging after you to relieve his wounded feelings."

Though Jessica very much doubted Dain had any feelings to be wounded, she was also aware that Genevieve had several decades' more experience with men. A great many men.

The invitation was accepted.

Dain could not decide what to do with Lady Wallingdon's invitation.

A part of his mind recommended he burn it.

Another part suggested he urinate on it.

Another advised him to shove it down Her Ladyship's throat.

In the end, he threw it into a trunk, which contained, along with various souvenirs of his travels, one mangled bonnet and one frilly umbrella. Six months from now, he told himself, he would look at those things and laugh. Then he would burn them, just as, years earlier, he'd burned the gloves he'd been wearing when Susannah had first touched his hand, and the piece of a feather that had fallen from her bonnet, and the note inviting him to the fatal dinner party at her uncle's.

At present, all he had to decide was how best to settle accounts with Miss Trent, as well as with the pious hypocrites who expected her to effect the miracle of bringing Lord Beelzebub to his knees.

He knew that was why Lady Wallingdon had invited him. Respectable Paris would like nothing better than to see him fall. That his slayer was a slip of an English spinster made the prospect all the more delicious. He had very little doubt that every self-righteous blockhead in Paris was praying for his defeat—the more ignominious, the better—at her hands.

They wanted a morality play, the Triumph of Virtue or some such rubbish.

He could leave them waiting, let them hold their collective breath until they were asphyxiated, while the stage remained empty. He rather enjoyed that image: a few hundred souls dying of suspense while Beelzebub dallied elsewhere, laughing, drinking champagne, his lap filled with painted harlots.

On the other hand, it would be delightful to laugh in their faces, to stalk onto the stage and treat them to a performance they'd never forget. That image, too, had its appeal: an hour or so of satanic mayhem in one of the Faubourg St. Germain's most decorously exclusive ballrooms. Then, at the climax, he would sweep Miss Jessica Trent into his arms, stamp his cloven hoof, and disappear with her in a cloud of smoke.

He'd no sooner conjured the image than he discarded

it as antithetical to his purposes. She must be ignored, so that she and everyone else would understand she had no power over him. He would do better to collect an armful of women at random, drag them away, and leave them mindless with terror in a cemetery.

But that was rather a lot of bother, and Paris didn't deserve so much entertainment. Better to let it die of disappointment.

So his mind went, back and forth, right up to the evening of the ball.

Jessica arrived at the ball in a state of resentful frustration, which ensuing events did little to improve.

She had spent several hours before the party fussing about her hair, her gown, and her accessories. She spent more than two hours after her arrival enduring a lot of subtle innuendoes from the female guests and not so subtle ones from the males.

By half past eleven, Bertie had already lost a few hundred quid in the cardroom, drunk himself senseless, and been taken home. Genevieve, meanwhile, was dancing for the second time with the Duc d'Abonville. Her beatific expression told Jessica that her grandmother was not going to be of any assistance this night. The French aristocrat had made an impression. When Genevieve was impressed with a man, she could not concentrate on anything else.

Normally Jessica could view her grandmother's romantic frailties with a mildly amused detachment. Now she understood, viscerally, what Genevieve felt, and it wasn't at all amusing.

It wasn't amusing to be edgy and restless and lonely and bored past endurance because it was nearly midnight and one despicable brute couldn't be bothered to come. It wasn't amusing, either, to know it was better he didn't come, and to want him here all the same and to hate herself for wanting it.

She had even left two dances unclaimed, in the mortifying hope that His Satanic Majesty would take a whim to haul her about the dance floor. Now, watching Genevieve and the handsome French nobleman, Jessica's heart sank. With Dain, it would never be like that.

He would never gaze down upon her with such a melting smile as Abonville's, and if Jessica ever looked upon him with an expression as enraptured as Genevieve's, Dain would laugh in her face.

Crushing a despair she knew was irrational, Jessica yielded to her two most pressing suitors. She gave one of the reserved dances to Malcolm Goodridge and the other to Lord Sellowby.

As he wrote his name upon the last empty stick of her fan—it was to be a souvenir of the occasion, her last night in Paris—Sellowby said, *sotto voce*, "I see there is no dance left for Dain. Are you confident he will not appear?"

"Do you believe otherwise?" she said. "Have you detected a whiff of brimstone or a puff of smoke heralding his approach?"

"I have a hundred pounds riding on his appearance," said Sellowby. He took out his pocket watch. "At precisely—Well, we shall see in a moment."

Jessica saw the minute hand of his timepiece meet its shorter mate at the same instant she heard a clock somewhere loudly chiming.

On the tenth stroke, heads began swiveling toward the ballroom entrance, and the clamor of voices began to die away. With the twelfth chime, the room fell still as death.

Her heart thudding, Jessica made herself turn, too, toward the entrance.

It was an immense, ornate, arched affair.

It did not seem large enough for the dark, towering figure that paused beneath it.

It was a long, dramatic pause, in keeping with the dramatic midnight entrance. And in keeping with his Prince of Darkness reputation, Dain was garbed almost entirely in stark, uncompromising black. A bit of snowy linen showed at his wrists, and another bit about his neck and upper chest, but they only heightened the effect. Even his waistcoat was black.

Though she stood the room's length away, Jessica had no doubt the dark gaze sweeping carelessly over the assembly glittered with contempt, and the hard mouth was curled in the ever so faint, ever so scornful smile.

The recollection of what that dissolute mouth had done to her a fortnight ago sent a wave of heat up her neck. She fanned herself and tried to drive the memory away—along with the suspicion that Sellowby was watching her out of the corner of his eye. She told herself it didn't matter what Sellowby or anyone else thought, except Dain.

He had come and she was here, so he could have no complaint on that score. All she had to do now was figure out what game he meant to play, and play it by his rules, and hope the rules fell somewhere within the bounds of civilized behavior. Then, mollified, he would laugh and go on his merry way, and she could go home to England, and he would not come rampaging after her. She would pick up with her life precisely where she had left off, and in a very short time, she would forget that he'd ever existed. Or she would remember him as one did a bad dream or a bout of fever, and sigh with relief that it was over.

It *must* be that way, Jessica told herself. The alternative was ruin, and she would not let her life be destroyed on account of a temporary madness, regardless how virulent.

It took Dain exactly nine seconds to spot Miss Trent in the mob. She stood with Sellowby and several other notorious rakes at the far end of the ballroom. She wore a silver-blue gown that shimmered in the light, and there seemed to be a lot of shimmering and fluttering objects dancing about her head. He supposed she had it screwed up in the ridiculous coils again. But the coiffure, like exaggerated sleeves and bonnets heaped with gewgaws, was the current fashion, and he doubted it could be any more atrocious than the birds of paradise standing upon a topknot on Lady Wallingdon's fat head.

Lady Wallingdon's fat face was arranged in a rigidly polite expression of welcome. Dain stalked to her, made an extravagant bow, smiled, and pronounced himself enchanted and honored and, generally, beside himself with rapture.

He gave her no excuse for retreating, and when he sweetly asked to be introduced to her guests, he took a malicious pleasure in the consternation that widened her beady eyes and drained all the color from her jowly face.

By this time, the mob of frozen statues about them was beginning to stir back to life. His trembling hostess gave a signal, the musicians dutifully began playing, and the ballroom gradually returned to a state as close to normal as one could reasonably expect, given the monster in its midst.

All the same, as his hostess led him from one group of guests to the next, Dain was aware of the tension in the air, aware that they were all waiting for him to commit an outrage—and probably wagering on what kind of outrage it would be.

He wanted, very badly, to oblige them. It had been nearly eight years since he'd entered this world, and though they all looked and behaved as he remembered polite Society looking and behaving, he'd forgotten what it felt like to be a freak. He'd remembered the stiff courtesy that couldn't disguise the fear and revulsion in their eyes. He'd remembered the women turning pale at his approach and the false heartiness of the men. He had forgotten, though, how bitterly alone they made him feel, and how the loneliness enraged him. He had forgotten how it twisted his insides into knots and made him want to howl and smash things.

After half an hour, his control was stretched to the breaking point, and he decided to leave—just as soon as he put the author of his miseries in her place, once and for all.

The quadrille having ended, Malcolm Goodridge was leading Miss Trent back to her circle of admirers, who were loitering near an enormous potted fern.

Dain released Lady Wallingdon. Leaving her to totter to a chair, he turned and marched across the room in the direction of the grotesque fern. He kept on marching until the men crowding about Miss Trent had to give way or be trodden down. They gave way, but they didn't go away.

He swept one heavy-lidded glance over them.

"Go away," he said quietly.

They went.

He gave Miss Trent a slow, head-to-toe survey.

She returned the favor.

Ignoring the simmering sensation her leisurely grey gaze triggered, he let his attention drift to her bodice, and boldly studied the rampant display of creamy white shoulders and bosom.

"It must be held up with wires," he said. "Otherwise, your dressmaker has discovered a method of defying the laws of gravity."

"It is lined with a stiffening material and bones, like a corset," she said calmly. "It is horridly uncomfortable, but it is the height of fashion, and I dared not risk your displeasure by appearing a dowd."

"Ah, you were confident I'd come," he said. "Because you are irresistible."

"I hope I'm not so suicidal as to wish to be irresistible to you." She fanned herself. "The simple fact is that there seems to be a farce in progress, of which we are the principals. I am prepared to take reasonable measures to help put an end to it. You set the tongues wagging with the scene in the coffee shop, but I will admit that I provided provocation," she added quickly, before he could retort. "I will also admit that the gossip might have died down if I hadn't burst into your house and annoyed you." Her color rose. "As to what happened afterward, no one saw, apparently, which makes it irrelevant to the problem at hand."

He noted that she was gripping her fan tightly and that her bosom was rising and falling with a rapidity indicative of agitation.

He smiled. "You did not behave, at the time, as though it were irrelevant. On the contrary—"

"Dain, I kissed you," she said evenly. "I see no reason to make an issue of it. It was not the first time you've ever been kissed and it won't be the last."

"Good heavens, Miss Trent, you are not threatening to do it again?" He widened his eyes in mock horror.

She let out a sigh. "I knew it was too much to hope you would be reasonable."

"What a woman means by a 'reasonable' man is one she can manage," he said. "You are correct, Miss Trent. It is too much to hope. I hear someone sawing at a violin. A waltz, or an approximation thereof, appears to be in the offing."

"So it does," she said tightly.

"Then we shall dance," he said.

"No, we shan't," she said. "I had saved two dances because . . . Well, it doesn't matter. I already have a partner for this one."

"Certainly. Me."

She held up her fan in front of his face, to display the masculine scribbling upon the sticks. "Look carefully," she said. "Do you see 'Beelzebub' written there?"

"I'm not shortsighted," he said, extracting the fan from her tense fingers. "You needn't hold it so close. Ah, yes, is this the one?" He pointed to a stick. "Rouvier?"

"Yes," she said, looking past him. "Here he comes."

Dain turned. A Frenchman was warily approaching, his countenance pale. Dain fanned himself. The man paused. Smiling, Dain pressed thumb and forefinger to the stick with "Rouvier" written on it. It snapped.

Rouvier went away.

Dain turned back to Miss Trent and, still smiling, broke each stick, one by one. Then he thrust the demolished fan into the fern pot.

He held out his hand. "My dance, I believe."

It was a primitive display, Jessica told herself. On the scale of social development it was about one notch above hitting her over the head with a club and dragging her away by her hair.

Only Dain could get away with it, just as only he could clear the field of rivals simply by telling them, without the smallest self-consciousness or subtlety, to go away.

And only she, besotted lunatic that she was, would find it all dizzyingly romantic.

She took his hand.

They both wore gloves. She felt it all the same: a thrill of contact sharp as an electrical shock. It darted through her limbs and turned her knees into jelly. Looking up, she saw the startled expression in his eyes and wondered, as his knowing smile faded, whether he felt it, too.

But if he did, it caused him no hesitation, for he boldly grasped her waist and, on the next upbeat, whirled her out.

With a gasp, she caught hold of his shoulder.

Then the world swung away, out of focus, out of existence, as he swept her into a waltz unlike anything she'd ever experienced before.

His wasn't the sedate English mode of waltzing, but a surging, blatantly sensuous Continental style, popular, she supposed, at gatherings of the demimonde. It was the way, she guessed, he danced with his whores.

But Dain wouldn't change his ways merely to accommodate a lot of Society prudes. He would dance as he chose, and she, delirious, could only be happy he'd chosen her.

He moved with inherent grace: strong, powerful, and utterly sure. She never had to think, only let herself be swept endlessly round the ballroom while her body tingled with consciousness of him and only him: the broad shoulder under her hand . . . the massive, muscular frame inches from her own . . . the tantalizing scent of smoke and cologne and Male . . . the warm hand at her waist, drawing her nearer by degrees, so that her skirts swirled round his legs . . . and nearer still and into a swift turn . . . her thigh grazing his . . .

She looked up into glittering, coal black eyes.

"You're not putting up much of a struggle," he said.

"As though it would do any good," she said, swallowing a sigh.

"Don't you even want to try?"

"No," she said. "And there's the hell of it."

He studied her face for a long moment. Then his mouth curved into that aggravatingly mocking smile. "I see. You find me irresistible."

"I'll get over it," she said. "I'm going home tomorrow."

His hand tightened on her waist, but he made no answer.

The music was faltering to a close. In a moment, he'd laugh and walk away, and she could return to reality . . . and to a life in which he couldn't, mustn't, be a part, or else she'd have no life at all.

"I'm sorry I tarnished your reputation," she said. "But I didn't do it all by myself. You could have ignored me. You certainly didn't have to come tonight. Still, all you have to do now is laugh and walk away, and they'll see I mean nothing to you, and they had it all wrong."

He spun her into a last, sweeping turn as the music ended, and held her one hammering moment longer than he should have. Even when he released her at last, he didn't release her altogether, but kept her hand imprisoned in his.

"And what happens, Jess," he said, his voice deepening, "if it turns out they had it right?"

The throbbing undercurrent in the low baritone made her look up again. Then she wished she hadn't, because she thought she saw turmoil in the black depths of his eyes. It must be her own turmoil reflected there, she told herself. It couldn't be his, and so there was no reason her heart should ache to ease it.

"It doesn't turn out that way," she said shakily. "You only came to make fools of them—and of me, especially. You marched in and took over and made everyone kowtow to you, like it or not. You made me dance to your tune as well."

"You seemed to like it," he said.

"That doesn't mean I like *you*," she said. "You had better let go of my hand before people start thinking you like *me*."

"I don't care what they think. *Andiamo*."

Her hand firmly imprisoned in his, he started walking, and she had no choice but to go with him—or be dragged along.

He was leading her to the entryway.

Jessica was looking frantically about her, debating whether it would do any good to scream for help, when a loud crash came from the cardroom. Then someone screamed and several others shouted and there were more loud crashes. And in the next instant, everyone in the ballroom was rushing toward the noise.

Everyone except Dain, who merely picked up his pace and continued toward the entrance.

"It must be a fight," she said, trying to pull her hand free. "A riot, by the sounds of it. You'll miss the fun, Dain."

He laughed and tugged her through the entryway.

Seven

$\mathcal{D}$ain knew the house. It had belonged to the previous Marquess of Avory, and had been the scene of more than one drunken orgy. It was promising to become one of the most notorious residences in Paris when the marquess had met his untimely death. That had been about two years ago, and the furnishings were vastly different now. Still, Dain had no trouble recognizing the small sun parlor on the ground floor whose French doors opened into the garden.

That was where he took Jessica.

To negotiate.

Because—as he *should* have expected and prepared for—matters were not proceeding as he'd planned.

He had planned to wreak havoc and mayhem. Within five minutes of his arrival, he'd found that the combined pride of the Ballisters and Usignuolos wouldn't let him.

No matter how much he was goaded, he would not be reduced to behaving like an animal.

Not in front of her, at any rate.

He had remembered the scornful look she'd given her brother two weeks ago, and the contemptuously amused look she'd given Dain himself, and how it had made him behave like a complete idiot.

He'd tried to forget it, but every moment and emotion of the episode was branded upon his mind: humiliation, rage, frustration, passion . . . and one stunning moment of happiness.

He had experienced a host of disagreeable emotions this evening . . . and forgotten them all the instant he'd danced with her.

She'd been slender and supple and light in his arms. So easy to hold. Her skirts had swirled about his legs, and he'd thought of slim white limbs entangled with his amid the rustle of sheets. Her scent, the provocatively innocent blend of chamomile soap and Woman, had whirled in his head, and he'd thought of pearly skin glimmering in the light of a single candle and long black hair tumbled upon a pillow . . . and himself wrapped in her clean, sweet womanliness, touching, tasting, drinking her in.

He had told himself these were ludicrous fantasies, that clean, sweet women did not lie in his bed and never would, willingly.

But she had seemed willing enough to dance with him. Though she couldn't have enjoyed it, and must have had a typically underhand feminine motive for seeming to, she'd made him believe she did and that she was happy. And when he'd gazed into her upturned countenance, he'd believed, for a moment, that her silver-grey eyes had been glowing with excitement, not resentment, and she had let him draw her closer because that was where she wanted to be.

It was all lies, of course, but there were ways to make certain lies half-true. Dain knew the ways. She, like every other human being since the Creation, had a price.

Consequently, all he had to do was find out what it was and decide whether he was willing to pay.

He led her to a corner of the garden farthest from the blazing lights of the house. Most of the late Lord Avory's collection of Roman artifacts was still picturesquely strewn among the shrubbery, doubtless because it would cost a fortune to move the mammoth pieces.

Dain picked his companion up and sat her upon a stone sarcophagus. Standing upon an ornate base, it was tall enough to bring them nearly eye to eye.

"If I do not return very soon," she said tightly, "my reputation will be in tatters. Not that you care, certainly. But I warn you, Dain, that I will not take it docilely and you—"

"My reputation is already in tatters," he said. "And *you* don't care."

"That is completely wrong!" she cried. "I tried to tell you before: I do sympathize, and I was willing to help mend matters. Within reason, that is. But you refuse to listen. Because, like every other man, you can keep only one idea in your head at a time—usually the wrong one."

"Whereas women are capable of holding twenty-seven contradictory notions simultaneously," he returned. "Which is why they are incapable of adhering to anything like a principle."

He took her hand and began to peel off her glove.

"You'd better stop that," she said. "You're only going to make matters worse."

He pulled away the glove, and at the first glimpse of her fragile, white hand, all thoughts of negotiation fled. "I don't see how matters could become worse," he muttered. "I am already besotted with a needle-tongued, conceited, provoking ape leader of a *lady*."

Her head jerked up, her grey eyes widening. "Besotted? You're nothing like it. *Vengeful* is more like it. Spiteful."

He went to work with speedy efficiency on the other glove. "I must be besotted," he said evenly. "I have the imbecilic idea that you're the prettiest girl I've ever seen. Except for your coiffure," he added, with a disgusted glance at the coils and plumes and pearls. "That is ghastly."

She scowled. "Your romantic effusions leave me breathless."

He lifted her hand and pressed his mouth to her wrist. "*Sono il tuo schiavo*," he murmured.

He felt the jump of her pulse against his lips. "It means, 'I am your slave,'" he translated, as she snatched her hand away. "*Carissima*. Dearest."

She swallowed. "I think you had better stick to English."

"But Italian is so moving," he said. "*Ti ho voluto dal primo momento che ti vedi.*"

I've wanted you from the first moment I saw you.

"*Mi tormenti ancora.*"

You've tormented me ever since.

He went on telling her, in words she couldn't understand, all he'd thought and felt. And while he talked, watching her eyes soften and hearing her breath quicken, he swiftly removed his own gloves.

"Oh, don't," she breathed.

He leaned in closer, still speaking the language that seemed to mesmerize her.

"You shouldn't use masculine wiles," she said in a choked voice. She touched his sleeve. "What have I done that's so unforgivable?"

You made me want you, he told her in his mother's language. *You've made me heartsick, lonely. You've made me crave what I vowed I would never need, never seek.*

She must have heard the rage and frustration throbbing beneath the longing words, but she didn't recoil or try to escape. And when he wrapped his arms about her, she only caught her breath, and let it out on a sigh, and he tasted that sigh when his mouth closed over hers.

Jessica had heard the turmoil in his voice, and required no powers of divination to understand that it boded ill. She'd told herself a hundred times already to run away. Dain would let her go. He had too much pride to force her into his embrace or chase her if she fled.

She simply couldn't do it.

She didn't know what he needed, and even if she had known, she doubted she could provide it. Yet she felt— and the feeling was as certain as her awareness of imminent disaster—that he needed it desperately, and she couldn't, despite common sense and reason, abandon him.

Instead, she abandoned herself, as she had been tempted to do the first time she'd seen him, and as she'd been more painfully tempted when he'd unbuttoned her impossible glove, and as she'd wanted past endurance when he'd kissed her in the storm.

He was big and dark and beautiful and he smelled of smoke and wine and cologne and Male. Now she found that she'd never wanted anything so desperately in all her life as she wanted his low voice sending shivers up and down her back and the lashing strength of his arms about her and his hard, depraved mouth crushing hers.

She couldn't keep herself from answering the fierce tenderness of his kiss, any more than she could keep her hands from straying over wool and linen, warm with his body's warmth, until she found the place where his heart beat, fast and hard, like her own.

He shuddered at her touch, and pushed between her thighs, pulling her closer while he dragged scorching kisses over her mouth and down, to her neck. She was aware of hot masculinity throbbing against her belly and of the pulsing heat that contact generated in the intimate place between her legs. She heard the rational voice in her head telling her matters were escalating too swiftly, and urging her to draw back, to retreat while she still could, but she couldn't.

She was wax in his hands, melting under the kisses simmering over the swell of her breast.

She'd thought she understood what desire was: attraction, a potent magnetic current between male and female, drawing them together. She'd thought she understood lust: a hunger, a craving. She'd been feverish at night, dreaming of him, and restless and edgy by day, thinking of him. She'd called it animal attraction, primitive, mad.

She found she'd understood nothing.

Desire was a hot, black whirlpool, tearing her this way and that, and all the while, inevitably, and with perilous swiftness, dragging her down, beneath intellect, beneath will and shame.

She felt the impatient tug at the ties of her bodice, felt the fastenings give way, and it only made her impatient, too, to yield, to give whatever he needed. She felt his fingers trembling as they slid over the skin he'd bared, and she trembled as well, aching under his shatteringly gentle touch.

"*Baciami.*" His voice was rough, his touch a silken caress. "Kiss me, Jess. Again. As though you mean it."

She lifted her hands and slid her fingers into his thick, curling hair and brought his mouth to hers. She kissed him with all the shameless meaning she had in her. She answered the bold thrust of his tongue as eagerly as her body answered the gentler ravishment of his caress, lifting and arching into him to press her aching breast against his big, warm hand.

This was what she'd needed, hungered for, from the moment she'd met him. He was a monster, but she'd missed him all the same. She'd missed every terrible thing about him . . . and every wonderful thing: the warm, massive, muscular body vibrating power, insolence, and animal grace . . . the bold, black eyes, stone-cold one moment and blazing hellfire the next . . . the low rumble of his voice, mocking, laughing, icy with contempt or throbbing with yearning.

She had wanted him from the start, without understanding what desire was. Now he'd taught her what it was and made her want more.

She broke away and, pulling his head down, kissed his beautiful, arrogant nose and his haughty brow and trailed her mouth over his hard jaw.

"Oh, Jess." His voice was a moan. "*Sì. Ancora. Baciami. Abbracciami.*"

She heard nothing else, only the need in his voice. She felt nothing else, only the heat of desire pressed to her own heat. She was aware only of the taut power of his frame, and the warm hands moving over her while his mouth claimed hers again, and of the rustle of silk and cambric as he pushed up her skirts and slid his hand over her knee, and of the warmth of that hand grazing the skin above her stocking.

Then his hand tightened and froze and his warm body turned to stone.

His mouth jerked from hers, and startled, Jessica opened her eyes . . . in time to see the fire die in his, leaving them as cold as the onyx of his stickpin.

Then, too late, she heard as well: the swish of a gown brushing against shrubbery . . . and muffled whispers.

"It seems we have an audience, Miss Trent," Dain said. His voice dripped scorn. Coolly he pulled her bodice back up, and yanked her skirts back down. There was nothing protective or gallant in the gesture. He made her feel as though, having had a look at and a sampling of what she had to offer, he'd decided it wasn't worth having. She might have been a trumpery toy displayed upon Champtois' counter, not worth a second glance.

And that, Jessica understood as she took in the chilling expression on his countenance, was what he wanted those watching to think. He was going to throw her to the wolves. That was his revenge.

"You know we're equally to blame," she said, keeping her voice low so that the onlookers couldn't hear. "You helped get me into this, Dain. You can bloody well help get me out of it."

"Ah, yes," he said in carrying tones. "I am to announce our betrothal, am I not? But why, Miss Trent, should I pay the price of a wedding ring for what I might have, *gratis?*"

She heard gasps behind him, and a giggle. "I shall be ruined," she said tightly. "This is unworthy of you—and unforgivable."

He laughed. "Then shoot me." And with one mocking glance at the figures standing in the shadows, he walked away.

His mind roiling with humiliation and rage, Dain made his way blindly through the garden, wrenched the locked gate from its hinges, and marched through the narrow alleyway and on down the street, and down the next and the next.

It wasn't until he neared the Palais Royal that his breathing began to return to normal and black fury gave way to stormy thought.

She was like all the others—like Susannah, but worse, a better actress, and more crafty in setting the self-same trap. And he, with years of experience behind him, had walked straight into it. Again. To be snared in worse circumstances.

With Susannah, he'd simply stolen a peck on the cheek in view of her greedy family. This time, several of Paris' most elite sophisticates had watched him make a cake of himself, heard him groaning and panting and babbling desire and devotion like a feverish schoolboy.

Even as a schoolboy, at thirteen, he had not behaved like a moonstruck puppy. Even then, he had not nearly wept with longing.

Oh, Jess.

His throat tightened. He paused and ruthlessly swallowed the burning ache, composed himself, and walked on.

At the Palais Royal, he collected a trio of plump tarts and an assortment of male comrades, and plunged into dissipation. Harlots and gambling hells and champagne: his world. Where he belonged, he told himself. Where he was happy, he assured himself.

And so he gambled and drank and told bawdy jokes and, swallowing his revulsion at the familiar smell of perfume, powder, and paint, filled his lap with whores, and buried his grieving heart, as he always did, under laughter.

Even before Dain's laughter had faded and he'd disappeared into the garden's shadows, Jessica was dragging herself from the black pit of humiliated despair into which he'd dropped her. There was no choice but to lift her chin and face the next moment and all the moments to come. She faced the onlookers, daring them to utter an insult. One by one, they turned their backs and silently retreated.

Only one came forward. Vawtry was shrugging out of his coat as, clutching her bodice to cover herself, Jessica leapt down from the sarcophagus. He hastened toward her with the coat.

"I tried," he said unhappily, his eyes tactfully averted while she wrapped his coat about her. "I told them Dain had left alone and you had gone to look for your grandmother, but one of the servants had seen you enter the sun parlor . . ." He paused. "I'm sorry."

"I should like to make a discreet exit," she said, keeping her voice expressionless. "Would you be kind enough to find Lady Pembury?"

"I hate to leave you alone," he said.

"I don't faint," she said. "I don't indulge in hysterics. I'll be quite all right."

He gave her a worried glance, then hurried away.

As soon as he was gone, Jessica pulled off his coat and restored her gown to rights as best she could without her maid. She couldn't reach all the fastenings, most of which were in back, but she found enough to secure the bodice, so that she didn't have to hold it up. While she struggled with the ties and hooks, she reviewed her situation with brutal objectivity.

She knew it hardly mattered that Dain hadn't ravished her. What mattered was that it had been Dain with whom she'd been caught. That was enough to make her damaged goods in the eyes of all the world.

Within less than twenty-four hours, the story would reach every corner of Paris. Within a week, it would reach London. She could see well enough what the future held.

No self-respecting gentleman would sully his family name by marrying Dain's leavings. After this, she wouldn't have a prayer of attracting to her shop the hosts of rich, respectable people her success—and her own respectability—depended upon. Ladies would hold their skirts to keep from brushing against her when they passed, or cross the street to avoid contamination. Gentlemen would cease being gentlemen and subject her to the same indignities they offered the lowliest street-walker.

With a handful of words, in short, Dain had destroyed her life. On purpose.

All he'd needed to do was sweep one of his deadly glances over them and tell them they'd seen nothing, and they would have decided it was healthiest to agree with him. All the world feared him, even his so-called friends. He could make them do and say and believe what he wanted.

But all he'd wanted was revenge—for whatever it was his twisted mind believed Jessica had done to him. He'd taken her to this garden with no other purpose. She wouldn't have put it past him to have dropped a hint beforehand to somebody, to make sure the discovery would take place at the most humiliating moment: her bodice undone and sagging to her waist, his tongue down her throat, his filthy hand up her skirt.

Though her face heated at the recollection, she refused to feel ashamed of what she'd done. Her behavior might be accounted indecent by Society's rules, and misguided according to her own, but it wasn't evil. She was a healthy young woman who had simply yielded to feelings countless other women yielded to—and might do with impunity if they were married or widowed and discreet about it.

Even though she wasn't married or widowed, and by

normal rules should have been considered out of bounds, she couldn't, in all fairness, blame him for taking advantage of what was offered so willingly.

But she could and would blame him for refusing to shield her. He had nothing to lose, and he'd known very well that she had everything to lose. He could have helped her. It would have cost him nothing, scarcely an effort. Instead, he'd insulted and abandoned her.

That was the evil. That was the base, unforgivable act.

And that, she resolved, was what he'd pay for.

At half past four in the morning, Dain was holding court in Antoine's, a restaurant in the Palais Royal. His circle of companions had by this time widened to include a handful of Lady Wallingdon's guests: Sellowby, Goodridge, Vawtry, and Esmond. The subject of Jessica Trent was scrupulously avoided. Instead, the fight in the cardroom, which Dain had missed—between a drunken Prussian officer and a French republican— and the ensuing mayhem were discussed in detail and at argumentative length.

Even the tarts felt obliged to express their opinions, the one on Dain's right knee taking the republican side, while the one on the left was squarely with the Prussian. Both argued with a level of ignorance, both political and grammatical, that would have made Bertie Trent seem an intellectual prodigy.

Dain wished he hadn't thought of Trent. The instant the brother's image flickered in Dain's mind, the sister's arose: Jessica gazing up into his eyes from under an overdecorated bonnet . . . watching his face while he unbuttoned her glove . . . hitting him with her bonnet and her small gloved fist . . . kissing him while lightning flashed and thunder crashed . . . whirling round a dance floor with him, her skirts rustling about his legs, her face glowing with excitement. And later, in his arms . . . a firestorm of images, feelings, and one sweet, anguished moment . . . when she had kissed his big, loathsome nose . . . and cut his heart to pieces and put it back together again and made him believe he was not a monster to her. She had made him believe he was beautiful.

Lies, he told himself.

They were all lies and tricks, to trap him. He'd ruined her brother. She had nothing left. Thus, like Susannah, whose brother had gambled away the family fortune, Jessica Trent was desperate enough to set the oldest trap in history to catch herself a rich, titled husband.

But now Dain found himself considering the circle of men about him. All were better looking, better behaved, better prospects altogether.

His gaze lingered upon Esmond, who sat beside him, and was the most beautiful man on three continents, and also very possibly—though no one knew for sure—even wealthier than the Marquess of Dain.

Why not Esmond? Dain asked himself. If she needed a rich spouse, why should a quick-witted female like Jessica Trent choose Beelzebub over the Angel Gabriel, hell rather than heaven?

Esmond's blue gaze met his. "*Amore è cieco*," he murmured in perfect Florentine accents.

Love is blind.

Dain recollected Esmond telling him a few weeks ago about "bad feelings" regarding *Vingt-Huit*, and recalled the events that had taken place almost immediately thereafter. Gazing at him now, Dain had an uncomfortable feeling of his own: that the angelic count was reading his mind, just as he'd read clues, invisible to everyone else, about the now defunct palace of sin.

Dain was opening his mouth to deliver a crushing

setdown when Esmond stiffened, and his head turned slightly, his gaze fixing elsewhere while his smile faded.

Dain looked that way, too—toward the door—but at first he could see nothing, because Sellowby had leaned over to refill his glass.

Then Sellowby lounged back again in his chair.

Then Dain saw her.

She wore a dark red gown, buttoned up to the throat, and a black shawl draped like a mantilla over her head and shoulders. Her face was white and hard. She strode toward the large table, chin high, silver eyes flashing, and paused a few feet away.

His heart crashed and thundered into a hectic gallop that made it impossible to breathe, let alone speak.

Her glance flicked over his companions.

"Go away," she said in a low, hard voice.

The whores leapt from his lap, knocking over glasses in their haste. His friends bolted up from their places and backed away. A chair toppled and crashed to the floor unheeded.

Only Esmond kept his head. "Mademoiselle," he began, his tones gentle, mollifying.

She flung back the shawl and lifted her right hand. There was a pistol in it, the barrel aimed straight at Dain's heart. "Go away," she told Esmond.

Dain heard the click as she cocked the weapon and the scrape of a chair as Esmond rose. "Mademoiselle," he tried again.

"Say your prayers, Dain," she said.

His gaze lifted from the pistol to her glittering, furious eyes. "Jess," he whispered.

She pulled the trigger.

Eight

The shot threw Dain back against his chair, which crashed to the floor with him.

Jessica brought the pistol down, let out the breath she'd been holding, then turned and walked away.

It took the onlookers a few moments to make their brains comprehend what their eyes and ears told them. In those moments, she made her way unhindered across the restaurant, out the door, and down the stairs.

A short time later, she found the hackney she'd ordered to wait for her, and told the driver to take her to the nearest police station.

There, she asked for the officer in charge. She turned over the pistol and told what she had done. The officer did not believe her. He sent two *gendarmes* to Antoine's, and gave her a glass of wine. The men returned an hour later, with copious notes they'd taken at the scene of the crime, and the Comte d'Esmond.

Esmond had come to release her, he said. It was all a misunderstanding, an accident. The Marquess of

Dain's wound was not mortal. A scratch, that was all. He would not bring charges against Mademoiselle Trent.

Naturally not, Jessica thought. He would lose a court battle against her. This was Paris, after all.

"Then I shall bring charges against myself," she said, chin high. "And you may tell your friend—"

"Mademoiselle, I shall be honored to convey any message you wish," Esmond said smoothly. "But you will communicate more comfortably in my carriage, I think."

"Certainly not," she said. "I insist upon being jailed, for my own protection, so that he can't kill me to keep me quiet. Because, monsieur, that is the only way *anyone* is going to keep me quiet."

She turned to the officer in charge. "I shall be happy to write a full and detailed confession for you. I have nothing to hide. I shall be delighted to speak with the reporters who will no doubt be mobbing the place in the next half hour."

"Mademoiselle, I am sure the matter can be settled to your satisfaction," said Esmond. "But I recommend you let your temper cool before you speak to anyone."

"Very wise," said the officer in charge. "You are agitated. It is understandable. An affair of the heart."

"Quite," she said, meeting Esmond's enigmatic blue gaze. "A crime of passion."

"Yes, mademoiselle, as everyone will deduce," said Esmond. "If the police do not release you immediately, there will be more than reporters storming the place. All of Paris will rise up to rescue you, and the city will be plunged into riot. You do not wish innocent people to be killed on your account, I am sure."

There was a clamor outside—the first contingent of reporters, she guessed. She drew out the moment, letting tension build in the room.

Then she shrugged. "Very well. I shall go home. For the sake of the endangered innocents."

By midmorning, the Comte d'Esmond was with Dain, who lay upon a sofa in the library.

The wound was nothing, Dain was sure. He'd scarcely felt it. The bullet had gone clean through. Though his arm had bled a great deal, Dain was used to the sight of blood, including his own, and should not have swooned.

But he had, several times, and each time he'd come to, he'd felt hotter. A physician had come and examined the wound and treated it and bandaged it and told Dain he was very lucky.

It was clean. No bones had been shattered. Muscle and nerve damage was negligibly minor. There was no danger of infection.

Dain should not, therefore, be feverish, but he was. First his arm burned, then his shoulder and neck caught fire. Now his head was ablaze.

Amid this internal hellfire, he heard Esmond's voice, smooth and soothing as always.

"She knows, *naturellement*, that no jury in France would convict her," said Esmond. "Here, it is easier to pass a camel through the eye of a needle than to convict a beautiful woman of any crime which appears to be in any way connected to *l'amour*."

"Of course she knows." Dain gritted out the words. "Just as I know she didn't do it in the heat of the moment. Did you see her hand? Not a hint of trembling. Cold and steady as you please. She was not in a mindless rage. She knew precisely what she was doing."

"She knows very well what she is doing," Esmond agreed. "Shooting you was only the beginning. She means to make a spectacle of you. I am to tell you that she will make public—in the courtroom if she can get the trial she insists upon, or in the papers if she cannot—every detail of the episode. She says she will repeat all you said to her and describe in full detail everything you did."

"In other words, she'll exaggerate and twist words to her purpose," said Dain, angrily aware that all she had to utter was the truth. And that, in the eyes of the world, would reduce Lord Beelzebub to a lovesick, panting, groaning, sweating schoolboy. His friends would howl with laughter at his mawkish outpourings, even the Italian.

She would remember what the words sounded like—she was adept in Latin, wasn't she?—and do an apt imitation, because she was quick and clever . . . and vengeful. Then all his mortifying secrets, dreams, fantasies, would be translated into French and English—and soon, every other language known to humankind. The words would be printed in bubbles over his head in printshop caricatures. Farces of the episode would be enacted upon the stage.

That was merely a fraction of what he'd face, Dain knew.

He had only to recollect how the press had pilloried Byron a dozen years earlier—and the poet had been a model of social rectitude compared to the Marquess of Dain. Furthermore, Byron had not been obscenely wealthy, terrifyingly big and ugly, and infuriatingly powerful.

The bigger they are, the harder they fall. And the better the world liked seeing them fall.

Dain understood the way of the world very well. He could see plainly enough what the future held. Miss Jessica Trent saw, too, undoubtedly. That was why she hadn't killed him. She wanted to make sure he suffered the torments of hell while he lived.

She knew he would suffer, because she had struck in the only place where he could be hurt: his pride.

And if he couldn't endure it—which she knew, of course, he couldn't—she'd get her satisfaction in private, no doubt. She would make him *crawl.*

She had him exactly where she wanted him, the she-devil.

Amid the hellfire raging over half his body, his head began to pound. "I'd better deal with her directly," he said. His tongue was thick, slurring the words. "Negotiate. Tell her . . ." He swallowed. His throat burned, too. "Terms. Tell her . . ."

He shut his eyes and searched his throbbing, roiling mind for words, but they wouldn't come. His head was a red-hot mound of metal a hellish blacksmith was hammering upon, pounding intellect, thought, into nothingness. He heard Esmond's voice, very far away, but couldn't make sense of the words. Then the satanic hammer struck one shattering blow, and knocked Dain into oblivion.

Consumed by the feverish illness he shouldn't have had, Dain drifted in and out of consciousness for most of the next four days.

On the morning of the fifth day, he woke fully, and more or less recovered. That was to say, the fire and throbbing were gone. His left arm refused to move, though. It dangled uselessly at his side. There was feeling in it, but he couldn't make it do anything.

The physician returned, examined, made wise noises, and shook his head. "I can find nothing wrong," he said.

He summoned a colleague, who also found nothing wrong, and summoned another, with the same result.

By late afternoon, Dain had seen eight medical men,

all of whom told him the same thing. By then, Dain was beside himself. He had been poked and questioned and muttered over for most of the day, and spent a great deal of money on physicians' fees to no purpose.

To cap it off, a law clerk arrived minutes after the last quack left. Herbert delivered the message the clerk had brought just as Dain was attempting to pour himself a glass of wine. His eye upon the note on the silver salver, Dain missed the glass, and splattered wine on his dressing gown, slippers, and the Oriental carpet.

He hurled imprecations, as well as the salver, at Herbert's head, then stormed out of the drawing room and on to his own room, where he worked himself into a fury trying to unseal and unfold the note with one hand. By then, he was so enraged, he could scarcely see straight.

There was little enough to see. According to the note, Mr. Andrew Herriard wished to meet with His Lordship's solicitor on behalf of Miss Jessica Trent.

Lord Dain's insides turned to lead.

Andrew Herriard was a famous London solicitor with an extensive clientele of powerful expatriates in Paris. He was also a pillar of rectitude—incorruptible, loyal, and indefatigable in serving his clients. Lord Dain was aware, as were a great many people, that beneath the lawyer's saintly exterior loomed a steel trap with jaws and teeth a shark would envy. The trap was reserved primarily for men, because Mr. Andrew Herriard was a gallant knight in the service of the weaker sex.

It didn't matter to the solicitor that the law was squarely on the side of male prerogative, and that a woman, to all intents and purposes, had no rights under that law and nothing she could call her own, including her offspring.

Herriard created the rights he believed women were

entitled to—and got away with it. Even Francis Beaumont, devious swine that he was, could not touch the tenth part of a farthing of his wife's income, thanks to Herriard.

This was because Herriard's approach, when a fellow balked at outrageous demands, was to subject the poor sod to an endless stream of barristers and petty litigation, until the sod caved in from sheer exhaustion, was ruined by legal fees, or was carried, screaming, to a lunatic asylum.

Miss Trent, in short, was not only going to make Lord Dain crawl, but she would have Herriard do the dirty work for her, and have it all done legally, with not a loophole for Dain to wriggle out of.

"There is no animal more invincible than a woman," Aristophanes had said, "nor fire either, nor any wildcat so ruthless."

Ruthless. Vicious. *Fiendish.*

"Oh, no, you don't," Dain muttered. "Not via gobetweens, you demon spawn." He wadded the note into a tight ball and hurled it at the grate. Then he stomped to his writing desk, grabbed a sheet of notepaper, scrawled an answer, and shouted for his valet.

In his note to Mr. Herriard, Dain had declared that he would meet with Miss Trent at seven o'clock that evening at her brother's house. He would not, as Herriard had requested, send his solicitor to meet with hers, because the Marquess of Dain had no intention, he wrote, "of being sworn, signed, and bled dry by proxy." If Miss Trent had terms to dictate, she could bloody well do it in person. If that didn't suit, she was welcome to send her brother to Dain, who would be happy to settle the matter at twenty paces—with *both* combatants armed this time.

Given the last suggestion, Jessica decided it would be best if Bertie spent the evening elsewhere. He still had no idea what had happened.

She had returned from the police station to find her brother suffering painful consequences of his alcohol consumption during Lady Wallingdon's ball. His constitution weakened by months of dissipation, he had succumbed to a violent dyspepsia, and had not left his bed until teatime yesterday.

Even in the best of circumstances, his brain functions were unreliable. At present, the effort to comprehend Dain's anomalous behavior might trigger a relapse, if not apoplexy. Equally important, Jessica dared not risk Bertie's bumbling after Dain with the misguided idea of avenging her honor.

Genevieve had agreed. She had, accordingly, taken Bertie to dine with her at the Duc d'Abonville's. The duc could be relied upon to hold his tongue. It was he, after all, who'd advised Jessica to hold hers until she spoke with a lawyer.

It was also the duc who was paying Mr. Herriard's fee. If Jessica had not agreed to let him do so, Abonville would have called Dain out himself. That offer had told Jessica all she needed to know about the French nobleman's feelings about Genevieve.

At seven o'clock, therefore, Bertie was safely out of the way. Only Mr. Herriard was with Jessica in the drawing room. They were standing before a table upon which a neat pile of documents lay when Dain stalked in.

He swept Herriard one contemptuous glance, then bent his sardonic obsidian gaze upon Jessica. "Madam," he said, with a short nod.

"My lord," she said, with a shorter one.

"That takes care of the social niceties," he said. "You may proceed to the extortion."

Mr. Herriard's lips set in a thin line, but he said nothing.

He took up the papers from the table and gave them to Dain, who moved across the room to a window. He set the papers upon the wide sill, took up the topmost one, and leisurely read it. When he was done, he put it down and took up the next.

Minutes ticked by. Jessica waited, growing edgier with each passing moment.

Finally, nearly a half hour later, Dain looked up from the documents it should have taken him a fraction of that time to comprehend.

"I wondered how you meant to play it," he told Herriard. "If we spare ourselves the legalisms and Latinisms, what it boils down to is a defamation suit—if I don't agree to settle the matter privately, according to your exorbitant terms."

"The words you uttered in the hearing of six other parties could be construed in only one way, my lord," said Herriard. "With those words, you destroyed my client's social and financial credit. You have made it impossible for her to wed or earn a respectable independent livelihood. You have made her an outcast from the society to which she was bred and properly belongs. She will be obliged, therefore, to live in exile from her friends and loved ones. She must build a new life."

"And I'm to pay for it, I see," said Dain. "Settle all of her brother's debts, amounting to six thousand pounds." He glanced over the pages. "I am to support her to the tune of two thousand per annum and . . . ah, yes. There was something about securing and maintaining a place of residence."

He leafed through the pages, dropping several on the floor in the process.

It was then Jessica realized he wasn't using his left hand at all, and that he held the arm oddly, as though something were wrong with it. There shouldn't be, except for a minor bullet wound. She'd aimed carefully, and she was an excellent markswoman. Not to mention he was a very large target.

He looked her way then, and caught her staring. "Admiring your handiwork, are you? I daresay you'd like a better look. Regrettably, there's nothing to see. There's nothing wrong with it, according to the quacks. Except that it doesn't work. Still, I count myself fortunate, Miss Trent, that you didn't aim a ways lower. I'm merely disarmed, not unmanned. But I have no doubt Herriard here will see to the emasculation."

Her conscience pricked. She ignored it. "You got—and *will* get exactly as you deserve, you deceitful, spiteful brute."

"Miss Trent," Herriard said gently.

"No, I will not guard my tongue," she said. "His Lordship wanted me present because he wanted a row. He knows very well he's in the wrong, but he's too curst stubborn to admit it. He wants to make me out to be a scheming, greedy—"

"Vindictive," said Dain. "Don't leave out vindictive."

"*I*, vindictive?" she exclaimed. "I was not the one who arranged to have the biggest gossips in Paris 'happen along' while I was half-undressed and being led—fool that I was—straight to ruination."

His black brows rose a fraction. "You're not implying, Miss Trent, that *I* arranged that farce."

"I don't have to imply anything! It was obvious. Vawtry was there. *Your* friend. And the others—those snide Parisian sophisticates. I know who arranged for them to watch me be disgraced. And I know why. You did it for spite. As though everything that's happened—all the gossip, every dent in your precious reputation—were *my fault!*"

There was a short, taut silence. Then Dain threw the rest of the papers to the carpet, stalked to the decanter tray, and helped himself to a glass of sherry. He needed only one hand to do that, and only one swallow to empty it.

When he turned back to her, the irritating mockery of a smile was in place. "It would appear that we've been laboring under the same misapprehension," he said. "I thought *you* had arranged for the—er—interruption."

"I'm not surprised," she said. "You also seem to labor under the misapprehension that you are a splendid catch—in addition to mistaking me for a lunatic. *If* I were desperate for a husband—which I have not been and never will be—I should not have to resort to such ancient, pathetic tricks."

She drew herself up. "I may appear a negligible, dried-up spinster to you, my lord, but yours, I assure you, is the minority view. I am unwed by choice, not for lack of offers."

"But now you won't get any," he said. His sardonic gaze drifted lazily over her, making her skin prickle. "Thanks to me. And that's what all this is about."

He set down the empty glass and turned to Herriard. "I've damaged the goods, and now I must pay what you deem the value of the merchandise, or else you will heap me with documents, plague me with barristers and clerks, and drag me through endless months of litigation."

"If the law regarded women in a proper light, the process would not be endless," said Mr. Herriard, unruffled. "The punishment would be severe and swift."

"But we live in benighted times," said Dain. "And I

am, as Miss Trent will assure you, the most benighted of men. I have, among other quaint beliefs, the antiquated notion that if I pay for something, it ought to belong to me. Since I seem to have no choice but to pay for Miss Trent—"

"I am not a pocket watch," she said tightly. She told herself she ought not feel in the least surprised that the cocksure clodpole proposed to settle matters by making her *his mistress*. "I am a human being, and you will never own me, no matter what you pay. You may have destroyed my honor in the eyes of the world, but you will not destroy it in fact."

He lifted an eyebrow. "Destroy your honor? My dear Miss Trent, I am proposing to *redeem* it. We shall be wed. Now, why don't you sit down and be quiet like a good girl and let the men sort out the details."

Jessica experienced a moment of numb incomprehension before the words struck, sharp and stunning as a blow to the head. The room darkened and everything within it wobbled drunkenly. She had to struggle to focus. "Wed?" Her voice sounded very far away, weak, plaintive.

"Herriard demands that I bail out your brother, and house and support you for the rest of your life," he said. "Very well. I agree—but on the same terms any other man would insist upon: exclusive ownership and breeding rights."

His hooded gaze dropped to her bodice, and heat simmered there and spread, just as though it had been his hands, not his eyes, upon her.

She summoned her composure. "I see what you are about," she said. "It's not a genuine offer at all, but a strategy to tie our hands. You know we can't sue you if you offer to do the allegedly honorable thing. You also know I won't marry you. And so you think you have us at *point non plus*."

"I do," he said, smiling. "If you refuse me and attempt litigation, you'll only humiliate yourself. Everyone will believe you're a money-hungry slut."

"And if I accept your make-believe offer of marriage, you'll play along until the last minute—and leave me waiting at the altar," she said. "And humiliate me anyhow."

He laughed. "And open the door to a long, expensive breach-of-promise suit? Make Herriard's job easier for him? Think again, Jess. And keep it simple, why don't you? Marriage or nothing."

She snatched up the first thing at hand—a small but heavy brass figure of a horse.

Mr. Herriard stepped toward her. "Miss Trent," he said quietly. "I beg you will resist the temptation."

"Might as well," said Dain. "It won't do a bit of good. I can duck a missile, if not a bullet."

She set down the statue and turned to Herriard. "You see, don't you?" she asked. "He's not offering in order to make amends, because he doesn't think he owes me any. All he wants is to get the better of me—and getting the better of you in the bargain will make his triumph all the sweeter to him."

"It hardly matters what you think of me," said Dain. "There are only two choices. And if you're waiting for me to make it more palatable by falling to my knees and begging for your hand, Jess, you may wait until Judgment Day," he added with a laugh.

She heard it then, faint but recognizable. She'd heard it before, in boyish boasts and taunts: the small, discordant note of uncertainty beneath the laughter. She swiftly reviewed the words he'd uttered, and wondered if that was all his pride would allow him to say. Masculine pride was an exceedingly precious and fragile item. That was why males built fortresses about it, practically from infancy.

I'm not afraid, boys said, laughing, when they were sick with terror. They laughed off floggings and pretended to feel nothing. They also dropped rodents and reptiles into the laps of little girls they were infatuated with, and laughed in that same uncertain way when the little girls ran away screaming.

His proposal was, perhaps, the equivalent of a gift of a reptile or rodent. If she indignantly rejected it, he would laugh, and tell himself that was precisely what he wanted.

But maybe it wasn't.

Jessica reminded herself that "maybe" was hardly a reliable basis for marriage.

On the other hand, Genevieve had advised her to reel him in. Even as late as this morning, after all that had happened, Genevieve had not changed her mind. "I know he behaved abominably, and I do not blame you for shooting him," she said. "But recollect that he was interrupted at a time a man most dislikes interruption. He was not thinking rationally. He could not. All the same, I am certain he cares for you. He did not look so insolent and cynical when he danced with you."

"Marriage or nothing," Dain's impatient voice broke into her thoughts. "Those are the terms, the only terms. Take your pick, Jess."

Dain told himself it didn't matter. If she consented, he could at least exorcise his idiotic lust in exchange for the extortionate sum he had to pay. Then he could leave her in Devon and pick up his life again. If she refused, he'd pay nothing, and she would go away and stop plaguing him, and he would forget the lust and her. Either way, he won and she lost.

But his heart pounded all the same, and his gut twisted with a chill, throbbing dread he had not felt since his boyhood.

He set his jaw and endured while he watched her move away from Herriard toward a chair. But she didn't sit down. She simply stared at it, her beautiful face a blank.

Herriard frowned. "Perhaps you want some time, Miss Trent. A few minutes of privacy. I am sure His Lordship would concede that much," he said, turning the frown upon Dain. "After all, the lady's entire future is at stake."

"I don't need more time," said Miss Trent. "It is easy enough to calculate the assets and liabilities on either side."

She looked up at Dain and, to his astonishment, smiled. "I find the prospect of a life of poverty and obscurity in a remote outpost of civilization singularly unattractive. I can think of nothing more absurd than living so merely for the sake of my pride. I had much rather be a wealthy marchioness. You are perfectly awful, of course, Dain, and I don't doubt you'll strive to make my life a misery to me. However, Mr. Herriard will see that I am well provided for in the mercenary sense. Also, I shall derive some personal satisfaction from knowing that you will have to eat every last contemptuous word you ever uttered about men who let themselves be trapped into marriage and entanglements with respectable women. I should give anything to be a fly on the wall when you explain your betrothal to your friends, my lord Beelzebub."

He stared at her, afraid to trust his hearing.

"The answer is yes," she said impatiently. "Do you

think I'm such a sapskull as to say no, and let you off scot-free?"

He found his voice. "I knew that was too much to hope."

She approached him. "What will you tell your friends, Dain? Something about marriage being less bother than having me chasing after you and shooting you, I suppose."

She lightly touched his coat sleeve, and the small gesture made his chest constrict painfully.

"You ought to put it in a sling," she said. "Make a show of it. Not to mention you'll be less likely to damage it accidentally."

"A sling would spoil the line of my coat," he said stiffly. "And I don't need to make a show of or explain anything."

"Your friends will roast you unmercifully," she said. "I should give anything to hear it."

"I shall announce our betrothal to them tonight, at Antoine's," he said. "And they may make what they like of it. It's nothing to me what those morons think. Meanwhile, I advise you to run along and pack. Herriard and I have business to discuss."

She stiffened. "Pack?"

"We'll leave for England the day after tomorrow," he said. "I'll see to the travel arrangements. We'll be married in London. I won't have a mob descending upon the Dartmoor countryside and agitating the cattle. We can leave for Devon after the wedding breakfast."

Her eyes darkened. "Oh, no, you don't," she said. "We can be wed here. You might allow me to enjoy Paris for a while at least, before you exile me to Devon."

"We will be wed in St. George's, Hanover Square," he said. "In a month's time. I'll be damned if I'll plead with the sodding Archbishop of Canterbury for a special license. The banns will be read. And you may enjoy London in the interim. You are not staying in Paris, so just put that idea out of your head."

The idea of the Marchioness of Dain living in the stewpot he called home on the Rue de Rivoli made his flesh creep. His lady wife would *not* sit at the table where half the degenerates of Paris had caroused and eaten and drunk until they were sick—and retched upon carpets and furniture. She would not embroider or read by the fire in a drawing room that had housed orgies the Romans would have envied.

He made a mental note to order a new mattress for the ancestral bed in Devon, and to have all the present bedclothes and hangings burnt. He would not have the Marchioness of Dain contaminated by the objects amid which he'd fathered a bastard upon Charity Graves.

"I have had a perfectly wretched time in Paris, thanks to you," she said, her grey eyes sparking. "You might at least allow me to make up for it. I should not dream of expecting you to live in my pocket, but I should think I might be permitted to go to parties and enjoy my newly redeemed honor and—"

"You can go to parties in London," he said. "You may have as grand a wedding breakfast as you like. You may buy all the frocks and fripperies you like. What the devil do you care where you are, so long as I pay the bills?"

"How can you be so insensitive?" she cried. "I do not wish to be hustled away from Paris as though I were a mortifying secret."

"A *secret?*" His voice rose. "In St. George's, Hanover Square? How much more bloody public and respectable can this infernal match be?"

He looked over her head at Herriard, who was at the table, tucking papers into his leather document case, his countenance expressing studied oblivion to the row. "Herriard, perhaps you can explain what harrowing crime I shall perpetrate with a London wedding."

"This dispute is not within my jurisdiction," said Herriard. "No more than is the number of wedding guests or any of the other disagreements which usually attend upon a betrothal. You will have to negotiate on your own."

Lord Dain thought he'd endured enough "negotiating" for one day. He had not come intending to marry the author of his misery. Not consciously, at any rate. He had offered, he'd thought, only because he couldn't bear to be cornered and harried and beaten by a vengeful little spinster and her diabolical lawyer.

He had not realized, until he offered, how very much her answer did matter. He had not realized until now how boring and depressing Paris and the weeks and months to come would appear when he contemplated her gone . . . forever.

Though she'd consented, he was still anxious, because she wasn't his yet, and she might escape after all. Yet his pride wouldn't let him yield to her. Yield an inch, and a woman would take an ell.

He must begin as he meant to go on, he told himself, and he meant to be master in his own house. He would not be managed. He would not change his ways for anybody, even her. Dain gave the orders; others obeyed.

"*Cara*," he said.

She met his gaze, her expression wary.

He took her hand. "Pack your bags," he said softly.

She tried to pull her hand away. He let it go, but only to wrap his good arm about her waist and pull her close and up, off the floor, and clamp his mouth over hers.

It was over in an instant. She scarcely had time to struggle. One swift, brazen kiss . . . and he let her down and released her. She tottered back a step, her face flushed.

"That's all the negotiating you get, Jess," he said, hastily smothering the heat and hunger the too short embrace had stirred. "If you go on arguing, I shall assume you want more."

"Very well, London it is—but that will cost you, Dain," she said.

She turned away. "Mr. Herriard, show him no mercy. If he wants blind obedience, he will not get it cheap. I shall expect a king's ransom in pin money. My own carriages and cattle. Ample portion to issue, female as well as male. Make him howl, Mr. Herriard. If he does not roar and stomp about like an outraged elephant, you may be certain you are not demanding enough."

"I should pay a great deal," Dain said, grinning evilly, "for *blind obedience.* I shall begin making a list of commands this very night." He made her an extravagant bow. "Until the day after tomorrow, then, Miss Trent."

She curtsied. "Go to blazes, Dain."

"I shall, undoubtedly—eventually." He looked to the solicitor. "You may call upon me at two o'clock tomorrow with your infernal documents, Herriard."

Without waiting for a reply, Dain sauntered from the room.

Nine

On the way to Calais, Dain had ridden with Bertie outside the coach. At the inns, Dain had retired to the taproom with Bertie while Jessica dined with her grandmother. During the Channel crossing, His Lordship had kept to the opposite end of the French steamer. En route to London, he had again ridden outside the luxurious carriage he'd hired. Once in London, he had deposited her, Bertie, and Genevieve at the door of Uncle Arthur and Aunt Louisa's house. Jessica had not seen her betrothed since.

Now, a full fortnight after leaving Paris—fourteen days during which her affianced husband seemed determined to ignore her out of existence—he arrived at two o'clock in the afternoon and expected her to drop whatever she was doing to attend to him.

"He wants me to go for a drive?" Jessica said indignantly when her flustered aunt returned to the sitting room to relay Dain's message. "Just like that? He has suddenly recollected my existence and expects me to

come running at the snap of his fingers? Why didn't
you tell him to go to the devil?"

Aunt Louisa sank into a chair, pressing her fingers
to her forehead. In the few minutes she'd spent with
him, Dain had evidently managed to undermine even
her autocratic composure.

"Jessica, pray look out the window," she said.

Jessica set down her pen upon the writing desk
where she'd been battling with the wedding breakfast
menu, rose, and went to the window. Upon the street
below she saw a handsome black curricle. It was attached to two very large, very temperamental black
geldings, which Bertie was struggling mightily to hold.
They were snorting and dancing restlessly about. Jessica had no doubt that in a very few minutes they'd be
dancing on her brother's head.

"His Almighty Lordship says he will not leave the
house without you." Aunt Louisa's voice throbbed
with outrage. "I advise you to hurry, before those mur-
derous beasts of his kill your brother."

In three minutes, a seething Jessica had a bonnet
upon her head and her green pelisse snugly fastened
over her day frock.

In another two, she was being helped onto the
carriage seat. Or *shoved* was more like it, for Dain
promptly flung his huge body onto the seat, and she
had to wedge herself into a corner to avoid his brawny
shoulder. Even so, in the narrow space it was impossible
to escape physical contact. His useless left hand lay
upon his thigh, and that muscled limb pressed brazenly
against hers, as did the allegedly crippled left arm.
Their warmth penetrated the thick fabric of her pelisse
as well as the muslin frock beneath, to make her skin
tingle.

"Comfortable?" he asked with mocking politeness.

"Dain, this curricle is not big enough for the two of us," she said crossly. "You're crushing me."

"Maybe you'd better sit on my lap, then," he said.

Suppressing the urge to slap the smirk off his face, she turned her attention to her brother, who was still fumbling about the horses' heads. "Confound you, Bertie, get away from there!" she snapped. "Do you want them to mash your skull upon the paving stones?"

Dain laughed and gave the beasts leave to start, and Bertie hastily stumbled back to the safety of the sidewalk.

A moment later, the curricle was hurtling at a breakneck pace through the crowded West End streets. Jammed, however, between the high, cushioned side of the carriage seat and the rock-hard body of her demonic betrothed, Jessica knew she was in small danger of tumbling out. She leaned back and contemplated Dain's Steeds from Hell.

They were the worst-tempered horses she'd ever encountered in her life. They fussed and snorted about and objected to everything and everybody that strayed into their path. They tried to trample pedestrians. They exchanged equine insults with every horse they met. They tried to knock over lampposts and curb posts, and strove to collide with every vehicle that had the effrontery to share the same street with them.

Even when they reached Hyde Park, the animals showed no signs of tiring. They tried to run down the workmen finishing the new archway at Hyde Park Corner. They threatened to stampede down Rotten Row—upon which no vehicle but the monarch's was permitted.

They succeeded in none of their fiendish enterprises, however. Though he waited until the last minute, Dain quelled all attempts at mayhem. To Jessica's mingled annoyance and admiration, he did so without seeming to make the slightest effort, despite having to drive with only one hand.

"I suppose there wouldn't be any challenge in it," she said, thinking aloud, "if your cattle behaved themselves."

He smoothly drew the right one back from imminent collision with the statue of Achilles and turned the satanic beasts westward into the Drive. "Perhaps your ill temper has communicated itself to them, and they're frightened. They don't know where to run, what to do. Is that it, Nick, Harry? Afraid she'll shoot you?"

The beasts tossed their heads and answered with evil horsey laughter.

Leave it to Dain, she thought, to give his horses Lucifer's nicknames. And leave it to him to own animals who fully merited the names.

"You'd be ill tempered, too," she said, "if you'd spent the last week wrestling with guest lists and wedding breakfast menus and fittings and a lot of pestering relatives. You'd be cross, too, if every tradesman in London were besieging your house, and if your drawing room had come to look like a warehouse, heaped with catalogs and samples. They have been plaguing me since the morning our betrothal announcement appeared in the paper."

"I shouldn't be ill tempered in the least," he said, "because I should never be so cork-brained as to let myself be bothered."

"You're the one who insisted upon the grand wedding at St. George's, Hanover Square," she said. "Then you left it all to me. You haven't made the smallest pretense of helping."

"*I?* Help?" he asked incredulously. "What the devil are servants for, you little nitwit? Did I not tell you to send the bills to me? If no one else in the household is competent to do the work, then hire somebody. If you want to be a wealthy marchioness, why don't you act like one? The working classes work," he explained with exaggerated patience. "The upper classes tell them what to do. You should not upset the social order. Look at what happened in France. They overthrew the established order decades ago, and what have they to show for it? A king who dresses and behaves like a bourgeois, open sewers in their grandest neighborhoods, and not a decently lit street, except about the Palais Royal."

She stared at him. "I had no idea you were such a Tory snob. Certainly one couldn't tell, given your choice of companions."

He kept his gaze upon the horses. "If you're referring to the tarts, may I remind you that they're hired help."

The last thing she wanted was to be reminded of his bed partners. Jessica did not want to think about how he'd amused himself at night while she lay sleepless in her bed, fretting about the wedding night and her lack of experience—not to mention her lack of the Rubenesque figure he was so revoltingly partial to.

Gloomily certain that her marriage would be a debacle—no matter what Genevieve said—Jessica did not want to care whether she pleased him in bed or not. She could not get the better of her pride, though, and that feminine vanity couldn't bear the prospect of failing to captivate a husband. Any husband, even him. Neither of Genevieve's spouses had ever dreamt of straying, nor had any of the lovers she'd discreetly taken during her long widowhood.

But now was hardly the time to wrestle with that daunting problem, Jessica told herself. It made more sense to take the opportunity to get some practical matters sorted out. Like the guest list.

"I know where your female companions fit on your social scale," she said. "The men are another matter. Mr. Beaumont, for instance. Aunt Louisa says one may not invite him to the wedding breakfast because he isn't good ton. But he is your friend."

"You bloody well better not invite him," Dain said, his jaw hardening. "Buggering sod tried to spy on me when I was with a whore. Invite him to the wedding and the swine will think he's invited to attend the wedding night as well. What with the opium and drink, he probably can't get his own rod to stand to attention— so he watches someone else do it."

Jessica discovered that the image of Rubenesque trollops writhing in his lap wasn't nearly so agitating as what now appeared in her mind's eye: six and a half feet of dark, naked, *aroused* male.

She had a good idea of what arousal looked like. She'd seen some of Mr. Rowlandson's erotic engravings. She wished she hadn't. She didn't want so vivid an image of Dain doing with a voluptuous whore what the men in Rowlandson's pictures had been doing.

The picture hung in her mind, bold as the illuminations displayed during national celebrations, and it twisted her insides into knots and made her want to kill somebody.

She was not simply jealous, she was madly so—and he'd put her into this mortifying state with but a few careless words. Now she looked into the future, and saw him doing it again and again, until he made her completely insane.

She should not let him do it to her, Jessica knew. She should not be jealous of his tarts. She should thank her lucky stars for them, because he'd spend as little time as possible with her, while she would be a wealthy noblewoman, free to conduct her life as she wished. She'd told herself this a thousand times at least, since the day he'd so insolently proposed and she'd stupidly let her heart soften.

Lecturing herself didn't do any good. She knew he was perfectly awful and he'd used her abominably and he was incapable of affection and he was wedding her mainly for revenge ... and she wanted him to want only her, all the same.

"Have I finally shocked you?" Dain asked. "Or are you merely sulking? The silence has become deafening."

"I am shocked," she said tartly. "It would never occur to me that you would mind being watched. You seem to delight in public scenes."

"Beaumont was watching through a *peephole*," Dain said. "In the first place, I can't abide sneaks. In the second, I paid for a whore—not to perform, gratis, for an audience. Third, there are certain activities I prefer to conduct in private."

The carriage drive at this point began to veer northward, away from the banks of the Serpentine. The horses struggled to continue along the riverbank, aiming at a stand of trees. Dain smoothly corrected their direction without appearing to take any notice of what he was doing.

"At any rate, I felt obliged to clarify my rules with the aid of my fists," he went on. "It's more than possible Beaumont holds a grudge. I shouldn't put it past him to take out his ill feeling on you. He's a coward and a sneak and he has a nasty habit of . . ." He trailed off, frowning. "At any rate," he went on, his expression grim, "you're to have nothing to do with him."

It took her a moment to grasp the implications of the command, and in that moment the world seemed to grow marginally brighter and her heart a cautious degree lighter. She shifted sideways to scrutinize his glowering profile. "That sounds shockingly . . . protective."

"I paid for you," he said coldly. "You're mine. I look after what's mine. I shouldn't let Nick or Harry near him either."

"By gad—do you mean to say I am as important a possession as your *cattle?*" She pressed her hand to her heart. "Oh, Dain, you are too devastatingly romantic. I am altogether overcome."

He brought his full attention upon her for a moment, and his sullen gaze dropped to where her hand was. She hastily returned it to her lap.

Frowning, he turned back to the horses. "That overgarment thing, the what-you-call-it," he said testily.

"My pelisse? What's wrong with it?"

"You filled it better the last time I saw it," he said. "In Paris. When you burst into my party and bothered me." He steered the beasts right, into a tree-lined avenue a few yards south of the guardhouse. "When you assaulted my virtue. Surely you remember. Or did it merely seem to fit better because you were wet?"

She remembered. More important, *he* did—in sufficient detail to notice a few pounds' shrinkage. Her mood lightened another several degrees.

"You could throw me into the Serpentine and find out," she said.

The short avenue led to a small, thickly shaded circular drive. The trees ringing it shut out the rest of the park. In a short while, the five o'clock promenade would begin, and this secluded area, like the rest of Hyde Park, would be crammed with London's fashionables. At present, however, it was deserted.

Dain drew the curricle to a halt and set the brake. "You two settle down," he warned the horses. "Make the least bother, and you'll find yourselves hauling barges in Yorkshire."

His tone, though low, carried the clear signal of Obedience or Death. The animals responded to it just as though they were human. Instantly they became the most subdued, docile pair of geldings Jessica had ever seen.

Dain turned his moody black gaze upon her. "Now, as to you, Miss Termagant Trent—"

"I love these pet names," she said, gazing soulfully up into his eyes. "Nitwit. Sapskull. Termagant. How they make my heart flutter!"

"Then you'll be in raptures with a few other names I have in mind," he said. "How can you be such an idiot? Or have you done it on purpose? Look at you!" He addressed this last to her bodice. "At this rate, there won't be anything left of you by the wedding day. When was the last time you ate a proper meal?" he demanded.

Jessica supposed that, in Dain's Dictionary, this qualified as an expression of concern.

"I did not do it on purpose," she said. "You have no idea what it's like under Aunt Louisa's roof. She conducts wedding preparations as generals conduct warfare. The household has been in pitched battle since the day we arrived. I could leave them to fight it out among themselves, but I should not care for the result—and you would detest it. My aunt's taste is appalling. Which means I have no choice but to be involved, night and day. Then, because it takes all my will and energy to maintain control, I'm too tired and vexed to eat a proper meal—even if the servants were capable of making one, which they aren't, because she's worn them to a frazzle, too."

There was a short silence. Then, "Well," he said, shifting a bit in his place, as though he were not altogether comfortable.

"You told me I should hire help," she said. "What good will that do, when she'll interfere with them as well? I shall still be involved—and driven—"

"Yes, yes, I understand," he said. "She's bothering you. I'll make her stop. You should have told me before."

She smoothed her gloves. "Until now, I was unaware you had any inclinations to slay dragons for me."

"I don't," he said. "But one must be practical. You'll want all your strength for the wedding night."

"I cannot think why I should need strength," she said, ignoring a host of spine-tingling images rising in her mind's eye. "All I have to do is lie there."

"*Naked*," he said grimly.

"Truly?" She shot him a glance from under her lashes. "Well, if I must, I must, for you have the advantage of experience in these matters. Still, I do wish you'd told me sooner. I should not have put the modiste to so much trouble about the negligee."

"The *what?*"

"It was ghastly expensive," she said, "but the silk is as fine as gossamer, and the eyelet work about the neckline is exquisite. Aunt Louisa was horrified. She said only Cyprians wear such things, and it leaves nothing to the imagination."

Jessica heard him suck in his breath, felt the muscular thigh tense against hers.

"But if it were left to Aunt Louisa," she went on, "I should be covered from my chin to my toes in thick cotton ruffled white monstrosities with little pink bows and rosebuds. Which is absurd, when an evening gown reveals far more, not to mention—"

"What color?" he asked. His low voice had roughened.

"Wine red," she said. "With narrow black ribbons

threaded through the neckline. Here." She traced a plunging *U* over her bosom. "And there's the loveliest openwork over my . . . well, *here*." She drew her finger over the curve of her breast a bare inch above the nipple. "And openwork on the right side of the skirt. From here"—she pointed to her hip—"down to the hem. And I bought—"

"Jess." Her name was a strangled whisper.

"—slippers to match," she continued. "Black mules with—"

"*Jess*." In one furious flurry of motion, he threw down the reins and hauled her into his lap.

The movement startled the horses, who tossed their heads and snorted and commenced an agitated dance. "Stop it!" Dain said sharply. They stilled.

His powerful right arm tightened round Jessica's waist and he pulled her close.

It was like sitting in the throbbing heat of a furnace: Brick-hard and hot, his body pulsed with tension. He slid his hand down over her hip and clasped her thigh.

She looked up. He was scowling malevolently at his big, gloved hand. "You," he growled. "Plague take you."

She tilted her head back. "I'll return it, if you wish. The nightgown."

His furious black gaze moved up, to her mouth. His breathing was harsh. "No, you won't," he said.

Then his mouth, hard and hungry, fell upon hers, dragging over her lips as though to punish her.

But what Jessica tasted was victory. She felt it in the heat he couldn't disguise, and in the pulsing tension of his frame, and she heard it clear as any declaration when his tongue pushed impatiently for entry.

He wanted her. Still.

Maybe he didn't want to, but he couldn't help it, any more than she could help wanting him.

And for this moment, she needn't pretend otherwise. She squirmed up to wrap her arms round his neck, and held tightly while he ravaged her mouth. And while she ravaged his.

They might have been two furious armies, and the kiss a life-or-death battle. They both wanted the same: conquest, possession. He gave no quarter. She wanted none. She couldn't get enough of the hot sin of his mouth, the scorching pressure of his hand, dragging over her hip, brazenly claiming her breast.

She claimed, too, her hands raking over his massive shoulders and down, digging her fingers into the powerful sinews of his arms. *Mine*, she thought, as the muscles bunched and flexed under her touch.

And *mine*, she vowed, as she splayed her hands over his broad, hard chest. She would have him and keep him if it killed her. A monster he may be, but he was *her* monster. She would not share his stormy kisses with anyone else. She would not share his big, splendid body with anyone else.

She squirmed closer. He tensed and, groaning deep in his throat, moved his hand down and clasped her bottom, pulling her closer still. Even through the leather driving gloves and several layers of fabric, his bold grasp sent sizzling ripples of sensation over her skin.

She wanted his touch upon her naked flesh: big, bare, dark hands moving over her, everywhere. Rough or gentle, she didn't care. As long as he wanted her. As long as he kissed her and touched her like this . . . as though he were starving, as she was, as though he couldn't get enough of her, as she couldn't of him.

He dragged his mouth from hers and, muttering what sounded like Italian curses, took his warm hand off her buttock.

"Let go of me," he said thickly.

Swallowing a cry of frustration, she brought her hands down, folded them upon her lap, and stared at a tree opposite.

Dain gazed at her in furious despair.

He should have known better than to come within a mile of her. They'd be wed in thirteen days, and he would have the wedding night and as many nights thereafter as he needed to slake his lust and be done with it. He had told himself it didn't matter how much she haunted and plagued him meanwhile. He had endured worse, for smaller reward, and he could surely endure a few weeks of frustration.

He had to endure it, because he had a far too vivid image of the alternative: the Marquess of Dain hovering about and panting over his bride-to-be like a starving mongrel at a butcher's cart. He would be fretting and yapping at her doorstep by day and howling at her window by night. He would be trotting after her to dressmakers and milliners and cobblers and haberdashers, and snarling and growling about her at parties.

He was used to getting what he wanted the instant he wanted it, and to wisely ignoring or rejecting what he couldn't get that instant. He had found he could no more disregard her than a famished hound could disregard a slab of meat.

He should have realized that the day he met her, when he'd lingered in Champtois' shop, unable to take his eyes off her. He should at least have discerned the problem the day he'd gone to pieces just taking off her damned glove.

In any case, there was no escaping the truth now, when he'd given himself—and her—so mortifyingly eloquent a display. All she had to do was describe a bit of lingerie, and he lost his mind and tried to devour her.

"Do you want me to get off your lap?" she asked politely, still gazing straight ahead.

"Do you want to?" he asked irritably.

"No, I am perfectly comfortable," she said.

He wished he could say the same. Thanks to the small, round bottom perched so confounded *comfortably* upon his lap, his loins were experiencing the fiery torments of the damned. He was throbbingly aware that release was mere inches away. He had only to turn her toward him and lift her skirts and . . .

And she might as well have been in China, for all the chance there was of that happening, he thought bitterly. That was the trouble with ladies—one of the legion of troubles. You couldn't just do the business when you wanted to. You had to court and persuade, and then you had to do it in a proper bed. In the dark.

"You may stay, then," he said. "But don't kiss me again. It's . . . provoking. And don't tell me about your sleeping apparel."

"Very well," she said, glancing idly about her, just as though she were sitting at a tea table. "Did you know that Shelley's first wife drowned herself in the Serpentine?"

"Is my first wife considering the same?" he asked, eyeing her uneasily.

"Certainly not. Genevieve says that killing oneself on account of a man is inexcusably gauche. I was merely making conversation."

He thought that, despite the torments, it was rather pleasant to have a soft, clean-smelling lady perched upon his knee, making idle conversation. He felt a smile tugging at his mouth. He quickly twisted it into a scowl. "Does that mean you've left off being cross for the moment?"

"Yes." She glanced down at his useless left hand,

which had slid onto the seat during their stormy embrace. "You really ought to wear a sling, Dain. So that it doesn't bang into things. You could do it a serious injury, and never notice."

"I've only banged it once or twice," he said, frowning at it. "And I noticed, I assure you. I feel everything, just as though it worked. But it doesn't. Won't. Just lies there. Hangs there. Whatever." He laughed. "Conscience bothering you?"

"Not in the least," she said. "I thought of taking a horsewhip to you, but you wouldn't have felt a thing, I daresay."

He studied her slim arm. "That would want a good deal more muscle than you could hope for," he said. "And you'd never be quick enough. I'd skip out of your way and laugh."

She looked up. "You'd laugh even if I managed to strike. You'd laugh if your back were torn to shreds. Did you laugh after I shot you?"

"Had to," he answered lightly. "Because I swooned. Ridiculous."

It had been ridiculous, he realized now, as he searched the cool grey depths of her eyes. It had been absurd to be outraged with her. The scene in the Wallingdons' garden hadn't been her doing. He was beginning to suspect whose it had been. If the suspicion was correct, he had not only behaved abominably, but had been unforgivably stupid.

He'd deserved to be shot. And she'd done it well. Dramatically. He smiled, recollecting. "It was neatly done, Jess. I'll give you that."

"It was splendidly done," she said. "Admit it: brilliantly planned and executed."

He looked away, toward Nick and Harry, who were pretending to be sleepily at peace with the world. "It was very well done," he said. "Now I think of it. The red and black garments. The Lady Macbeth voice." He chuckled. "The way my courageous comrades bolted up in terror at the sight of you. Like a lot of ladies at a tea party invaded by a mouse."

His amused gaze came back to her. "Maybe it was worth being shot, just to see that. Sellowby—Goodridge—in a panic over a little female in a temper fit."

"I am not *little*," she said sharply. "Just because you are a great gawk of a lummox, you needn't make me out to be negligible. For your information, my lord Goliath, I happen to be taller than average."

He patted her arm. "You needn't worry, Jess. I'm still going to marry you, and I'll manage to make do somehow. You are not to be anxious on that score. In fact, I've brought proof."

He slid his hand into the deep carriage pocket. It took him a moment to find the package he'd hidden there, and the moment was enough to set his heart pounding with anxiety.

He'd spent three agitated hours selecting the gift. He'd rather be stretched upon a rack than return to Number Thirty-two, Ludgate Hill, and endure that hellish experience again. At last his fingers closed upon the tiny box.

Still, his heart didn't stop pounding, even when he drew it out and clumsily pressed it into her hand. "You'd better open it yourself," he said tightly. "It's a deuced awkward business with one hand."

Her grey glance darting from him to the package, she opened it.

There was a short silence. His insides knotted and his skin grew clammy with sweat.

Then, "Oh," she said. "Oh, Dain."

His helpless panic eased a fraction.

"We're betrothed," he said stiffly. "It's a betrothal ring."

The clerk at Rundell and Bridge had made appalling suggestions. A birthstone—when Dain had no idea when her birthday was. A stone to match her eyes— when there was no such stone, no such object in existence.

The obsequious worm had even dared to suggest a row of gems whose initials formed a message: Diamond-Emerald-Amethyst-Ruby-Epidote-Sapphire-Turquoise . . . for DEAREST. Dain had very nearly lost his breakfast.

Then, finally, when he'd been driven to the last stage of desperation, poring over emeralds and amethysts and pearls and opals and aquamarines and every other curst mineral a craftsman could clamp onto a ring . . . then, in the last of what seemed like a thousand velvet-padded trays, Dain had found it.

A single cabochon ruby, so smoothly polished that it seemed liquid, surrounded by heartbreakingly perfect diamonds.

He had told himself he didn't care whether she liked it or not. She'd have to wear it anyway.

He'd found it a great deal easier to pretend when she wasn't near. Easier to make believe he'd chosen that particular ring simply because it was the finest. Easier to hide in his dark wasteland of a heart the real reason: that it was a tribute, its symbolism as mawkish as any the jeweler's clerk had proposed.

A bloodred stone for the brave girl who'd shed his blood. And diamonds flashing fiery sparks, because lightning had flashed the first time she'd kissed him.

Her gazed lifted to his. Silver mist shimmered in her

eyes. "It's beautiful," she said softly. "Thank you." She pulled off her glove and took the ring from the box. "You must put it on my finger."

"Must I?" He tried to sound disgusted. "Some sentimental twaddle, I suppose."

"There's no one to see," she said.

He took the ring from her and slipped it over her finger, then quickly drew his hand away, afraid she'd discern the trembling.

She turned her hand this way and that, and the diamonds took fire.

She smiled.

"At least it fits," he said.

"Perfectly." Turning her head, she darted one quick kiss at his cheek, then hastily returned to her seat. "Thank you, Beelzebub," she said very softly.

His heart constricted painfully. He snatched up the reins. "We'd better get out of here, before the fashionable stampede begins," he said, his voice very gruff. "Nick! Harry! You can stop playing dead now."

They could play anything. They'd been trained by a circus equestrian, and they loved to perform, responding instantly to the subtle cues Dain had spent three full days learning from their former master. Though he knew how it was done, even he sometimes had trouble remembering that it was a certain flick of the reins or a change in tone they reacted to, and not his words.

At any rate, they were fondest of the role they'd played en route to Hyde Park, and he let them play it again, all the way back. That took his betrothed's attention away from him, and fixed it on praying she'd arrive alive at her aunt's doorstep.

With Jessica preoccupied, Dain had leisure to collect his shattered composure, and address his intelligence to putting two and two together, as he should have done weeks ago.

There had been six onlookers, Herriard had said.

Now Dain tried to remember the faces. Vawtry, yes, looking utterly thunderstruck. Rouvier, the man Dain had publicly embarrassed. Two Frenchmen he recalled having seen many times at *Vingt-Huit*. And two French-women, one unfamiliar. The other had been Isobel Callon, one of Paris' most vicious gossips . . . and one of Francis Beaumont's favorite female companions.

What had Jessica said that night? Something about how the gossip would have died down if she hadn't burst into his house.

But maybe it wouldn't have died down, Dain reflected. Maybe public interest in his relations with Miss Trent had swelled to insane proportions because someone had fed the rumor mill. Maybe someone had kept the gossip stirred and encouraged the wagers, knowing the rumors would drive Beelzebub wild.

All Beaumont would have needed to do was drop a word to the right party. Isobel Callon, for instance. She'd seize the delicious tidbit and make a campaign of it. She wouldn't need much encouragement to do so, because she hated Dain. Then, having sown the seeds, Beaumont could retire to England and enjoy his revenge at a safe distance . . . and laugh himself sick when letters arrived from his friends, detailing the latest events in the Dain-versus-Trent drama.

When the suspicion had first arisen, Dain had thought it far-fetched, the product of an agitated mind.

Now it made a good deal more sense than any other explanation. It did explain at least why jaded Paris had become so obsessed with one ugly Englishman's hand-ful of encounters with one pretty English female.

He glanced at Jessica.

She was trying to ignore Nick and Harry's Steeds of Death performance by concentrating on her betrothal ring. She hadn't put her glove back on. She turned her hand this way and that, making the diamonds spark rainbow fire.

She liked the ring.

She had bought a red silk nightgown, trimmed with black. For her wedding night.

She had kissed him back and touched him. And she hadn't seemed to mind being kissed and touched.

Beauty and the Beast. That's what Beaumont would call it, the poison-tongued sod.

But in thirteen days, this Beauty would be the Marchioness of Dain. And she would lie in the Beast's bed. Naked.

Then Dain would do everything he'd been dying to do for what seemed an eternity. Then she would be his, and no other man could touch her, because she belonged to him exclusively.

True, he could have bought Portugal for what "exclusive ownership" was costing him.

On the other hand, she was prime quality. A lady. His lady.

And it was very possible Dain owed it all to the sneaking, corrupt, cowardly, spiteful Francis Beaumont.

In which case, Dain decided, it would be pointless—as well as a waste of energy better saved for the wedding night—to take Beaumont apart and break him into very small pieces.

By rights, Dain ought to thank him instead.

But then, the Marquess of Dain was not very polite.

He decided the swine wasn't worth the bother.

Ten

On a bright Sunday morning on the eleventh day of
May in the Year of Our Lord Eighteen Hundred
Twenty-Eight, the Marquess of Dain stood before the
minister of St. George's, Hanover Square, with Jessica,
only daughter of the late Sir Reginald Trent, baronet.

Contrary to popular expectation, the roof did not
fall in when Lord Dain entered the holy edifice, and
lightning did not strike once during the ceremony.
Even at the end, when he hauled his bride into his arms
and kissed her so soundly that she dropped her prayer
book, no clap of thunder shook the walls of St. George's,
although a few elderly ladies fainted.

As a consequence, on the evening of that day, Mr.
Roland Vawtry gave Francis Beaumont his note of
hand for three hundred pounds. Mr. Vawtry had previously written and delivered other notes of varying
amounts to Lord Sellowby, Captain James Burton, Au-
gustus Tolliver, and Lord Avory.

Mr. Vawtry did not know where or how he would get
the money to cover the notes. Once, a decade earlier,

he'd gone to the moneylenders. The way that worked, he learned—and learning it had cost him two years of wretchedness—was, in a nutshell, that if they lent you five hundred pounds, you were obliged to pay back one thousand. He had rather blow out his brains than repeat the experience.

He was painfully aware that he would have no trouble covering his present debts of honor if he hadn't had to settle so very many others before he left Paris. He wouldn't have had the present debts at all, he reflected miserably, if he had learned his lesson in Paris and left off wagering on any matter involving Dain.

He had won exactly once, and that had not been much of a victory. He had lost two hundred pounds to Isobel Callon when she insisted Dain had lured Miss Trent to Lady Wallingdon's garden to make love to her.

Vawtry had simply won it back when Dain, contrary to Isobel's confident prediction, had failed, when caught, to enact the role of chivalrous swain. He had behaved, for once, like himself.

Unfortunately for Vawtry's finances, that had happened only the once. Because not a week later, after vowing he wouldn't have Miss Trent if she were served on a platter of solid gold—after the incomprehensible female had *shot* him—Dain had strolled into Antoine's and coolly announced his betrothal. He had said that someone had to marry her because she was a public menace, and he supposed he was the only one big and mean enough to manage her.

Moodily wondering just who was managing whom, Vawtry settled into a corner table with Beaumont at Mr. Pearke's oyster house in Vinegar Yard, on the south side of Drury Lane Theater.

It was not an elegant dining establishment, but Beaumont was partial to it because it was a favorite haunt of artists. It was also very cheap, which made Vawtry partial to it at the moment.

"So Dain gave you all a show, I hear," said Beaumont, after the tavern maid had filled their glasses. "Terrified the minister. Laughed when the bride vowed to obey. And nearly broke her jaw kissing her."

Vawtry frowned. "I was sure Dain would drag it out to the last minute, then loudly announce, 'I don't.' And laugh and stroll out the way he came."

"You assumed he would treat her as he did other women," said Beaumont. "You forgot, apparently, that all the other women had been tarts, and that, in Dain's aristocratic dictionary, the tarts are mere peasant wenches, to be tumbled and forgotten. Miss Trent, however, is a gently bred maiden. Completely different situation, Vawtry. I do wish you'd seen."

Vawtry saw now. And now it seemed so obvious, he couldn't believe he hadn't worked it out for himself ages ago. A lady. A different species altogether.

"If I had seen, you would be out three hundred quid at present," he said, his voice light, his heart heavy.

Beaumont picked up his glass and studied it before taking a cautious sip. "Drinkable," he said, "but just barely."

Vawtry took a very long swallow from his own glass.

"Perhaps what I actually wish," Beaumont went on, after a moment, "is that I'd known the facts. Matters would be so different now."

He frowned down at the table. "If I'd known the truth then, I might at least have dropped a hint to you. But I didn't know, because my wife tells me nothing. I truly believed, you see, that Miss Trent was penniless. Right up until last night, when an artist friend who does sketches for Christie's corrected my misapprehension."

Mr. Vawtry eyed his friend uneasily. "What do you mean? Everyone knows Bertie Trent's sister hadn't a feather to fly with, thanks to him."

Beaumont glanced about. Then, leaning over the table, he spoke in lower tones. "You recall the moldering little picture Dain told us about? The one the wench got for ten sous from Champtois?"

Vawtry nodded.

"Turned out to be a Russian icon, and one of the finest and most unusual works of the Stroganov school in existence."

Vawtry looked at him blankly.

"Late sixteenth century," Beaumont explained. "Icon workshop opened by the Stroganov family, Russian nobility. The artists made miniatures for domestic use. Very delicate, painstaking work. Costly materials. Highly prized these days. Hers is done with gold leaf. The frame is gold, set with precious gems."

"Obviously worth more than ten sous," Vawtry said, trying to keep his tone casual. "Dain did say she was shrewd." He emptied his glass in two swallows and refilled it. Out of the corner of his eye, he saw the tavern maid approaching with their meal. He wished she'd hurry. He didn't want to hear any more.

"Value, of course, is in the eye of the beholder," Beaumont went on. "I'd put it at a minimum of fifteen hundred pounds. At auction, several times that, very likely. But I know of at least one Russian who'd sell his firstborn to have it. Ten, possibly twenty thousand."

Lady Granville, daughter of the Duke of Sutherland, one of the richest men in England, had brought her husband a dowry of twenty thousand pounds.

Such women, the daughters of peers, were far beyond Mr. Vawtry's reach, along with their immense dowries. Miss Trent, on the other hand, the daughter of an insignificant baronet, belonged to the same class of country gentry as Mr. Vawtry himself.

He saw now that he'd had a perfect opportunity to cultivate her, after Dain had publicly insulted and humiliated her. She had been vulnerable then. Instead of merely handing her his coat, Vawtry might have enacted the role of chivalrous knight. He might, in that case, have stood before the preacher with her this very day.

Then the icon would have been his, and clever Beaumont could have helped him turn it into ready money . . . ready to be invested. Roland Vawtry could have settled down with a pretty enough wife, and lived in tranquil comfort, no longer dependent on Dame Fortune—or, more to the point, the whims of the Marquess of Dain.

Instead, Roland Vawtry was five thousand pounds in debt. Though this was not very much by some people's standards, by his, it might have been millions. He was not concerned about the tradesmen he owed, but he was deeply anxious about the notes of hand he'd given his friends. If he did not make good on them very soon, he would not have any friends. A gentleman who failed to pay debts of honor ceased being deemed a gentleman. That prospect was even more harrowing to him than the threat of moneylenders, sponging houses, or debtors' prison.

He viewed his situation as desperate.

Certain people could have told him that Francis Beaumont could detect another's desperation at twenty paces, and took great personal pleasure in exacerbating it. But those wise persons were not about, and Vawtry was not an overly intelligent fellow.

Consequently, by the time they'd finished their meal and emptied half a dozen bottles of the barely drinkable wine, Mr. Beaumont had dug his pit, and Mr. Vawtry had obligingly toppled headfirst into it.

At about the time Roland Vawtry was tumbling into a pit, the new Marchioness of Dain's hindquarters were showing symptoms of rigor mortis.

She sat with her spouse in the elegant black traveling chariot in which they'd been riding since one o'clock in the afternoon, when they'd left their guests at the wedding breakfast.

For a man who viewed marriage and respectable company with unmitigated contempt and disgust, he had behaved with amazing good humor. In fact, he had seemed to find the proceedings infinitely amusing. Three times he'd asked the trembling minister to speak up, so that the audience didn't miss anything. Dain had also thought it a great joke to make a circus performance of kissing his bride. It was a wonder he hadn't thrown her over his shoulder and carried her out of the church like a sack of potatoes.

If he had, Jessica thought wryly, he would have still managed to look every inch the aristocrat. Or monarch was more like it. She had learned that Dain had an exceedingly high opinion of his consequence, in which the standard order of precedence played no role whatsoever.

He'd made his views very clear to her aunt, not long after he'd given Jessica the heartachingly beautiful betrothal ring. After taking Jessica home and spending an hour with her in the parlor, perusing her lists and menus and other wedding annoyances, he'd sent her away and had a private conversation with Aunt Louisa. He'd explained how the future Marchioness of Dain was to be treated. It was simple enough.

Jessica was not to be pestered and she was not to be contradicted. She answered to nobody but Dain, and he answered to nobody but the king, and then only if he was in the mood.

The next day, Dain's private secretary had arrived with a brace of servants and taken over. After that, all Jessica had had to do was give an occasional order and accustom herself to being treated like an exceedingly precious and delicate, all-wise and altogether perfect princess.

Not by her husband, though.

They had been traveling for more than eight hours, and though they stopped frequently to change horses, that was for not a second more than the one to two minutes it took to make the change. At Bagshot, at about four o'clock, she'd needed to use the privy. She'd returned to find Dain pacing impatiently by the carriage, pocket watch in hand. He had strongly objected to her taking five times longer to answer nature's call than the stablemen did to unhitch four horses and hitch up four fresh ones.

"All a male need do," she'd told him patiently, "is unfasten his trouser buttons and aim somewhere, and it's done. I am a female, however, and neither my plumbing nor my garments are so accommodating."

He had laughed and stuffed her into the carriage and told her she was an infernal bother, but she was born that way, wasn't she?—being born female. Nonetheless, the second time she'd needed to relieve herself, a few miles back at Andover, he'd grumblingly told her to take her time. She'd returned to find him patiently sipping a tankard of ale. He had laughingly offered her a sip, and laughed harder when she drained the quarter pint he'd left.

"That was a mistake," he'd said when they were once more upon the road. "Now you'll be wanting to stop at every necessary from here to Amesbury."

That had led to a series of privy and chamber pot

jokes. Jessica had never before understood why men found those sorts of anecdotes so gut-busting hilarious. She had moments ago discovered that they could be funny enough if related by an evilly clever storyteller.

She was at present recovering from an altogether immature fit of whooping laughter.

Dain was lounging back in the seat, which, as usual, he took up most of. His half-closed eyes were crinkled up at the corners and his hard mouth had curved into an endearingly crooked smile.

She wanted to be vexed with him for making her laugh so intemperately at the crass, puerile story. She couldn't be. He looked so adorably pleased with himself.

She was in a sorry case, to find Beelzebub *adorable*, but she couldn't help it. She wanted to crawl into his lap and cover his wicked countenance with kisses.

He caught her studying him. She hoped she didn't look as besotted as she felt.

"Are you uncomfortable?" he asked.

"My backside and limbs have fallen asleep," she said, shifting her position a fraction away. Not that one could get away, even in this coach, which was roomier than his curricle. There was still only one seat, and there was a great deal of him. But the air had cooled considerably with evening, and he was very warm.

"You should have asked to step out to stretch your limbs when we stopped at Weyhill," he said. "We shan't stop again until Amesbury."

"I scarcely noticed Weyhill," she said. "You were telling one of the most moronic anecdotes I'd ever heard."

"Had it been less moronic, the joke would have gone over your head," he said. "You laughed hard enough."

"I didn't want to hurt your feelings," she said. "I

thought you were trying to impress me by displaying the uppermost limits of your intellect."

He turned an evil grin upon her. "When I set out to *impress* you, my lady, believe me, intellect will have nothing to do with it."

She met his gaze stoically, while her insides went into a feverish flurry. "You are referring to the wedding night, no doubt," she said composedly. "The 'breeding rights' for which you've paid so extortionate a price. Well, it will be easy enough to impress me, since you're an expert and I have never done it, even once."

His grin faltered a bit. "Still, you know all about it. You weren't in the least puzzled by what the lady and gentleman in your grandmama's pocket watch were doing. And you seem to have an excellent notion of the services the tarts are employed to perform."

"There is a difference between intellectual knowledge and practical experience," she said. "I will admit I'm a trifle anxious in the latter regard. Yet you are not at all inhibited, and so I am sure you will not be shy about instructing me."

Jessica hoped he wouldn't be too impatient to do so. She was a quick learner, and she was sure she could discover how to please him in a relatively short time. If he gave her the chance. That was all she was truly worried about. He was used to professionals who were trained to satisfy. He might easily become bored and irritated with her ignorance, and abandon her for women who were less . . . bother.

She knew he was taking her to Devon with the intention of leaving her there when he'd had his fill of her.

She knew she was asking for heartache to hope and try for more.

Most of the world—all but a handful of the wedding guests, certainly—viewed him as a monster, and her marriage to the Bane and Blight of the Ballisters as a narrow notch above a death sentence. But he was not a monster when he held her in his arms. And so Jessica couldn't stop herself from hoping for more of that, at least. And hoping, she was determined to try.

His gaze had slid away. He was rubbing his thumb over his knee, and frowning at it as though a wrinkle had had the audacity to appear in his trousers.

"I think we'd better continue this discussion later," he said. "I had not . . . Gad, I should think it was simple enough. It's not as though you're competing at university for a first in Classics or Mathematics."

Only for first in his black heart, she thought.

"When I do something, I want to do it well," she said. "Actually, I always want to be the best. I am terribly competitive, you see. Perhaps it comes of having to manage so many boys. I had to beat my brother and cousins at everything, including sports, or they wouldn't respect me."

He looked up—not at her, but at the coach window. "Amesbury," he said. "About bloody time, too. I'm starving."

What the Bane and Blight of the Ballisters was, at the moment, was terrified.

Of his wedding night.

Now, when it was too late, he saw his mistake.

Yes, he knew Jessica was a virgin. He could hardly forget it, when that had been one of the most mortifying aspects of the entire situation: one of Europe's greatest debauchees mindless with lust for a slip of an English spinster.

He had known she was a virgin just as he had known her eyes were the color of a Dartmoor mist, and as changeable as the atmosphere of those treacherous expanses. He knew it in the same way he knew her hair was silken jet and her skin was creamy velvet. He'd known it, and the knowing was sweet, when he'd looked down at his bride as they stood before the minister. She'd worn a silver-grey gown and a faint pink had glowed in her cheeks, and she was not only the most beautiful creature he'd ever seen, but she was pure as well. He had known no other man had possessed her, that she was his and his alone.

He had also known he would bed her. He'd dreamt of it long and often enough. Moreover, having waited what seemed like six or seven eternities, he had made up his mind to do it properly, in a luxurious inn, in a big, comfortable bed with clean linens, after a well-prepared supper and a few glasses of good wine.

Somehow, he had neglected to take into account what being a virgin meant, beyond being untouched. Somehow, through all those heated fantasies, he'd left out one critical factor: No series of men had gone before him to make the way easy. He had to break her in himself.

And that, he feared, was just what he'd do: break her.

The carriage halted. Suppressing a desperate urge to scream at the coachman to keep on driving—until Judgment Day, preferably—Dain helped his wife out.

She took his arm as they started toward the entrance. Her gloved hand had never seemed so woefully small as it did at this moment.

She had insisted she was taller than average, but that wasn't the least bit reassuring to a man as big as a house, and likely to have the same impact when he fell upon her.

He would crush her. He would break something, tear something. And if he somehow managed not to kill her and if the experience did not turn her into a babbling lunatic, she would run away screaming if he ever tried to touch her again.

She would run away, and she would never again kiss him and hold him and—

"Well, stand me up and knock me down again—either a coal barge just hove into view or it's Dain."

The raucous voice jolted Dain back to the moment and to his forgotten surroundings. He'd entered the inn without noticing and heard the landlord's greeting without attending, and was, in the same distracted way, following his host to the stairway that led to the chambers Dain had reserved.

Coming down the stairs was the voice's owner: his old Eton schoolfellow Mallory. Or, rather, the Duke of Ainswood now. The previous duke, all of nine years old, had fallen victim to diphtheria a year ago. Dain recalled signing the condolence note his secretary had written to the mother and the tactfully combined condolences and congratulations to Mallory, the cousin. Dain hadn't bothered to point out that tact was wasted on Vere Mallory.

Dain hadn't seen the man since Wardell's funeral. His former schoolfellow had been drunk then and he was drunk now. Ainswood's dark hair was a greasy rat's nest, his eyes puffy and bloodshot, and his jaw rough with at least two days' growth of beard.

Dain's nerves were already in a highly sensitive state. The realization that he must introduce this repellent figure to his dainty, elegant, *pure* wife stretched those frayed nerves another dangerous notch.

"Ainswood," he said with a curt nod. "What a charming surprise."

"Surprise is hardly the word." Ainswood stomped down to the foot of the stairs. "I'm knocked acock. Last time I saw you, you said you wouldn't come back to England again on anybody's account, and if anyone else wanted you at his funeral, he'd better contrive to keel over in Paris." His bloodshot gaze fell upon Jessica then, and he grinned in what Dain considered an intolerably obscene manner. "Why, bless me if hell hasn't truly frozen over. Dain not only back in England, but traveling with a bit of muslin, to boot."

The threads of Dain's control began to unravel. "I won't ask what hermit's cave you've been living in, that you don't know I've been in London for nearly a month and wed this morning," he said, his voice cool, his insides roiling. "The *lady* happens to be *my* lady."

He turned to Jessica. "Madam, I have the dubious honor of presenting—"

The duke's loud guffaw cut him off. "Wed?" he cried. "Quick, tell me another. Mayhap this bird of paradise is your sister. No, better yet, your great aunt Mathilda."

Since any female out of the schoolroom would know that "bird of paradise" was a synonym for "harlot," Dain had no doubt his wife was aware she'd just been insulted.

"Ainswood, you have just called me a liar," he said in ominously mild tones. "You have slandered my lady. Twice. I will give you precisely ten seconds to compose an apology."

Ainswood stared at him for a moment. Then he grinned. "You always were good with the daring and daunting, my lad, but that cock won't fight. I know a hoax when I see one. Where was your last performance, my dove?" he asked Jessica. "The King's Theatre, Haymarket? You see, I don't slander you a bit. I can tell you're above his usual Covent Garden wares."

"That's three times," said Dain. "Innkeeper."

Their host, who'd withdrawn to a dark corner of the hall, crept out. "My lord?"

"Kindly show the lady to her chamber."

Jessica's fingers dug into his arm. "Dain, your friend's half-seas over," she whispered. "Can't you—"

"*Upstairs*," he said.

She sighed and let go of his arm and did as she was told.

He watched until she'd passed the landing. Then he turned back to the duke, who was still gazing upward at her, his expression lewdly expressive of his thoughts.

"Prime piece," said His Grace, turning back to him with a wink. "Where'd you find her?"

Dain grabbed his neckcloth and shoved him against the wall. "You stupid, filthy piece of horse manure," he said. "I gave you a chance, *cretino*. Now I have to break your neck."

"I'm quaking in my boots," Ainswood said, his bleary eyes lighting at the prospect of battle. "Do I get the chit if I win?"

A short while later, oblivious to her maid's protests, Jessica stood on the balcony overlooking the inn's courtyard.

"My lady, I beg you to come away," Bridget pleaded. "It isn't a fit sight for Your Ladyship. You'll be ill, I know you will, and on your wedding night, too."

"I've seen fights before," said Jessica. "But never one on my account. Not that I expect they'll do much damage. I calculate they're evenly matched. Dain is bigger, of course, but he must fight one-armed. And Ainswood is not only well built, but drunk enough not to feel much."

The cobblestoned yard below was rapidly filling with men, some in dressing gowns and nightcaps. Word had quickly spread, and even at this late hour, few males could resist the lure of a mill. Not just any mill, either, for the combatants were peers of the realm. This was a rare treat for boxing aficionados.

Each man had drawn a circle of supporters. Half a dozen well-dressed gentlemen were gathered about Dain. They were offering the usual loud and contradictory advice while Dain's valet, Andrews, helped his master out of his upper garments.

Bridget let out a shriek, and scuttled back against the balcony door. "Heaven preserve us—they're *naked!*"

Jessica didn't care about "they." Her eyes were upon one man only, and he, stripped to the waist, took her breath away.

The torchlight gleamed upon sleek olive skin, over broad shoulders and brawny biceps, and spilled lovingly over the hard angles and flexing curves of his chest. He turned, displaying to her dazzled eyes a smooth expanse of back, gleaming like dark marble and sculpted in clean lines of bone and rippling muscle. He might have been a marble Roman athlete come to life.

Her insides tightened, and the familiar heat coiling through her was a thrumming mixture of yearning and pride.

Mine, she thought, and the thought was an ache, bittersweet, of hope and despair at once. He was hers in name, by law both sacred and secular. But no law could make him truly, fully hers.

That would want a long and dogged battle.

The drunken Ainswood, she thought ruefully, stood a better chance of winning than she did. On the other hand, he did not seem overly intelligent, and her struggle wanted brains, not brawn.

Jessica did not lack brains, and the mouthwatering sight below constituted more than sufficient motivation.

She watched one of the men secure Dain's left arm in a makeshift sling. Then the two combatants stood up to each other, nearly toe to toe.

The signal was given.

Ainswood instantly made a fierce rush at his opponent, head down and fists flailing. Dain, smiling, retreated, carelessly dodging the shower of blows, simply letting the duke come on as hard as he could.

But hard as the man came, he got nowhere. Dain was light on his feet, his reflexes lightning-fast—as they must be, for Ainswood was surprisingly quick, despite his insobriety. Nonetheless, Dain led him a merry chase. Blow after blow that seemed certain to connect struck only air, infuriating the duke.

He came on harder yet, throwing more power into the assault, trying every angle. One blow glanced off Dain's arm. Then there was a blur of movement and a loud *thwack!* And Ainswood staggered backward, blood streaming from his nose.

"A conker, by gad," Jessica muttered. "And I never saw it coming. Nor did His Grace, to be sure."

Bloody but undaunted, Ainswood laughed and bounded back for yet another dogged attack.

By this time, Bridget had returned to her new mistress's side. "Mercy on us," she said, her round face wrinkled with distaste. "Isn't once enough to be hit?"

"They don't feel it." Jessica turned back to the fight. "Until it's over, that is. Oh, well done, Dain," she cried as her lord's powerful right slammed into the duke's side. "That's what he wants. To the body, my dear. The oaf's head is thick as an anvil."

Fortunately, her cries could not be heard over the shouts of the assembled onlookers, or Dain might have been distracted—with unfortunate results—by his dainty wife's bloodthirsty advice.

In any case, he'd evidently worked out the matter on his own, and one—two—three—brutal body blows at last brought Ainswood to his knees.

Two men rushed forward to haul His Grace up. Dain backed away.

"Give it up, Ainswood," someone in Dain's circle shouted.

"Aye, before he *really* hurts you."

From her vantage point, Jessica could not be certain how much damage Dain had done. There was a good deal of blood spattered about, but the human nose did tend to bleed profusely.

Ainswood stood, swaying. "Come along, Big Beak," he taunted, gasping. "I'm not done with you." Clumsily he waved his fists.

Dain shrugged, strode forward and, in a few swift motions, knocked the flailing hands away and planted his fist in his opponent's gut.

The duke folded up like a rag doll and toppled backward. Fortunately, his friends reacted quickly, catching him an instant before his head could hit the cobblestones. When they'd pulled him up into a sitting position, he grinned stupidly up at Dain. Sweat mingled with blood trickled down the duke's face.

"Apologize," said Dain.

Ainswood took several heaving breaths. "Beg pardon, Beelz," he croaked.

"You will also take the first opportunity to apologize to my lady."

Ainswood sat, nodding and breathing hard for a long moment. Then, to Jessica's chagrin, he looked up toward the balcony. "Beg pardon, my lady Dain!" he called out hoarsely.

Then Dain looked up, too. Damp black curls clung to his forehead, and a fine sheen of sweat glistened on his neck and shoulders.

His eyes widened briefly in astonishment when

they lit upon her, and an odd, pained look crossed his features. But in the next instant, the familiar, mocking expression was in place. "My lady," he said, and swept her a theatrical bow.

The crowd cheered.

She nodded. "My lord." She wanted to leap down from the balcony and into his arms.

One-armed, he had fought his own friend, because of her. He had fought cleverly, splendidly. He was magnificent. She wanted to cry. She mustered a tremulous smile, then turned and hurried through the door Bridget held open for her.

Not certain at first what to make of his bride's troubled smile, Dain took stock of the situation and his appearance, and ended by making the worst of it.

The smile and the cool composure, he decided, were for the audience's benefit. It was a cover-up smile, as so many of his own were, and he could easily imagine what she was covering up.

Her new husband was an animal.

He'd been brawling in an innyard like a common ruffian.

He was dirty and spattered with Ainswood's blood and sweating and *stinking*.

He was also half-naked, and the torchlights had given her a lurid view of what he'd intended to conceal in darkness: his gross blackamoor's body.

By now, she was probably clutching a chamber pot, casting up her accounts—if she wasn't bolting the door and helping Bridget push heavy furniture against it.

Dain decided against washing up in the room. Instead, he marched to the pump, deaf to his valet's warnings about the night air and fatal chills.

Not to be outdone, Ainswood joined him there. They

silently doused themselves while their friends gathered round them to exclaim and argue about the fight.

When the two had completed their cold ablutions, they stood eyeing each other and shrugging their shoulders to conceal their shivering.

Ainswood spoke first. "Wed, by gad," he said, shaking his head. "Who'd have thought it?"

"She shot me," said Dain. "She had to be punished. 'Pardon one offense,' says Publilius, 'and you encourage the commission of many.' Can't have every female who feels vexed with me running after me with pistol cocked. Had to make an example of her, didn't I?"

He glanced round at the others. "If one female gets away with shooting Beelzebub, others might start thinking they can get away with shooting any male, on any trifling pretext."

The men about him fell silent. As they pondered this outrageous prospect, their expressions grew very grave.

"I wed her as a public service," he said. "There are times when a man must rise above his own petty concerns and act on behalf of his friends."

"So he must," said Ainswood. He broke into a grin. "But it doesn't seem so great a sacrifice to me. That is a prime—I mean to say, your lady is exceedingly handsome."

Dain affected indifference.

"I should say *beautiful*," said Carruthers.

"Quality," said another.

"Her bearing is elegant," another volunteered.

"Graceful as a swan."

While his chest expanded and his shoulders straightened, Dain managed to appear disgusted. "I give you leave to cudgel your brains, composing lyrical odes to her perfection," he said. "I, however, mean to have a drink."

Eleven

*J*essica's dinner appeared about twenty minutes after the mill. Her husband did not. He was in the bar parlor with some companions, according to the innkeeper, and had requested Her Ladyship not to wait for him.

Jessica was not surprised. In her experience, after trying desperately to knock each other's brains from their skulls, men promptly became the very dearest of friends and celebrated their intimacy by becoming cockeyed drunk.

She ate her dinner, washed, and dressed for bed. She didn't bother to don the red and black nightgown. She doubted His Lordship would arrive in a suitable condition to appreciate it. Instead she put on a less interesting cream-colored one and a pastel brocade dressing gown over it, and settled down in a comfortable chair by the fire with Byron's *Don Juan*.   •

It was long past midnight when she heard a trio of clumsy footsteps in the hall outside and a trio of drunken voices slurring over a bawdy song. She rose and opened the door.

Dain, who'd been leaning upon his two comrades, pushed himself off and lurched toward her. "Behold, the bridegroom cometh," he announced thickly. He flung his arm over Jessica's shoulder. "Go away," he told his friends.

They staggered away. He kicked the door shut. "Told you not to wait," he said.

"I thought you might want help," she said. "I sent Andrews to bed. He was asleep on his feet. And I was awake, reading, anyhow."

His coat and previously pristine shirt were rumpled, and he'd lost his neckcloth. His blood-spattered trousers were damp, his boots caked with dried mud.

He released her, and swaying, stared at his boots for a long moment. Then he swore under his breath.

"Why don't you sit down on the bed?" she suggested. "I can help you get your boots off."

He moved unsteadily toward the bed. Clutching the bedpost, he carefully lowered himself onto the mattress. "Jess."

She approached, and knelt at his feet. "Yes, my lord."

"Yes, my lord," he echoed with a laugh. "Jess, m'lady, I believe I'm castaway. Lucky you."

She began tugging at his left boot. "We'll see about my luck. We've only the one bed, and if drink makes you snore the way it does Uncle Arthur, I'm in for a ghastly night—or what's left of the night."

"Snoring," he said. "Worried about *snoring*. Henwit."

She got the boot off and started on the other.

"Jess," he said.

"At least you recognize me."

The right boot proved more stubborn. Yet she dared not yank too hard, lest he topple forward and crash down on her. "You'd better lie down," she said.

He grinned stupidly at her.

"*Down*," she said firmly.

"Down," he repeated, giving the room the same vacant grin. "Where's that?"

She rose and set her hands on his chest and gave him a hard shove.

He fell back, setting the mattress bouncing. He chuckled.

Jessica bent and renewed her struggle with the boot.

"Dainty," he said, gazing up at the ceiling. "Dainty Lady Dain. She tastes like rain. She is a great pain. In the arse. *Ma com' è bella. Molto bella.* Very beautiful . . . pain . . . in the arse."

She yanked the boot off. "That doesn't rhyme." She rose. "Byron you are not."

A soft snore answered.

"Behold the bridegroom," she muttered. "Thank heaven it's a large bed. My conjugal devotion does not extend to sleeping on the floor."

She moved away to the washstand. After washing the mud from her hands, she took off her dressing gown and hung it on a chair.

Then she walked round to the other side of the bed, and pulled back the bedclothes as far as she could. It wasn't quite far enough. The upper half of his body sprawled diagonally across the mattress.

She pushed at his shoulder. "Move over, you lummox."

Mumbling, he rolled first onto one side, then onto the other.

Jessica shoved harder. "*Move*, drat you."

He grumbled something and rolled a bit more. She

kept pushing, and eventually—and unconscious all the while—he got his head upon the pillow and his feet off the floor. Then he curled up in a fetal position, facing her side of the bed.

She climbed in beside him and angrily yanked the blankets up. "Pain in the hindquarters, am I?" she said under her breath. "I'd have done better to push you onto the floor."

She turned to look at him. Tangled black curls fell over his brow, which, in sleep, was as smooth as an innocent babe's. His right hand clutched a corner of the pillow. He was snoring, but very softly, a low, steady murmur.

Jessica closed her eyes.

Even though his body wasn't touching hers, she was acutely aware of him, of his weight upon the mattress . . . and the mingled masculine scents of smoke and spirits and himself . . . and the warmth his immense body generated.

She was also aware of a most irrational frustration . . . and hurt, if she were to be completely honest.

She had expected Dain to toss back a few glasses with his friends. She'd expected him to arrive the worse for drink. She would not have minded. He would not be the first or the last bridegroom to come tipsy to the bridal bed, and it had occurred to her that hazy perception might make him more tolerant of her inexperience.

Actually, if truth be told, she would have preferred to have him as close to unconscious as possible. Deflowering a virgin was not the most aesthetic of experiences, and Genevieve had told her that it was often the biggest, most thick-skinned brutes who became hysterical over a few drops of maidenly blood. She had also explained how to deal with the hysteria—and everything else.

Aware that her entire future with Dain could hinge upon this night's experience, Jessica had prepared for it as any wise general would prepare for a crucial battle.

She was well informed, and fully determined to do her very best. She was prepared to be cheerful, willing, responsive, and attentive.

She was not prepared for this.

He was no schoolboy. He knew his drinking limits. He knew how much it took to incapacitate him.

Yet he hadn't stopped. On his wedding night.

Reason told her there must be a typically crack-brained masculine reason for his behavior, and sooner or later she'd figure it out, and it would turn out to have nothing to do with trying to hurt her feelings or make her feel undesirable or any of the other gloomy sensations she was experiencing at the moment.

But it had been a long day, and she realized now that she'd spent most of that time tense with mingled anticipation and anxiety about what, it turned out, wasn't going to happen.

She was exhausted and she couldn't sleep, and she must ride another million miles tomorrow at the same hectic pace, in the same agitated emotional state. She wanted to cry. She wanted, even more, to scream and beat him and pull his hair and make him as hurt and angry as she was.

She opened her eyes and sat up and looked about for something she could hit him with without doing permanent damage. She could dump the contents of the water pitcher on him, she thought, as her gaze fell upon the washstand.

Then she realized she shouldn't have been able to see the washstand. She'd left the lamp burning on the bedstand beside her. She moved to the edge of the bed and put it out.

She sat there, staring into the darkness. From outside the window came the predawn chirping of birds.

He grumbled and stirred restlessly.

"Jess." His voice was thick with sleep.

"At least you know I'm here," she muttered. "I suppose that's something." With a sigh, she lay down again. She was tugging the blankets up when she felt the mattress shift and sink. There was more incoherent grumbling. Then he flung his arm over her midriff and his leg over hers.

He was on top of the bedclothes. She was under them.

His big limbs were heavy, but very warm.

She felt marginally better.

In a few moments, she fell asleep.

Dain's first conscious sensations were of a small, soft bottom nestled against his groin and a deliciously rounded breast under his hand. In the instant it took him to mentally connect the agreeable parts with the female they belonged to, a host of other recollections flooded in, and his mood of sleepy amorousness swept away on a tide of self-loathing.

He'd brawled in an innyard like a common yokel while his wife looked on. He had consumed enough wine to float an East Indiaman and, instead of considerately passing out in the bar parlor, he'd let his oafish friends haul him up to the bridal chamber. As though it hadn't been enough for his new bride to see him filthy and rank with sweat, he must also display himself in all his drink-sodden grossness. Even then, he hadn't shown the courtesy of collapsing on the floor, well away from her. He'd dropped his great wine- and smoke-reeking elephant's body onto the bed, and let his dainty lady wife haul off his boots.

His face burned.

He rolled away and stared at the ceiling.

At least he hadn't violated her. He'd drunk a good deal more than even he was accustomed to, in order to make sure of that. It was a miracle he'd made it up the stairs.

He could have done without that miracle. He could have done without a few other things, such as remembering anything at all. He wished the rest of him were as paralyzed as his left arm.

Satan's blacksmith was using his head as an anvil again. Lucifer's chief cook was mixing a foul brew in his mouth. At some point during Dain's pitifully few hours of sleep, the Prince of Darkness had apparently ordered a herd of raging rhinoceroses to stampede over his body.

Beside him, the source of Dain's troubles stirred.

Cautiously he hauled himself up, grimacing as thousands of vicious needles jabbed his left arm and burned and pricked his hand.

He got out of bed, every bone, muscle, and organ viciously protesting, and staggered to the washstand.

He heard a rustle of movement from the bed. Then came a sleep-clogged feminine voice. "Do you want any help, Dain?"

Whatever conscience Lord Dain possessed had sunk into a fatal decline and expired sometime about his tenth birthday. At the sound of his wife's voice offering assistance, it rose, like Lazarus, from the dead. It fastened its gnarled fingers upon his heart and let out a shriek that should have shattered the window, the water jug, and the small washstand mirror into which Dain was gazing.

Yes, he answered silently. He wanted help. He wanted help being born over again and coming out right this time.

"I daresay you've the very devil of a head," she said after a long, silent moment. "Bridget will be up and about by now. I'll send her down to mix a remedy for you. And we'll order you a light breakfast, shall we?"

While she spoke, there was more rustling. Without looking, he was aware of her leaving the bed. When she approached to get her dressing gown from a chair, he turned his gaze to the window. Hazy sunlight dappled the sill and floor. He guessed it was past six o'clock. Monday. Twelfth of May. The day after his wedding.

It was also his birthday, he recollected with an unpleasant jolt of surprise. His thirty-third birthday. And he'd wakened in the same condition with which he'd greeted the last twenty, and in which he'd greet the next twenty, he thought bleakly.

"There's no cure," he muttered.

She had started toward the door. She paused and turned. "Would you care to place a small wager on that?"

"You're only looking for an excuse to poison me." He lifted the pitcher and clumsily splashed water into the basin.

"If you are not afraid to try it, I promise close to full recovery by the time we set out," she said. "If you are not feeling worlds better by then, you may claim a forfeit of your own choosing. If you are better, you will thank me by stopping at Stonehenge, and letting me explore—without having to listen to sarcastic remarks and complaints about delays."

His glance strayed to her, then quickly away. But not quickly enough. Her tangled black hair hung loose about her shoulders, and the faint flush of sleep yet clung to her cheeks, a wash of pearly pink on creamy white porcelain. Never had she appeared more fragile.

Though tousled, her face unwashed, her slim body sagging with fatigue, she had never, either, appeared more beautiful.

Here were Beauty and the Beast with a vengeance, Dain thought as he met his reflection in the mirror.

"If I'm not better," he said, "I shall use your lap as a pillow all the way to Devon."

She laughed and left the room.

At half past seven o'clock in the morning, two miles past Amesbury, Dain was leaning against a monolithic stone on a rise overlooking the Salisbury Plain. Below and beyond spread an undulating blanket of green with a few rectangular patches of bright yellow rape fields. A small number of houses dotted the landscape, along with the occasional lonely herd of sheep or cattle, all looking as though some giant hand had idly strewn them. Here and there, the same careless hand had stuck a cluster of trees against the horizon or thrust it into the cleavage between the gently swelling slopes.

Dain grimaced at his choice of metaphors: blankets and cleavage and big, clumsy hands. He wished he hadn't swallowed the mugful of odoriferous liquid Jessica had given him. The instant he'd begun to feel better, the itch had started again.

He hadn't had a woman in weeks . . . months.

If he didn't get relief soon, he would have to hurt somebody. A lot of somebodies. Beating Ainswood had not relieved the condition one iota. Drinking himself blind had only deadened the itch temporarily. Dain supposed he could find a proper-sized whore between here and Devon, but he had a disagreeable suspicion that wouldn't do much more good than fighting or drinking.

It was his slim, woefully fragile wife he wanted, and

hadn't been able to stop wanting from the instant he'd met her.

The place was quiet. He could hear the swish of her carriage dress when she moved. The teasing rustle was coming nearer. He kept his eye on the vista straight ahead until she paused a few feet away.

"I understand that one of the trilithons fell not so very long ago," she said.

"Seventeen hundred ninety-seven," he said. "A friend at Eton told me about it. He claimed the stone toppled over in fright the day I was born. So I checked. He was wrong. I was a full two years old at the time."

"I daresay you beat the true facts into your school-fellow." She tilted her head back to look at him. "Was it Ainswood, I wonder?"

Despite a walk in the brisk morning air, she looked tired. Too pale. Shadows ringed her eyes. His fault.

"It was someone else," he said shortly. "And you're not to think I brawl with every fool who tries to exercise his feeble wit upon me."

"You don't brawl," she said. "You're a most scientific fighter. Intellectual, I should say. You knew what Ainswood would do before he knew it himself."

She moved away, toward a fallen stone. "I'd wondered how you would manage it, with but one arm." She dropped her umbrella onto the stone and posed, fists clenched, one held closer to her body. "How, I asked myself, can he shield himself and strike simultaneously? But you didn't do it that way." She ducked her head to the side, as though dodging a blow, and backed off. "It was dodge and retreat, luring him on, letting him waste his strength."

"It wasn't hard," he said, swallowing his surprise. "He wasn't as alert as he might have been. Not nearly so quick as he is when sober."

"I'm sober," she said. She leapt onto the stone. "Come, let's see if I'm quick enough."

She was wearing an immense leghorn hat, with flowers and satin ribbons sprouting from the top. It was tied under her left ear in an enormous bow. The carriage dress was the usual fashionable insanity of flounces and lace and overblown sleeves. A pair of satin straps buckled each sleeve above the elbow, so that her upper arms appeared to be made of balloons. The satin cords lacing up the lower sleeves ended in long tassels that dangled from the middle of her forearms.

He could not remember when he'd seen anything so ludicrous as this silly bit of femininity gravely poised upon a stone in approved boxing stance.

He walked up to her, his mouth quivering. "Come down, Jess. You look like a complete addlepate."

Her fist shot out. His head went back, reflexively, and she missed . . . but only by a hairsbreadth.

He laughed—and something struck his ear. He eyed her narrowly. She was smiling, and twin glints of mischief lit her grey eyes. "Did I hurt you, Dain?" she asked with patently false concern.

"Hurt me?" he echoed. "Do you actually believe you can hurt me with *that*?"

He grabbed the offending hand.

She lost her balance and stumbled forward and caught hold of his shoulder.

Her mouth was inches from his.

He closed the distance and kissed her, fiercely, while he let go of her hand to wrap his arm around her waist.

The morning sun beat down warmly, but she tasted like rain, like a summer storm, and the thunder he heard was his own need, his blood pounding in his ears, his heart drumming the same unsteady beat.

He deepened the kiss, thirstily plundering the sweet heat of her mouth, and instantly intoxicated when she answered in kind, her tongue curling over his in a teasing dance that made him dizzy. Her slender arms wound about his neck and tightened. Her firm, round breasts pressed against his chest, sending whorls of heat down, to throb in his loins. He slid his hand down, cupping her small, deliciously rounded derriere.

Mine, he thought. She was light and slender and curved to sweet perfection . . . and she was his. His very own wife, ravishing him with her innocently wanton mouth and tongue, clinging to him with intoxicating possessiveness. As though she wanted him, as though she felt what he did, the same mindless, hammering need.

His mouth still locked with hers, he swept her down from her stony pedestal and would have swept her onto the hard ground as well . . . but a raucous cry from above jolted him back to reality.

He broke away from her mouth and looked up.

A carrion crow fearlessly alit on one of the smaller bluestones, and offered a beaky profile from which one glinting eye appeared to regard Dain with mocking avian amusement.

Big Beak, Ainswood had called him last night. One of the old Eton epithets—along with "Earwig," "Black Buzzard," and a host of other endearments.

His face burning, he turned away from his wife. "Come along," he said, his voice sharp with bitterness. "We can't dawdle here all day."

Jessica heard the bitterness and discerned the flush under his olive skin. For a few moments, she fretted that she'd done something to offend or disgust him. But halfway down the incline, he slowed to let her catch up with him. And when she took his hand—the crippled one—and squeezed it, he glanced at her, and said, "I hate crows. Noisy, filthy things."

She supposed that was as close to an explanation or apology as he could come. She glanced back at the ancient temple. "I collect it's because you're a high-strung thoroughbred. He was merely part of the atmosphere to me. I thought it all very romantic."

He gave a short laugh. "You mean 'gothic,' I think."

"No, I don't," she said. "There was I in the arms of a dark, dangerous hero, amid the ruins of Stonehenge, an ancient place of mystery. Byron himself could not have painted a more romantic scene. I'm sure you believe there isn't a romantic bone in your body," she added with a sidelong glance. "If you found one, you'd break it. But you needn't worry. I shouldn't dream of declaring otherwise to anyone else."

"I'm not romantic," he said tightly. "And I most certainly am not *high-strung*. As to thoroughbreds—you know very well I'm half-Italian."

"The Italian half is blue-blooded, too," she said. "The Duc d'Abonville told me your mother's line is very old Florentine nobility. That, apparently, reconciled him to our marriage."

He uttered a series of words she couldn't understand, but guessed were curses in his mother's tongue.

"He means to marry Genevieve," she said mollifyingly. "That's what made him so overprotective of me. But there are benefits to the attachment. He's taken Bertie in hand, which means you won't be bothered with my brother's financial difficulties in future."

Dain brooded silently until they'd reentered the carriage. Then, releasing a sigh, he leaned back and closed his eyes. "Romantic. High-strung. And you think it's reassuring that your grandmother's *lover* means to take your brainless brother in hand. I do believe, Jess, that you are as demented as every other member—and prospective member—of your entire lunatic family."

"Are you going to sleep?" she asked.

"I might, if you could manage to hold your tongue for three minutes."

"I'm tired, too," she said. "Do you mind if I lean on your arm? I can't sleep sitting bolt upright."

"Take off that idiotic bonnet first," he muttered.

She took it off and rested her head on his brawny arm. After a moment, he shifted sideways a bit and tucked her head against his chest. That was more comfortable.

It was also all the reassurance Jessica needed for now. Later, she'd try to figure out what had upset him during their embrace—and why he'd become so very tense when she spoke of his mother's family. At present she was content to enjoy what felt delightfully like husbandly affection.

They slept through most of the journey, until they reached the Devon border. Despite the delay in setting out, they reached Exeter by late afternoon. They crossed the River Teign shortly thereafter, then wended down to Bovey Tracey, and across the River Bovey. A few winding miles west, Jessica had her first glimpse of the strange rock formations of Dartmoor.

"Haytor Rocks," he said, pointing out his window at an immense stone outcropping at the top of a hill. She climbed onto his lap to get a better view.

He laughed. "You needn't worry about missing it. There are plenty more. Hundreds of those things, everywhere you look. Tors and cairns and barrows and bogs. You married me, only to wind up in precisely the 'remote outpost of civilization' you wished to avoid.

Welcome, Lady Dain, to the howling wilderness of Dartmoor."

"I think it's beautiful," she said softly.

Like you, she wanted to add. In the orange glow of the lowering sun, the rugged landscape was dark and harshly beautiful, as he was.

"I'll have to win another wager," she said into the moody silence. "So that you'll take me to those rocks."

"Where you'll contract a lung fever," he said. "It's cold, windy, and wet, and the climate changes from brisk autumn to bitter winter and back again ten times in an hour."

"I never take ill," she said. "I'm not a high-strung thoroughbred—unlike certain individuals who shall remain nameless."

"You'd better get off my lap," he said. "We'll be at Athcourt very shortly, and the staff will be out in full battle regalia. I shall make a poor enough appearance as it is. You've rumpled and wrinkled me past repair. You squirm and fidget even more asleep than awake. I scarcely closed my eyes the entire way to Exeter."

"Then you must have been snoring with your eyes open," she said as she returned to her place beside him.

"I was not snoring."

"On my head," she said. "And several times, straight into my ear." She had found the deep, masculine rumble inexpressibly endearing.

He scowled at her.

Jessica ignored it, returning her gaze to the passing landscape. "Why is your home called Athcourt?" she asked. "After a great battle, like Blenheim?"

"The Ballisters originally lived further north," he said. "One of them took a fancy to the Dartmoor property as well as the daughter and sole surviving issue of Sir Guy de Ath, a powerful fellow in this area.

The name, incidentally, was originally Death. It was changed for obvious reasons. My ancestor got the daughter and the estate on condition he keep the quaint name alive. That's why the males of the family get Guy de Ath stuck on just before 'Ballister.' "

She'd read his name on countless marriage-related documents. "Sebastian Leslie Guy de Ath Ballister," she said, smiling. "And here I thought you had all those names because there's so much of you."

She felt his body stiffen. She looked up. His jaw was tight, too, his mouth set in a hard line.

She wondered what nerve she'd struck inadvertently.

She didn't have time to work out the riddle, because Dain snatched up her forgotten bonnet and shoved it on her head backwards, and she had to right the hat and tie the ribbons. Then she had to try to make a dress she'd traveled in since early morning look presentable, because the carriage was turning in to a gateway, and Dain's ill-concealed agitation told her the drive beyond led to his home.

Twelve

$\mathcal{D}$espite the unplanned-for pause at Stonehenge, Dain's carriage drew up at Athcourt's front entrance at precisely eight o'clock, as scheduled. By twenty past eight, he and his bride had inspected the domestic army, all turned out in trim ceremonial array, and had been discreetly inspected in turn. With a very few exceptions, none of the present staff had ever clapped eyes on their master before. Nonetheless, they were too well trained and well paid to show any emotion, including curiosity.

All was ready, exactly as Dain had ordered, and every requirement provided precisely to the minute, according to the schedule he'd sent ahead. Their baths had been readied while they reviewed the staff. Their dinner clothes were pressed and neatly laid out.

The first course was served the instant lord and lady took their seats at opposite ends of the long table in the cavernous dining room. The cold dishes arrived cold, the warm, warm. Andrews, the valet, stood near His

Lordship's chair throughout the meal and assisted with all tasks requiring two hands.

Jessica did not appear in the least daunted by a dining room the size of Westminster Abbey, or the dozen liveried footmen waiting at attention near the sideboard while each course was consumed.

At a quarter to eleven she rose from the table to leave Dain to his port. As coolly as though she'd been mistress there for centuries, she informed the house steward, Rodstock, that she would have tea in the library.

The table had been cleared before she was through the door, and the decanter appeared before Dain almost in the same instant. His glass was filled with the same silent unobtrusiveness, and his host of attendants vanished in the same ghostly quiet and quick way when he said, "That will be all."

It was the first time Dain had had anything like privacy for two days, and the first chance to think properly about the problem of deflowering his bride since he'd realized it was a problem.

What he thought was that it had been a long day and his paralyzed arm was throbbing and the dining room was too quiet and he didn't like the color of the drapes and the landscape hanging over the mantle was too small for the location.

At five minutes to eleven, he pushed away his untouched wineglass, rose, and went to the library.

Jessica stood at a book stand, where the immense family Bible lay open to a page containing the customary entries of weddings, births, and deaths. When her husband entered, she threw him a reproachful look. "Today is your birthday," she said. "Why didn't you tell me?"

He approached, and his stony expression settled into the usual mocking mask as he glanced down at the place she pointed to. "Fancy that. My estimable sire didn't black my name out. I'm all amazement."

"Am I to believe you've never once looked in this book?" she asked. "That you weren't interested in your forebears—when you knew all about Guy de Ath?"

"My tutor told me about my ancestors," he said. "He tried to enliven the history curriculum with regular strolls through the portrait galley. 'The first Earl of Blackmoor,' he would solemnly announce as he paused before a portrait of a chevalier with long golden curls. 'Created during the reign of King Charles II,' I would be informed. Then my tutor would expound upon the events of that reign and explain how my noble ancestor fit in and what he'd done to win his earldom."

His tutor had told him, not his father.

"I should like to be tutored in the same way," she said. "Perhaps tomorrow you will take me for a stroll through the portrait gallery. I collect it must be about ten or twelve miles long."

"One hundred eighty feet," he said, his eye returning to the page. "You seem to have an exaggerated view of the size of Athcourt."

"I'll get used to it," she said. "I managed not to gape and gawk too much when introduced to the cathedral village otherwise known as Her Ladyship's Apartments."

He was still staring at the page where his birth had been recorded. His sardonic expression hadn't changed, but there was turmoil in his dark eyes. Jessica wondered whether it was the entry directly below that troubled him. It had saddened her, and she had grieved for him.

"I lost my parents in the year after you lost your mother," she said. "They were killed in a carriage accident."

"Fever," he said. "She died of fever. He entered that event, too." Dain sounded surprised.

"Who entered your father's death?" she asked. "That isn't your hand."

He shrugged. "His secretary, I suppose. Or the vicar. Or some officious busybody." He pushed her hand away and slammed the ancient Bible shut. "If you want family history, we've volumes of it on the shelves at the far end of this room. It's recorded in tedious detail, going back to the Roman conquest, I daresay."

She opened the Bible again. "You are the head of the family and you must put me in it now," she said gently. "You've acquired a wife, and you must write it down."

"Must I, indeed, this very minute?" He lifted an eyebrow. "And suppose I decide not to keep you after all? Then I should have to go back and blot out your name."

She left the bookstand, crossed to a study table, took up a pen and inkwell, and returned to him. "I should like to see you try to get rid of me," she said.

"I could get an annulment," he said. "On grounds that I was of unsound mind when the marriage was contracted. Lord Portsmouth's marriage was annulled on those grounds, only the day before yesterday."

He took the pen from her all the same, and made a grand ceremony of recording their marriage in his bold script, with a few flourishes to heighten the effect.

"Ah, handsomely done," she said, leaning over his arm to look at the entry. "Thank you, Dain. Now I shall be part of the Ballisters' history." She was aware that her breasts were resting on his arm.

So was he. He jerked away as though they'd been a pair of hot coals.

"Yes, you have been immortalized in the Bible," he said. "I expect you'll be demanding a portrait next, and I shall have to move a famous ancestor into storage to make room for you."

Jessica had hoped that a bath, dinner, and a glass or two of port would calm him down, but he was as skittish now as he'd been when they'd entered Athcourt's gates.

"Is Athcourt haunted?" she asked, strolling with studied casualness to a tall set of bookshelves. "Should I be prepared for clanking chains or hideous wails at midnight or quaintly attired ladies and gentlemen wandering the corridors?"

"Gad, no. Who put such an idea into your head?"

"You." She stood on tiptoe to examine a shelf of poetic works. "I cannot tell whether you're bracing yourself to tell me something ghastly, or you're in expectation of something ghastly. I thought the something might be Ballister ghosts popping out of the woodwork."

"I'm not bracing myself for anything." He stalked to the fireplace. "I am not *braced*. I am perfectly at ease. As I should be, in my own damned house."

Where he'd learned his family's history from a tutor, instead of his father, she thought. Where his mother had died when he was ten years old . . . a loss that still seemed to hurt him deeply. Where there was an immense, ancient family Bible he'd never looked into.

She wondered if he'd known his dead half-siblings' names, or whether he'd read them this day, as she had, for the first time.

She took out a handsome, very expensively bound volume of *Don Juan*.

"This must have been your purchase," she said. "The last cantos of *Don Juan* were published scarcely four years ago. I didn't know you had a taste for Byron's work."

He had wandered to the fireplace. "I don't. I met

him during a trip to Italy. I bought the thing because its author was a wicked fellow and its contents were reputedly indecent."

"Which is to say, you haven't read it." She opened the book and selected a stanza from the first canto. " 'Wedded she was, some years, and to a man / of fifty, and such husbands are in plenty; / And yet, I think, instead of such a ONE / 'T were better to have TWO of five and twenty.' "

Dain's hard mouth quirked up. Jessica flipped through the pages. " 'A little she strove, and much repented, / And whispering "I will ne'er consent"—consented.' "

A stifled chuckle. But she had him, Jessica knew. She settled down onto the sofa and skipped ahead to the second canto, where she'd left off reading the night before.

The sixteen-year-old Don Juan, she explained, was being sent away because of his affair with the beautiful Donna Julia, wife of the fifty-year-old gentleman.

Then Jessica began to read aloud.

At Stanza III, Dain left the fireplace.

By the eighth stanza, he was sitting beside her. By the fourteenth, he had arranged himself into an indolent sprawl, with a sofa pillow under his head and a padded footstool under his feet. In the process, his crippled left hand had in some mysterious manner managed to land on her right knee. Jessica pretended not to notice, but read on—about Don Juan's grief as his ship sailed from his native land, and of his resolve to reform, and of his undying love for Julia, and how he would never forget her or think of anything but her.

" ' "A mind diseased no remedy can physic—" / Here the ship gave a lurch, and he grew seasick." ' "

Dain snickered.

" ' "Sooner shall Heaven kiss earth—"(here he fell

sicker) / "Oh Julia! What is every other woe?—(For God's sake let me have a glass of liquor; Pedro, Battista, help me down below.)"'"

If she'd been reading alone, Jessica would have giggled, as she'd done last night. But for Dain's benefit, she spouted Don Juan's lovesick declarations with a melodramatic anguish that grew increasingly distracted as the hero's *mal de mer* got the better of undying love.

She pretended not to notice the large body shaking with silent laughter, so close to hers, or the occasional half-smothered chuckle that sent a tickling breeze over her scalp.

"'"Beloved Julia, hear me still beseeching!" / (Here he grew inarticulate with retching.)'"

The breeze tickled the top of her ear, and she did not have to look up to be aware of her husband leaning nearer, looking over her shoulder at the page. She read on into the next stanza, conscious of his warm breath on her ear and of the vibrations his low, rumbling chuckle set off inside her.

"'No doubt he would have been more pathetic,—'"

"'But the sea acted as a strong emetic,'" he gravely finished the stanza. Then she let herself look up, but his gaze slipped away in the same instant and the expression on his harshly handsome face was inscrutable.

"I can't believe you bought it and never read it," she said. "You had no idea what you were missing, did you?"

"I'm sure it was more amusing hearing it read in a ladylike voice," he said. "Certainly it's less work."

"Then I'll read to you regularly," she said. "I shall make a romantic of you yet."

He drew back, and his inert hand slid to the sofa. "You call that *romantic*? Byron's a complete cynic."

"In my dictionary, romance is not maudlin, treacly

sentiment," she said. "It is a curry, spiced with excitement and humor and a healthy dollop of cynicism." She lowered her lashes. "I think you will eventually make a fine curry, Dain—with a few minor seasoning adjustments."

"Adjustments?" he echoed, stiffening. "Adjust *me?*"

"Certainly." She patted the hand lying beside her. "Marriage requires adjustments, on both sides."

"Not this marriage, madam. I paid—and through the nose—for blind obedience, and that is precisely—"

"Naturally, you are master of your own household," she said. "I have never met a man more adept at managing everything and everybody. But even you can't think of everything, or look for what you've never experienced. I daresay there are benefits you've never imagined to having a wife."

"There's only one," he said, his eyes narrowing, "and I assure you, my lady, I've thought of it. Often. Because it's the only damned thing—"

"I devised a remedy for your indisposition this morning," she said, stifling a surge of irritation . . . and anxiety. "You thought there was no cure. You have just discovered Byron, thanks to me. And that put you into a better humor."

He kicked the footstool away. "I see. So that's what you've been about—humoring me. Softening me up—or trying to."

Jessica closed the book and set it aside.

She had resolved to be patient, to do her duty by him, to look after him because he badly needed it, whether he realized it or not. Now she wondered why she bothered. After last night—after this morning—after exiling her to the foot of a mile-long dining table—the blockhead had the effrontery to reduce her superhuman efforts to *manipulation*. Her patience snapped.

"Trying . . . to . . . soften . . . you." She dragged the words out, and they slammed inside her, making her heart pump with outrage. "You cocksure, clodpated *ingrate*."

"I'm not blind," he said. "I know what you're about, and if you think—"

"If you think that I could not do it," she said tightly, "that I could not make you eat out of my hand, if that's what I wanted, I recommend you think again, Beelzebub."

There was a short, thundering silence.

"Out of your hand," he repeated very, very quietly.

She recognized the quiet tone and what it boded, and a part of her brain screamed, *Run!* But the rest of her mind was a red mass of anger. Slowly, deliberately, she laid her left hand, palm up, upon her knee. With her right index finger she traced a small circle in the center.

"There," she said, her own voice just as quiet as his, her own mouth curved in a taunting smile. "Like that, Dain. In the palm of my hand. And then," she went on, still stroking the center of her palm, "I would make you crawl. And *beg*."

Another silence thundered through the room and made her wonder why the books didn't topple from their shelves.

Then it came, velvet-soft, the one answer she hadn't expected, and the one, she knew in an instant, she should have predicted.

"I should like to see you try," he said.

His brain was trying to tell him something, but Dain couldn't hear it past the clanging in his ears: *crawl . . . and beg.* He couldn't think past the mockery he heard in her soft tones and the fury twisting his gut.

And so he locked himself in frigid rage, knowing he was safe there, impervious to hurt. He had not crawled and begged when his eight-year-old world shattered to pieces, when the only thing like love he'd ever known had fled from him and his father had thrust him away. The world had thrust him into privies, taunted and mocked and beat him. The world had recoiled from him and made him pay for every pretty deceit that passed for happiness. The world had tried to beat him down into submission, but he would not submit, and the world had had to learn to live with him on his terms.

As she must. And he would endure whatever he must, to teach her so.

He thought of the great rocks he'd pointed out to her hours ago, which centuries of drumming rain and beating wind and bitter cold could not wear down or break down. He made himself a mass of stone like them, and, as he felt her move beside him, he told himself she would never find a foothold; she could no more scale him than she could melt him or wear him down.

She came onto her knees beside him, and he waited through the long moment she remained motionless. She was hesitating, he knew, because she wasn't blind. She knew stone when she saw it, and maybe, already, she saw her mistake . . . and very soon, she'd give it up.

She lifted her hand and touched his neck—and snatched her hand away almost in the same instant, as though she felt it, too, as he did: the crackling shock darting under the skin to shriek along his nerve endings.

Though he kept his gaze fixed straight ahead, Dain saw her puzzled reaction in the periphery of his vision, caught her frown as she studied her hand, discerned her thoughtful glance moving to his neck.

Then, his heart sinking, he perceived the slow upturn

of her mouth. She edged nearer, and her right knee slid behind him against his buttock, while her left pressed against his thigh. Then she slipped her right arm round his shoulders and draped her left over his upper chest, and leaned in closer. Her sweetly rounded bosom pressed against his arm while she touched her lips to the too sensitive skin at the corner of his eye.

He kept himself rigid, concentrated hard on breathing steadily, to keep himself from howling.

She was warm and so soft, and the faint apple scent of chamomile swirled like a net about him . . . as though the slenderly curved body enveloping his weren't snare enough. She trailed her parted lips down, over his cheek, along his unyielding jaw to the corner of this mouth.

And *Fool!* he silently berated himself, for daring her, when he knew she could not back away from a challenge and he had never come away unscathed after issuing one.

He had walked into a trap, again, for the hundredth time, and this time it was worse. He could not turn to drink in her sweetness, because that would be yielding, and he would not. He must sit like a granite monolith, while her soft bosom rose and fell against his arm, and while her warm breath, her soft mouth, teased over his skin in brushstroke kisses.

Like a block of stone he remained, while she sighed softly against his ear, and the sigh hissed through his blood. And so he continued, immovable outwardly, wretched inwardly, while she slowly worked loose the knot of his neckcloth and drew it away.

He saw it drop from her fingers and tried to keep his attention on the tangled white fabric at his feet, but she was kissing the back of his neck, and sliding her hand under his shirt at the same time. He couldn't focus his eyes or concentrate his mind because she was everywhere, a fever coiling over him and throbbing inside him.

"You're so smooth," her murmuring voice came from behind him, her breath warm on the nape of his neck while she stroked his shoulder. "Smooth as polished marble, but so warm."

He was on fire, and her low, foggy tones were oil drizzled upon the flames.

"And strong," she went on, while her serpent hands went on, too, sliding over taut muscles that tightened and quivered under her touch.

He was weak, a great, stupid ox, sinking into the mire of a virgin's seduction.

"You can pick me up with one hand," the throaty voice continued. "I love your big hands. I want them all over me, Dain. Everywhere." She flicked her tongue over his ear, and he trembled. "On my skin. Like this." Under his fine cambric shirt, her fingers stroked over his pounding heart. She brushed her thumb over the taut nipple, and his breath hissed out between clenched teeth.

"I want you to do that," she said, "to me."

He wanted to, sweet Mother of Jesus, how he wanted to. The knuckles of his tightly fisted hand were white, and his clenched jaw was aching, and those sensations were pure delight compared to the vicious throbbing in his loins.

"Do what?" he asked, willing the syllables past his thickened tongue. "Was I . . . supposed . . . to feel something?"

"You bastard." She pulled her hand away, and he felt one coursing thrill of relief, but before he could draw the next breath, she was scrambling onto his lap, drawing up her skirts as she straddled him.

"You want me," she said. "I can feel it, Dain."

She could hardly fail to. There was nothing between

hot, aroused male and warm female but a layer of wool and a scrap of silk. His trousers. Her drawers . . . soft thighs pressing against his. God help him.

He knew what was there, beneath the drawers: a few inches of stocking above her knee, the knot of a garter, the silken skin above. Even the fingers of his crippled left hand twitched.

As though she could read his mind, she lifted that useless hand and dragged it over the rumpled silk of her skirt.

Under, he wanted to cry. The stocking, the garter, the sweet, silken skin . . . *please*.

He clamped his mouth shut.

He wouldn't beg, wouldn't crawl.

She pushed him back against the sofa cushions and he went down easily. All his strength was focused on keeping the cry from escaping.

He saw her hand move to the ties of her bodice.

"Marriage requires adjustments," she said. "If it's a tart you want, I must act like one."

He tried to close his eyes, but he hadn't the strength even for that. He was riveted upon her slim, graceful fingers and their wicked work . . . the tapes and hooks giving way, the fabric slipping down . . . the swell of creamy flesh spilling from the lace and sagging silk.

"I know my . . . charms . . . aren't as immense as what you're used to," she said, pushing the bodice down to her waist.

He saw twin moons, alabaster smooth and white.

His mouth was dry, his head thick, filled with cotton wool.

"But if I come very close, maybe you'll notice." She lifted herself up and bent over him . . . very near, too near.

One taut rosebud . . . inches from his parched lips . . .

woman-scent, rich, coiling in his nostrils, swirling in his head.

"Jess." His voice was cracked and harsh, parched.

His mind was a desert. No thought. No pride. He was mere sand, whirling in a windstorm.

With a choked cry, he pulled her down, and captured her mouth . . . sweet oasis . . . *oh, yes, please* . . . and she parted to his frantic plea. He raked her sweetness thirstily. He was dry, burning, and she cooled him and inflamed him at once. She was the rain, and she was hot brandy, too.

He dragged his hand down over her smooth, supple back, and she shivered, and sighed against his mouth. "I love your hands." Low, the caressing whisper of her voice.

"*Sei bella*," he answered roughly, his fingers curling and tightening at her waist. So firm and supple, but oh, so small under his big hand.

There was so little of her, but he wanted it all, and wanted it desperately. He raked his famished mouth over her face, her shoulder, her throat. He rubbed his cheek against the velvety slopes of her breasts and nuzzled the fragrant valley between. He made a winding path with his tongue to the rosy nipple that had teased him moments ago, and captured it. He caressed it with his lips, his tongue, and held her shuddering body fast while he suckled.

From above him came a soft, startled cry. But her fingers were tangling in his hair, moving restlessly over his scalp, and he knew the cry was not pain, but excitement.

The tormenting she-devil liked it.

Then, heated and maddened as he was, he knew he wasn't powerless.

He could make her beg, too.

His heart was racing at a gallop and his mind was

thick and drunk, but somehow he summoned a fragment of control and, instead of hurrying on, he laid siege to her other breast, more slowly and deliberately . . .

She went to pieces.

"Oh. Oh, Dain. Please." Her fingers moved spasmodically, over his neck, his shoulders.

Yes, beg. He took the quivering nipple lightly between his teeth, and gently tugged.

"Dear God. Please . . . don't. Yes. Oh." She was squirming helplessly, arching toward him one instant and trying to twist away in the next.

He slid his hand up under the rumpled, tangled skirt and stroked over the silken drawers. She moaned.

He released her breast and she sank down and dragged her parted lips over his until he answered, and welcomed her in, and let jolts of pleasure shake his frame while she ravished his mouth.

And while he drank in the hot liquor of her kiss, he was pushing up the flimsy silk leg of her drawers, stroking over stocking and upward, to the knot of her garter. He swiftly untied it and pushed it away, and drew the stocking down, and slid his fingers over her thigh and up, over the bunched-up silken drawers, to grasp her sweetly rounded buttock.

She came away from his mouth, her breathing shallow, uneven.

Still grasping her bottom, he shifted position, moving her with him, so that she lay on her side, trapped between his big frame and the sofa back. He kissed her again, deeply, while he moved his hand to the fastenings of her drawers, and untied them, and eased them down. He felt her body tense, but he held her mouth captive, distracting her with a slow, tender kiss, and all the while his fingers were moving over her thigh, stroking, caressing, stealing toward her innocence.

She squirmed, pulling away from his mouth, but he would not let her escape, and he could not keep from touching her . . . the fine, taut skin at the juncture of her thigh . . . a wanton tangle of silky curls . . . and sweet womanliness, warm, butter-soft . . . and butter-slick . . . the delicious evidence of desire.

He had stirred her, roused her. She wanted him.

He began to stroke the tender feminine folds, and she went very, very still.

Then, "Oh." Her voice was soft with surprise. "Oh. That's . . . *wicked*. I did not—" The rest was lost in a smothered cry, and the sweet warmth pressed against his finger. Her slender body twisted and turned restlessly, toward him, away. "Oh, Lord. *Please*."

He scarcely heard the plea. He was beyond hearing. His blood pounded in his veins, thundered in his ears.

He found the tender bud and the narrow parting beneath, but it was so small, so tight against his great, intruding finger.

He caressed the sensitive peak, and it swelled. She was clutching his coat, making soft, breathless sounds, trying to burrow into his hard body. Like a frightened kitten. But she wasn't frightened. She trusted him. His own trusting kitten. Innocent. So fragile.

"Oh, Jess, you're so tiny," he murmured, despairing.

He stroked gently inside her, but slick and hot as she was, the way was too small, too tight for him.

His lust-swollen rod strained furiously against his trousers, a great, monstrous invader that would tear her to pieces. He wanted to weep, to howl.

"So tight," he said, his voice raw with misery, because he couldn't stop touching her, couldn't stop caressing what he couldn't, dare not, have.

She didn't hear him. She was lost in the fever he was feeding. She was touching him, kissing him.

So restless her hands, her innocently wanton mouth. She was smoldering in the fire he'd built to conquer her, and he could not stop adding fuel to the blaze.

"Oh, don't . . . yes . . . *please*."

He heard her gasp, then a sob . . . and her body shuddered, and the tight flesh clenched against his fingers . . . and eased . . . and clenched again, as another climax shook her slender frame.

He drew his hand away and found it was shaking. Every muscle in his body was taut with strain, aching with the effort it had cost him to keep from ripping her apart. His groin felt as though it had been clamped in Satan's own vise.

He drew a ragged breath. And another. And another, waiting for her to come back to the world, and hoping his loins would calm before then, before he had to move.

He waited, but nothing happened. He knew she wasn't dead. He could hear, feel, her breathing . . . slow, steady, peaceful . . . too peaceful.

He stared at her incredulously. "Jess?"

She murmured and burrowed in, nestling her head in the cradle of his shoulder.

For another full minute he gazed, slack-jawed, into her beautiful tranquil, *slumbering* face.

Just like a damned man, he thought exasperatedly. She got what she wanted, then curled up and went to sleep.

That was what *he* was supposed to do, blast and confound her bloody impudence. And now—curse her for a selfish ingrate—he would have to figure out how—with only one arm working—to get her to bed without waking her.

Thirteen

Jessica wasn't sure when exactly she'd become aware she was being carried up the stairs. It all seemed part of a dream or part of long ago, when she was a sleepy little girl, so tiny that even Uncle Frederick, who was the smallest of her uncles, could easily scoop her up in one arm and carry her up the stairs to the nursery. An uncle's arm made a hard seat, true, and the ride was bumpy, but she was perfectly safe, snugly braced against a big male body, her head nestled upon a broad shoulder.

Gradually the fog of sleep cleared, and even before she opened her heavy eyes, Jessica knew who was carrying her.

She also remembered what had happened. Or most of it. A great deal was lost in the delirious whirlpool Dain had pulled her into.

"I'm awake," she said, her voice heavy with sleep. She was still weary, and her mind was thick as pudding. "I can walk the rest of the way."

"You'll tumble down the stairs," Dain said gruffly. "At any rate, we're nearly there."

There, it turned out, was Her Ladyship's Apartments. The Grand Catacombs, she silently renamed them, as Dain carried her into the dimly lit cavern of her bedchamber.

He set her down very carefully upon the bed.

Then he rang for her maid . . . and left. Without another word, and in rather a hurry.

Jessica sat gazing at the empty doorway, listening to his carpet-muffled footsteps as he strode down the long hallway, until she heard the faint thud of his door closing.

Sighing, she bent to remove the stocking he'd loosened, which had slid down to her ankle.

She had known from the minute she'd agreed to marry him that it wouldn't be easy, she reminded herself. She had known he was in an exceedingly prickly humor this evening—all day, in fact. She could not expect him to behave rationally . . . and bed her properly . . . and sleep with her.

Bridget appeared then, and without appearing to notice her mistress's disordered state of dress or distracted state of mind, quietly and efficiently prepared Her Ladyship for bed.

Once tucked in, the maid gone, Jessica decided there was no point in fretting about Dain's failure to deflower her.

What he had done had been very exciting and surprising, especially the last part, when he'd made her have a little earthquake. She knew what that was, because Genevieve had told her. And thanks to her grandmother, Jessica was well aware that those extraordinary sensations did not always occur, especially early in marriage. Not all men took the trouble.

She could not believe Dain had taken the trouble merely to score a point, like proving his power over her. According to Genevieve, it was extremely painful for an aroused male to deny himself release. Unless Dain had an esoteric way of relieving his arousal that Genevieve had failed to mention, he'd surely suffered acute discomfort.

He must have had a compelling reason for doing so.

Jessica could not begin to imagine what it was. He wanted her, beyond a doubt. He had tried to resist, but he couldn't—not after she'd shamelessly bared her breasts and stuck them right under his arrogant Florentine nose . . . not after she'd hiked up her skirts and sat on his breeding organs.

She flushed, recalling, but the heat she felt wasn't embarrassment. At the time, she'd felt wonderfully free and wicked . . . and she'd been hotly, deliciously rewarded for her boldness.

Even now, she felt he'd given her a gift. As though it were her birthday, not his. And after gifting his wife with a little earthquake and enduring acute physical discomfort, he had—with no small difficulty, she was sure—contrived to get her up the stairs without waking her.

She found herself wishing he hadn't done so. It would have been easier if he'd roughly wakened her and laughed at her and let her make her own way upstairs, dazed, stumbling . . . besotted. It would have been easier still if he had simply pushed her down, rammed into her, rolled away, and fallen asleep.

Instead, he'd taken pains. He'd taught her pleasure and taken care of her after. Sweet and chivalrous he'd been, truly.

Her husband was transforming simple animal attraction into something much more complicated.

And soon, if she was not very careful, she might make the fatal error of falling in love with him.

Midafternoon of the following day, Lady Dain discovered that Athcourt did have ghosts.

She knelt on a threadbare carpet in the uppermost chamber of the North Tower. The room was one of Athcourt's furnishings graveyards. About her were trunks filled with clothing of bygone eras, draperies, and linens, as well as assorted odds and ends of furniture, crates of mismatched dinnerware, and a number of household utensils of enigmatic function. Beside her knelt Mrs. Ingleby, the housekeeper.

They were both gazing at a portrait of a young woman with curling black hair, coal black eyes, and a haughty Florentine nose. Jessica had found it in a dark corner of the room, hidden behind a stack of trunks, and thickly wrapped in velvet bed hangings.

"This can be no one but His Lordship's mother," Jessica said, wondering why her heart hammered as though she were afraid, which she wasn't. "The gown, the coiffure—last decade of the eighteenth century, no question."

There was no need to remark upon the physical resemblance. The lady was simply the feminine version of the present marquess.

This was also the first portrait Jessica had seen that bore any resemblance to him.

After Jessica's solitary breakfast—Dain had eaten and vanished before she'd come down—Mrs. Ingleby had given her a partial tour of the immense house, including a leisurely stroll through the long second-floor gallery opposite their bedrooms, which housed the family portraits. Except for the first Earl of Blackmoor, whose heavy-lidded gaze had reminded her of Dain's, Jessica had detected no likenesses.

Nowhere among these worthies had she spied a female who could have been Dain's mother. Mrs. Ingleby, when questioned, had told her there wasn't such a portrait, not that she knew of. She'd been at Athcourt since the present marquess came into the title, when he'd replaced most of the previous staff.

This portrait, then, had been hidden away during his father's time. Out of grief? Jessica wondered. Had it been too painful for the late marquess to see his wife's image? If so, he must have been a very different man from the one she'd seen in his portrait: a fair, middle-aged gentleman, garbed in somber Quaker-like simplicity. But the humble dress was in stark contrast to his expression. No gentle Friend had lived behind the stern countenance with its narrowed, wintry blue eyes.

"I know nothing about her," Jessica said, "except the date she was wed and the date she died. I hadn't expected her to be so young. I had assumed the second wife was a more mature woman. This is little more than a girl."

And who, she wondered angrily, had shackled this ravishing child to the horrid, pious old block of ice?

She drew back, startled by the vehemence of her reaction. Quickly she stood up.

"Have it brought down to my sitting room," she told the housekeeper. "You may have it lightly dusted before, but no further cleaning until I've had a chance to examine it in better light."

Mrs. Ingleby had been imported from Derbyshire. She'd heard nothing about old family scandals before she'd come and, because she would not tolerate belowstairs

gossip, she'd heard nothing since. Lord Dain's agent
had hired her, not simply because of her sterling reputation as a housekeeper, but because of her strict princi-
ples: In her view, the care of a family was a sacred trust,
which one did not abuse by whispering scandal behind
one's employers' backs. Either the conditions were good
or they were not. If they were not, one politely gave
notice and departed.

Her strict views did not, however, prevent the rest of
the staff from gossiping when her back was turned.
Consequently, most of them had heard about the previous Lady Dain. One of them was one of the footmen
summoned to move the portrait to the present Lady
Dain's sitting room. He told Mr. Rodstock who the
portrait subject was.

Mr. Rodstock was much too dignified to dash his
head against the chimneypiece as he wished to. All he
did was blink, once, and order his minions to alert him
the instant His Lordship returned.

Lord Dain had spent most of the day in Chudleigh. At
the Star and Garter, he'd met up with Lord Sherburne,
who was making his meandering way south to Devonport for a wrestling match.

Sherburne, who'd been wed less than a year, had left
his young wife in London. He was the last person in
the world to find anything odd about a very recently
married man's deserting his bride for the bar parlor of
a coaching inn several miles from home. On the contrary, he invited Dain to journey with him to Devonport. Sherburne was awaiting a few other fellows, who
were to arrive this evening. He suggested Dain pack,
collect his valet, and join them for dinner. Then they
could all leave together first thing tomorrow morning.

Dain had accepted the invitation without hesitation,

ignoring the skull-splitting shriek of his conscience. Hesitation was always a sign of weakness and, in this case, Sherburne might think Beelzebub needed his wife's *permission* first, or that he couldn't bear to be away from her for a few days.

He could bear it easily, Dain thought now, as he hurried up the north staircase to his room. Furthermore, she needed to be taught that she could not manipulate him, and this lesson would be considerably less painful for him than the one he'd given her last night. He'd rather let carrion crows feast on his privates than go through that horrific experience again.

He would go away, and calm down, and put matters into perspective, and when he returned he would . . .

Well, he didn't know precisely what he would do, but that was because he wasn't calm. When he was, he would figure it out. He was certain there must be a simple solution, but he could not contemplate the problem coolly and objectively while she was nearby, bothering him.

"My lord."

Dain paused at the head of the stairs and looked down. Rodstock was hurrying up after him. "My lord," he repeated breathlessly. "A word, if you please."

What the steward had to say was more than a word, yet no more than what was needed. Her Ladyship had been exploring the North Tower storage room. She had found a portrait. Of the previous marchioness. Rodstock thought His Lordship would wish to be informed.

Rodstock was a paragon, the soul of discretion and tact. Nothing in his tone or demeanor indicated any consciousness of the bomb he had just dropped at his master's feet.

His master, likewise, evidenced no awareness of any explosion whatsoever.

"I see," Dain said. "That is interesting. I had no idea we had one about. Where is it?"

"In Her Ladyship's sitting room, my lord."

"Well, then, I might as well look at it." Dain turned and headed down the Long Gallery. His heart was beating unsteadily. Other than that, he felt nothing. He saw nothing, either, during the endless walk past the portraits of the noble line of men and women he had never felt a part of.

He walked on blindly to the end of the hall, opened the last door on the left, and turned left again into the narrow passageway. He continued past one door, and on to the next, then through it, and on through the second passage to the door at its end, which stood open.

The portrait that wasn't supposed to exist stood before the sitting room's east-facing window on a battered easel, which must have been unearthed from the schoolroom.

Dain walked up to the painting and gazed at it for a long while, though it hurt, badly—more than he could have guessed—to look into the beautiful, cruel face. His throat burned and his eyes as well. If he could, he would have wept then.

But he couldn't because he wasn't alone. He did not have to take his eyes from the portrait to know his wife was in the room.

"Another of your finds," he said, choking a short laugh past his seared throat. "And on your first treasure hunt here, too."

"Luckily, the North Tower is cool and dry," she said. Her voice was cool and dry as well. "And the painting was well wrapped. It will need minimal cleaning, but I should prefer another frame. This one is much too dark and overornate. Also, I had rather not put her in the portrait gallery, if you don't mind. I'd prefer she had a place to herself. Over the dining room mantel, I think. In place of the landscape."

She came nearer, pausing a few paces to his right. "The landscape wants a smaller room. Even if it didn't, I'd much rather look at her."

He would, too, though it was eating him alive to do so.

He would have been content merely to look at his beautiful, impossible mother. He would have asked nothing . . . or so very little: a soft hand upon his cheek, only for an instant. An impatient hug. He would have been good. He would have tried . . .

Mawkish nonsense, he angrily reproached himself. It was only a damned piece of canvas daubed with paint. It was a painting of a whore, as all the household, all of Devon, and most of the world beyond knew. All except his wife, with her fiendish gift for turning the world upside down.

"She was a whore," he said harshly. And quickly and brutally, to have it said and done and over with, he went on. "She ran away with the son of a Dartmouth merchant. She lived openly with him for two years and died with him, on a fever-plagued island in the West Indies."

He turned and looked down into his wife's pale, upturned face. Her eyes were wide with shock. Then, incredibly, they were glistening . . . with tears.

"How dare you?" she said, angrily blinking the tears back. "How dare you, of all men, call your mother a whore? You buy a new lover every night. It costs you a few coins. According to you, she took but one—and he cost her everything: her friends, her honor. Her son."

"I might have known you could make even this romantic," he said mockingly. "Will you make the hot-blooded harlot out to be a martyr to—to what, Jess? *Love?*"

He turned away from the portrait, because the howling had started inside him, and he wanted to scream, *Why?* Yet he knew the answer, always had. If his mother had loved him—or pitied him at least, if she could not love him—she would have taken him with her. She would not have left him alone, in hell.

"You don't know what her life was like," she said. "You were a child. You couldn't know what she felt. She was a foreigner, and her husband was old enough to be her father."

"Like Byron's Donna Julia, you mean?" His voice dripped acid irony. "Perhaps you're right. Perhaps Mama would have done better with two husbands, of five and twenty."

"You don't know whether your father treated her well or ill," his wife persisted, like a teacher with a stubborn student. "You don't know whether he made the way easy for her or impossible. For all you know, he may have made her wretched—which is more than likely, if his portrait offers an accurate indication of his character."

And what of me? he wanted to cry. *You don't know what it was like for me, the hideous thing she left behind, shut out, shunned, mocked, abused. Left . . . to endure . . . and pay, dearly, for what others took for granted: tolerance, acceptance, a woman's soft hand.*

He was appalled at his own inner rage and grief, the hysteria of a child . . . who had died five and twenty years ago.

He made himself laugh and meet her steady grey gaze with the mocking mask he wore so well. "If you've taken my sire in dislike, feel free to exile him to the

North Tower. You may hang her in his place. Or in the chapel, for all I care."

He headed for the door. "You needn't consult me about redecorating. I know no female can live two days in a house and leave anything as it was. I shall be much astonished if I can find my way about when I return."

"You're going away?" Her tones remained steady. When he paused and turned at the threshold, she was looking out the window, her color back to normal, her countenance composed.

"To Devonport," he said, wondering why her composure chilled him so. "A wrestling match. Sherburne and some other fellows. I'm to meet them at nine o'clock. I need to pack."

"Then I must change orders for dinner," she said. "I think I'll dine in the morning room. But I had better have a nap before then, or I shall fall asleep into my plate. I have been over only about one quarter of the house, yet I feel as though I had walked from Dover to Land's End."

He wanted to ask what she thought of the house, what she liked—apart from the soul-shattering portrait of his mother—and what she didn't like—besides the offensive landscape in the dining room, which he hadn't liked, either, he recalled.

If he were not going away, he could have found out over dinner, in the cozy intimacy of the morning room.

Intimacy, he told himself, was the last thing he needed now. What he needed was to get away, where she could not turn him upside down and inside out with her heart-stopping "discoveries" . . . or torment him with her scent, her silken skin, the soft curves of her slender body.

It took all his self-control to walk, not run, from the room.

Jessica spent ten minutes trying to calm down. It didn't work.

Unwilling to cope with Bridget or anyone else, she ran her own bath. Athcourt, fortunately, boasted the rare luxury of hot and cold running water, even on the second floor.

Neither solitude nor the bath calmed her down, and napping was impossible. Jessica lay on her large, lonely bed, stiff as a poker, glaring up at the canopy.

Barely three days wed, and the great jackass was abandoning her. For his friends. For a *wrestling match*.

She got up, pulled off her modest cotton nightgown, and stalked, naked, to her dressing room. She found the wine red and black silk negligee and put it on. She slipped into the black mules. She shrugged into a heavy black and gold silk dressing gown, tied the sash, and loosely draped the neckline so that a bit of the negligee peeped above it.

After running a brush through her hair, she returned to her bedchamber and exited through the door that opened into what Mrs. Ingleby had called the Withdrawing Chamber. At present, it housed part of Dain's collection of artistic curios. It also adjoined His Lordship's apartments.

She crossed the huge, dim room to the door that led to Dain's rooms. She rapped. The muffled voices she'd heard while approaching abruptly ceased. After a moment, Andrews opened the door. As he took in her dishabille, he let out a gasp, which he quickly turned into a small, polite cough.

She turned a sweet, artless smile upon him. "Ah, you haven't gone yet. I am so relieved. If His Lordship can spare a minute, I need to ask him something."

Andrews glanced to his left. "My lord, Her Ladyship wishes—"

"I'm not deaf," came Dain's cross voice. "Get away from there and let her in."

Andrews backed away and Jessica strolled in, glancing idly about her while she made her way slowly into the room and around the immense seventeenth-century bed to her husband. The bed was even larger than hers, about ten feet square.

Dain, in shirt, trousers, and stockinged feet, stood near the window. He was glaring down at his traveling case. It stood open upon a heavily carved table which she guessed had been built about the same time as the bed. He would not look at her.

"It is a . . . delicate matter," she said, her voice hesitant, shy. She wished she could command a blush as well, but blushes did not come easily to her. "If we might be . . . private?"

He shot a glance at her, and back to the valise almost in the same instant. Then he blinked, and turned his head toward her once more, stiffly this time. Slowly he surveyed her, up and down and up again, pausing at the revealing neckline of her dressing gown. A muscle jumped in his cheek.

Then his face set, hard as granite. "Ready for your nap, I see." He glowered past her at Andrews. "What are you waiting for? 'Private,' Her Ladyship said. Are you deaf?"

Andrews left, closing the door after him.

"Thank you, Dain," Jessica said, smiling up at him. Then she stepped closer, took a handful of starched and neatly folded neckcloths from the valise, and dropped them on the floor.

He looked at her. He looked at the linen upon the floor.

She took out a stack of pristine white handkerchiefs and, still smiling, threw them down, too.

"Jessica, I don't know what game you're at, but it is not amusing," he said very quietly.

She collected an armful of shirts and flung them onto the floor. "We have been wed scarcely three days," she said. "You do *not* desert your new bride for your sap-skull friends. You will not make a laughingstock of me. If you are unhappy with me, you say so, and we discuss it—or quarrel, if you prefer. But you do not—"

"You do not dictate to me," he said levelly. "You do not tell me where I may and may not go—or when—or with whom. I do not explain and you do not question. And you do *not* come into my room and throw temper fits."

"Yes, I do," she said. "If you leave this house, I will shoot your horse out from under you."

"Shoot my—"

"I will not permit you to desert me," she said. "You will not take me for granted as Sherburne does his wife, and you will not make all the world laugh at me—or pity me—as they do her. If you cannot bear to miss your precious wrestling match, you can jolly well take me with you."

"Take you?" His voice climbed. "I'll bloody well take you, madam—straight to your room. And lock you in, if you can't behave yourself."

"I should like to see you tr—"

He lunged at her, and she dodged an instant too late. In the next instant, she was slung up under one brawny arm, and he was hauling her like a sack of rags to the door she'd entered.

It stood open. Luckily, it opened into the room, and only one of her arms was trapped against his body.

She pushed the door shut.

"Bloody hell!"

Swearing was all he could do about it. He had only one usable hand, which was occupied. He couldn't move the door handle without letting go of her.

He swore again. Turning, he marched to the bed and dumped her there.

As she fell back onto the mattress, her dressing gown fell open.

Dain's furious black gaze stormed over her. "Damn you, Jess. Curse and confound you." His voice was choked. "You will not—you cannot—" He reached out to grab her hand, but she scrambled back.

"You're not going to put me out," she said, retreating to the center of the huge bed. "I'm not a child and I will not be locked in my room."

He knelt on the edge of the mattress. "Don't think, just because you've crippled me, I can't teach you a lesson. Don't make me chase you." He dove at her, grabbing for her foot. She pulled away, and the black mule came off in his hand. He threw it across the room.

She snatched the other one off and threw it at him. He ducked, and the slipper hit the wall.

With a low growl, he flung himself at her. She rolled away to the opposite side of the bed, and he lost his balance. He fell face-first, sprawling across the lower half of the big mattress.

She could have leapt from the bed and escaped then, but she didn't. She had come prepared for a battle royal, and she would fight this one to the bitter end.

He dragged himself up onto his knees. His shirtfront had fallen open, revealing a tautly muscled neck and the dark web of tantalizingly silky hair her fingers had played with the night before. His big chest rose and fell with his labored breathing. She had only to glance up at his eyes to understand that anger was but the smallest part of what worked on him at this moment.

"I'm not going to wrestle with you," he said. "Or quarrel. You will go to your room. Now."

She'd lost the sash of her dressing gown, and the top part had slid down to her elbows. She shrugged out of it, then sank down upon the pillows and gazed up at the canopy, her mouth set mulishly.

He moved closer, the mattress sagging under his weight. "Jess, I'm warning you."

She wouldn't answer, wouldn't turn her head. She didn't have to. That deadly tone of his wasn't quite as ominous and intimidating as he wanted it to be. She didn't have to look, either, to understand why he'd paused.

She knew he didn't want to look at her, but he couldn't help it. He was a man, and had to look, and what he saw could hardly fail to distract him. She was aware that one of the narrow ribbons holding up the bodice of her negligee had slipped down over her shoulder. She was aware that the gauzy skirt was tangled about her legs.

She heard his breath hitch.

"Damn you, Jess."

She heard the indecision in the husky baritone. She waited, still fixed upon the black and gold dragons above her, leaving him to battle it out with himself.

A full minute and more he remained unmoving and silent, but for the harsh, unsteady breathing.

Then the mattress shifted and sank, and she felt his knees against her hip and heard his muffled moan of defeat. His hand fell upon her knee and slid upward, the silk whispering under his touch.

She lay still while he slowly stroked up over her hip,

over her belly. The warmth of the caress stole under her skin and made her feverish.

He paused at her bodice, and traced the eyelet work over her breast. It tautened under his touch, her nipple hardening and thrusting up against the thin silk . . . yearning for more, as she did.

He pushed the fragile fabric down, and brushed his thumb over the hard, aching peak. Then he bent and took it in his mouth, and she had to clench her hands to keep from holding him there, and clench her jaw as well, to keep from crying out as she had done the night before: *Yes . . . please . . . anything . . . don't stop.*

He had made her beg last night, yet he had not made her his. And today he thought he could turn his back and walk away, and do as he pleased. He thought he could desert her, leave her wretched and humiliated, a bride, but not a wife.

He didn't want to want her, but he did. He wanted her to beg for his lovemaking, so that he could pretend he was in control.

But he wasn't. His mouth was hot on her breast, her shoulder, her neck. His hand was shaking, his touch roughening, because he was feverish, too.

"Oh, Jess." His voice was an anguished whisper as he sank down beside her. He pulled her to him, and dragged hot kisses over her face. "*Baciami.* Kiss me. *Abbracciami.* Hold me. Touch me. Please. I'm sorry." Urgent, desperate, his voice, while he struggled with the narrow ribbon ties.

I'm sorry. He'd actually said it. But he didn't know what he was saying, Jessica told herself. He was lost in simple animal hunger, as she had been, last night.

He wasn't sorry, merely mindless with primitive male lust. His hand worked feverishly, pulling the gown down, moving over her back, her waist.

He grabbed her hand and kissed it. "Don't be angry. Touch me." He pushed her hand under his shirt. "The way you did last night."

His skin was on fire. Hot and smooth and hard . . . feathery masculine hair . . . muscles quivering under her fingers . . . his big body shuddering under her lightest touch.

She wanted to resist, to remain angry, but she wanted this more. She'd wanted to touch and kiss and hold him from the day she'd met him. She'd wanted him to burn for her, just as she'd wanted him to set her ablaze.

He was pulling the negligee down, over her hips.

She grasped the edges of his shirtfront and, with one fierce yank, tore it in half.

His hand fell from her hip. She tore the shirt cuff away, and rent the seam up to the shoulder. "I know you like to be undressed," she said.

"Yes," he gasped, and shifted back to give her access to the other, useless arm. She was no more gentle with that sleeve. She ripped it off.

He pulled her against him, pressing her bared breasts to the powerful chest she'd exposed. His heart beat next to hers, to the same frenetic rhythm. He grasped the back of her head and crushed her mouth to his, and drove out anger, pride, and thought in that long, devouring kiss.

The ragged remains of his shirt came away in her hands. He stripped away her negligee in the same frantic moment. Their hands became tangled, tearing at his trouser buttons. Wool ripped and buttons tore from the cloth.

He pushed her legs apart with his knee. She felt the hard shaft throbbing hotly against her thigh while her own heat pulsed against his questing hand. He found the place where he'd tormented her last night, and sweetly tormented her again, until she cried out and her body spilled its feminine tears of desire.

She clung to him, shaking and desperate, and "*Please,*" she begged. "*Please.*"

She heard his voice, ragged with longing . . . words she couldn't understand . . . then a shaft of pain as he thrust into her.

Her mind went black and *Please, God, don't let me faint*, was all she could think. She dug her nails into his back, clinging to him for consciousness.

His damp cheek pressed against hers, and his breath was hot on her ear. "Sweet Jesus, I can't—Oh, Jess." He lashed his arm about her and rolled onto his side, taking her with him. He hooked his arm under her knee, and lifted her leg up and around his waist. The searing pressure eased, and her panic faded with it. She shifted upward and buried her face in the curve of his neck. She held on tightly, savoring the sweat-slickened heat of his skin, the musky scent of passion.

She was aware of him moving again, inside her, but her untutored body was yielding, and pain was a distant memory. He'd pleasured her already, and she expected no more, but gradually it came, pulsing through her with each slow, possessive stroke.

Pleasure bubbled up inside her, warm and tingling, and her body arched up to welcome it, and joy bolted through her, sharp and sweet.

It wasn't the same joy he'd taught her before, but every instinct recognized it and hungered for more. She rocked against him, matching his rhythm, and more came, faster and harder, and faster still . . . a furious race to the peak . . . a lightning blast of rapture . . . and the sweet rain of release.

Fourteen

*H*ell and damnation," Dain muttered as he gingerly withdrew from her. "I'll never make it to Chudleigh in time for dinner now."

He rolled onto his back and focused intently upon the embroidered gold dragons above, to keep himself from leaping up and subjecting his wife to a thorough physical examination. Fortunately, with his lust appeased, for the moment, his intellect had resumed normal operation. And with the return of reason, he could sort out the simple facts.

He had not forced himself on her. Jessica had invited him.

He had crashed into her like a battering ram and been incapable of exercising much restraint thereafter, yet she hadn't screamed or wept. On the contrary, she had seemed to get right into the spirit of the thing.

He looked at her. Her hair had fallen over her eyes. Turning toward her, he brushed it away. "I collect you've survived," he said gruffly.

She made an odd sound—a cough or a hiccup, he couldn't tell. Then she flung herself against him and, "Oh, Dain," she choked out.

The next he knew, her face was pressed against his chest and she was sobbing.

"*Per carita.*" He wrapped himself about her and stroked her back. "For God's sake, Jess, don't . . . This is very . . . troublesome." He buried his face in her hair. "Oh, very well. Cry if you must."

She would not weep forever, he told himself. And upsetting as it was to hear it and feel the tears trickling over his skin, he knew matters might have been worse. At least she had turned to him, not away. Besides, she was entitled to cry, he supposed. He had been rather unreasonable these last few days.

Very well, more than that. He'd been a beast.

Here she was, a new bride in this mammoth house with its grand army of servants, and he had not helped her. He had not tried to make the way easy . . . just as she'd said about his father.

He'd been acting like his *father*. Cold and hostile and rejecting every effort to please.

For Jessica had been trying to please, hadn't she? She had read to him and tried to talk to him and she'd probably thought the portrait of his mother would be a lovely surprise for him. She had wanted him to stay, when any other woman would have been in raptures to be rid of him. She had offered herself to him, when any other woman would have swooned with relief to escape his attentions. And she'd given herself willingly and passionately.

He was the one who ought to be weeping, with gratitude.

The cloudburst ended as abruptly as it had begun. Jessica squirmed away, rubbed her face, and sat up.

"Lud, how emotional one becomes," she said shakily. "Is my nose red?"

"Yes," he said, though the light was failing and he could scarcely see straight anyhow.

"I had better wash my face," she said. She climbed off the bed, picked up her dressing gown, and put it on.

"You can use my bath. I'll show you the way." He started to get out of bed, but she waved him back.

"I know where it is," she said. "Mrs. Ingleby explained the layout." She headed unerringly across the room, opened the correct door, and hurried through.

While she was gone, Dain quickly examined the bedclothes and cleaned himself off with a piece of his shirt, which he threw in the fire.

Whatever the cause of her weeping fit, it hadn't been a reaction to serious physical injury, he comforted himself. He'd found a spot of blood on one of the coverlet's gold dragons and there had been a bit on him, but it was nothing like the carnage his overwrought imagination had pictured these last three days.

He could not believe his mind had been so disordered. In the first place, any cretin might have understood that if the female body could adapt to dropping brats, it must certainly be able to adapt to the breeding instrument—unless the man was an elephant, which he wasn't, quite. In the second place, any imbecile might have recollected that this woman had never, since the time under the lamppost in Paris, recoiled from his advances. She had even spoken plainly enough—more than once, without a blink—about his breeding rights.

Where in the name of heaven had he obtained the idea she was fragile or missish? This was the woman who'd *shot him!*

It was the strain, Dain decided. The trauma of finding himself married, combined with crazed lust for his bride, had been more than his mind could cope with. The portrait of his mother had finished him off. With that, his brain had shut down altogether.

By the time Jessica returned, Dain had himself and everything else in proper order. Andrews had carried away the heaps of discarded traveling clothes, the valise was put away, the lamps had been lit, a footman was on his way to Chudleigh, and dinner was being prepared.

"It seems you've been busy," she said, glancing about as she came up to him. "How tidy the room is."

"You were gone rather a while," he said.

"I had a bath," she said. "I was agitated, as you saw." She studied the knot of his sash, her brow furrowed. "I think I was hysterical. I wish I hadn't cried, but I couldn't help it. It was a . . . deeply moving experience. I daresay you're used to it, but I am not. I was much affected. I had not expected . . . Well, frankly, I was expecting the worst. When it came to the point, I mean. But you did not seem to experience any difficulty, and you did not seem inhibited by my inexperience or annoyed, and, except for a moment, it did not feel like the first time at all. At least, not what I'd imagined the first time to be like. And what with having my anxieties relieved and the extraordinary sensations . . . The long and the short of it is, I could not contain my feelings."

He had read the signs more or less correctly, then, for once, finally. The world was in order. All he needed to do was step carefully, to keep it that way.

"My temper has not been altogether even, either," he said. "I'm not used to having a female about. It's . . . distracting."

"I know, and I've taken that into account," she said. "Nonetheless, Dain, you cannot expect me to go through this again."

He stared at the top of her head and watched his

neatly ordered world tumble back into chaos. In an instant, his previously light heart became a lead casket, bearing the corpse of a fragile infant hope. He should have known better than to hope. He should have realized he'd make everything go wrong. But he didn't understand now, any more than he ever had, how he had turned everything so very wrong. He didn't understand why she'd been sent into his life, to give him hope, and kill it in the first moment he dared to believe it.

His face set and his body turned to stone, but he couldn't muster the callous laughter or the clever witticism needed to complete this too familiar scene. He had tasted happiness in her arms, and hope, and he could not let them go without knowing why.

"Jessica, I know I've been . . . difficult," he said. "All the same—"

"Difficult?" She looked up, her grey eyes wide. "You have been impossible. I begin to think you are not right in the upper storey. I knew you wanted me. The one thing I've never doubted was that. But getting you into bed—you, the greatest whoremonger in Christendom— gad, it was worse than the time I had to drag Bertie to the tooth-drawer. And if you think I mean to be doing that the rest of our days, you had better think again. The next time, my lord, you will do the seducing—or there won't be any, I vow."

She stepped back and folded her arms over her bosom. "I mean it, Dain. I am sick to death of throwing myself at you. You like me well enough. And if the first bedding didn't prove we suit in that way at least, then you are a hopeless case, and I wash my hands of you. I will *not* permit you to make a wreck of me."

Dain opened his mouth, but nothing came out. He shut it and walked to the window. He sank onto the cushioned seat and stared out. "Worse than . . .

Bertie . . . to the tooth-drawer." He gave a shaky laugh. "The *tooth-drawer*. Oh, Jess."

He heard her slippered footsteps approaching.

"Dain, are you all right?"

He rubbed his forehead. "Yes. No. What an idiot." He turned and met her frowning gaze. "High-strung," he said. "That's the trouble, isn't it? I'm high-strung."

"You're overwrought," she said. "I should have realized. We've both been under a strain. And it's harder on you because you are so sensitive and emotional."

Sensitive. Emotional. He had the hide of an ox—and about the same intelligence, apparently. But he didn't contradict her.

"A strain, yes," he said.

"Why don't you have a bath, too?" she suggested. She smoothed his hair back from his forehead. "And while you enjoy a good long soak, I'll order dinner."

"I've ordered it," he said. "They should be up with it soon. I thought we might dine here. It would save the bother of dressing for dinner."

She studied his face, and slowly her mouth eased into a smile. "Perhaps you're not quite as hopeless a case as I thought. What about Sherburne?"

"I sent a footman to Chudleigh with a note," he said. "I informed Sherburne I'd see him at the wrestling match. Saturday."

She stepped back, her smile fading. "I see."

"No, you don't." He rose. "You're coming with me."

He watched her chilly composure ebb as she took in the last sentence and decided to believe him. Her soft mouth curved upward again and silver mist shimmered in her eyes.

"Thank you, Dain," she said. "I should like that very much. I've never seen a proper wrestling match before."

"I daresay it will be a novel experience all round," he said, gravely eyeing her up and down. "I can't wait to see Sherburne's face when I arrive with my lady wife in tow."

"There, you see?" she said, unoffended. "I told you there were other benefits to having a wife. I can come in very handy when you wish to shock your friends."

"There is that. But my own comfort was my first consideration," he added as he edged away. "I shall want you about to cater to my whims and soothe my sensitive nerves and . . ." He grinned. "And warm my bed, of course."

"How romantic." She pressed her hand to her heart. "I believe I shall swoon."

"You'd better not." Dain headed toward the door she'd entered. "I can't wait around to pick you up. My bladder is about to explode."

With the world securely in order, Dain was able to devote the leisurely bath time to editing his mental dictionary. He removed his wife from the general category labeled "Females" and gave her a section of her own. He made a note that she didn't find him revolting, and proposed several explanations: (a) bad eyesight and faulty hearing, (b) a defect in a portion of her otherwise sound intellect, (c) an inherited Trent eccentricity, or (d) an act of God. Since the Almighty had not done him a single act of kindness in at least twenty-five years, Dain thought it was about bloody time, but he thanked his Heavenly Father all the same, and promised to be as good as he was capable of being.

His expectations in this regard were, like most of his expectations, very low. He would never be an ideal husband. He had almost no idea how to be a husband at all—beyond the basics of providing food, clothing, shelter, and protection from life's annoyances. And getting brats.

As soon as offspring came into his mind, Dain slammed his dictionary shut. He was in a good humor. He didn't want to spoil it by fretting, and working himself into another fit of insanity over the inevitable. Besides, there was an even chance the brats would come out like her rather than him. In any case, he wouldn't be able to prevent their coming because there was no way he could keep his hands off her.

He knew a good thing when he had it. He knew that tumbling his wife was about as close to experiencing heaven as he'd ever get. He was far too selfish and depraved by nature to give it up. As long as she was willing, he wasn't going to worry about consequences. Something horrible was bound to happen, of course, sooner or later. But that was how his life worked. Since he couldn't prevent it, whatever it was, he might as well take his motto from Horace: *Carpe diem, quam minimum credula postero.* Seize the day, put no trust in the morrow.

Accordingly, with matters properly sorted out and settled for the present, Dain joined his wife for dinner. During the meal, he further revised his dictionary. To her odd list of accomplishments he had already added a comprehension of the art of boxing. At dinner he discovered she possessed a knowledge of wrestling as well, gleaned from sporting periodicals and male conversations. She had reared not only her brother, she explained, but ten boy cousins as well—because she was the only one who could "manage the lot of ignorant savages." Yet not one of the ingrates would take her to a professional match.

"Not even Polkinhorne's bout with Carr," she told Dain indignantly.

That famous match had also taken place in Devonport, two years ago.

"There were seventeen thousand spectators," she said. "Would you please explain to me how one female would attract notice in such a crowd?"

"You are bound to attract notice, even amid seventy thousand," he said. "You are the prettiest girl I've ever seen, as I distinctly recall telling you in Paris."

She sat back, startled, her smooth cheeks turning pink. "Good grief, Dain, that was a flat-out compliment—and we're not even making love."

"I am a shocking fellow," he said. "One never knows what astonishing thing I'll say. Or when." He sipped his wine. "The point is, you will attract notice. In normal circumstances, you would have a lot of drunken louts bothering you and distracting your escort. But since I shall be your escort, there will be no bothering or distracting. All the louts, however drunk they may be, will keep their eyes upon the wrestlers and their hands to themselves." He set down his wineglass and took up his fork again.

"The tarts had better do the same," she said, returning her attention to her food. "I am not as big and intimidating as you, but I have my methods. I won't tolerate such annoyances, either."

Dain kept his gaze on his plate and concentrated on swallowing the morsel he'd just very nearly choked on.

She was possessive . . . about *him*.

The beautiful, mad creature—or blind and deaf creature, or whatever she was—coolly announced it as one might say, "Pass the salt cellar," without the smallest awareness that the earth had just tilted on its axis.

"These large sporting events tend to attract Cyprians in droves," he said. "I fear you'll have your hands full . . ." His mouth twitched. "Fighting them off."

"I suppose it's too much to ask you not to encourage them," she said.

"My dear, I wouldn't dream of encouraging them," he said. "Even I know it's very bad ton to—to cast lures at other women while one's wife is about. Not to mention you'd probably shoot me." He shook his head sadly. "I only wish my self-restraint were enough. But the vexing thing is, they don't seem to want any encouragement. Everywhere I go—"

"It does not vex you," she said with a reproachful glance. "You are well aware of your effect on women, and I'm sure it gratifies you no end to watch them sigh and salivate over your magnificent physique. I do not wish to spoil your fun, Dain. But I do ask you to consider my pride, and refrain from embarrassing me in public."

Women . . . sighing and salivating . . . over his magnificent physique.

Maybe the brutal bedding had destroyed a part of her brain.

"I don't know what you're thinking of," he said. "Did I not pay a king's ransom for you? Why in blazes should I waste money and energy luring other females, when I've bought one for permanent use?"

"A few hours ago, you were prepared to desert me," she pointed out. "After only three days' marriage—and before you'd consummated it. You did not seem to regard money and energy any more than you regarded my pride."

"I was not thinking clearly then," he said. "I was at the mercy of my delicate nerves. Also, I'm not accustomed to regarding anybody else's feelings. But now that my mind has cleared, I see your point, and it's a sound one. You are the Marchioness of Dain, after all, and it will not do for anyone to laugh at you or pity you. It is one thing for me to behave like a jackass. It is quite another, however, when my behavior reflects ill upon you." He set down his fork and leaned toward her. "Have I got that right, my lady wife?"

Her soft mouth curved. "Perfectly," she said. "What a keen mind you have, Dain, when it is clear. You go direct to the heart of the issue."

The approving smile shot directly to his heart and curled warmly there.

"Good heavens, that sounds like a flat-out compliment." He laid his hand over his melting heart. "And on my intellect, no less. My primitive, male intellect. I do believe I shall swoon." His gaze slid to her décolletage. "Maybe I'd better lie down. Maybe . . ." He lifted his eyes to hers. "Are you finished, Jess?"

She let out a small sigh. "I daresay I was finished the day I met you."

He rose and moved to her chair. "Anyone might have told you that. I can't imagine what you were thinking of, to keep plaguing me as you did." He lightly trailed his knuckles along her silken cheek.

"I wasn't thinking clearly," she said.

He took her hand and drew her up from the chair. "I begin to doubt you are capable of any kind of thinking," he said. He wasn't either, at present. He was too achingly aware of her skin, flawless porcelain white, and of the small, graceful hand in his own.

He was painfully conscious of his great, clumsy bulk, and his crude ways, and of his darkness, inside and out. He still had trouble believing that only a few hours earlier, he'd been pounding into her, slaking his bestial lust upon her innocent body. He could scarcely believe his lust was aroused again, so fiercely, so soon. But he was an animal. She had only to smile at him and the monstrous, brutal need swelled inside him, smothering intellect and demolishing the woefully thin veneer of civilized male.

He told himself to calm down, to talk, to woo. She wanted to be seduced, and it was the least he could do. He ought to be able to. He ought to have that much control. But the best he could do was lead her to the bed, instead of grabbing her and throwing her down on the table and himself on top of her.

He drew back the bedclothes and sat her down upon the mattress. Then he gazed at her helplessly while he searched the turgid mire of his mind for the right words.

"I couldn't keep away," she said, her grey eyes searching his. "I knew I should, but I couldn't. I thought you understood that, but it seems you didn't. You got that part wrong, too, didn't you? What on earth have you been thinking, Dain?"

He had lost track of the conversation. He wondered what she read in his face. "What did I get wrong?" he asked, essaying an indulgent smile.

"Everything, it seems." Her sooty lashes lowered. "And so it's no surprise that I misjudged."

"Is that why you didn't keep away? Because you misjudged me?"

She shook her head. "No, and it's not because I'm addled upstairs, either. You are not to think I'm mad, Dain, because I'm not. I know it looks that way, but there's a perfectly reasonable explanation. The intellect, as you of all men ought to know, is no match for the intensity of the animal drive. I've been in lust with you from the moment I met you."

His knees grew wobbly. He crouched down in front of her and took a firm grip of the edge of the mattress. He cleared his throat. "Lust." He managed to keep the one syllable low and steady. He decided not to try any more syllables of anything.

She was searching his eyes again. "You didn't know, did you?"

Dissembling was utterly beyond his powers. He shook his head.

She brought her hands up to cup his face. "You must be blind. And deaf. Or terribly confused. Everyone in Paris knew. You poor man. I don't want to begin to imagine what's been going through your mind."

He managed to laugh. "I thought it was me they knew about. That I was . . . besotted. I was. I told you so."

"But, darling, you lust after every female you see," she said ever so patiently. "Why should Paris work itself into a frenzy about that? It was because of my behavior, don't you understand? They saw I was too infatuated to keep away, as a sensible, strong-moraled lady should. That's what made the business interesting to them."

Darling. The room was whirling merrily about him.

"I wanted to be sensible," she went on. "I didn't want to bother you. I knew it would lead to trouble. But I couldn't help it. You are so . . . virile. You are so thoroughly a *male*. You're big and strong and you can pick me up with one hand. I cannot describe what an extraordinary sensation that is."

Virile he understood. He was that. He also understood there was no accounting for tastes. Until she'd come along, he'd always been attracted to largish women. Very well, then. Her tastes inclined to big, strong men. He was certainly that, too.

"I'd heard all about you," she said. "I thought I was prepared. But no one had described you properly. I was expecting a gorilla." She drew her index finger down his nose. "You were not supposed to have the face of a dé Medici prince. You were not supposed to have the physique of a Roman god. I wasn't prepared for that. I had no defenses ready." With a small sigh, she brought her hands to his shoulders. "I still haven't. Physically, I cannot resist you at all."

He tried to find a place in his dictionary under "Dain" for dé Medici princes and Roman gods, but the phrases fit nowhere, and merely contemplating them made him want to howl with laughter. Or weep. He couldn't decide which. He decided he was becoming hysterical. He wasn't surprised. She had a knack for doing that to him.

He stood up. "No need to worry, Jess. Lust is no problem. Lust I can deal with very well, thank you."

"I know." She eyed him up and down. "You deal with it to perfection."

"In fact, I'm prepared to deal with it this very minute." He began heaping pillows against the headboard.

"That is most . . . understanding of you," she said, her glance darting from the pillows to him.

He patted the heap. "I want you to lie here."

"Naked?"

He nodded.

Without the smallest hesitation, she stood up and undid the sash of her dressing gown. He watched the robe fall open. She gave a lazy shrug.

Femme fatale, he thought as, entranced, he watched the heavy black silk slither down past her slim shoulders, over the creamy skin and achingly feminine curves, and fall with a sensuous hiss at her feet.

He watched the graceful movement of her slight body as she climbed onto the bed and settled back against the pillows, unashamed, uninhibited, unafraid.

"I almost wish I could be naked all the time," she said softly. "I love the way you look at me."

"You mean the panting and salivating?" He untied his own sash.

"I mean that sleepy, sulky look you get." She laid her hand upon her belly. "It makes my insides hot and muddled."

He flung off his dressing gown.

She inhaled sharply.

His swelling shaft sprang up, just as though she'd called to it. Dain looked down and laughed. "You want virile. Virile you get."

"And big and strong." Her voice was husky. Her softened grey gaze traveled up and down his frame. "And beautiful. How the devil was I to resist you? How could you think I could?"

"I didn't realize you were so shallow." He climbed onto the bed and straddled her legs.

"I suppose it's just as well," she said. "Otherwise . . ." She slid her hand up his thigh. "Oh, Dain, if you had guessed what was going through my mind when I met you . . ."

Gently but firmly he removed her hand and set it upon the mattress. "Tell me."

"In my mind, I took off all your clothes. I couldn't help it. It was a dreadful few moments. I was terrified my reason would snap, and I'd actually do it. There, in the shop. In front of Champtois. In front of Bertie."

"You took off my clothes," he said. "In your mind."

"Yes. Ripped them off, actually. As I did a short while ago."

He bent over her. "Do you want to know what went through my mind, *cara?*"

"Something equally depraved, I hope." She stroked his chest. Again he took her hand away.

"I wanted . . . to . . . lick you," he said slowly. "From the top of your head . . . to the tips of your toes."

She shut her eyes. "Depraved, yes."

"I wanted to lick you and kiss you and touch you . . . everywhere." He kissed her forehead. "Everywhere it's white. Everywhere it's pink. Everywhere else."

He trailed his tongue over one sleek eyebrow. "That's

what I'm going to do now. And you must lie there. And take it."

"Yes." One sibilant sound of acquiescence and a shiver—of pleasure, apparently, because her soft, ripe mouth curled upward.

He brushed his lips over that small, cat-in-the-cream-pot smile, and said no more, but gave himself up to realizing his fantasy.

The reality, he found, was sweeter, and the taste and scent of her more intoxicating by far, than the dream.

He kissed her nose and savored the satin of her cheek. He inhaled her and tasted her and discovered her all at once, all over again: the perfect oval of her face, the slant of her cheekbones, the skin so fine and flawless that he'd wanted to weep when first he beheld her.

Perfection, he'd thought then, and it had nearly broken his heart, because he couldn't have her.

But he could, for now at least. He could touch his lips to that perfection . . . the heartbreaking face . . . the tantalizingly dainty ear . . . the smooth column of her neck.

He remembered how he'd stood in the shadows and hungered for the white skin exposed in the lamplight. He trailed his parted lips down over the snowy shoulder he'd gazed at from his hiding place, and down her right arm to her fingertips and back up again. He made the same lingeringly possessive path up and down her left arm. Her fingers curled and her breath came in sweet little sighs that murmured in his veins and made his heart thrum like a violincello.

He lavished kisses over her firm, round breasts, rising and falling with her quickened breathing. He trailed his tongue over the taut, blushing nipples and savored her tiny moans briefly, then made himself move on, because there was more, and he would take nothing for granted. He'd experience it all, because the world could end tomorrow, for all he knew, and Hell open up and swallow him.

He continued downward, washing kisses over her smooth belly and the luscious curve of her hips . . . down the outside of her slender, shapely leg, to the slim ankle and on to the tips of her toes, as he'd promised. Then slowly he worked his way up again to her satiny inner thigh.

She was trembling now, and his loins were heavy and hot and more than ready.

But he wasn't done, and only the present could be trusted. This moment might be all he had. And so again he kissed and savored, all the way to her toes and back.

Then he trailed his tongue over the velvety skin just above the dark nest of curls between her legs.

"You're beautiful, Jess," he said thickly. "Every inch of you." He slid his fingers into the damp, dusky curls.

She moaned.

He brought his mouth to the warm, moist core.

She gave a low cry, and her fingers caught in his hair.

The feminine cry of pleasure sang in his veins. The rich scent and taste of Woman flooded his senses. She was all he wanted in the world, and she was his, wanting him, slick and hot for him.

He worshipped her with his mouth for wanting him. He pleasured her for the delirious joy of doing so, until her hands fisted in his hair and she cried out his name, and he felt the tremors shake her.

Then, finally, he sheathed himself in her hotly welcoming softness, and joined her.

Then the world shook for him as well, and if it had ended in that instant, he would have gone to damnation happily, because she clung to him and kissed him as though there were no tomorrow and she would hold and want him forever.

And when the world exploded, and he spilled himself into her, it was as though his soul spilled, too, and he would have given up that soul gladly, if that were the price for the moment of pure happiness she gave him.

The next day, Jessica gave him the icon.

Dain found it at his place when he came into the breakfast room. It stood between his coffee cup and the plate. Even in the weak light of an overcast morning, pearls shimmered, topaz and rubies sparkled, diamonds shot rainbow sparks. Beneath the glimmering golden halo, the grey-eyed Madonna smiled wistfully upon the scowling infant in her arms.

A small, folded piece of notepaper was tucked under the bottom of the jeweled frame. His heart racing, Dain took it out and opened it.

"Happy Birthday," it read. That was all.

He looked up from the note to his wife, who sat opposite, her sleek hair framed by the hazy light from the window.

She was buttering a piece of scone, oblivious, as usual, to the cataclysm she'd just set off.

"Jess." He could scarcely force the one syllable past his tight throat.

"Yes?" She set down the knife and spooned a lump of preserves onto the scone.

He thumbed frantically through his mental dictionary, looking for words, but he couldn't find what he wanted because he didn't know what he was looking for.

"Jess."

The bit of scone paused halfway to her lips. She looked at him.

Dain pointed at the icon.

She looked at that. "Oh. Well, better late than never, I thought. And yes, I know it isn't truly a gift because it belongs to you anyway. Everything of mine—or nearly everything—became yours legally when we wed. But we shall have to pretend, because I hadn't time to think of, let alone find, a suitable birthday present." She popped the buttered and lavishly sweetened tidbit into her mouth . . . as though everything had been thoroughly explained and settled and not a single fragment of the sky had fallen.

For the first time, Dain had an inkling of what it must feel like to be Bertie Trent, owning the necessary human quantity of grey matter, but possessing no notion how to make it function. Perhaps, Dain thought, Trent hadn't been born that way after all. Perhaps he had simply been incapacitated by a lifetime of explosions.

Perhaps the term *femme fatale* ought to be taken more literally. Perhaps it was the brain she was fatal to.

Not my brain, Dain resolved. *She is not going to turn me into a blithering imbecile.*

He could handle this. He could sort it out. He was merely taken aback, that was all. The last birthday present he'd received had come from his mother, when he was eight. The tart Wardell and Mallory had supplied on Birthday Thirteen didn't count, because Dain had wound up having to pay for her.

He was surprised, no more. Greatly surprised, admittedly, because he'd truly believed Jessica would sooner throw the icon into a cauldron of boiling acid than let him have it. He hadn't even asked about it during the marriage negotiations, because he'd assumed she'd sold it long since, and he'd adamantly refused to let himself imagine or hope, even for one half second, that she hadn't.

"This is a . . . delightful surprise," he said, as any

intelligent adult would say in the circumstances. "*Grazie*. Thank you."

She smiled. "I knew you would understand."

"I cannot possibly understand all the implications and symbolic significance," he said very, very calmly. "But then, I am a male, and my brain is too primitive for such complicated calculations. I can see, however— as I did as soon as the filth had been removed—that it is an exquisite work of art, and I doubt I shall ever grow tired of looking at it."

That was gracious, he thought. Adult. Intelligent. Reasonable. He had only to keep his hand upon the table and it would not tremble.

"I hoped you would feel so," she said. "I was sure you'd recognized how remarkable and rare it was. That's because it's more evocative, do you not agree, than the usual run of Stroganovs, fine as they are."

"Evocative." He gazed at the richly painted figures. Even now, though it was his, he was uneasy, unwilling to lose himself in it or examine the feelings it evoked.

She rose and came to him and laid her hand on his shoulder.

"When I first saw it, after it had been repaired and cleaned, I was much affected," she said. "The sensations were very odd. Apparently, at this level of artistry, I am out of my depth. You are the connoisseur. I am merely a species of magpie, and I am not always certain why my eye is drawn to certain objects, even when I have no doubt of their value."

He glanced up, bewildered. "You are asking me to explain what makes this so extraordinary?"

"Besides the unusual color of her eyes," she said. "And the lavish use of gold. And the workmanship. None of these explains why it elicits such strong emotion."

"It elicits strong emotion in you because you are

sentimental," he said. Reluctantly he brought his eyes back to the icon.

He cleared his throat and continued in the patient tones of a tutor. "One is accustomed to the classic Russian pout. But this is altogether different, you see. Baby Jesus looks truly cross and sulky, as though he's tired of posing, or hungry—or merely wants attention. And his mama doesn't wear the conventional tragic expression. She's half-frowning, yes. Mildly irritated, perhaps, because the boy's being troublesome. Yet she wears a glimmer of a smile, as though to reassure or forgive him. Because she understands that he doesn't know any better. Innocent brat, he takes it all for granted: her smiles and reassurances, her patience . . . forgiveness. He doesn't know what he has, let alone how to be grateful for it. And so he frets and scowls . . . in blissful infant ignorance."

Dain paused, for the room seemed to have grown too quiet suddenly, and the woman beside him too still.

"It is altogether natural and human a pose," he went on, careful to keep his tone light and neutral. "We forget that this pair represent holy figures, and focus instead upon the simple human drama within the artistic conventions and rich trappings. If this Madonna and child were merely saintly, the work would not be half so rare and interesting."

"I see what you mean," his wife said softly. "The artist has captured his models' personalities, and the mother's love for her little boy, and the mood of a moment between them."

"That is what awakens your sentiment," he said. "Even I find them intriguing, and can't resist theorizing about what their countenances express—though they're long dead, and the truth hardly signifies. That is the artist's talent: He makes one wonder. It's rather as though he played a joke on the viewer, isn't it?"

Glancing up from the icon at Jessica, he made himself laugh, as though this heartachingly beautiful portrait of maternal love were merely an amusing artistic riddle.

She squeezed his shoulder. "I knew there was more to it than met my untrained eye," she said, too gently. "You are so perceptive, Dain." Then she quickly moved away and returned to her seat.

Not quickly enough, though. He had caught it, in the flicker of time before she masked it. He'd seen it, in her eyes, just as he'd heard it in her voice a moment ago: sorrow . . . pity.

And his heart twisted and churned into rage—with himself, because he'd somehow said too much, and with her, because she'd been too quick—quicker than he—to perceive what he'd said, and worse, what he'd felt.

But he was not a child, Dain reminded himself. He wasn't helpless. No matter what he'd unwittingly revealed to his wife, his character had not changed. *He* had not changed, not a whit.

In Jessica, he had found a good thing, that was all, and he meant to make the most of it. He would allow her to make him happy, certainly. He would let himself be flayed alive and boiled in oil, however, before he'd allow his wife to *pity* him.

Fifteen

Andrews entered then, and the first footman, Joseph, with him. His Lordship's beefsteak was set before him, and his ale. Andrews cut the steak while Jessica, who had wanted to perform that small service, sat uselessly in her chair, pretending to eat a breakfast that tasted like sawdust and was about as easily swallowed.

She—the expert on interpreting men—scarcely understood her husband at all. Even last night, when she'd discovered he was not vain, as she'd believed, and that the love of women had not come easily to him, as she'd supposed, she had not guessed the extent of the trouble.

She had merely reminded herself that many men couldn't see themselves clearly. When Bertie, for instance, looked into a mirror, he thought a man with a brain looked back. When Dain looked into his, he somehow missed the full extent of his physical beauty. Odd in a connoisseur, but then, men were not altogether consistent creatures.

As to the love of women, Jessica had never been exactly thrilled at the prospect of falling in love with him herself. It was understandable, then, that other women—even hardened professionals—might decide he was more than they cared to tackle.

She should have also realized, though, that the difficulty lay deeper. She should have put the clues together: his acute sensibility, his mistrust of women, his edginess in his family home, his bitterness toward his mother, the portrait of his forbidding father, and Dain's contradictory behavior toward Jessica herself.

She'd known—hadn't every instinct told her?—he badly needed her, needed something from her.

He needed what every human being needed: love.

But he needed it far more than many, because, apparently, he hadn't had so much as a whiff of it since he was a babe.

. . . he takes it all for granted: her smiles and reassurance, her patience, forgiveness.

Jessica knew she should have laughed, as he had, and kept matters light, no matter what she'd felt. She should not have spoken of mamas and little boys they loved. Then Dain wouldn't have looked up at her as he had, and she wouldn't have seen the lonely little boy in him. She would not have grieved for that child, and Dain would not have seen the grief in her eyes.

Now he would think she felt sorry for him—or worse, that she'd deliberately lured him into betraying himself.

He was probably furious with her.

Don't, she prayed silently. *Be angry if you must, but don't turn your back and walk away.*

Dain didn't leave.

All the same, if Jessica had been a fraction less

accustomed to male irrationality, his behavior during
the next few days would have destroyed every hope
she'd cherished of building anything remotely like a
proper marriage. She would have decided he was Beelzebub in truth, and had never been a little boy at all—
let alone a heartbroken and lonely one—but had
sprung fully grown from the skull of the Prince of
Darkness, much as Athena had popped out of Zeus'
head.

But that, she soon understood, was what Dain
wanted her to believe: that he was a heartless debauchee whose primary interest in her was lascivious,
and who viewed her as an amusing toy, no more.

By Friday, he had debauched her in the window
seat of his bedroom, an alcove off the portrait gallery,
under the pianoforte in the music room, and against
the door of her sitting room—in front of his mother's
portrait, no less. And that was only the daytime de-
pravity.

At least when they were making love he was consistently passionate. Whatever he might be able to pretend when cool and rational, he could not pretend he
didn't want her—badly—or that making her equally
lust-crazed wasn't a crucial element of the business.

The rest of the time, however, he was the Dain everyone believed he was. For hours at a stretch he could be
amiable, even charming. Then, for no ascertainable
reason, he'd turn on her, trickling sarcasm over her like
acid, or patronizing her, or casually uttering a handful
of words nicely calculated to turn her mind black with
rage.

The message, in other words, was that Jessica was
permitted to desire him; she was not, however, to insult him with any softer emotions, such as affection or
compassion. She was not, in short, to try to get under

his skin or—heaven forfend!—weasel her way into his black, rotten heart.

This was not in the least fair, considering that the beast had already crept under her skin and was rapidly fastening like a pernicious parasite upon her heart. He didn't even have to work at it. She was falling in love with him—in spite of everything and against her better judgment—more slowly, yes, but just as inexorably as she'd fallen in lust with him.

That didn't mean, however, that she wasn't strongly tempted to do him a violent injury. When it came to being exasperating, Dain was a genius. By Friday, she was debating the relative merits of putting another bullet through him and trying to decide which portion of his anatomy she could most easily live without.

By Saturday, she'd decided that his brain was probably the most dispensable.

He had awakened in the wee hours, randy, and wakened her to remedy the ailment. Which, it turned out, required two treatments. Consequently, they'd overslept.

As a result of their late start for Devonport, they arrived at the wrestling match minutes after it began, and failed to get a suitable place in the crowd. And everything was Jessica's fault—because he wouldn't have become randy, Dain had complained, if she hadn't been sleeping with her hindquarters squashed against his privates.

"We're too close," he complained now, his arm protectively about her shoulders. "In another few rounds, you'll be spattered with sweat—and very possibly blood, if Sawyer doesn't stop kicking Keast in the knees."

Jessica did not remind him that he was the one who'd insisted on elbowing his way to the front.

"That's how Cann dealt with Polkinhorne," she

said. "I understood kicking was permissible in west country wrestling."

"I wish that someone in this crowd believed soap and water were permissible," he muttered, glancing about him. "I'll wager fifty quid there isn't a human being within a mile who's had a bath in the last twelve-month."

All Jessica noticed were the usual male odors of spirits, tobacco, and musk—and she had to concentrate hard to notice, because she was pressed against her husband's side, and his distinctive scent was making her toes curl. It took considerable effort to remain focused on the match, when his warm body was conjuring heated recollections of feverish lovemaking in the small hours of the morning. His big hand dangled but a few inches from her breast. She wondered whether anyone in the crowd pressing about them would notice if she shifted to close the distance.

She hated herself for wishing to close it.

"This match is pathetic," Dain grumbled. "I could bring Sawyer down with both hands tied and one leg broken. Gad, even you could do it, Jess. I cannot believe Sherburne traveled two hundred miles to witness this abysmal spectacle, when he might have stayed comfortably at home and pumped his wife. One might understand if the girl were bracket-faced or spotty—but she's well enough, if one has a taste for those China doll creatures. And if she isn't to his taste, then why in blazes did the fool marry her? It wasn't as though she had a bun in the oven—nor is she like to have, when he's never home to do the business."

The speech was typical of Dain's mood this day: All the world was in conspiracy to annoy him. Even Sherburne, because he had not . . . stayed comfortably home with his wife.

Comfortably? Jessica blinked once in astonishment. Good grief, had she actually made progress with her thickheaded husband after all?

Suppressing a smile, she looked up into his cross countenance. "My lord, you do not seem to be enjoying yourself."

"The stench is intolerable," he said, glaring past her. "And that sodding swine Ainswood is leering at you. I vow, the man is *begging* to have his sotted head separated from his shoulders."

"Ainswood?" She craned her neck, but she could not recognize any faces in the mob.

"You needn't look back at him," Dain said. "He is such an idiot, he'll take it for encouragement. Oh, lovely, now Tolliver's at it. And Vawtry, too."

"I'm sure it's you they're looking at," Jessica said mollifyingly, while her spirits soared. The brute was actually *jealous*. "They probably had wagers going as to whether you'd come, and Ainswood is not leering, but gloating, because he's won."

"Then I wish I'd stayed at home. In bed." Dain frowned down at her. "But no, my wife's existence will be rendered meaningless if she cannot see a wrestling match, and so—"

"And so you sacrificed your comfort to indulge me. Then, after all the bother, it turns out not to be a proper match at all. You are vexed because you meant this to be a treat for me, and you think it's spoiled."

His frown deepened. "Jessica, you are humoring me. I am not a child. I have a strong aversion to being humored."

"If you do not wish to be humored, then you should stop fussing about everything in the world and say plainly what the matter is." She returned her attention to the wrestlers. "I am not a mind reader."

"Fussing?" he echoed, his hand falling away from her. "*Fussing?*"

"Like a two-year-old who's missed his nap," she said.

"*A two-year-old?*"

She nodded, her eyes ostensibly upon the match, her consciousness riveted upon the outraged male beside her.

He took one—two—three furious breaths. "We're leaving," he said. "Back to the carriage. *Now.*"

Dain did not make it to the carriage. He barely made it to the outer edge of the spectators, and the carriage was a good distance beyond, thanks to their late arrival and the mass of vehicles that had preceded them. Crested coaches were jammed against lowly farm wagons, and the disgruntled beings left to mind the cattle were relieving their vexations by quarreling loudly among themselves.

Having vexations of his own to relieve, and convinced he'd explode long before he found the carriage, Dain hurried his wife to the first unoccupied area he spotted.

It was a burial ground, attached to a tiny, crumbling church in which Dain doubted any services had been conducted since the Armada. The gravestones, their inscriptions long since eroded by salt air, listed drunkenly in every direction but upright. Those, that is, making any pretense of standing. Nearly half had given up the attempt ages ago, and sprawled where they'd fallen, with the tall weeds huddled about them like pickpockets about a gin-sotted sailor.

"It's as though the place didn't exist," Jessica said, looking about her and apparently oblivious to the big, angry hand clutching her arm as he relentlessly marched her along. "As though no one has noticed or cared that it's here. How odd."

"You won't find it so odd in a moment," he said. "You'll wish you didn't exist."

"Where are we going, Dain?" she asked. "I'm sure this isn't a shortcut to the carriage."

"You'll be very lucky if it isn't a shortcut to your funeral."

"Oh, look!" she cried. "What splendid rhododendrons."

Dain did not have to follow her pointing finger. He'd already spotted the gigantic shrubs, with their masses of white, pink, and purple blooms. He'd also discerned the pillared gateway in their midst. He supposed a wall had once been attached to the gateway, either enclosing the church property or the property beyond. For all he knew, the wall might still be there, or parts of it, hidden by the thick mass of rhododendrons. All he cared about was the "hidden" part. The shrubs formed an impenetrable screen from passersby.

He marched his wife to the gateway and hauled her to the right pillar, which was better concealed, and backed her up against it.

"A two-year-old, am I, my lady?" He tore off his right glove with his teeth. "I'll teach you how old I am." He stripped off the other glove.

He reached for his trouser buttons.

Her glance shot to his hand.

He swiftly undid the three buttons of his small falls, and the flap fell open.

He heard her suck in her breath.

His rapidly swelling shaft was pushing against the fabric of his French bearer. It took him nine seconds to release the nine buttons. His rod sprang out, throbbing hotly at attention.

Jessica sank back against the pillar, her eyes closed.

He dragged up her skirts. "I've wanted you the whole curst day, drat you," he growled.

He had waited too long to bother with drawer strings or anything like finesse. He found the slit of her drawers and thrust his fingers inside and tangled them in the silky curls.

He had but to touch her—a few impatient caresses—and she was ready, pushing against his fingers, her breathing quick and shallow.

He thrust into her, and scorching joy bolted through him at the slick, hot welcome he found, and the low moan of pleasure he heard. He grasped her bottom and lifted her up.

She wrapped her legs round him and, clutching his shoulders, threw back her head and gave a throaty laugh. "I've wanted you, too, Dain. I thought I'd go mad."

"Fool," he said. Mad she was, to want such an animal.

"Your fool," she said.

"Stop it, Jess." She was nobody's fool, least of all his.

"I love you."

The words shot through him and beat upon his heart. He couldn't let them in.

He withdrew almost completely, only to drive again, harder this time.

"You can't stop me," she gasped. "I love you."

Again and again he stormed into her in hard, fierce thrusts.

But he couldn't stop her.

"I love you," she told him, repeating it at every thrust, as though she would drive the words into him, as he drove his body into hers.

"I love you," she said, even as the earth shook, and the heavens opened up and rapture blasted through him like lightning.

He covered her mouth to shut out the three fatal words, but they were spilling into his parched heart even while his seed spilled into her. He couldn't stop his heart from drinking in those words, couldn't keep it from believing them. He had tried to keep her out, just as he'd tried not to need more from her than was safe. Futile.

He never had been, never would be, safe from her. *Femme fatale.*

Still, there were worse ways to die.

And *Carpe diem*, he told himself, as he collapsed against her.

As he might have expected, Dain emerged from paradise and walked straight into a nightmare.

By the time they'd left the churchyard and begun hunting for their carriage, the ludicrous match had ended, ludicrously, in a technical dispute. The spectators were streaming out in all directions, a part of the mob heading toward the town proper and another part away toward the mass of vehicles.

A short distance from the carriage, Vawtry hailed him.

"I'll wait in the carriage," Jessica said, slipping her hand from Dain's arm. "I cannot possibly be expected to conduct a rational conversation at present."

Though he doubted he could, either, Dain managed a knowing chuckle. Letting her go on to the vehicle, he joined Vawtry.

They were soon joined by several others, Ainswood included, and in a moment Dain was caught up in the general indignation about the grievously disappointing wrestlers.

Vawtry was in the midst of reviewing the disputed throw when Dain noticed that Ainswood was not attending at all, but staring past him.

Sure the man was gawking at Jessica again, Dain bent a warning frown upon him.

Ainswood didn't notice. Turning back, grinning, to Dain, he said, "Looks like your footman's got himself a bit more than a handful."

Dain followed the duke's amused glance. Jessica was in the carriage, out of reach of His Grace's leering gaze.

Meanwhile, though, Joseph—who, as first footman, danced attendance upon Lady Dain—was struggling with a ragged, filthy urchin. A pickpocket, by the looks of it. Sporting events attracted them, like the whores, in droves.

Joseph managed to get the ragamuffin by the collar, but the brat twisted about and kicked him. Joseph bellowed. The guttersnipe answered with a stream of profanity that would have done a marine credit.

At that moment, the carriage door opened, and Jessica started out. "Joseph! What in blazes are you about?"

Though well aware she could handle the contretemps—whatever it was—Dain was also aware that he was supposed to be the authority figure . . . and his friends were watching.

He hurried over to intercept her.

A bloodcurdling scream came from behind him.

It startled Joseph, loosening his grasp. The ragamuffin broke free, and was off like a shot.

But Dain charged at the same moment and, catching the shoulder of his filthy jacket, hauled the brat to a stop. "See here, you little—"

Then he broke off, because the boy had looked up,

and Dain was looking down . . . into sullen black eyes, narrowed above a monstrous beak of a nose, in a dark, scowling face.

Dain's hand jerked away.

The boy didn't move. The sullen eyes widened and the scowling mouth fell open.

"Yes, lovey," came a strident female voice at the edges of the waking nightmare. "That's your pa, just like I said. Just like you. Aren't you, my lord? And isn't he just like you?"

Hideously like. As though the space between them were not air, but five and twenty years, and the face below his own, looking back from some devil's mirror.

And it was the voice of Satan's own whore he'd heard, Dain knew, even before he met Charity Graves' malevolent gaze—just as, when he saw that malevolence, he knew she'd done this on purpose, as she'd done everything, including bringing this monstrous child into the world.

He opened his mouth to laugh, because he must, because it was the only way.

Then he remembered they were not alone upon a nightmare island in Hell, but upon a public stage, enacting this ghastly farce before an audience.

And one of the spectators was his wife.

Though a lifetime seemed to have passed, it was but a moment, and Dain was already moving, instinctively, to block Jessica's view of the boy. But the brat had also come out of his daze and, in the same instant, darted away into the crowd.

"Dominick!" his accursed mother screamed. "Come back, lovey."

Dain's gaze shot to his wife, who stood about twenty feet away, looking from the woman to him—then beyond, to the mob into which the boy had disappeared.

Dain started toward her, sending a glance in Ainswood's direction.

Drunk he may be, as usual, but the duke got the message. "By gad, is that you, Charity, my flower?" he called.

Charity was hurrying toward the carriage—toward Jessica—but Ainswood had moved quickly. He caught the bitch by the arm and firmly drew her back. "By heaven, it *is* you," he loudly announced. "And here I thought you were still locked up in the asylum."

"Let me go!" she screeched. "I got something to say to Her Ladyship."

But Dain had reached his wife's side by this time. "Into the carriage," he told Jessica.

Her eyes were very wide, very grave. She threw a look toward Charity, whom Ainswood was hustling away, with the assistance of several comrades who'd also grasped the situation.

"She isn't right in the head," said Dain. "It's not important. Into the carriage, my dear."

Jessica sat rigidly in the carriage, her hands tightly folded in her lap. She remained so, her mouth compressed in a taut line, while the vehicle lurched into motion, and she did not utter a syllable or change her frigid posture thereafter.

After twenty minutes of riding with a marble statue, Dain could bear it no longer. "I beg your pardon," he said stiffly. "I promised you would not be embarrassed in public, I know. But I didn't do it on purpose. I should think that was obvious."

"I know very well you didn't sire the child on purpose," she said icily. "That is rarely the first thing a male thinks of when he's tumbling a trollop."

So much for hoping she hadn't been able to see the boy's face.

He might have known. Her keen eyes missed nothing. If she could discern a priceless icon under inches of mold and dirt, she could easily spot a bastard at twenty paces.

She had seen, beyond a doubt. Jessica would not have judged the matter on a tart's words alone. If she hadn't seen, she would have given Dain a chance to defend himself. And he would have denied Charity's accusation.

But now there would be no denying the blackamoor skin and the monstrous nose—visible, easily identifiable for miles. No hope of denying, when Jessica had observed as well that the mother was fair, green-eyed and auburn-haired.

"And it is no good trying to pretend you didn't know the child was yours," Jessica went on. "Your friend Ainswood knew, and he moved quickly enough to get the woman out of the way—as though I were a half-wit, and could not see what was before me. 'Asylum,' indeed. It's the lot of you who belong in Bedlam. Running about like overwrought hens—and meanwhile the boy gets away. You had him." She turned to him, her eyes flashing angry reproach. "But you let him go. How could you, Dain? I could not believe my eyes. Where the devil were your wits?"

He stared at her.

She turned back to the window. "Now we've lost him, and heaven only knows how long it will take to find him again. I could just scream. If I had not gone with you to the churchyard, I might have been able to catch him. But I could scarcely walk, let alone run— and I must not contradict you in public, so I could hardly shout, 'After him, idiot!' in front of your friends—even if it had not been too late, anyhow. I cannot recollect when I've seen a little boy take off so fast. One moment he was there. The next, he'd vanished."

His heart was a fist, beating mercilessly against his ribs.

Find him. Catch him.

She wanted him to go after the hideous thing he'd made with that greedy, vengeful slut. She wanted him to look at it and touch it and . . .

"No!" The word exploded from him, a roar of denial, and with it, Dain's mind turned black and cold.

The small, dark face he'd looked into had turned his insides into a seething pit of emotion it had wanted every iota of his will to contain. His wife's words had sent the lava spilling through the crevices.

But the frigid darkness had come, as it always did, to preserve him, and it smothered feeling, as it always did.

"No," he repeated quietly, his voice cold and controlled. "There will be no finding. She had no business having him in the first place. Charity Graves knew well enough how to get rid of such 'inconveniences.' She'd done it countless times before I happened along and countless times thereafter, I don't doubt."

His wife was staring at him now, her face pale and shocked, just as she'd looked when he told her about his mother.

"But wealthy aristocrats don't come Charity's way very often," he went on, telling this tale in the same coldly brutal way he'd related his mother's. "And when she found she was breeding, she knew the brat was either mine or Ainswood's. Either way, she imagined she had a ripe pigeon to pluck. When the brat turned out to be mine, she didn't waste a minute finding out the name of my solicitor. She wrote to him promptly enough, proposing an allowance of five hundred a year."

"Five hundred?" Jessica's color returned. "To a professional? And not even your mistress, either, but a common trollop you shared with your friend?" she added indignantly. "And one who had the babe on purpose—not a respectable girl got in the family way—"

"*Respectable?* Did you imagine, even for an instant, Jess, that I—gad, what? I seduced—*lured* an innocent— and left her breeding?"

His voice had begun to rise. Clenching his fist, he added levelly, "You know very well I had managed to avoid entanglements with respectable females until you exploded into my life."

"Certainly I never imagined you would go to the bother of seducing an innocent," she said crisply. "It simply hadn't occurred to me that a trollop might have a babe through pure greed. Even now I have difficulty imagining a woman being so wrongheaded. Five hundred pounds." She shook her head. "I doubt even the Royal Dukes support their by-blows in such luxury. No wonder you are so outraged. And no wonder, either, there is so much ill feeling between you and the boy's mother. I had a suspicion she went out of her way to embarrass you. She must have heard—or seen—that you had your wife with you."

"If she tries it again," he said grimly, "I'll have her and the guttersnipe she spawned transported. If she comes within twenty miles of you—"

"Dain, the woman is one matter," she said. "The child is another. He did not ask to have her for a mother, any more than he asked to be born. She was exceedingly unkind to use him as she did today. No child

should be subjected to such a scene. Still, I strongly
doubt she considers anybody's feelings but her own. I
noticed that she was far better dressed than her so-
called 'lovey.' Dirt is one thing—little boys cannot remain clean above two and a half minutes—but there is
no excuse for the child to wear rags, when his mother
is garbed like a London high-flyer."

She looked up at him. "How much do you give her,
by the way?"

"Fifty," he said tightly. "More than enough to feed
and clothe him—and let her spend all she makes on
her back on herself. But I daresay the rags were all part
of her game: to make me appear the villain of the
piece. Too bad I'm accustomed to the role, and that
what other fools think does not concern me in the
least."

"Fifty a year is more than generous. How old is he?"
Jessica demanded. "Six, seven?"

"Eight, but it makes no—"

"Old enough to notice his appearance," she said. "I
cannot excuse his mother for dressing him so shabbily.
She has the money, and ought to know how a boy of
that age would feel. Mortified, I don't doubt—which is
why he annoyed Joseph. But she does not consider the
child, as I said, and all you have told me only convinces
me she is an unfit mother. I must ask you, Dain, to set
aside your feelings toward her, and consider your son.
He is yours by law. You can take him away from her."

"No." He had smothered feeling, but his head had
begun to pound, and his useless arm was throbbing.
He could not freeze and smother physical pain. He
could scarcely think past it. Even if he could have rea-
soned coolly, there was no explanation he could give
for his behavior that would satisfy her.

He shouldn't have tried to explain, he told himself.

He could never make her understand. Above all, he didn't want her to comprehend, any more than he wanted to himself, what he'd felt when he'd looked down into that face, into the devil's mirror.

"No," he repeated. "And stop fussing about it, Jess. None of this would have happened if you hadn't insisted on coming to the bedamned wrestling match. By gad, I cannot seem to stir a foot when you are by without"—he gestured wearily—"without things going off in my face. No wonder I have a headache. If it isn't one thing, it's another. *Women.* Everywhere. Wives and Madonnas and mothers and whores and—and you're plaguing me to death, the lot of you."

By this time, Roland Vawtry had relieved Ainswood and the others of responsibility for Charity Graves and was marching her into the inn where she claimed to be staying.

She was not supposed to be staying at an inn in Devonport. She was supposed to be where he'd left her two days earlier, in Ashburton, where she'd said nothing about Dain or Dain's bastard. There, all she had done was sashay into the public room and settle at a table nearby with a fellow who seemed to know her. After a while, the fellow had left, and Vawtry's comrades having departed for assignations of their own, he had found himself sharing the table with her and buying her a tankard of ale. After which they had adjourned for a few rollicking hours of what Beaumont had claimed Vawtry badly needed.

Beaumont had been right on that count, as he seemed to be on so many others.

But Beaumont didn't have to be here now to point out that what Charity Graves badly needed was to be beaten within an inch of her life.

The inn, fortunately, was not a respectable one, and no one made a murmur when Vawtry stomped up after her to her room. As soon as he'd shut the door, he grabbed her shoulders and shook her.

"You lying, sneaking, troublemaking little strumpet!" he burst out. Then he broke away, fearing he *would* kill her, and certain that he did not badly need to be hanged for murdering a tart.

"Oh, my," she said with a laugh. "I fear you're not happy to see me, Rolly, my love."

"Don't call me that—and I'm not your love, you stupid cow. You're going to get me killed. If Dain finds out I was with you in Ashburton, he's sure to think I put you up to that scene."

He flung himself into a chair. "Then he'll take me apart, piece by piece. And ask questions later." He raked his fingers through his hair. "And it's no use hoping he won't find out, because nothing ever goes right when it comes to him. I vow, it must be a curse. Twenty thousand pounds—slipped through my hands—I didn't even know it was there—and now *this*. Because I didn't know you were there—here—either. And the brat—his bastard. Who knew he had one? But now everyone does—thanks to you—including *her*—and if he doesn't kill me, the bitch will shoot me."

Charity approached. "Did you say 'twenty thousand,' lovey?" She sat on his lap and drew his arm around her and pressed his hand against her ample breast.

"Leave me alone," he grumbled. "I'm not in the mood."

Roland Vawtry's mood was one of black despair.

He was mired in debt, with no way of getting out, ever, because he was Dame Fortune's dependent, and she was capricious, as Beaumont had so wisely warned. She gave a priceless icon to a man who already had more than he could spend in three lifetimes. She took away from a man who had next to nothing, and left him with less than nothing. She could not even give him a tart without making that female the author of his demise.

Mr. Vawtry truly believed himself to be at the last stages of desperation. The modest stock of common sense and self-confidence he'd once possessed had been ruthlessly vandalized in a matter of days by a man whose primary delight in life was making other people miserable.

Vawtry was incapable of recognizing that his situation wasn't half so catastrophic as it appeared, any more than he recognized Francis Beaumont as the insidious agent destroying his peace of mind.

His mind poisoned, Vawtry believed that his friendship with Dain was the source of his troubles. "'He must have a long spoon that must eat with the devil,'" Beaumont had quoted, and Roland Vawtry had promptly realized that his spoon had been too short for dining with the likes of Dain, and that his own case was the same as Bertie Trent's. Association with Beelzebub had ruined them both.

Now, Vawtry was not only ruined, but—thanks to Charity—in imminent danger of a violent death. He needed to think—or better yet, run for his life. He knew he couldn't do either of those things properly while his lap was filled with a buxom trollop.

All the same, angry as he was with her, he felt disinclined to push her off. Her luxurious bosom was warm and soft, and she was stroking his hair back, just as though he had not nearly killed her minutes earlier. A woman's touch—even that of a brazen whore—was very comforting.

Under the comforting touch, Vawtry's mind softened

toward her. After all, Dain had done Charity an ill turn as well. At least she'd had the courage to confront him.

Besides, she was pretty—very pretty—and exceedingly jolly company in bed. Vawtry squeezed her breast and kissed her.

"There now, you see how naughty you've been," she said. "As though I wouldn't look after you. Silly boy." She ruffled his hair. "He won't think anything like what you say. All I have to do is tell people how Mr. Vawtry paid me . . ." She considered. "Paid me twenty pounds to keep out of the way and not bother his very dear friend, Lord Dain. I'll tell 'em how you said I wasn't to spoil the honeymoon."

How clever she was. Vawtry buried his face in her plump, pretty bosom.

"But I come—came—anyhow, because I'm a wicked, lying whore," she continued. "And you was—were—that vexed with me, you beat me." She kissed the top of his head. "That's what I'll say."

"I wish I had twenty pounds," he mumbled to her bodice. "I'd give it to you. I would. Oh, Charity, what am I to do?"

She, possessing an innate skill for her profession, showed him what to do, and he, having a knack for misconstruing the obvious, interpreted professional skill as feeling for him. Before many hours had passed, he'd confided all his troubles to her, and for hours after, while he lay asleep in her arms, Charity Graves lay awake planning how to make all her dreams come true.

Sixteen

Half an hour after he'd stormed into his bedroom and slammed the door, Dain stood upon the threshold of Jessica's dressing room. He bent a frigid stare upon Bridget, who was taking the pins from Jessica's hair. "Get out," he said very quietly.

Bridget fled.

Jessica stayed were she was, upon the chair at her dressing table. Spine stiff, she lifted her hands and continued removing the pins. "I am not going to quarrel with you about this any longer," she said. "It's a waste of time. You refuse to listen to a word I say."

"There's nothing to listen to," he ground out. "It's none of your bloody business."

That was how he'd responded during the drive home to her efforts to make him understand the problem . . . because one short scene with a female from his past had cancelled all the progress Jessica had made with him. They were back to where they'd been when she'd shot him.

"*You* are my business," she said. "Let me put it to you simply." She turned in her seat and met his gaze squarely. "You made the mess, Dain. You clean it up."

He blinked once. Then his mouth curled into the horrid smile. "You are telling me it is my duty. May I remind you, madam, that you—that *no one*—tells me—"

"That boy is in trouble," she said. "His mother will be the ruin of him. I have explained this to you every way I could, but you refuse to listen. You refuse to trust my instincts about this, of all matters, when you know I have brought up, virtually single-handed, ten boys. Which includes having to deal with dozens of their beastly friends as well. If there is one thing I understand, my lord, it is boys—good ones, horrid ones, and all the species in between."

"What you can't seem to understand is that I am not a little boy, to be ordered about and told my curst duty!"

She was wasting her breath. She turned back to the mirror, and took out the last of the pins.

"I am tired of this," she said. "I am tired of your mistrust. I am tired of being accused of manipulating and patronizing and . . . bothering. I am tired of trying to deal with a consistently unreasonable man as though he were a reasonable one. I am tired of having every effort to reach you thrown back at me with insult."

She took up her brush and began drawing it through her hair with slow, steady strokes. "You don't want anything I have to offer, except physical pleasure. Everything else is a vexation. Very well, then. I shall cease vexing you. There will be no more attempts at that laughable thing, a rational adult discussion."

He gave a short, bitter laugh. "Certainly not. There will be the icy silence instead. Or the reproachful silence. Or the sulking. The same pleasant manner, in short, to which you treated me the last ten miles to Athcourt."

"If I was disagreeable, I beg your pardon," she said composedly. "I shall not behave so again in future."

He came up to the dressing table and set his right hand down upon it. "Look at me," he said, "and tell me what that's supposed to mean."

She looked up into his rigidly set countenance. Emotion churned in the depths of his eyes, and her heart ached for him, more than ever. He wanted her love. She'd given it. Today she'd declared it, in no uncertain terms, and he had believed her. She had seen that in his eyes as well. He had let the love in and—though he hadn't been sure what to do with it, and probably wouldn't be sure for months, years maybe—he hadn't tried to thrust it away.

Until Charity Graves made her spiteful entrance.

Jessica was not about to spend more weeks working on him, only to have her efforts flung in her face the next time someone or something set him off. He would have to stop viewing the present—and her especially—through the warped spectacles of the past. He would have to learn who his wife was and deal with that woman, not the general species, Female, he viewed with such bitter contempt. He would have to learn it all the hard way, because she had a more urgent problem to spend her energy upon at present.

Dain was a grown man, ostensibly able to look after himself and presumably capable of sorting matters out rationally . . . eventually.

His son's situation, however, was far more perilous, for little boys were entirely at the mercy of others. Someone must act on Dominick's behalf. It was all too clear that the someone must be Jessica. As usual.

"What it means is that you win," she said. "It goes

your way from now on, my lord. You want blind obedience. That is what you'll get."

He treated her to another mocking laugh. "I'll believe that when I see it," he said. Then he stalked out.

It took Dain a week to believe it, though he saw it and heard it every day and every night.

His wife agreed with everything he said, regardless how imbecilic. She would dispute nothing, regardless how much he goaded her. She was perfectly amiable, regardless how obnoxious he was.

If Dain had been in the least superstitious, he might have believed that another woman's soul had entered Jessica's beautiful body.

A week with this amiable, blindly obedient stranger left him acutely uncomfortable. After two weeks, he was wretched.

Yet he had nothing to complain about. Nothing, that is, that his pride would let him complain about.

He could not say she was plaguing him to death when she never so much as hinted at disagreement or displeasure.

He could not say she was cold and unresponsive in bed, when she behaved as willingly and lustily as she had from the start.

He could not complain that she was unkind, when any hundred outside observers would have unanimously agreed that her behavior was nothing short of angelic.

Only he—and she—knew he was being punished, and why.

It was all because of the unspeakable thing he'd made with Charity Graves.

It did not matter to Jessica that the thing was as foul inwardly as it was hideous outwardly, that there was not a scrap of good it could have inherited from its depraved monster of a sire and its vicious whore of a mother. It would not have mattered to Jessica if the thing had two heads and maggots crawling out of its ears—which, in Dain's view, would make it no more repellent than it already was. It might have crawled on its belly and been covered with green slime and it would be all the same to Jessica: Dain had made it; therefore, Dain must take care of it.

It was the same way she'd viewed her brother's case. It didn't matter that Bertie was a thorough nincompoop. Dain had lured the fool in over his head; ergo, Dain must fish the fool out.

It was the same way she'd viewed her own case: Dain had ruined her; Dain must repair the damage.

And once again, just as in Paris, Jessica had devised his punishment with diabolical precision. This time, everything he'd insisted he didn't want, she didn't give. There was no plaguing, pestering, or disobedience. There was no uncomfortable sentiment, no pity . . . and no love—for never once, after hammering the words into his brain and heart in the burial ground in Devonport, did Jessica again say, "I love you."

To his everlasting shame, he tried to make her say it. During lovemaking, Dain tried everything he could think of to make the words come. But no matter how tender he was, or passionately creative, no matter how much aching Italian lyricism he poured into her ears, she wouldn't say them. She sighed, she moaned, she groaned. She cried out his name, and the Almighty's, and even, at times, the Fallen One's . . . but never the three sweet words his heart hungered for.

After three weeks, he was desperate. He would have settled for anything vaguely like affection: one "block-head" or "clodpole"—a priceless vase hurled at his head—his shirts in shreds—a row, please God, just one.

The trouble was, he dared not goad her too far. If he rose to the truly heinous heights of which he was capable, he might provoke the row he craved; he might also drive her away. For good. He couldn't risk it.

As it was, Dain knew her patience wouldn't hold out indefinitely. Being the world's most perfect wife to the world's most impossible husband was a Herculean task. Even she could not keep at it forever. And when her patience snapped, she would leave. For good.

After a month, panic set in, as Dain perceived the first signs of strain in her flawless, angelically patient and amiable countenance. His own features bleakly composed, he sat at the breakfast table on a Sunday morning in mid-June, covertly noting the fine taut lines that had appeared in her forehead and at the corners of her eyes. Her posture was taut as well, as stiff as the dutiful smile she wore during the gruesomely cheerful conversation about nothing in particular, and most certainly, about nothing that mattered to either of them.

I'm losing her, he thought, and his hand came up, instinctively, to reach for her and draw her back. But he reached for the coffeepot instead. He filled his cup and stared helplessly at the dark liquid and saw his black future there, because it was not in him to give her what she wanted.

He could not accept the monstrosity she called his *son*.

Dain knew his behavior was irrational in her eyes. Even to himself he could not explain it, though he'd been trying all this last hellish week. But he couldn't reason past the revulsion. Even now, panicked and heartsick, he could not reason past the bile rising inside, instantly, at the image in his mind's eye: the dark, sullen face with its hideous beak . . . the malformed, freakish little body. It was all he could do to remain quietly in his chair, pretending to be a civilized adult, while inwardly the monster raged and howled, craving destruction.

"I had better make haste," Jessica said, rising. "Otherwise I shall be late for church."

He rose, too, the polite husband, and escorted her downstairs, and watched while Bridget helped Her Ladyship into shawl and bonnet.

He made the same joke he'd made every previous Sunday, about Lady Dain's setting a good example for the community and Lord Dain's considerateness in keeping away, so that the church roof didn't collapse upon the pious souls of Athton.

And when Her Ladyship's carriage set off, he stood as he had the four previous Sundays, at the top of the drive, watching until it had disappeared from view.

But this Sabbath, when he returned to the house, he did not go to his study as usual. This day, he entered Athcourt's small chapel and sat on the hard bench where he'd shivered countless Sundays in his childhood while trying desperately to keep his mind on heavenly things and not upon the hunger gnawing at his belly.

This time, he felt as lost and helpless as that little boy had been, trying to understand why his Heavenly Father had made him wrong inside and out and wondering what prayer must be prayed, what penance must be paid, to make him right.

And this time, the grown man asked, with the same despair a little boy had asked, decades ago: *Why will You not help me?*

While Lord Dain was struggling with his inner demons, his wife was preparing to snare one of flesh-and-blood.

And, while Jessica had faith enough in Providence, she preferred to seek help from more accessible sources. Her assistant was Phelps, the coachman.

He was one of the very few staff members who'd been at Athcourt since the time of the previous marquess. Then, Phelps had been a lowly groom. That he'd been retained and promoted was proof of Dain's regard for his abilities. That he was called "Phelps," rather than the standard "John Coachman," evidenced high regard for the man personally.

The regard was returned.

This did not mean that Phelps considered His Lordship infallible. What it meant, Jessica had learned, shortly after the contretemps at Devonport, was that Phelps understood the difference between doing what the master ordered and doing what was good for him.

The alliance between Jessica and the coachman had begun on the first Sunday she'd attended church in Athton. After she'd alit from the carriage, Phelps had asked permission to do his own kind of "meditatin'," as he put it, at the Whistling Ghost public house.

"Certainly," Jessica replied, adding with a rueful smile, "I only wish I could go with you."

"Ess, I reckon," he said in his broad Devon drawl. "That muddle yesterday with that fool woman'll be all over Dartymoor by now. But Your Ladyship don't mind a bit of gawkin' 'n tongue waggin', do you? Shot him, you did." His leathery faced creased into a smile. "Well, then. You be teachin' the rest of 'em, too, what you be made of."

A few days later, when he drove her to the vicarage for tea, Phelps further clarified his position by sharing with Jessica what he'd heard at the Whistling Ghost about Charity Graves and the boy, Dominick, along with what he himself knew about the matter.

Thus, by this fifth Sunday, Jessica had a good idea of the kind of woman Charity Graves was, and more than ample confirmation that Dominick needed rescuing.

According to Phelps, the boy had been left in the care of the elderly Annie Geach, a midwife, while Charity wandered Dartmoor like a gypsy. Annie had died about a month before Dain had returned to England. Since then, Charity had been hovering in the Athton vicinity. Though she was rarely seen in the village itself, her son, left mostly on his own, was encountered all too often, and too often making trouble.

About a month and a half ago, a few well-meaning folks had attempted to settle him in school. Dominick refused to settle, wreaking havoc and mayhem during the three times he'd attended. He picked fights with the other children and played nasty tricks on master and pupils alike. He couldn't be schooled into good behavior because he answered with laughter, taunts, and obscenities. He couldn't be whipped into obedience either, because one had to catch him first, and he was diabolically quick.

In the last few weeks, his behavior had grown increasingly flagrant, the incidents more numerous. During one week, Dominick had, on Monday, torn Mrs. Knapp's laundry from the line and trampled it in the mud; on Wednesday he'd dropped a dead mouse into Missy Lobb's market basket; on Friday he'd thrown horse droppings at Mr. Pomeroy's freshly painted stable doors.

Most recently, Dominick had blackened the eyes of two youths, bloodied the nose of another, urinated on the front steps of the bakehouse, and exposed his bottom to the minister's housemaid.

Thus far, the villagers had kept their complaints to themselves. Even if they had been able to catch

Dominick, they were baffled what to do with the lord
of the manor's fiendish son. No one yet had mustered
the courage to confront Dain with his offspring's crimes.
No one yet could overcome codes of decency and deli-
cacy to complain of Dain's bastard to his wife. No one,
moreover, could find Charity Graves and make *her* do
something about her Demon Seed.

It was this last that troubled Jessica most. Charity
had not been seen in the last fortnight, during which
time Dominick's bids for attention—as she viewed his
atrocities—had grown increasingly desperate.

Jessica was sure it was his father's attention he sought.
Since Dain was inaccessible, the only way to get it was to
throw the village into an uproar. Jessica also suspected
the mother had instigated or encouraged the disturbances in some way. Still, the method seemed stupidly
risky. Dain was far more likely to carry out his threat
of having Charity transported than to pay her to go
away, if that was what she wanted.

The alternative explanation, even more disturbing,
made less sense. Charity may have simply abandoned
the child, and for all one knew, he'd been sleeping in
stables or out on the moors, in the shelter of the rocks.
Yet Jessica couldn't believe the woman had simply left,
empty-handed. She could not have snared a rich lover,
else all Dartmoor would know about it. Discretion was
not at all in Charity's style, according to Phelps.

In either case, Jessica had decided last night, the boy
could not be permitted to run amok any longer.

The patience of Athton's inhabitants was being
stretched to its limits. One day, very soon, a mob of
outraged villagers would be pounding at Athcourt's
doors. Jessica had no more intention of waiting for
that event than she did for a possibly abandoned child
to die of exposure or starvation or be sucked down

into one of Dartmoor's treacherous mires. She could not wait any longer for Dain to come to his senses.

Accordingly, she had come down to breakfast wearing the same tautly haggard expression Aunt Claire wore when suffering one of her deadly headaches. All of the servants had noticed, and Bridget had asked twice en route to church whether Her Ladyship was feeling poorly. "A headache, that's all," Jessica had answered. "It won't last, I'm sure."

After disembarking, Jessica dawdled until Joseph departed, as he usually did, for the bake-house, where his younger brother was employed, and the other servants were either in church or on their way to their own Sunday morning diversions. That left only one unwanted guardian, Bridget.

"I believe I had better excuse myself from services," Jessica said, rubbing her right temple. "Exercise always clears a headache, I find. What I need is a good, long walk. An hour or so ought to do it."

Bridget was a London-trained servant. Her idea of a good, long walk was the distance from the front door to the carriage. It was easy enough for her to calculate that "an hour or so," at her mistress's usual pace, meant three to five *miles*. Thus, when Phelps "volunteered" to accompany the mistress in Bridget's place, the maid agreed with no more than a token protest, and hurried into the church before Phelps could change his mind.

When Bridget was out of sight, Jessica turned to Phelps. "What did you hear last night?" she asked.

"Friday arternoon he let Tom Hamby's rabbits loose. Tom chased him up to the far south wall of His Lordship's park. Yester' arternoon, the lad raided Jem Furse's rag and bone bins, and Jem chased him up to nigh the same place."

Phelps' gaze shifted northward, in the direction of

the park. "The boy goes where they daren't chase him, right into His Lordship's private property."

The boy was seeking his father's protection, in other words, Jessica thought.

"There be one of 'em little summerhouse things not far from the place where they lose him," the coachman went on. "His Lordship's grampa built it for the ladies. I 'spect a lad might get in easy 'nough, if he made up his mind on it."

"If the summerhouse is his lair, then we'd better make haste," said Jessica. "It's nearly two miles from here."

"That be by way of the main road 'n the estate road," he said. "But I knows a shorter way, if you don't mind a steepish climb."

A quarter of an hour later, Jessica stood on the edge of a clearing, gazing at the fanciful summerhouse the second marquess had built for his wife. It was an octagonal stone structure, painted white, with a steep conical red roof nearly as tall as the house itself. Round windows with elaborately carved frames adorned every other side of the octagon. The unwindowed sides held medallions of similar size and shape, carved with what appeared to be medieval knights and ladies. Climbing roses, planted at alternating corners of the octagon, artfully framed windows and medallions. Tall yew hedges bordered the winding gravel path to the door.

Aesthetically speaking, it was rather a hodgepodge, yet it had a certain sweet charm. Certainly Jessica could see how this fanciful place would appeal to a child.

She waited while Phelps completed his slow circuit of the building, peeping cautiously through the windows. When he was done, he shook his head.

Jessica swallowed an oath. It had been too much to

hope that the boy would actually be here, even though it was Sunday morning, and he usually limited his assaults upon the village to weekday afternoons. She was about to leave her hiding place to consult with Phelps when she heard a twig snap and the faint thudding of hurried footsteps. She waved Phelps back and he promptly ducked down behind the hedge.

In the next instant, the boy darted into the clearing. Without pausing once or looking about him, he raced up the path to the door. Just before he reached it, Phelps leapt up from his hiding place and caught him by the sleeve.

The child drove his elbow into Phelps' privates, and Phelps, doubling over, let go with a choked oath.

Dominick tore back down the path and bolted across the clearing toward the trees at the back of the summerhouse. But Jessica had seen immediately where he'd go, and she was already running in that direction. She chased him down a bridle path, over a bridge, and down the winding narrow pathway beside the stream.

If he had not been running all the way up the steep hill to the summerhouse, she wouldn't have had a prayer of catching him now, but he was winded and down to a vaguely human pace rather than his usual demonic one. At a fork in the pathway, he hesitated briefly—it was unfamiliar ground, evidently—and in the few seconds he did, Jessica pushed herself a notch faster. Then she leapt and tackled him.

He went down—into the grass, fortunately—and she on top of him. Before he could think of trying to wriggle free, she grabbed his hair and gave a sharp yank. He let out a howl of outrage.

"Girls don't fight fair," she gasped. "Be still or I'll snatch you bald."

He treated her to a breathless stream of obscenities.

"I've heard all those words before," she said between gulps of air. "I know worse ones, too."

There was a short silence while he digested this unexpected reaction. Then, "Get off me!" he burst out. "Get *off* me, you cow!"

"That is the wrong way to say it," she said. "The polite way is 'Please get off me, my lady.'"

"Bugger you," he said.

"Oh, dear," she said. "I fear I shall have to take desperate measures."

Releasing his hair, she planted a loud, smacking kiss on the back of his head.

He gave a shocked gasp.

She dropped another noisy kiss on the back of his grimy neck. He tensed. She kissed his dirty cheek.

He let out the breath he'd been holding in a stream of obscenities, and furiously squirmed out from under her. Before he could scramble away, though, she caught the shoulder of his ragged jacket and quickly came to her feet, hauling him up with her.

His shabby boot shot out at her shins, but she dodged, still holding fast.

"Quiet down," she said in her best Obedience or Death tones, giving him a shake for good measure. "Try kicking me again and I shall kick back—and I won't miss, either."

"Piss on you!" he cried. He made a violent effort to wrench away, but Jessica had a firm grip, not to mention plenty of practice with squirming children.

"Let me go, you stupid sow!" he shrieked. "Let me go! Let me *go!*" He was pulling and twisting frantically. But she grasped one scrawny arm and managed to draw him back firmly against her and wrap her arms about him.

The squirming stopped, but the outraged howls did not.

It occurred to Jessica that he was truly alarmed, yet she could not believe he was afraid of her.

His cries were growing more desperate when the answer appeared.

Phelps came round a turn in the bridle path with a woman in tow. The child broke off midscream and froze.

The woman was Charity Graves.

It was the boy's mother who had been chasing him this time and, unlike the hapless Athcourt villagers, she had a very good idea what to do with him. For starters, she would beat him within an inch of his life, she announced.

He'd run away a fortnight ago, and Charity claimed she'd been looking for him everywhere. Finally, she'd ventured to Athton—though she knew it was as much as her life was worth to come within ten miles of His Lordship, she said. She'd come as far as the Whistling Ghost when Tom Hamby and Jem Furse came running out, leading a dozen other angry men, who quickly surrounded her.

"And they give—gave—me an earful," Charity said, bending a threatening look upon her son.

Jessica no longer had him by the collar. At his mother's appearance, the boy had grabbed her hand. He was gripping it hard now. Except for the fierce pressure of that little hand, he was immobile, his body rigid, his dark eyes riveted upon his mother.

"Everyone in Dartmoor knows what he's been up to," Jessica said. "You cannot expect me to believe you heard nothing. Where were you, in Constantinople?"

"I'm a working woman," said Charity, tossing her head. "I can't be watching him every second, and I got no nanny to do it for me, neither. I sent him to school, didn't I? But Schoolmaster couldn't make him mind, could he? And how am I to do it, I ask you, when the boy bolts on me and I don't know where he's keeping himself?"

Jessica doubted that Charity cared where the boy was keeping himself, until she'd heard his refuge was Athcourt's park. If His Lordship found out the "guttersnipe" was hiding out in the second marquess's ornate, immaculately maintained summerhouse, there would be hell to pay, and Charity knew it.

Even now, she was not so boldly defiant as she pretended. Her green glance skittered away from time to time to take in their leafy surroundings, as though she expected Dain to explode through the trees at any moment.

Uneasy she was, yet she did not seem in any great hurry to be gone, either. Though Jessica could not guess what exactly was going through the woman's mind, it was clear enough that she was sizing up the Marchioness of Dain and adjusting her approach accordingly. Having quickly perceived that the threats of dire punishment for Dominick were not meeting with approval, she had promptly shifted to blaming her difficult circumstances.

Even while Jessica was noting these matters, Charity was making further adjustments.

"I know what you're thinking," the woman said, her tones softening. "That I don't look after him proper and a child don't—doesn't—run away unless he's wretched. But it weren't—wasn't—me made him so, but the stuck-up brats at school. They told him what his mama's trade was—as though their own papas and brothers didn't come knocking at my door, and mamas and sisters, too, to get their 'mistakes' fixed. And them precious little prigs made it out like I was nothing but filth. And they called him names, too. Didn't they, lovey?" she said with a pitying glance at Dominick.

"Do you wonder, then, he was vexed and made trouble?" she went on, when the boy didn't respond. "And it's just what they deserve, for picking on a poor tyke and giving him nightmares. But now he don't like his own mama no more, either, and won't stay. And look where the fool child comes, my lady. And won't his pa have my head for it?—as though I done—did—it on purpose. He'll have me taken up, he will, and sent to the workhouse. And he'll cut off the boy's keeping money, and then what's to become of us, I ask you?"

Phelps was gazing at Charity in patent disgust. He opened his mouth to say something, but caught Jessica's warning glance. He relieved his feelings by rolling his eyes heavenward.

"You've spent a good deal of breath telling me nothing I hadn't figured out for myself," Jessica said crisply. "What you have not told me is what you proposed to gain by coming to Athton in the first place, when you understood His Lordship's sentiments, or why, in the second place, you have lingered in the vicinity, when you were aware of Dominick's distress and the means he chose of expressing it. There must be something you want very badly, to take such risks."

Charity's hunted expression instantly vanished. Her countenance hardening, she gave Jessica an insolent head-to-toe survey.

"Well, then, Dain didn't marry no feather-wit, did

he?" Charity said with a smile. "Maybe I did have plans, my lady, and maybe the lad spoilt 'em. But maybe there's no harm done, either, and we can fix it, you and me."

A few minutes later, Dominick having been persuaded to release his death grip on Jessica's hand, the group was slowly making its way back toward the main road. Phelps had drawn the boy a discreet distance ahead of the two women, so that the latter could negotiate in private.

"I'm no feather-wit, either," Charity said, with a furtive glance about her. "I can see easy enough that you want the little devil. But Dain don't want him, else he'd 've come and took—taken—him by now, wouldn't he? And you know you can't just up and steal my boy from me, because I'll make a fuss—and make sure Dain hears it. And there's no one hereabouts'll hide Dominick away and mind him for you, if that's what you're wondering. I know. I tried it. No one'll have him, because they're scared. They're scared of Dain and they're scared of the boy, because he looks like a little goblin and acts like one, too."

"I am not the only one with a problem," Jessica said coldly. "When Dain finds out you've been letting that child run wild in Athton, you'll *wish* the workhouse were your next residence. What he has in mind is a one-way voyage to New South Wales."

Charity laughed. "Oh, I won't be staying to find out what he has in mind. You should've heard Tom and Jem a while back—and the others. They won't be waiting on His Lordship's wishes. They want me gone, and they'll hunt me all over Dartmoor, they say, and have the dogs helping 'em. And if they don't chase me into a bog, they'll have me tied to a cart and whipped from here to Exeter, they promised. So I decided I'll be on the first London coach tomorrow."

"A wise decision," said Jessica, suppressing a shudder at the prospect of little Dominick roaming the thieves' kitchens of London. "Having encountered me, however, you have guessed that you need not leave empty-handed."

"Gracious me, if you aren't the quick one." The smile she bent upon Jessica was perfectly amiable. Charity, clearly, was a businesswoman, and she was delighting in the challenge of a tough customer. "Being so quick, I guess you'll figure out what to do with my little lovey if I give him up easy-like, with no fuss. Just like I'll figure out what to do with him in London if you decide he isn't worth the trouble.

"I do not wish to hurry you, but I am obliged to be at the church when services end," Jessica said. "Perhaps you would be good enough to describe my 'trouble' in simple pounds, shillings, and pence."

"Oh, it's much simpler than that," said Charity. "All you have to do is give me the picture."

Seventeen

At two o'clock that afternoon, Dain stood with his wife at the top of a rise overlooking the moors.

She had asked him to take her to the Haytor Rocks after luncheon. Her pallor and the lines of fatigue about her eyes and mouth had told him she was not up to the climb—or the climate, for even in mid-June, the moors could be bone-numbingly cold and wet. Along Devon's south coast, subtropical flowers and trees flourished as though in a hothouse. Dartmoor was another matter altogether. It made its own weather, and what went on in the highlands had little to do even with the conditions in a valley not two miles away.

Dain had kept his concern to himself, though. If Jessica wanted to climb one of the peaks of the great ridge bounding the moors, she had a good reason. If he hoped to mend the damage between them, he must show some evidence of trusting her judgment.

She had said, hadn't she, that she was tired of his mistrust . . . among a great many other things.

And so he held his tongue now as well, instead of telling her she'd be warmer in the shelter of the immense rock than on the edge of the ridge, facing the arctic blasts.

The brutal wind had sprung up when they'd reached the massive granite outcropping that crowned the hill. The clouds were churning into a sinister grey mass, promising a Dartmoor storm—while a few miles west, at Athcourt, the sun was no doubt shining brightly at this moment.

"I thought it would be like the Yorkshire moors," she said. Her gaze swept the rock-strewn landscape below them. "But it seems altogether different. Rockier. More . . . volcanic."

"Dartmoor is basically a heap of granite," he said. "According to my tutor, it is part of a broken chain extending to the Scilly Islands. A good part of it utterly defies cultivation, as the flora, I was told, amply demonstrates. Not much else besides gorse and heather is stubborn enough to obtain a roothold. The only plush patches of greenery—" He pointed to a lush green spot in the distance. "There, for instance. Looks like an oasis in a very rocky desert, doesn't it? But at its best, it's a bit of marsh. At the worst, it's quicksand. That's only a small patch. A few miles northwestward is the Grimspound Bog, just one of many that have swallowed sheep, cows, and men whole."

"Tell me how you'd feel, Dain," she said, never taking her eyes from the rugged vista stretching out below them, "if you'd learned a child had been left to wander these moors, unattended, for days, even weeks."

A dark, sullen child's face rose in his mind's eye.

A chill sweat broke out over his flesh and an immense weight filled his insides, as though he'd just swallowed lead.

"Christ, Jess."

She turned and looked up at him. Under the wide bonnet brim, her eyes were as dark as the lowering clouds overhead. "You know what child I mean, don't you?"

He couldn't keep himself upright under the weight within. His limbs were trembling. He forced himself to move away, to the mountainous rock. He set his clenched fist against the blessedly ungiving granite and pressed his throbbing forehead to his fist.

She came to him. "I misunderstood," she said. "I thought your hostility was toward the boy's mother. Consequently, I was sure you'd understand soon enough that the child was more important than an old grudge. Other men seem to deal easily enough with their by-blows, even boast of them. I thought you were merely being obstinate. But that, obviously, is not the case. This seems to be a problem of cosmic proportions."

"Yes." He swallowed a gulp of stinging air. "I know, but I can't think it out. My brain . . . seizes up. Paralyzed." He forced out a short laugh. "Ridiculous."

"I had no idea," she said. "But at least you are telling me now. That is progress. Unfortunately, it is not very helpful. I am in a bit of a predicament, Dain. I am prepared to act, of course, but I could not possibly do so without informing you of the situation."

The clouds were spitting chill drops of rain, which the gusting wind spattered against his neck. He lifted his head and turned to her. "We'd better get back into the carriage, before you take a fatal ague."

"I am dressed very warmly," she said. "I know what to expect from the weather."

"We can discuss this at home," he said. "Before a warm fire. I should like to get there before the heavens open up and drench us."

"No!" she burst out, stamping her foot. "We're not *discussing* anything! I am going to tell you, and you are going to *listen!* And I don't give a damn if you contract a lung fever and whooping cough besides. If that little boy can bear the moors—on his own—wearing rags and boots full of holes, with nothing in his belly but what he can steal to put there, then you can bloody well bear it!"

Again the face flashed in his mind.

Revulsion, sour and thick, was rising inside him. Dain made himself drag in more air, in long, labored breaths.

Yes, he bloody well could bear it. He had told her weeks ago to stop treating him like a child. He had wanted her to stop behaving like an amiable automaton. He'd received his wishes, and he knew now he could and would endure anything, as long as she didn't leave him.

"I'm listening," he said. He leaned against the rock.

She studied him with troubled eyes. "I am not trying to torture you, Dain, and if I had a clue what your problem was, I would try to help. But that obviously wants a good deal of time, and there isn't time. At present, your son is more desperately in need of help than you are."

He made himself focus on the words, and push the sickening image to the back of his mind. "I understand. On the moors, you said. On his own. Not acceptable. Quite."

"And so you must understand that when I heard of it, I was obliged to act. Since you made it clear you didn't want to hear anything about him, I was obliged to act behind your back."

"I understand. You had no choice."

"And I should not distress you now, if I were not obliged to do something that you might never forgive."

He swallowed nausea and pride in one gulp. "Jess, the only unforgivable thing you can do is leave me," he said. "*Se mi lasci mi uccido*. If you leave me, I'll kill myself."

"Don't be ridiculous," she said. "I should never leave you. Really, Dain, I cannot think where you get such addled ideas."

Then, as though this explained and settled everything, she promptly returned to the main subject, and told him what had happened that day: how she'd stalked the beast to its lair—in Dain's own park, no less, where the little fiend had broken into the summerhouse, and had been more or less living there for the last week at least.

Dain's sickness swiftly subsided, and the unendurable weight with it, swept away on a tide of shocked disbelief. The Demon Seed he'd planted in Charity Graves had been terrorizing his own village, skulking about his own park—and Dain had heard not so much as a whisper about it.

Speechless, he could only gape at his wife while she briskly related her capture of the boy, and went on to describe the encounter with the guttersnipe's mother.

Meanwhile, the atmosphere about them had darkened ominously. The spitting rain had built to a steady drizzle. Under it, the spray of feathers and ribbons adorning her bonnet had sagged and collapsed, to cling soggily to the brim. But Jessica was as oblivious to the state of her bonnet as she was to the fiercely gusting wind, the fine beating rain, and the black mass roiling above their heads.

She had reached the crisis point in her tale, and that was all that troubled her at present. A crease had appeared between her gracefully arched eyebrows and her gaze had dropped to her tightly folded hands.

"Charity wants the icon in exchange for the boy," she said. "Otherwise, if I try to take him, she threatened to scream blue murder—because that would bring you into it, and she knows you'll send him—and her—away. But that I cannot permit, and I brought you here to tell you so. I will find a way to keep him out of your sight, if you insist. I will not, however, let him go away with his irresponsible mother to London, where he will fall into the hands of cutpurses, perverts, and murderers."

"The icon?" he said, scarcely heeding the rest. "The bitch wants my Madonna—a Stroganov—for that hideous little—"

"Dominick is not hideous," Jessica said sharply. "True, he has behaved monstrously, but he received no discipline at home in the first place and he has been much provoked in the second. He was blissfully unaware he was a bastard, or what that meant, just as he did not grasp the meaning of his mother's trade—until he went to school, where the village children enlightened him in the cruelest possible way. What he is, is frightened and confused, and painfully aware that he is not like other children—and no one wants him." She paused. "Except me. If I had pretended I didn't want him, his mother might not have demanded so much. But I could not pretend, and add to the child's misery."

"Plague take the black whoreson!" he shouted, pulling away from the rock. "That bitch will not have my icon!"

"Then you will have to take the child away from her yourself," said Jessica. "I do not know where she is hiding, but I strongly doubt she can be found in less than twenty-four hours. Which means that someone must be at the Postbridge coach stop early tomorrow morning. If the someone is not me, with the icon, it must be you."

He opened his mouth for a roar of outrage, then shut it and counted to ten instead.

"You are proposing," he said levelly, "that I toddle

down to Postbridge at the crack of dawn . . . and patiently await Charity Graves' entrance . . . and there, before a crowd of bog-trotters, *negotiate* with her?"

"Certainly not," said Jessica. "You need not negotiate. He's your son. All you have to do is take him, and there will be nothing she can do about it. She could not claim she was being tricked—as she easily might if anyone but you attempts it."

"Take him—just like that? In front of *everybody?*"

She peered up at him from under her soggy bonnet. "I do not see what is so shocking. I am merely suggesting you behave in your customary style. You stomp in and take over and tell Charity to go to blazes. And to hell with what everyone else thinks."

He clung doggedly to the fraying threads of his control. "Jessica, I am not an idiot," he said. "I see what you are about. You are . . . managing me. The idea of mowing Charity Graves down is supposed to be irresistibly appealing. Also, perfectly logical, since I have no intention of giving up my icon. Which I don't."

"I'm aware of that," she said. "Which is why I could not possibly steal it. I cannot believe the woman actually thought I would. But she is completely amoral, and I daresay the word 'betrayal' means nothing to her."

"Yet you mean to take the icon if I do not do as you ask," he said.

"I must. But I could not do so without telling you."

He tilted her chin up with his knuckle and, bending his head, gave her a hard stare.

"Did it never occur to you, Mistress Logic, that I wouldn't *let* you take it?"

"It occurred to me that you might *try* to stop me," she said.

With a sigh he released her chin and turned his gaze upon the mountainous mass of granite. "And I should have about the same success, I collect, as I would in trying to persuade this rock to trot over to Dorset."

Dain heard a low rumble in the distance, as though the heavens themselves agreed that the situation was hopeless.

He felt as bewildered and angry and helpless as he had in Paris, when another storm had been rolling toward him.

He could not even think about the loathsome thing he'd made with Charity Graves without becoming physically ill. How in Lucifer's name was he to go to it and look at it and talk to it and touch it and *take the thing into his keeping?*

The Haytor storm followed them back to Athcourt. It pounded on the roof and beat at the windows and flashed demonic bolts that lit the house with blazing white light.

Those who heard His Lordship raging through the house might have easily believed that he was truly Beelzebub, whose wrath had stirred the very elements themselves.

But then, Jessica thought, Dain did not handle his emotional problems well. He had only three methods for dealing with "bother": knock it down, frighten it away, or buy it off. When the methods didn't work, he was at a loss. And so he had a tantrum.

He raged at the servants because they weren't quick enough in assisting his wife out of her wet outer garments, and then let everything drip on the marble floor of the vestibule—as though sodden garments weren't bound to drip or muddy boots leave dirty footprints.

He was in fits because their baths had not been drawn and weren't steaming and ready the instant they reached their apartments—as though anyone had any idea of the precise moment lord and lady would return.

He bellowed because his boots were *ruined*—as though he hadn't two dozen pairs at least.

Jessica heard his outraged voice rumbling through several walls while she took her bath and changed and wondered whether poor, abused Andrews would give notice at last.

But Dain's own bath must have calmed him down a degree or two, for by the time he stalked into her chambers, the deafening outraged elephant roar had dropped to a growl, and the thunderous expression had softened to a surly glower.

He entered with his crippled arm in a sling. "Adjustments," he said after Bridget had wisely fled without waiting to be chased out. "Marriage requires bloody adjustments. You want a sling, Jess, you get a sling."

"It does not spoil the line of your coat," she said, surveying him with a critical eye. "It looks rather dashing, actually." She didn't add that it also looked as though he were planning to go out, for he was dressed for riding.

"Don't humor me," he said. Then he stalked into her sitting room, took the portrait of his mother from the easel, and carried it out—and kept on walking out the door.

She followed him down the passage, down the south stairs, and into the dining room.

"You want Mama in the dining room," he said. "Mama hangs in the dining room."

He set the painting against a chair and pulled the bell rope. A footman instantly appeared.

"Tell Rodstock I want the bloody landscape down and the portrait in its place," Dain said. "And tell him I want it done *now*."

The footman instantly vanished.

Dain walked out of the dining room and across the short hall to his study.

Jessica hurried after him.

"The portrait will look very handsome over the mantel," she said. "I found a lovely set of drapes in the North Tower. I'll have them cleaned and hung in the dining room. They'll complement the portrait better than what's there."

He had moved to his desk, but he didn't sit down. He stood before it, half-turned from her. His jaw was set, his eyes hooded.

"I was eight years old," he said tightly. "I sat there." He nodded at the chair in front of the desk. "My father sat there." He indicated his own usual place. "He told me my mother was Jezebel, that the dogs would eat her. He told me she was on her way to Hell. That was all the explanation he gave me of her departure."

Jessica felt the blood draining from her face. She, too, had to turn away while she summoned her composure. That wasn't easy.

She had guessed that his father had been harsh, unforgiving. She had never imagined that he—that any father—could be so brutally cruel . . . to a little boy . . . bewildered, frightened, grieving for his lost mother.

"Your father was angry and humiliated, no doubt," she made herself say evenly. "But if he'd truly cared for her, he would have gone after her, instead of venting his spleen on you."

"If you run away," Dain said fiercely, "I shall hunt you down. I shall follow you to the ends of the earth."

If she could manage not to topple over in shock when he had threatened to kill himself on her account, she could manage it now, she told herself.

"Yes, I know that," she said. "But your father was a miserable, bitter old man who married the wrong woman, and you are not. Obviously she was high-strung—and that's where you get it from—and he made her wretched.

But I am not in the least high-strung, and I would never permit you to make me wretched."

"Just as you will not permit that bedamned female to take her Satan's spawn to wicked London."

Jessica nodded.

He leaned back against the desk and directed a glare at the carpet. "It does not occur to you, perhaps, that the child may not wish to leave its—his—mother. That such an event may . . ." He trailed off, his hand beating against the edge of the desk as he sought the words.

He didn't have to finish. She knew he referred to his own case: that his mother's desertion had devastated him . . . and he hadn't altogether recovered yet.

"I know it will be traumatic," Jessica said. "I asked his mother to try to prepare him. I suggested she explain that where she was going was much too dangerous for a little boy and it was better to leave him where he would be safe, and where she was sure he'd be provided for."

He shot her one quick look. Then his gaze dropped again to the carpet.

"I wish it were true," Jessica said. "If she truly loved him, she would never subject him to such a risk. She would put his welfare first—as your own mother did," she dared to add. "*She* did not drag a little boy off on a dangerous sea voyage, with no assurance she could provide for him—if, that is, he managed to survive the journey. But her case was tragic, and one must grieve for her. Charity Graves . . . Ah, well, in some ways she is a child herself."

"My mother is a tragic heroine and Charity Graves a child," Dain said. He pushed away from the edge of the desk and moved behind it, not to the chair but to the window. He looked out.

The storm was abating, Jessica noticed.

"Charity wants pretty clothes and trinkets and the attention of all males in the vicinity," she said. "With her looks and brains—and charm, for she has that, I admit—she might have been a famous London courtesan by now, but she is too lazy, too much a creature of the moment."

"Yet this creature of the moment is single-mindedly bent upon my icon, you informed me on the way home," he said. "Which she has never seen. And for whose existence she relies upon the word of a village looby who heard it from someone else, who heard it from one of our servants. Yet she is convinced the thing is worth twenty thousand pounds. Which amount, she told you, was the only counteroffer you could make—and you had better make it in sovereigns, because she had no faith in paper. I should like to know who put this twenty thousand pounds into her head."

Jessica joined him at the window. "I should, too, but we haven't time to find out, have we?"

With a short laugh, he turned to her. "*We?* It isn't 'we' at all, as you know perfectly well. It's 'Dain,' the pitiable, henpecked fellow who must do exactly as his wife tells him, if he knows what's good for him."

"If you were henpecked, you would obey me blindly," she said. "But that is not the case at all. You have sought an explanation of my motives, and you are now attempting to deduce Charity's. You are also preparing to deal with your son. You are trying to put yourself in his shoes, so that you may quickly make sense of any troublesome reactions and respond intelligently and efficiently."

She drew closer and patted his neckcloth. "Go ahead. Tell me that I'm 'humoring' you or 'managing' you or whatever other obnoxious wifely thing I am doing."

"Jessica, you are a pain in the arse, do you know that?" He scowled at her. "If I were not so immensely fond of you, I should throw you out the window."

She wrapped her arms about his waist and laid her head against his chest. "Not merely 'fond,' but 'immensely fond.' Oh, Dain, I do believe I shall swoon."

"Not now," he said crossly. "I haven't time to pick you up. Get off me, Jess. I've got to go to bleeding Postbridge."

She drew back abruptly. "Now?"

"Of course now." He edged away. "I'll lay you any odds the bitch is there already—and the sooner I get this damn nonsense over with, the better. The storm's letting up, which means I should have something like light for a few more hours. Which means I'm less likely to ride into a ditch and break my neck." He quickly skirted the desk and headed for the door.

"Dain, try not to explode upon them," she called after him.

He paused and threw her an exasperated look.

"I thought I was supposed to mow her down," he said.

"Yes, but try not to terrify the child. If he bolts, you'll have the devil's own time catching him." She hurried up to him. "Maybe I should come along."

"Jessica, I can handle this," he said. "I am not completely incompetent."

"But you are not accustomed to dealing with children," she said. "Their behavior can be very puzzling at times."

"Jessica, I am going to collect the little beast," he said grimly. "I am not going to puzzle about anything. I shall collect him and bring him to you, and you may puzzle over him to your heart's content."

He moved to the door and jerked it open. "For starters, you can figure out what to do with him, because I'm hanged if I have a clue."

Dain decided to take his coachman with him, but not the coach. Phelps knew every road, path, and cattle track in Dartmoor. Even if the storm rebuilt and headed west with them, Phelps would get them promptly to Postbridge.

Besides, if he could help his mistress make trouble for her husband, Phelps could damned well help Dain get out of it.

Dain wasn't sure how Jessica had managed to talk his loyal coachman into betraying his trust these last weeks, but he saw soon enough that she didn't have the man completely wrapped around her finger. When Jessica rushed out to the stables to make a last plea to accompany them, Phelps negotiated the compromise.

"Mebbe if Her Ladyship could make up a parcel for the lad, she'll feel some'at easier in her mind," the coachman suggested. "She be worried he'll be hungry, 'n mebbe cold, 'n you be in too much hurry to heed it. Mebbe she might find a toy or some'at to keep him busy."

Dain looked at Jessica.

"I suppose that must do," she said. "Though it would be better if I were there."

"You will *not* be there, so just put that idea out of your head," said Dain. "I will give you a quarter hour to make up the damned parcel, and that's all."

Fifteen minutes later, Dain sat upon his horse, glaring at the front door of Athcourt. He waited another five minutes, then set out down the long drive, leaving Phelps to deal with parcels and Her Ladyship.

Phelps caught up with him a few yards past Athcourt's main gateway. "'Twere the toy what slowed her," he explained as they rode on. "Went up to the

North Tower, she did, 'n found one o' them paper peepshows. A sea battle, 't were, she said."

"That must be Nelson and Parker at Copenhagen," said Dain. "If it was one of mine, that is," he added with a laugh. "I daresay that's the only one I hadn't time to destroy before I was sent to school. Got it on my eighth birthday. One needn't wonder how she found it. My lady could find the proverbial needle in a haystack. That's one of her special talents, Phelps."

"Ess, I reckon it don't work out so bad, seeing as how Your Lordship loses some'at now and again." Phelps eyed his master's left arm, which Dain had freed from the sling the instant he was out of sight of the house. "Lost your arm saddle, did you, me lord?"

Dain glanced down. "Good heavens, so I have. Well, no time to look for it, is there?"

They rode on for a few minutes in silence.

"Mebbe I shouldn't've helped her look for the lad," Phelps said finally. "But I been worrit ever since I heerd ol' Annie Geach'd cocked up her toes at last."

Phelps explained that the elderly midwife had been all the mother Dominick had known.

"When Annie passed on, there weren't no one else wanted to look after the tyke," said Phelps. "As I reckon, his ma made trouble in front o' your new bride, figurin' you'd have to do some'at—mebbe give her money to go away or get a nuss for the lad. But you never sent nobody lookin' for her, not even when the boy were raisin' hell in the village—"

"I didn't know he was raising hell," Dain interrupted irritably. "Because no one bloody *told* me. Not even you."

" 'T weren't my place," said Phelps. "Not to mention which, how were I to know you wouldn't go about it all wrong? Transportin', Her Ladyship said. That's what you had in mind. Both on 'em—ma and boy. Well, I reckon it didn't set right with me, me lord. I stood by once, watchin' your pa go about it all wrong. I were young when your pa sent you off, and skeered o' losin' me place. And I reckoned the gentry knowed better 'n an ignorant village boy. But I be past the half-century mark now, 'n I sees things some'at different 'n before."

"Not to mention that my wife could persuade you to see pixies in your pockets, if that suited her plans," Dain muttered. "I should count myself lucky she didn't talk you into secreting her in one of your saddlebags."

"She tried," Phelps said with a grin. "I tole her she'd do more good gettin' ready for the lad. Like findin' the rest o' them wooden soldiers o' yours. 'N pickin' a nussmaid 'n fixin' up the nuss'ry."

"I said I would fetch him," Dain coldly informed the coachman. "I did not tell her the filthy beggar could live in *my* house, sleep in *my* nursery—" He broke off, his gut churning.

Phelps made no answer. He kept his gaze upon the road ahead.

Dain waited for his insides to settle. They covered another mile before the inner knots eased to a tolerable level.

"A problem 'of cosmic proportions,' she called it," Dain grumbled. "And yet I must solve it, it seems, somewhere between here and Postbridge. We're coming to the West Webburn River, aren't we?"

"Another quarter mile, me lord."

"And from there, Postbridge is what—less than four miles, isn't it?"

Phelps nodded.

"Four miles," Dain said. "Four bleeding miles to solve a problem of cosmic proportions. God help me."

Eighteen

An accomplished strumpet Charity Graves certainly was, Roland Vawtry thought. Clever, too, to come up with a fresh plan on the spur of the moment, with the village louts bearing down on her on one side and Lady Dain on the other.

As a mother, however, she was utterly useless.

Vawtry stood at the window overlooking the inn-yard, trying to ignore the revolting sounds behind him and the more revolting stench.

Immediately after the encounter with Lady Dain, Charity had hied to her tiny cottage in Grimspound, collected her belongings, and hurled them into the broken-down Dennet gig she'd bought a week ago, along with an equally broken-down pony.

The brat, however, had balked at getting into the gig, because of the thunder miles away.

Unwilling to risk his bolting from the vehicle and disappearing into the moors, Charity had pretended to sympathize. Promising they'd wait until the thunder stopped, she'd calmly set out a bit of bread and a mug of ale for him. To the ale, she'd added "the tiniest bit—not half a drop—of laudanum," she claimed.

The "half a drop" had quieted Dominick to the point of unconsciousness. She'd stuffed him into the gig and he'd slept the whole way to the inn at Post-bridge and for some time after, while Charity explained to Vawtry what had happened to destroy their original plans and what she'd contrived instead.

Vawtry trusted her. If she said Lady Dain wanted the loathsome child, then it was true.

If Charity said Her Ladyship would tell Dain nothing about it, that must be true as well, although Vawtry had rather more difficulty accepting this truth. He'd gone to the window more than once to survey the innyard for signs of Beelzebub or his minions.

"The worst that can happen is he'll turn up tomorrow instead of her," she'd told him. "But you only have to keep a sharp lookout. It's not like you can't see him coming from a mile away, is it? Then all we do is make ourselves scarce, quick-like. And if we can keep the pesky boy quiet another week, we can go back to the first plan."

The first plan involved criminal acts.

The second plan merely required keeping a sharp lookout—and listening to common sense, meanwhile. Even if Lady Dain had tattled, even if Dain decided to hunt Charity down, the bad weather would keep him at home for the present. In another two hours, the sun would set, and he was not likely to set out in the dark, through the mud, for Postbridge, especially when he couldn't know Charity was there already. That, anyone would agree, was too much bother for Dain.

All the same, Vawtry couldn't help wishing that Charity's common sense extended to child care. If she'd minded the boy properly in the first place, matters wouldn't have reached a crisis with Athton's populace. If she'd beaten the brat in the second place, instead of dosing him with laudanum, he wouldn't now be vomiting up the dinner he'd just wolfed down and working on spewing up whatever he'd had for breakfast as well.

Vawtry turned away from the window.

Dominick lay on a narrow cot, clutching the edge of the thin mattress, his head hanging over the chamber pot his mother held. The retching had stopped, for the moment at least, but his dirty face was grey, his lips blue, his eyes red.

Charity met her lover's gaze. "It weren't—wasn't— the laudanum," she said defensively. "It was the mutton he ate for dinner. Spoiled, it must've been—or the milk. He said everything tasted bad."

"He's got rid of everything," said Vawtry, "and he doesn't look any better. He looks worse. Maybe I'd better fetch a physician. If he D-I-E-S," he added, hoping Charity's spelling abilities were better than her mothering ones, "Her Ladyship won't be pleased. And someone I know might find herself closer to a gibbet than she likes."

The mention of the gallows washed the color from Charity's rosy cheeks. "Leave it to you to look for the worst in everything," she said, turning back to the sick child. But she made no objection when Vawtry collected his hat and left the room.

He had just reached the top of the stairs when he heard an ominously familiar rumble . . . which might as well have come from the bowels of the inferno, for it was Beelzebub's own voice.

Vawtry did not need a whiff of brimstone or a puff of smoke to inform him that during the moment he'd looked away from the window, the Golden Hart Inn had turned into the black pit of Hell and that, in a very few more moments, he would be reduced to a shriveled bit of ash.

He raced back to the room and flung open the door. "He's here!" he cried. "Downstairs. Terrifying the landlord."

The boy sat up abruptly, to gaze wide-eyed at Vawtry, who ran frantically about the room, snatching up belongings.

Charity rose from the boy's side. "Never mind the things," she said calmly. "Don't fly into a panic, Rolly. Use your head."

"He'll be here in a minute! What are we to do?"

"We're going to hustle out real quick-like," she said, moving to the window and surveying the innyard. "You take Dominick out this window and scoot along the ledge down to that hay wagon and jump."

Vawtry darted to the window. The hay wagon looked to be miles below—with not very much hay in it, either. "I can't," he said. "Not with him."

But she'd left the window while he was assessing the risk, and she'd already opened the door. "We daren't chance meeting up tonight. But you must take my boy—I can't carry him, and he's worth money, remember—and look for me in Moretonhampstead tomorrow."

"Charity!"

The door shut behind her. Vawtry stared at it, listening in numb horror to her footsteps racing toward the back stairs.

He turned to find the boy staring at the door, too. "Mama!" he cried. He crawled off the cot, managed to stagger three steps to the door, then swayed and crumpled upon the floor. He let out a gagging sound Vawtry had heard all too often in the last hours.

Vawtry hesitated, halfway between the sick child

and the window. Then he heard Dain's voice in the hall outside.

Vawtry ran to the window, unlatched it, and climbed out. Not ten seconds later, as he was edging cautiously along the ledge, he heard the door to the room crash open. He heard the bellowed oath as well. Forgetting caution, he scuttled hastily to the spot above the hay wagon and leapt.

Roaring into the room like the juggernaut, intent upon mowing Charity Graves down, Lord Dain very nearly crushed his son under his boots. Fortunately, one angry stride away, he noted the obstacle in his path and paused. In that pause, his glance took in the chamber, strewn with various items of female attire, the remains of a meal on a tray, an empty wine bottle, an over-turned cot, and some unidentifiable odds and ends, in-cluding the disgusting heap of dirt and rags at his feet.

Which appeared to be alive, for it was moving.

Dain hastily looked away and took three deep breaths to quell the bile rising within him. That was a mistake, because the air was rancid.

He heard a whimper from the animate pile of filth.

He made himself look down.

"Mama," the thing gasped. "Mama."

Ave Maria, gratia plena, Dominus tecum, benedicta tu in mulieribus, et benedictus fructus ventris tui, Iesus.

Dain remembered a child lost, alone and despairing, seeking comfort from the Virgin Mother, when his own was gone.

Sancta Maria, Mater Dei, ora pro nobis peccatori-bus, nunc et in hora mortis nostrae.

That child had prayed, not knowing what he prayed for. He had not known what his sin was, or what his mother's was. He had known, though, that he was alone.

Dain knew what it was to be alone, unwanted, frightened, confused, as Jessica had said of his son.

He knew what this hideous child felt. He, too, had been hideous and unwanted.

"Mama's gone," he said tightly. "I'm Papa."

The thing raised its head. Its black eyes were swollen and red-rimmed, the great beak dripping snot.

"Plague take you, you're filthy," Dain said. "When was the last time you had a bath?"

The brat's narrow face twisted into a scowl that would have sent Lucifer running for cover. "Sod off," he croaked.

Dain grabbed him by the collar and hauled him up. "I am your father, you little wretch, and when I say you're filthy and need a bath, you say, 'Yes, sir.' You do not tell me—"

"Bugger yourself." The boy choked out a sound halfway between a sob and a laugh. "Bugger you. Bugger, bugger, bugger. Sod, sod, sod."

"This is not puzzling behavior," Dain said. "I am not in the least puzzled. I know exactly what to do. I shall order a bath—and have one of the stablemen up to scrub you. And if you happen to take in a mouthful of soap in the process, that will be all to the good."

At this, the wretch let out a hoarse stream of invective and began writhing like a fresh-caught fish on a hook.

Dain's grip remained firm, but the boy's threadbare shirt did not. The ragged collar tore off and its wearer broke free—for exactly two seconds, before Dain caught him and swung him up off the floor and under his arm.

Almost in the same heartbeat Dain heard an ominous rattling sound.

Then the boy threw up . . . all over His Lordship's boots.

Then the squirming bundle under Dain's arm turned into a dead weight.

Alarm swept through him and surged into blind panic.

He'd killed the child. He shouldn't have held him so tightly. He'd broken something, crushed something . . . murdered his own son.

Dain heard approaching footsteps. His panicked gaze went to the door.

Phelps appeared.

"Phelps, look what I've done," Dain said hollowly.

"Got them fancy boots mucked up, I see," Phelps said, approaching. He peered down at the lifeless form still wedged against Dain's hip.

"What'd you do, skeer his dinner out o' him?"

"Phelps, I think I've killed him." Dain could scarcely move his lips. His entire body was paralyzed. He could not make himself look down . . . at the corpse.

"Then why's he breathin'?" Phelps looked up from the boy's face into his master's. "He be'nt dead. Only sick, I reckon. Mebbe took a chill comin' here in the bad weather. Whyn't you put him down over there on the bed so we can have a look at him?"

Addled, Dain thought. Jessica would say he was addled. Or high-strung. His face burning, he carefully shifted the boy up, carried him to the bed, and gently laid him down.

"He looks a mite feverish," said Phelps.

Dain cautiously laid his hand over the lad's grime-encrusted forehead. "He's—he's rather overwarm, I think," said His Lordship.

Phelps' attention was elsewhere. "Mebbe that be the trouble," he said, moving to the small fireplace. He took a bottle from the mantel and brought it to Dain. "As I recollect, laudynum didn't set right with you, neither. Nuss give it to you when your ma run off, 'n you was sick some'at fierce from it."

Dain, however, had not been half-starved at the time and had not been dragged through a Dartmoor drenching as well. He had been safe in his bed, with servants in attendance, and Nurse there to feed him tea and bathe his sweating body.

. . . it was better to leave him where he would be safe, and where she was sure he'd be provided for.

Dain had not been loved, but his mother had left him safe enough. He'd been looked after, provided for.

His mother had not taken him with her . . . where he would surely have died with her, of fever, upon an island on the other side of the world.

This boy's mother had left him to die.

"Go down and tell them we must have a pot of tea immediately," he told Phelps. "See that they send up plenty of sugar with it. And a copper tub. And every towel they can find."

Phelps started for the door.

"And the parcel," said Dain. "Fetch my lady's parcel."

Phelps hurried out.

By the time the tea arrived, Dain had stripped off his son's sweat-soaked garments and wrapped him in a bed sheet.

Phelps was ordered to build a fire, and set the tub near it. While he worked, his master spooned heavily sweetened tea into the boy, who lay limply against his arm, conscious again—thank heaven—but just barely.

Half a pot of tea later, he seemed to be reviving. His bleary gaze was marginally more alert, and his head had stopped lolling like a rag doll's. That head, an untidy mass of thick black curls like Dain's own, was crawling with vermin, His Lordship noticed, not much surprised.

But first things first, he counseled himself.

"Feeling better?" he asked gruffly.

A dazed black gaze rose to meet his. The sticky childish mouth trembled.

"Are you tired?" Dain asked. "Do you want to sleep for a bit? There's no hurry, you know."

The boy shook his head.

"Quite. You slept a good deal more than you wished, I daresay. But you'll be all right. Your mama gave you some medicine that didn't agree with you, that's all. Same thing happened to me once. Puked my guts out. Then, in a very short time, I was all better."

The boy's gaze dropped and he leaned toward the side of the bed. It took Dain a moment to realize the brat was trying to see his boots.

"There's no need to look," he said. "They're ruined. That's the second pair in one day."

"You *squashed* me," the child said defensively.

"And I turned you upside down," Dain agreed. "Bound to unsettle a queasy stomach. But I didn't know you were sick.

Because Jessica wasn't here to tell me, Dain added silently.

"Still, since you've found your tongue at last," he went on, "maybe you can find your appetite."

Another blank, shaky look.

"Are you hungry?" Dain asked patiently. "Does your belly feel empty?"

This won Dain a slow nod.

He sent Phelps down again, this time for bread and a bowl of clear broth. While Phelps was gone, Dain undertook to wash his son's face. It took rather a while, His Lordship being uncertain how much pressure to exert. But he managed to get most of the grime off without scraping half the skin away as well, and the boy endured it, though he shook like a new-foaled colt the whole time.

Then, after he'd consumed a few pieces of toasted bread and a cup of broth, and had stopped looking like a freshly dug-up corpse, Dain turned his attention to the small copper tub by the fire.

"Her Ladyship sent clean clothes for you," Dain said, indicating a chair upon which Phelps had heaped the garments. "But you must wash first."

Dominick's gaze darted from the clothes to the tub and back again several times. His expression became anguished.

"You must wash first," Dain said firmly.

The boy let out an unearthly howl that would have done an Irish banshee proud. He tried to struggle up and away. Dain caught hold of him and picked him up off the bed, oblivious to pounding fists, kicking feet, and deafening shrieks.

"Stop that racket!" he said sharply. "Do you want to make yourself sick again? It's only a bath. You won't die of it. I bathe every day and I'm not dead yet."

"No-o-o-o!" With that piteous wail, his son's louse-infested head sank onto Dain's shoulder. "No, Papa. *Please*. No, Papa."

Papa.

Dain's throat tightened. He moved his big hand up the lad's woefully thin back, and patted it gently.

"Dominick, you are crawling with vermin," he said. "There are only two ways to get rid of them. Either you have a bath in that handsome copper tub . . ."

His son's head came up.

"Or you must eat a bowl of turnips."

Dominick drew back and gazed at his father in blank horror.

"Sorry," said Dain, suppressing a grin. "It's the only other remedy."

The struggling and wails ceased abruptly.

Anything—even certain death—was preferable to turnips.

That was how Dain had felt as a child. If the boy had inherited his reaction to laudanum, one might reasonably deduce that he'd also inherited Dain's youthful aversion to turnips. Even now, he was not overly fond of them.

"You may have the hot water sent up now, Phelps," said His Lordship. "My son wishes to bathe."

The first wash Dain was obliged to handle himself, while Dominick sat rigid with indignation, his mouth set in a martyred line. When that was done, however, he was rewarded with a glimpse of the peepshow, and told he might play with it as soon as he was clean.

Dominick decided to conduct the second wash himself.

While he was making puddles about the tub under Phelps' watchful eye, Dain ordered dinner.

By the time it arrived, the boy had emerged from the tub, and Dain had towelled him dry, got him into the old-fashioned skeleton suit Jessica had found, and combed his unruly hair.

Then the coveted peepshow was put into Dominick's hands, and while he played with it, Dain sat down with his coachman to eat.

He took up his knife and his fork and was about to cut into his mutton when he realized he'd taken up his knife *and* his fork.

He stared at the fork in his left hand for a long moment.

He looked at Phelps, who was slathering butter on an enormous hunk of bread.

"Phelps, my arm works," said Dain.

"So it do," the coachman said expressionlessly.

Then Dain realized his arm must have been working for some time now, and he hadn't noticed. How else had he held his son's head up while spooning tea into him? How else had he carried him and patted his back at the same time? How else had he moved the boy's rigid body this way and that while bathing him and washing his hair? How else had he dressed him in that pestilentially impractical suit with its rows and rows of buttons?

"It stopped working for no known medical reason and now it's started working for no reason." Dain frowned at the hand. "Just as though there had never been anything wrong with it."

"Her Ladyship said 'tweren't nothing wrong with it. Said—meanin' no offense, me lord—'twere all in your head."

Dain's eyes narrowed. "Is that what you think? That it was all in my head? That, in other words, I am *addled?*"

"I only tole you what *she* said. Me, I reckon there were a sliver o' some'at them sawbones didn't get. Mebbe it just worked itself out."

Dain brought his attention back to his plate and commenced cutting the mutton. "Exactly. There was a medical explanation, but the French quack wouldn't admit he'd made a mistake, and all his friends stuck with him. There was something in there, and it simply worked itself out."

He was swallowing the first bite when his attention

drifted to Dominick, who lay on his belly on the rug before the fire, studying the Battle of Copenhagen.

The problem of cosmic proportions had shrunk to one sick and frightened little boy. And somehow, during that shrinking, something had worked itself out.

As he gazed at his son, Lord Dain understood that the "something" had not been a sliver of metal or bone. It had been in his head, or perhaps in his heart. Jessica had aimed left of his heart, hadn't she? Mayhap a part of that organ had been immobilized . . . with fear? he wondered.

Se mi lasci mi uccido, he'd told her.

He had been terrified, yes, that she'd leave him.

He realized now that he'd felt that way since the day she'd shot him. He'd feared then that he'd done the unforgivable, that he'd lost her forever. And he had not stopped being afraid. Because the only woman who'd ever cared for him before had abandoned him . . . because he was a monster, impossible to love.

But Jessica said that wasn't true.

Dain left the table and walked to the fire. Dominick looked up at his approach. In his son's dark, warily upturned countenance, Dain saw his own: the black troubled eyes . . . the hated beak . . . the sullen mouth. No, the child was not handsome by any stretch of the imagination. His face wasn't pretty and his body was awkwardly formed—scrawny limbs, overlarge feet and hands, and great bony shoulders.

He did not have a sunny disposition, either. Nor did his filthy vocabulary enhance his appeal. He wasn't a pretty child and he certainly wasn't a charming one.

He was just like his father.

And just like his father, he needed someone—anyone—to accept him. Someone to look upon him and touch him with affection.

It was not very much to ask.

"As soon as Phelps and I finish dinner, we're setting out for Athcourt," he told Dominick. "Do you feel strong enough to ride?"

The boy gave a slow nod, his eyes never leaving his father's.

"Good. I will take you up on my horse, and if you promise to be careful, I may let you hold the reins. Will you be careful?"

A quicker nod this time. And then, "Yes, Papa."

Yes, Papa.

And in Lord Beelzebub's dark, harsh Dartmoor of a heart, the sweet rain fell and a seedling of love sprouted in the once barren soil.

By the time Lord Dain finished his neglected dinner, Charity Graves should have reached Moretonhampstead. Instead, she was in Tavistock, some twenty miles in the opposite direction.

This was because Charity had collided with Phelps at the back entrance through which she'd planned to escape. He'd told her Lord Dain had come to collect his boy, and if Charity knew what was good for her, she would quietly and quickly disappear. Before Charity could summon up the required maternal tears and wails of grief at giving up her beloved son, Phelps had produced a small parcel.

The parcel had contained one hundred sovereigns, another fourteen hundred pounds in bank notes, and a note from Lady Dain. In the note, Her Ladyship pointed out that fifteen hundred quid was better than nothing and a great deal more agreeable than residence in New South Wales. She suggested that Miss Graves book passage to Paris, where her profession was better tolerated, and where her advanced age—Charity was

perilously near the dreaded thirty—would not be considered so great a drawback.

Charity had decided she was not a grieving mother
after all. She held her tongue and made herself scarce,
just as Phelps recommended.

By the time she'd found her gig, she'd done a simple
calculation. Sharing twenty thousand pounds with her
lover was an altogether different matter from sharing
fifteen hundred. She was fond of Rolly, yes, but not
that fond. And so, instead of heading northeast for
Moretonhampstead, on the road that would take her
to London, Charity had headed southwest. From Tavistock, her next stop would be Plymouth, she decided.
There she would find a vessel to take her to France.

Five weeks earlier, Roland Vawtry had tumbled into a
pit without realizing it. By now he was aware he was at
the bottom of a very deep hole. What he failed to see
was that the bottom was made of quicksand.

Instead, what he saw was that he'd betrayed Charity's trust.

Yes, she'd raced to Postbridge, straight to the inn
where she knew Vawtry was staying. Yes, she'd sent
for him, instead of discreetly hiring a room of her
own. And yes, that meant that the occupants of the
Golden Hart knew the tart and he were connected.
Still, since Vawtry had used a false name, there had
remained a chance Dain wouldn't discover the truth.

That chance, Vawtry belatedly discovered, had died
when he'd panicked and abandoned the brat.

The boy would have heard Charity call him "Rolly,"
and worse, would be able to describe him. Dominick
had stared at his mama's "friend" throughout the meal
he'd started spewing up minutes after finishing it.

Charity, being so quick-witted, had perceived the

problem. She'd told Vawtry to take the boy because that was the safest, wisest thing to do.

He was "worth money," she'd also said.

Vawtry had considered all this while cowering under a damp pile of hay, undecided which way to run and wondering whether he had a prayer of escaping the inn-yard unnoticed once he did decide.

But the place had not erupted with men commanded to hunt Roland Vawtry—or anyone else—down. No more satanic roars had issued from Vawtry's recently abandoned chamber.

Eventually, he had collected his courage and crept from the hay wagon.

No one accosted him. He walked as coolly as he could to the stables and asked for his horse.

It was there he learned of his reprieve.

The Marquess of Dain, he was informed, had all the inn servants—and not a few customers as well—running themselves ragged because his boy was sick.

Then Roland Vawtry saw that Fate had given him a chance to redeem himself in his beloved's eyes.

It did not take long to figure out how to accomplish that.

After all, he had nothing to lose now.

He was not only five thousand pounds in debt, but facing, he had no doubt, a rapid dismemberment at the Marquess of Dain's hands. Dain had other things on his mind now, but that wouldn't last forever. Then he would hunt his former comrade down.

Vawtry had one chance only and he must take it.

He must carry out Charity's plan . . . and he must do it all himself.

Nineteen

Mrs. Ingleby had told Jessica that when Athcourt had been enlarged and remodeled in the sixteenth century, the layout had been similar to that of Hardwick Hall in Derbyshire. The ground floor had been the service area primarily. The family apartments had occupied the first floor. The second floor, lightest and airiest, thanks to its high ceilings and tall windows, had held the state apartments.

In Dain's grandfather's time, the functions of the first and second floors were reversed, except for the Long Gallery, which continued to display the portrait collection.

The nursery, however, as well as the schoolroom and nursemaids' and governess's quarters, remained where they'd been since the late fifteen hundreds, at the northeast corner of the ground floor—the coldest and darkest corner of the main house.

That, Jessica told Mrs. Ingleby, shortly after Dain and Phelps had departed, was not acceptable.

"The child will be distressed enough at being separated from the only family he's known and brought to a cavernous place filled with strangers," she said. "I will not exile him to a dark corner two floors away, where he is sure to have nightmares."

After a consultation, the two women had agreed that the South Tower, just above Jessica's apartments, would be more suitable. Whatever needed to be moved out of the South Tower rooms could easily be transported across the roof walkway to one of the five other towers. The servants could do the same with items brought in from other storage rooms. That would leave a few very long trips from the present nursery to the new one, but only a few. Most of the room's furnishings had been put into storage twenty-five years earlier.

Thanks to Athcourt's grand army of servants, the project made rapid progress.

By the time the sun set, the new nursery was furnished with a bed, a rug, fresh linens, and handsome yellow draperies. The latter were not quite so fresh, but acceptable after a good shaking out in the twilight's clear air. Jessica had found a child-size rocking chair as well, rather battered but not broken, and a pull-along wooden horse minus half its tail, and most of the set of wooden soldiers Phelps had mentioned.

Mary Murdock, who'd been selected as nursemaid, was sorting through a trunkful of His Lordship's boyhood belongings for enough garments to see an active child through the days before a wardrobe could be made up for him. Bridget was removing the lace collar from a small nightshirt, because her mistress had told her that no boy of the present generation would be caught dead in that fussy thing.

They were working in the North Tower storage room, which had become the campaign's headquarters, for it was to this place the previous marquess had consigned most of the artifacts of his second wife's brief reign. Jessica had just unearthed a handsome set of picture books. She was piling them onto the windowsill when, out of the corner of her eye, she caught a flash of light in the darkness beyond.

She bent close to the thick glass. "Mrs. Ingleby," she said sharply. "Come here and tell me what that is."

The housekeeper hurried across the room to the west-facing window. She looked out. Then her hand went to her throat. "Mercy on us. That must be the little gate-house, my lady. And it looks to be . . . on *fire*."

The alarm was sounded immediately, and the house swiftly emptied as its inhabitants raced out to the gate-house.

The small pepperbox structure guarded one of Athcourt's lesser-used gates. Its gatekeeper normally spent Sunday evenings at a prayer meeting. If it burnt to the ground—which was likely, for the fire must rise high before anyone could see it—the loss would be no catastrophe.

However, His Lordship's timber yard was not far from that gate. If the fire spread thither, the timber stacks would be lost, along with the sheds filled with sawyers' tools. Since the timberyard supplied the lumber used to build and repair the homes of most of the estate's dependents, the fire was a community concern, drawing every able-bodied man, woman, and child from the village as well.

Everything happened, in other words, just as Charity Graves had promised Vawtry it would.

All of the small world of Athton descended upon the blazing gatehouse. In the excitement, Vawtry had no difficulty slipping into Lord Dain's house unnoticed.

It was not as easy, though, as it would have been a

week hence, as originally planned. For one, Vawtry couldn't pick his moment, but had to set the fire soon after a rainstorm. The wood and stone pepperbox was stubbornly slow to take fire at all, let alone blaze up to the heights necessary to be seen from miles around. Thanks to the damp, the blaze would also be slow to spread, which meant it would be under control a good deal more quickly than was comfortable for Mr. Vawtry.

Furthermore, the original scheme had required him only to make the conflagration. Charity had been responsible for getting into Athcourt and making off with the icon. Instead, Mr. Vawtry was obliged to play both roles, which meant a mad race from one end of the estate to the other—all the while praying the concealing darkness wouldn't also conceal an obstacle that would cause him to break his neck.

Thirdly, Charity had been in the house several times and knew the general layout. Vawtry had been there once, for the previous marquess's funeral, and one overnight stay was not enough to master the scores of stairways and passages of one of the largest houses in England.

The good news was that, as Charity had promised, no one had bothered to lock all the doors and windows before running off for firefighting heroics, and Mr. Vawtry got into the proper end of the house with no trouble.

The bad news was that he had to wander from one room to another before he discovered that the north back-stairs route Charity had described lay behind a door disguised as part of a wall of well-preserved Tudor-era printed paneling.

Not until after he'd found it did he recall Charity's laughing remark that all the servants' exits "pretended to be something else, like there were no servants at all, and the big house run itself."

Still, he managed to find it, and after that it was quick work to reach the second floor.

The door to Dain's apartments was the first on the left. As Charity had assured him, one needed but a moment to slip in and another to cross the vast chamber and collect the icon. Most important, the icon was precisely where she'd said it would be.

Lord Dain kept the heathenish picture his wife had given him on his bedstand, Joseph the footman had told his younger brother . . . who had told his betrothed . . . who had told *her* brother . . . who happened to be one of Charity's regular customers.

But never again, Vawtry vowed as he exited the bedchamber. After tonight, Charity would share her bed and stunning skills with only one man. That man was the daring, heroic Mr. Roland Vawtry, who would take her abroad, away from Dartmoor and its unwashed rustics. He'd show her the sophisticated world of Paris. The French capital would seem like fairyland to her, he thought as he hurried down the stairs, and he would be her knight in shining armor.

Lost in his fantasies, he pushed open a door, raced down a set of stairs . . . and found himself in a hallway he didn't remember. He hurried to the end, which turned out to be the music room.

After going through half a dozen more doors, he ended up in the ballroom, from whose entrance he saw the massive main staircase. He started toward it, then paused, undecided whether to try to find the back stairs again.

But it'd be hours before he found it, he told himself, and the house was empty. He made for the stairway, hurried down and across the broad landing, round the corner . . . and stopped short.

A woman stood on the stairs, looking up at him . . . then down, at the icon clutched against his breast.

In that instant's flicker of Lady Dain's glance from his face to the precious object he held, Vawtry regained his wits—and the use of his limbs.

He ran down the stairs, but she lunged at him, and he dodged too late. She grabbed his coat sleeve and he stumbled. The icon flew from his hands. He regained his balance in the next instant, and pushed her out of his way.

He heard a crash, but didn't heed it. His eyes on the picture at the foot of the carpeted stairs, he raced down and snatched it up.

Jessica's head had struck the wall and, grabbing blindly for balance, she knocked a Chinese vase from its pedestal. It struck the railing and shattered.

Though the world was reeling perilously toward darkness, she dragged herself upright. Firmly grasping the railing, she hurried down, ignoring the colored lights dancing about her head.

As she reached the great hall, she heard a door slam, and masculine curses, then the hurried tap of boots upon stone. Her mind clearing, she realized that her prey must have been trying to escape by the back way and got himself lost in the pantry instead.

She dashed down the hall toward the screens passage and reached the pantry door as he was running out.

This time he dodged her successfully. But even as he was bolting for the vestibule, she had grabbed the nearest object at hand—a porcelain Chinese dog—and it was out of her hand almost in the same instant, hurtling toward him.

It struck the side of his head, and he staggered, then sank to his knees, still clutching the icon. As she ran toward him, she saw blood trickling from his face. Even so, the wretched man wouldn't give up. He was crawling to the door and reaching for the handle. When she grabbed his collar, he twisted about and flung his arm up, knocking her away so violently that she lost her balance and fell over onto the tiles.

Jessica saw his fingers wrap around the handle, saw it move . . . and flung herself upon him. Grabbing a fistful of his hair, she slammed his head against the door.

He was pushing at her, screaming curses while he tried to twist free, but she was too furious to heed. The swine was trying to steal her husband's precious Madonna, and he was *not* going to get away with it.

"You will *not!*" she gasped, slamming his head against the door again. "Never!" Slam. "Never!" Slam.

Vawtry let go of the door and the icon and rolled sideways to get her off him.

She wouldn't be shaken loose. She dug her nails into his scalp, his face, his neck. He tried to roll on top of her. She thrust her knee into his groin. He jerked away and folded up onto his side, clutching his privates.

She had just grabbed his hair again, in order to dash his skull to pieces upon the marble tile, when she felt a pair of strong hands wrap around her waist and haul her up, off Vawtry, off the floor altogether.

"That's enough, Jess." Her husband's sharp tone penetrated her mindless fury, and she left off struggling to take in the world about her.

She saw that the great door stood open and a crowd of servants stood frozen just within it. In front of the mob of statues was Phelps . . . and Dominick, who was holding the coachman's hand and gazing up slack-jawed at Jessica.

That was all she saw, because Dain swiftly swung her up over his shoulder and marched through the screens passage and into the Great Hall.

"Rodstock," he said, without pausing or looking back, "the vestibule is a disgrace. Have someone see to it. *Now.*"

Once his wife was safely in her bath, with Bridget tending her and two sturdy footmen posted at the entrance to her apartments, Dain returned to the ground floor.

Vawtry, or what was left of him, lay on a wooden table in the old schoolroom, with Phelps standing guard. Vawtry's nose was broken and he'd lost a tooth and sprained a wrist. His face was caked with dried blood and one eye was swollen shut.

"All in all, you got off easy," Dain said, after surveying the damage. "Lucky she hadn't a pistol on her, aren't you?"

By the time he'd carried Jessica to her room, Dain had figured out what had happened. He'd seen the icon lying on the vestibule floor. He'd heard about the fire as he rode up to the house. He could put two and two together.

He did not have to interrogate his son to understand that Vawtry and Charity Graves were partners in crime.

Dain did not bother to interrogate Vawtry now, either, but told him what had happened.

"You let a greedy strumpet with great, fat udders turn you into a blithering idiot," Dain contemptuously summarized. "That's obvious enough. What I want to know is where you got the idea the thing was worth twenty thousand pounds. Confound it, Vawtry, couldn't you tell just by looking at it that it was worth five at most—and you know no pawnbroker would pay even half that."

"No time . . . to look." Vawtry was having a hard time getting the syllables around his swollen gums and mashed lips. His utterance sounded like "Oh—die—ooh—rook," but with Phelps' help, Dain was able to interpret.

"In other words, you never saw it before this night," said Dain. "Which means someone told you about it—Bertie most likely. And you *believed* him—which is imbecilic enough, for no one in his right mind listens to Bertie Trent—but then you had to go and tell Satan's own whore. And she, you have discovered, would sell her firstborn for twenty thousand quid."

"You was foolish, no mistake," Phelps chimed in mournfully, like a Greek chorus. "She sold her boy for only fifteen hundred. Now, don't you feel like a bit of a chucklehead, sir? Meanin' no offense, but—"

"Phelps." Dain turned a baleful eye upon his coachman.

"Aye, me lord." Phelps gave him a wide-eyed look that Dain did not believe for one minute.

"*I* did not give Charity Graves fifteen hundred pounds," His Lordship said very quietly. "As I recall, you most sensibly suggested that you head to the back of the inn, to prevent her escape in case she eluded me. I assumed you'd been too late and she'd fled. You did not volunteer information to the contrary."

"Her Ladyship were worrit the ma might make a fuss in front of the tyke," Phelps said. "Her Ladyship didn't want him upset no more than he was like to be already with you chargin' in. So she told me to give the gal some quietin' money. It were her pin money, Her

Ladyship said, 'n she could spend it how she liked. So she spent it on quietin' the ma, 'n wrote a note, tellin' the gal to take it 'n go to Paris 'n have a good time."

"Paris?" Vawtry sat up abruptly.

"Said the fellers there'd like her better and treat her kinder 'n them hereabouts. 'N I guess the gal liked the idea, cuz she lit up purty, 'n said Her Ladyship weren't a bad sort. 'N I was to tell Her Ladyship that she done what Her Ladyship said—tole the boy some'at or other like Her Ladyship asked her to."

. . . it was better to leave him where he would be safe . . . and provided for. Jessica had told the whore what to say and the whore had done it.

Then Dain saw how much trust his wife had placed in him. If she hadn't, she would have come with him, no matter what he said or did. But she'd trusted . . . that he'd make the boy feel safe, and make Dominick believe that what he'd been told was true.

Perhaps, Dain thought, his wife knew him a great deal better than he knew himself. She saw in him qualities he'd never discerned when he'd looked into a mirror.

If that was the case, he must believe she saw qualities in Charity he'd never suspected were there. Charity must possess something like a heart, if she'd taken the trouble to prepare Dominick for her desertion.

Jessica had also said that Charity was a child herself.

That seemed true enough. Plant an idea in her head, and she would run away with it.

He found himself grinning at Vawtry. "You should have found another bauble to distract her with," Dain said. "Something safer to scheme and dream about. She's a child, you know. Amoral, unprincipled. At present, she has fifteen hundred pounds in her hands, and she's forgotten all about the icon—and you. She'll never know—or if she hears, she won't care—that you risked your life and honor for . . ." Dain gave a short laugh. "What was it, Vawtry? Love?"

Beneath the bruises and lumps and caked blood, Vawtry's countenance turned a very dark red. "She *wouldn't*. She *couldn't*."

"I'll wager fifty quid she's on her way to the coast this very minute."

"I'll kill her," Vawtry croaked. "She can't leave me. She *can't*."

"Because you'll hunt her down," Dain said mockingly. "You'll follow her to the ends of the earth. If, that is, I don't see you hanged first."

The color abruptly drained from Vawtry's battered face, leaving a mottled landscape on a sickly grey background.

Dain studied his former comrade for a long moment. "The trouble is, I can think of no more fiendish a purgatory than the one you've stumbled into all by yourself. I can imagine no torment more hellish than being hopelessly besotted with Charity Graves." He paused. "Except one." Dain's mouth curled into a mocking smile. "And that is being married to her."

It was the most efficient solution, Dain decided. It was certainly a great deal less bother than prosecuting the besotted fool.

Vawtry had committed one crime, arson, and attempted another, theft.

Still, he had set fire to the least valuable structure on the estate and, thanks to the damp and the quick action of Dain's people, the damage was minimal.

As to the theft: Jessica had punished the inept criminal more brutally than Dain would have done. That a woman had administered the punishment added a lovely touch of humiliation to Vawtry's other woes.

Any gentleman possessing a modicum of masculine pride would rather have his ballocks torn off with red-hot pincers than allow the world to learn he'd been thrashed by a slip of a female.

Therefore, with the wisdom of Solomon—and a vivid recollection of Jessica's blackmail method in Paris—His Lordship pronounced sentence.

"You will find Charity Graves, wherever she is," Dain told his prisoner. "And you will marry her. That will make you legally responsible for her. And I will hold you legally and *personally* responsible if she ever comes within ten miles of my wife, my son, or any other member of my household. If she bothers us—any of us—ever again, I will throw a large dinner party, Vawtry."

Vawtry blinked. "Dinner?"

"To this dinner, I will invite all of our boon companions," Dain told him. "And when the port goes round, I shall stand up and regale the company with your fascinating adventures. I will provide a deliciously detailed account, in particular, of what I observed this evening from my front doorway."

After the moment it took him to comprehend, Vawtry went to pieces. "Find her?" he cried, looking wildly about him. "Marry her? *How?* Gad, can't you see? I wouldn't have got into this if I weren't three paces ahead of the bailiffs. I've *nothing*, Dain. Less than that." He groaned. "Five thousand less, to be precise. I'm *ruined*. Don't you see? I wouldn't have come to Devon at all if Beaumont hadn't told me I could win a fortune at the wrestling match."

"Beaumont?" Dain repeated.

Vawtry didn't heed him. "Fortune, indeed. With

those buffle-headed amateurs. Do you believe it?" He raked his fingers through his hair. "He was roasting me, the swine. 'Greatest match since Cann and Polkinghorne,' he said."

"Beaumont," Dain said again.

"Twenty thousand, he told me the thing was worth," Vawtry went on miserably. "But he was roasting me about that, too, wasn't he? Said he knew a Russian who'd sell his firstborn for it. And I *believed* him."

"So it wasn't Bertie Trent who put the idea in your head, after all, but Beaumont," Dain said. "I might have known. He bears me a grudge," he explained to the bewildered Vawtry.

"A grudge? But why pick on me?"

"To make you resentful of me, in hopes of creating ill will between us, I suppose," Dain said. "That he could add to your miseries at the same time simply made the business more delightful for him," Dain frowned. "He's nothing more than a sneaking troublemaker. He hasn't the nerve to seek revenge like a man. Which makes it all the more annoying that he has succeeded in his spiteful game far beyond his wildest dreams." His frown deepened. "I might have had you hanged. And he would have laughed himself sick."

While Vawtry was trying to digest this, Dain took a slow turn about the small room, reflecting.

"I believe I will pay your debts, Vawtry," he said finally.

"You'll *what?*"

"I will also make you a modest annual allowance," Dain went on. "For services rendered." He paused and folded his hands behind his back. "You see, my very dear, very loyal friend, I had no idea how valuable my icon was . . . until you told me. I had actually planned to give it to Mrs. Beaumont, in exchange for a portrait of my wife. Jessica had told me how much Mrs. Beaumont admired the icon. I thought it would be a more pleasing reward to the artist than mere coins." Dain smiled faintly. "But no portrait, even by the brilliant Leila Beaumont, is worth twenty thousand quid, is it?"

Vawtry had finally caught on. His battered face was creasing into a smile.

"Naturally, you will write to Beaumont, thanking him for sharing the information," Dain said. "It would be the polite thing to do. And naturally, as your very dear friend, he will be unselfishly delighted that you were able to profit from his wisdom."

"He'll be tearing his hair out when he reads it," Vawtry said. Then he flushed. "Pox take me, Dain, I hardly know what to say or think. Everything—gone so wrong—yet you've found a way to turn it right, in spite of what I did. If you'd dropped me into the nearest bog, there's not a fellow in England who'd blame you."

"If you do not keep that infernal female out of my way, I'll drop you both into a bog," Dain promised. He moved to the door. "Phelps will find someone to patch you up. I'll send one of the servants along to you with travel funds. And by the time the sun comes up, I will expect you to be gone, Vawtry."

"Yes, yes, of course. Thank—"

The door slammed behind Dain.

Twenty

At two o'clock in the morning, Lord Dain emerged from his bath. Then he was obliged to don his dressing gown and slippers and look for his wife because, as he might have expected, she was not in bed, where she was supposed to be.

He tried the South Tower first, but she was not hovering at Dominick's bedside. Mary was there, dozing in a chair. The boy was sound asleep, sprawled on his belly, the bedclothes kicked into a heap at the foot of the bed.

Grumbling under his breath, Dain untangled the sheets and blankets and briskly tucked them about his son. Then he gave the oblivious brat a pat on the head and left.

A quarter of an hour later, he found Jessica in the dining room.

Wrapped in her black and gold silk dressing gown, her hair carelessly piled and pinned atop her head, she stood before the fireplace. Her fingers cupped the bowl of a brandy snifter and she was gazing up at the portrait of his mother.

"You might have invited me to get drunk with you," he said from the doorway.

"This was between Lucia and me," she said, her eyes still upon the picture. "I came to raise a glass in her honor."

She lifted her glass. "To you, my dear Lucia: for bringing my wicked husband into the world . . . for giving him so much of what was best in you . . . and for giving him up, so that he would live and grow up into a man . . . and I would find him."

She swirled the amber liquid in the glass, and sniffed appreciatively. Then, with a small sigh of pleasure, she brought it to her lips.

Dain stepped into the room, closing the door behind him. "You don't know how lucky you were to find me," he said. "I am one of the few men in western Europe who could afford you. That, I have no doubt, is my very best brandy."

"I did take your wine cellar into account when I weighed your assets and liabilities," Jessica said. "It may well have tipped the scales in your favor."

She gestured with the glass at the painting. "Doesn't she look splendid there?"

Dain walked to the head of the table, sat in his chair, and studied the portrait. Then he got up and moved to the sideboard and considered it from that angle. He examined it from the doorway leading to the Musicians' Gallery, from the windows, and from the foot of the long dining table. Finally he joined his wife before the fireplace, folded his arms over his chest, and broodingly surveyed his mother from there.

But no matter what angle he viewed her from or how long and hard he stared, he no longer hurt inside. All he saw was a beautiful young woman who had loved him in her own temperamental way. Though he would never know the full truth of what had happened twenty-five years ago, he knew enough, believed enough, to forgive her.

"She was a handsome article, wasn't she?" he said.

"Exceedingly so."

"One can hardly blame the Dartmouth blackguard for making off with her, I suppose," he said. "At least he stayed with her. They died together. How that must have infuriated my father." He laughed. "But I don't doubt 'Jezebel's' son infuriated him far more. He couldn't disown me because he was too great a snob to leave his precious heritage in the vulgar hands of a sprig of the cadet branch. The great hypocrite couldn't even destroy her portrait—because she was part of the Ballisters' history, and he, like his noble ancestors, must preserve everything for his descendants, like it or not."

"He didn't even throw out your toys."

"He threw me out, though," Dain said. "The dust had scarcely settled behind my mother when he packed me off to Eton. Gad, what an obstinate old idiot. He could have cultivated me, won me over with the smallest effort. I was eight years old. Completely at his mercy. Clay in his hands. He could have molded me just as he liked. If he wanted revenge on her, that was the way to get it—and get the kind of son he wanted at the same time."

"I'm glad he didn't mold you," Jessica said. "You would not have turned out half so interesting."

He looked down into her smiling countenance. "Interesting, indeed. The Bane and Blight of the Ballisters, Lord of Scoundrels himself. The greatest whoremonger in Christendom. A cocksure, clodpated ingrate."

"The wickedest man who ever lived."

"A great gawk of a lummox. A spoiled, selfish, spiteful brute."

She nodded. "Don't leave out 'conceited clodpole.'"

"It does not matter what you think," he said loftily. "My son believes I am King Arthur and all the knights of the Round Table rolled into one."

"You are too humble, my dear," she said. "Dominick is convinced that you are Jupiter and the entire pantheon of Roman deities rolled into one. It is thoroughly nauseating."

"You don't know what nauseating is, Jess," he said with a laugh. "I only wish you might have seen the animate pile of filth I encountered at the Golden Hart Inn. If the thing had not spoken, I might have mistaken it for a moldering heap of refuse, and pitched it into the fire."

"Phelps told me," she said. "I went downstairs while you were bathing and cornered him when he was on his way out. He described the state Dominick had been in, and how you faced it and dealt with it, yourself . . . with your own *two* hands."

She slipped her arm through is, through the one that his own fears and need had paralyzed, and a little boy's greater fears and need had cured. "I did not know whether to laugh or cry," she said. "So I did both." Silver mist shimmered in her eyes. "I am so proud of you, Dain. And proud of myself," she added, looking away and blinking hard, "for having the good sense to marry you."

"Don't be ridiculous," he said. "Sense had nothing to do with it. But I will give you credit for making the best of a situation that would have driven any normal female to leap, screaming, from the top of the nearest tower."

"That would have been unforgivably gauche," she said.

"It would have meant admitting defeat, you mean,"

he said. "And that you cannot do. It isn't in your nature. As Vawtry has learned, to his everlasting mortification."

She frowned. "I know I took advantage of him. In spite of everything, he was too much the gentleman to fight back properly. All he could do was try to shake me off. But I should not have taken advantage if the curst fool had let go of the icon. Then, by the time he finally did, I was much too overwrought to stop smashing him. If you had not come when you did, I fear I might have killed him." She leaned her head against his brawny upper arm. "I do not think anyone else could have stopped me."

"Yes, we big, mean lummoxes have our uses," he said. He scooped her up and carried her to the dining room table. "Luckily, I had both arms working by then, else I doubt even I could have managed it." He plunked her down upon the gleaming wood surface. "What I should like to know, though, is why my level-headed wife hadn't the common sense to keep at least a few servants with her, fire or no fire."

"I did," she said. "But Joseph and Mary were up in the South Tower, too far away to hear anything. I should not have noticed Vawtry myself, if he hadn't come down the main staircase. But I had gone down to the ground floor to watch for you. Someone had to be there when you arrived, to make Dominick feel welcome. I wanted to be the one. I wanted to prove I was looking forward to his arrival." Her voice quavered. "I wanted to reassure him and—and give him a h-hug."

He tilted up her chin and gazed into her misty eyes. "I hugged him, *cara*," he said softly. "I took him up in front of me on my horse, and I held him close, because he is a child, needing reassurance. I told him I would take care of him . . . because he was my son. And I told

him you wanted him, too. I told him all about you—
that you could be kind and amazingly understanding,
but that you wouldn't tolerate any nonsense." He
smiled. "And when we came home, the first thing Dominick saw was active, incontrovertible proof of that last.
You proved that Papa was telling the truth, and Papa
knows everything about everybody."

"Then I shall hug Papa." She wrapped her arms
about his waist and laid her head against his chest. "I
love you, Sebastian Leslie Guy de Ath Ballister. I love
you, Lord Dain and Beelzebub, Lord Blackmoor, Lord
Launcells, Lord Ballister—"

"That's too many names," he said. "We've been wed
more than a month. Since it appears that you mean to
stay, I might as well give you leave to call me by my
Christian name. It is preferable, at any rate, to 'clodpole.'"

"I love you, Sebastian," she said.

"I'm rather fond of you, too," he said.

"Immensely fond," she corrected.

Her dressing gown was sliding down from her shoulders. He hastily drew it up. "Immense may well be the
word for it." He glanced down at where his shaft was
stirring against his dressing gown. "We had better get
upstairs quickly and go to sleep forthwith. Before my
feelings of fondness swell to an unreasonable degree."

"Going directly to sleep would be unreasonable,"
she said. She slid her hands up and into the opening of
his robe and stroked over his chest. The muscles there
tightened and pulsed, and the pulsations raced downward.

"You're exhausted from your ordeal," he said, swallowing a groan. "Also, I'm sure you must be bruised in
a hundred places. You don't want a fifteen-stone brute
heaving about on top of you."

She drew her thumb over his nipple.

He sucked in his breath.

"You could heave about *under* me," she said softly.

He told himself to ignore what she'd just said, but the image rose in his mind's eye, and his rod rose eagerly with it.

It had been a month since she'd told him she loved him. It had been a month since she had actually invited him, instead of simply cooperating. Enthusiastic as the cooperation had been, he'd missed her brazen overtures almost as much as he'd missed the three precious words.

Besides, he was an animal.

Already he was as randy as a rutting bull elephant.

He lifted her off the table. He meant to set her down, because carrying her would be too dangerously intimate. But she wouldn't be set down. She clung to his arms and wrapped her legs round his waist.

He tried not to look down, but he couldn't help it.

He saw soft white thighs encircling him, caught a glimpse of the sleek, dark curls just below the sash that was no longer holding the gown decorously in place.

She shifted a bit, and the robe slid from her shoulders again. She slipped first one, then the other arm from the loose sleeves. The elegant robe became a useless scrap of silk dangling from her waist.

Smiling, she brought her arms up to circle his neck. She rubbed her firm, white breasts against the opening of his dressing gown, and it gave way. The warm, feminine mounds pressed against his skin.

He turned and came back to the table and sank down upon it.

"Jess, how the devil am I to climb the stairs in this condition?" he asked hoarsely. "How is a man to see straight when you do such things to him?"

She licked the hollow of his throat. "I like the way

you taste," she murmured. She drew her parted lips over his collarbone. "And the way your skin feels against my mouth. And the way you smell . . . of soap and cologne and *male*. I love your big, warm hands . . . and your big, warm body . . . and your immense, throbbing—"

He dragged her head up and clamped his mouth over hers. She parted instantly, inviting him in.

She was wicked, a *femme fatale*, but the taste of her was fresh and clean. She tasted like rain, and he drank her in. He inhaled the chamomile scent mingled with the fragrance that was uniquely hers. He traced the delectable shape of her with his big, dark hands . . . the graceful column of her neck, the gentle slope of her shoulders, the silken curve of her breasts with their taut, dusky buds.

He slid back and down upon the table, and drew her down on top of him, and traced those feminine outlines again with his mouth, his tongue.

He stroked down her smooth, supple back and molded his hands to the sinuous turn of her slim waist and the gentle flare of her hips.

"I'm clay in your hands," she breathed against his ear. "I love you madly. I want you so much."

The soft voice, husky with desire, swam in his head and sang in his veins, and whirled its mad music through his heart.

"*Sono tutta tua, tesoro mio,*" he answered. "I'm all yours, my treasure."

He grasped her sweet rump and lifted her onto his manhood . . . and groaned as she guided him into her. "Oh, *Jess*."

"All mine." She sank, slowly, down upon his shaft.

"Sweet Jesus." Pleasure forked through him, jagged and white-hot. "*Oh, Dio.* I'm going to die."

"*All mine,*" she said.

"Yes. Kill me, Jess. Do it again."

She came up and sank again, with the same torturous slowness. Another lightning bolt. Scorching. Rapturous.

He begged for more. She gave him more, riding him, controlling him. He wanted it that way, because it was love that mastered him, happiness that shackled him. She was passionate chatelaine of his body, loving mistress of his heart.

When the storm broke at last and, trembling in the aftermath, she fell into his arms, he held her tight against the hammering heart she ruled . . . where the secret he'd hidden for so long pounded in his breast.

But he wanted no more such secrets. He could say the words now. So easy it was, when all that had been frozen and buried inside him had thawed and bubbled up, fresh as the Dartmoor streams in springtime.

With a shaky laugh, he brought her head up and lightly kissed her.

"*Ti amo,*" he said. And so ridiculously simple it was that he said it again, in English this time. "I love you, Jess."

If love had not exploded into his life, her husband informed Jessica a short time later, he might have made a mistake he'd never forgive himself for.

The sun was inching up from the horizon when they returned to the master bedroom, but Dain wasn't ready to sleep until the evening's events were clarified, explained, and settled.

He lay on his back, gazing up at the canopy's golden dragons. "Being besotted myself," he was saying, "I was forced to see how easily any man—especially one of Vawtry's limited intelligence—could stumble into a quagmire."

In a few contemptuous sentences, he told her of his suspicions about Beaumont's role in the Paris farce, and how the spitefulness had continued. Jessica wasn't much surprised. She had always considered Beaumont a particularly unpleasant human being and wondered why his wife hadn't left him long since.

She was, however, both surprised and amused by her husband's approach to the problem. By the time Dain had finished describing his intriguing methods for dealing with both Vawtry and the repellent Beaumont, Jessica was laughing helplessly.

"Oh, Sebastian," she gasped. "You are too wicked. I should give anything to see the expression on Beaumont's face when he reads Vawtry's th-thank you n-note," she sputtered. Then she went off into whoops again.

"Only you would appreciate the humor of the situation," he said when she'd quieted.

"And the artistry of it," she said. "Vawtry, Charity— even that spiteful sod Beaumont—all dealt with, settled in a matter of minutes. And all without your needing to lift a finger."

"Except to count out bank notes," Dain said. "It's costing me, remember?"

"Vawtry will be grateful to you for the rest of his life," she said. "He will race to the ends of the earth to do your bidding. And Charity will be content, because she'll be set up comfortably with a man who adores her. That's all she wanted, you know. A life of idle luxury. That's why she had Dominick."

"I know. She thought I'd pay her five hundred a year."

"I asked her how she came to that addled conclusion," Jessica said. "She told me it was when all the grand folks came to your father's funeral. Some of the gentlemen had brought their birds of paradise along and deposited them at nearby inns. Along with other London gossip, Charity heard tales—exaggerated, no doubt—of settlements and annuities made for certain noblemen's illegitimate offspring. That, she told me, is why she didn't employ the usual precautions with you and Ainswood, and why, when she found herself *enceinte*, she took no corrective measures."

"In other words, another brainless trollop put the idea in her head."

"Charity thought all she had to do was have one child, and she'd never have to work again. Five hundred pounds was unheard-of wealth to her."

"Which explains why she settled so easily for your fifteen hundred." Dain still had his eyes fixed upon the dragons. "You knew this, yet you threatened to give her my icon."

"If I'd had to deal with her by myself, I could not risk her creating an ugly scene in front of Dominick," Jessica explained. "Like you, he is acutely sensitive and emotional. The damage she could do with a few words in a few minutes might take years to repair. But with you there, that risk dropped considerably. Still, I preferred she go away quietly. That is why I armed Phelps with a bribe."

Dain turned onto his side and pulled her into his arms. "You did right, Jess," he said. "I doubt I could have dealt with a sick child and his screaming mother simultaneously. I had my hands full—both of them—and my mind fully occupied with him."

"You were there for him," she said, stroking his hard, warm chest. "His big, strong papa was there for him, and that's all that matters now. He's home. He's safe. We'll take care of him."

"Home." He looked down at her. "This is permanent, then."

"Lady Granville brought up her husband's two bastards—by her aunt, no less—along with their own legitimate brats. The Duke of Devonshire's by-blows have grown up in his household."

"And the Marchioness of Dain can do what she damn well pleases and the hell with what anyone else thinks," said her husband.

"I do not mind starting my family with an eight-year-old boy," she said. "One can communicate with children at that age. They are very nearly human."

At that moment, as though on cue, an inhuman howl rent the early morning quiet.

Dain pulled away from her and bolted up to a sitting position.

"He's having a nightmare, that's all," Jessica said, trying to tug her husband back down. "Mary's with him."

"That caterwauling is coming from the gallery." He scrambled from the bed.

While he was pulling on his dressing gown, Jessica heard another earsplitting shriek . . . coming from the gallery, as Dain said. She heard other sounds as well. Other voices. And thumps. And the faint thudding of hurried footsteps.

Dain had already stalked out barefoot while Jessica was still trying to disentangle herself from the bed-clothes. She quickly donned her dressing gown and mules and hurried out after him.

She found him standing just outside the door, his arms folded over his chest, his expression inscrutable while he watched a naked eight-year-old boy race toward the south stairs, three servants in hot pursuit.

Dominick was but a few feet from the entryway when Joseph abruptly appeared in it. The boy instantly turned and ran back the way he'd come, dodging the adults trying to catch him and shrieking when they missed.

"It would appear that my son is an early riser," Dain said mildly. "What did Mary feed him for breakfast, I wonder? Gunpowder?"

"I told you he was devilish quick," Jessica said.

"He ran past me a moment ago," Dain said. "He saw me. Looked straight up at me and laughed—those screeches are laughter, you will note—and never broke stride. He went headlong toward the north door, stopped one half second short of dashing his brains out against it—turned, and ran back the other way. I collect he wants my attention."

She nodded.

Dain strode out into the gallery. "Dominick," he said, without raising his voice.

Dominick darted into an alcove. Dain followed him, picked him off the draperies he was attempting to climb up, and hoisted the child over his shoulder.

He carried Dominick into the master bedroom, then into the dressing room.

Jessica followed them only as far as the bedroom. She could hear her husband's low rumble and the higher-pitched tones of his son, but couldn't make out the words.

When they emerged from the dressing room a few minutes later, Dominick was wearing one of his father's shirts. The pleated front extended below the boy's waist, while both sleeves and hem trailed upon the carpet.

"He ate his breakfast and washed, but he refuses to don the skeleton suit because it makes him choke, he claims," Dain explained, while Jessica nearly choked trying to keep a straight face.

"This is Papa's shirt," Dominick told her proudly. "It's too big. But I can't be bare-arsed—"

"*Naked,*" Dain corrected. "You don't refer to your hindquarters when there are ladies present. Just as you don't gallop about with your pump handle waving in the wind—even if it is vastly amusing to hear the shocked females scream. Also, you do not make a great row at dawn's crack when my lady and I are trying to sleep."

Dominick's attention immediately went to the immense bed. His black eyes widened. "Is that the biggest bed in the world, Papa?"

He pushed up the sleeves of his shirt and, grabbing up two fistfuls of the fabric billowing about his scrawny legs, trotted to the bed and gaped at it.

"It's the biggest one in the house," said Dain. "King Charles the Second slept in that bed once. When the king visits, one must give him the largest bed."

"Did you put a baby inside her in that bed?" Dominick enquired, directing his stare to Jessica's belly. "Mama said you put me inside her belly in the biggest bed in the world. Is there a baby in there now?" he demanded, pointing.

"Yes," said His Lordship. Turning away from his startled wife, he walked to the bed and scooped his son up. "But it is a secret. You must assure me you won't tell anybody until I give you leave. Will you promise?"

Dominick nodded. "I promise."

"I know it will be difficult to keep such an interesting secret," Dain said. "But I'll make it up to you. In return for that special favor, I will let you be the one to surprise everybody with the news. That's a fair trade, isn't it?"

After briefly weighing the matter, Dominick again bobbed his head up and down.

It was clear by now that the two males had no trouble communicating. It was also clear that Dominick was, to all intents and purposes, clay in his papa's big hands. And the papa knew it.

Dain turned a smugly superior smile upon his bemused wife, then carried his son out.

He returned alone a moment later, still smiling.

"You are very sure of yourself," she said as he approached her.

"I can count," he said. "We've been wed five weeks and you have not pleaded indisposition once."

"It's much too soon to tell," she said.

"No, it isn't." He scooped Jessica up as easily as he had his son and carried her to the bed. "It is easy enough to calculate. One fertile marchioness plus one virile marquess equals a brat, sometime between Candlemas and Lady Day."

He did not put her down, but sat on the edge of the mattress, cradling her in his muscular arms.

"So much for hoping I could surprise you," she said.

He laughed. "You have been surprising me, Jess, since the day I met you. Every time I turn around, something goes off in my face. If it isn't an obscene watch or a rare icon, it's a pistol—or my tragically misunderstood mother—or my hellion son. There have been times I've been convinced I didn't marry a female, but an incendiary device. This at least makes sense." He tucked a wayward strand of hair behind her ear. "It is not in the least astounding that two people with insatiable carnal appetites have made a baby. That is perfectly natural and reasonable. It does not distress my delicate sensibilities in the least."

"That's what you say now." She smiled up at him. "But when I begin to swell up and grow moody and short-tempered, your nerves will become completely unstrung. And when the birthing starts, and you hear me yelling and cursing and wishing you at the Devil—"

"I'll laugh," he said. "Like the conscienceless brute I am."

She reached up to caress his arrogant jaw. "Ah, well, at least you're a handsome brute. And rich. And strong. And virile."

"It's about time you saw how fortunate you are. You have married the most virile man in the world." He grinned, and in his eyes, black as sin, she saw the devil inside him laughing. But he was her devil, and she loved him madly.

"The most conceited, you mean," she said.

He bent his head until his great Usignuolo nose loomed an inch from hers. "The most virile," he repeated firmly. "You are pathetically slow if you haven't learned that by now. Fortunately for you, I am the most patient of tutors. I shall prove it to you."

"Your patience?" she asked.

"And my virility. Both. Repeatedly." His black eyes glinted. "I will teach you a lesson you'll never forget."

She tangled her fingers in his hair and brought his mouth to hers. "My wicked darling," she whispered. "I should like to see you try."

Bad girls who can be so good . . .

Admit it. Women have known since they were teenagers that a sultry look, some flirtatious banter and perhaps a quick coat of lip gloss is often all the arsenal they need to get what they want. It's really quite unfair . . . But there's nothing more dangerously seductive than a bad girl who knows exactly what she wants and how to get it. Our heroes don't stand a chance!

In these thrilling Romance Superleaders, meet four sexy and unstoppable heroines who are determined—by any means, legal or otherwise—to get the man of her dreams.

Love Letters From a Duke
Elizabeth Boyle
September 2007

Felicity Langley had set her sights on being the next Duchess of Hollindrake. But then she hires a mysterious footman and finds herself reluctantly drawn to him. Whatever is a girl to do when all she ever wanted was to marry a duke and suddenly finds herself falling in love with the unlikely man at her side?

As the bell jangled again, Tally groaned at the clamor. "Sounds as presumptuous as a duke, doesn't it? Should I check the window for a coach and four before you answer it?"

Felicity shook her head. "That could hardly be Hollindrake." She nodded toward the bracket clock their father had sent them the year before. "It's too early for callers. Besides, he'd send around his card or a note before he just arrived at our doorstep. Not even a duke would be so presumptuous to call without sending word."

Sweeping her hands over her skirt and then patting her hair to make sure it was in place, Felicity was actually relieved it couldn't be her duke calling—for she still hadn't managed a way to gain them new wardrobes, let alone more coal. But she had a good week to solve those problems, at least until the House of Lords reconvened . . . for then Hollindrake would have to come to Town to formally claim his title and take his oath of allegiance.

"So who do you think it is?" Tally was asking as she clung to a squirming Brutus.

Taking another quick glance at the clock, Felicity let out a big sigh. "How could I have forgotten? The agency sent around a note yesterday that they had found us a footman who met our requirements."

Tally snorted. "What? He doesn't need a wage and won't rob us blind?"

Felicity glanced toward the ceiling and shook her head. "Of course I plan on paying him—eventually—and since we have nothing worth stealing, that shouldn't be an issue."

The bell jangled again, and this time Brutus squirmed free of his mistress's grasp, racing in anxious circles around the hem of Tally's gown and barking furiously.

Well, if there was any consolation, Felicity mused as she crossed the foyer and caught hold of the latch, whoever was being so insistent was about to have his boots ruined.

Taking a deep breath, she tugged the door open and found herself staring into a dark green greatcoat, which her gaze dismissively sped over for it sported only one poor cape. The owner stood hunched forward, the brim of his hat tipped down to shield him from the wintry chill.

"May I help you?" Felicity asked, trying to tamp down the shiver that rose up her spine. It wasn't that she'd been struck by a chill, for this mountain of a man was blocking the razor cold wind. No, rather, it was something she didn't quite understand.

And then she did.

As this stranger slowly straightened, the brim of his hat rose, revealing a solid masculine jaw—covered in a hint of dark stubble that did little to obscure the strong cleft in his chin, nor hide a pair of firm lips.

From there sat a Roman nose, set into his features with a noble sort of craggy fortitude. But it was his eyes that finally let loose that odd shiver through her limbs with an abandon that not even she could tamp down.

His gaze was as dark as night, a pair of eyes the color of Russian sable, mysterious and deep, rich and full of secrets.

Felicity found herself mesmerized, for all she could think about was something Pippin had once confessed—that from the very moment she'd looked into Captain Dashwell's eyes, she'd just known he was going to kiss her.

A ridiculous notion, Felicity had declared at the time. But suddenly she understood what her cousin had been saying. For right now she knew there was no way on earth she was going to go to her grave without having once had her lips plundered, thoroughly and spectacularly, by this man, until her toes curled up in her slippers and she couldn't breathe.

She didn't know how she knew such a thing, but she just did.

"I'm here to see Miss Langley," he said. His deep voice echoed with a craggy, smoky quality. From the authority in his taut stance, to the arch of his brow as he looked down at her—clearly as surprised to find a lady answering her own door as she was to find him standing on her steps—he left her staggering with one unbelievable thought.

And her shiver immediately turned to panic.

This is him, her heart sang. *Please let this be him.*

Hollindrake!

She struggled to find the words to answer him, but for the first time in her life, Felicity Langley found herself speechless. She moved her lips, tried to talk, tried to be sensible, but it was impossible under this imposing man's scrutinizing gaze.

Yet how could this be? What was *he* doing here, calling on her? And at such an unfashionable hour?

And no wonder he was staring at her, for her hair wasn't properly fixed, her dress four years out of fashion, and her feet—dear God, she'd answered the door wearing red wool socks!

Tally nudged her from behind. "Felicity, say something."

Reluctantly wrenching her gaze away from his mesmerizing countenance, composing herself, she focused on what it was one said to their nearly betrothed.

But in those few moments, Felicity's dazzled gaze took in the coat once again—with its shockingly worn cuffs. *Worn cuffs?* Oh no, that wasn't right. And where there should be a pair of perfectly cut breeches, were a pair of patched trousers. *Patched?* But the final evidence that cooled her wayward thoughts more thoroughly than the icy floor that each morning met her toes was the pair of well-worn and thoroughly scuffed boots, one of which now sported the added accessory of a firmly attached, small, black affenpinscher dog.

Boots that looked like they'd marched across Spain and back, boots that had never seen the tender care of a valet. Boots that belonged to a man of service, not a duke.

And certainly not the Duke of Hollindrake.

She took another tentative glance back at his face, and found that his noble and arrogant features still left her heart trembling, but this time in embarrassed disappointment.

To think that she would even consider kissing such a fellow . . . well, it wasn't done. Well, she conceded, it was. But only in all those fairy tales and French novels Tally and Pippin adored.

And that was exactly where such mad passions and notions of "love at first sight" belonged—between the covers of a book.

"You must be the man we've been expecting," Tally was saying, casting a dubious glance in Felicity's direction. Obviously unaffected by this man's handsome countenance, she bustled around and caught up Brutus by his hind legs, tugging at the little tyrant. "Sorry about that. He loves a good pair of boots. Hope these aren't your only pair."

A Touch of Minx
Suzanne Enoch
October 2007

Samantha Jellicoe and Richard Addison are at it again! Sam knows Rick wants more of a commitment from her—it's just so hard for a barely reformed thief to resist a golden opportunity to test her skills. But is she willing to risk losing her sexy billionaire lover?

For a second she hung in the air before she smacked into the palm's trunk and wrapped her arms and legs around it. That would have hurt if she hadn't worn jeans and a long-sleeved shirt. Black, of course; not only was the dark color slimming, but it was the clothing of choice for disappearing into shadows. Sucking in another breath, she shimmied up the rough trunk until she was about four feet above the house's roof.

The roof here at the back of the house was flat and had a very nice skylight set into the ceiling of the room she needed to get into. Glancing over her shoulder to make sure she was lined up, she pushed off backward, twisting in midair to land on her hands and knees on the rooftop. Keeping her forward momentum going, she somersaulted and came up onto her feet.

Normally speed wasn't as important as stealth, but tonight she needed to get into Richard Addison's office before he tracked her down. And for an amateur, he had a pretty good nose for larceny. Of course she was a damned bloodhound, if she said so herself.

With another smile she crouched in front of the skylight and leaned over to peer into the dark office space below. Just because he'd announced that he would wait for her to show up outside the door didn't mean that he'd done so. The padlock he'd put on the skylight stopped her for about twelve seconds, most of that taken up by the time it took her to dig the paper clip out of her pocket.

Setting the lock aside, she unlatched the skylight and carefully shoved it open, gripping the edge to lean in headfirst. The large room with its conference table, desk, and sitting area at one end looked empty, and her Spider-Man senses weren't wigging out.

Pushing off with her feet, she flipped head over hands and landed in the middle of the room, bending her knees to cushion her landing and cut down on any sound. A small black box topped by a red bow sat on the desk, but after a glance and a quick wrestling match with her curiosity, she walked past it to the refrigerator set into the credenza and pulled out a Diet Coke. Deliberately she walked to the office door, leaned against the frame, and popped the soda tab.

A second later she heard the distinctive sound of a key sliding into a lock, and the door handle flipped down. "Surprise," she said, taking a swallow of soda.

The tall, black-haired Englishman stopped just inside the doorway and glared at her. Blue eyes darkened to black in the dimness, but she didn't need light to read his expression. *Annoyed.* Rick Addison didn't like to be bested.

"You used the skylight, didn't you?" he said, making the sentence a statement rather than a question.

"Yep."

"I padlocked it an hour ago."

"Hello," she returned, handing him the Diet Coke. "Thief. Remember?"

"Retired thief." He took a drink and gave it back to her before he continued past her to the desk. "You didn't peek?"

"Nope. The thought never crossed my mind." Well, it had, but she hadn't given in, so that counted. "I wouldn't ruin your surprise."

When he faced her again, his mouth relaxed into a slight smile. "I was certain you'd attempt to get around me in the gallery hall."

"I went out through the library window. If I'da been a bomb, you would have been blowed up, slick."

Grabbing her by the front of the shirt, he yanked her up against him, bent his face down, and kissed her. Adrenaline flowed into arousal, and she kissed him back, pulling off her black leather gloves to tangle her bare fingers into his dark hair. A successful B and E was a lot like sex, and when she could actually combine the two, hoo baby.

"You smell like palm tree," he muttered, sweeping her legs out from under her and lowering her onto the gray carpeted floor.

"How do you think I got in here?"

Rick's hands paused on their trek up under her shirt. "You climbed up the palm tree?"

"It's the fastest way to go." She pulled his face down over hers again, yanking open the fly of his jeans with her free hand. She loved his body, the feel of his skin against hers. It amazed her that a guy who spent his days sitting at conference tables and computers and arguing over pieces of paper could have the body of a professional soccer player, but he did. And he knew how to use it, too.

He backed off a little again. "This was supposed to be fun, Samantha. Not you climbing up a tree and jumping onto a roof thirty feet in the air."

"That *is* fun, Brit. Quit stalling. I want my present." She shoved her hand down the front of his pants. "Mm, feels like you want to give it to me, too."

Halfway to the Grave
Jeaniene Frost
November 2007

Catherine Crawfield has more than a few skeletons in her closet. She's a vampire slayer with a big attitude, who makes an unlikely alliance with a vampire named Bones to track down an even more menacing evil. Though their chemistry is sizzling hot, how long can their dangerous association last?

"Beautiful ladies should never drink alone," a voice said next to me.

Turning to give a rebuff, I stopped short when I saw my admirer was as dead as Elvis. Blond hair about four shades darker than the other one's, with turquoise-colored eyes. Hell's bells, it was my lucky night.

"I hate to drink alone, in fact."

He smiled, showing lovely squared teeth. *All the better to bite you with, my dear.*

"Are you here by yourself?"

"Do you want me to be?" Coyly, I fluttered my lashes at him. This one wasn't going to get away, by God.

"I very much want you to be." His voice was lower now, his smile deeper. God, but they had great intonation. Most of them could double as phone-sex operators.

"Well, then I was. Except now I'm with you."

I let my head tilt to the side in a flirtatious manner that also bared my neck. His eyes followed the movement, and he licked his lips. *Oh good, a hungry one.*

"What's your name, lovely lady?"

"Cat Raven." An abbreviation of Catherine and the hair color of the first man who tried to kill me. See? Sentimental.

His smile broadened. "Such an unusual name."

His name was Kevin. He was twenty-eight and an architect, or so he claimed. Kevin was recently engaged, but his fiancée had dumped him and now he just wanted to find a nice girl and settle down. Listening to this, I managed not to choke on my drink in amusement. What a load of crap. Next he'd be pulling out pictures of a house with a white picket fence. Of course, he couldn't let me call a cab, and how inconsiderate that my fictitious friends left without me. How kind of him to drive me home, and oh, by the way, he had something to show me. Well, that made two of us.

Experience had taught me it was much easier to dispose of a car that hadn't been the scene of a killing. Therefore, I managed to open the passenger door of his Volkswagen and run screaming out of it with feigned horror when he made his move. He'd picked a deserted area, most of them did, so I didn't worry about a Good Samaritan hearing my cries.

He followed me with measured steps, delighted with my sloppy staggering. Pretending to trip, I whimpered for effect as he loomed over me. His face had transformed to reflect his true nature. A sinister smile revealed upper fangs where none had been before, and his previously blue eyes now glowed with a terrible green light.

I scrabbled around, concealing my hand slipping into my pocket. "Don't hurt me!"

He knelt, grasping the back of my neck.

"It will only hurt for a moment."

Just then, I struck. My hand whipped out in a practiced movement and the weapon it held pierced his heart. I twisted repeatedly until his mouth went slack and the light faded from his eyes. With a last wrenching shove, I pushed him off and wiped my bloody hands on my pants.

"You were right." I was out of breath from my exertions. "It only hurt for a moment."

Much later when I arrived home, I was whistling. The night hadn't been a total waste after all. One had gotten away, but one would be prowling the dark no more. My mother was asleep in the room we shared. I'd tell her about it in the

morning. It was the first question she asked on the week-
ends. *Did you get one of those things, Catherine?* Well, yes,
I did! All without me getting battered or pulled over. Who
could ask for more?

I was in such a good mood, in fact, that I decided to try
the same club the next night. After all, there was a dangerous bloodsucker in the area and I had to stop him, right? So
I went about my usual household chores with impatience.
My mother and I lived with my grandparents. They owned a
modest two-story home that had actually once been a barn.
Turned out the isolated property, with its acres of land, was
coming in handy. By nine o'clock, I was out the door.

It was crowded again, this being a Saturday night. The
music was just as loud and the faces just as blank. My initial
sweep of the place turned up nothing, deflating my mood a
little. I headed toward the bar and didn't notice the crackle
in the air before I heard his voice.

"I'm ready to fuck now."

"What?"

I whirled around, prepared to indignantly scald the ears
of the unknown creep, when I stopped. It was *him*. A blush
came to my face when I remembered what I'd said last night.
Apparently he'd remembered as well.

"Ah yes, well . . ." Exactly how did one respond to that?
"Umm, drink first? Beer or . . . ?"

"Don't bother." He interrupted my hail of the bartender
and traced a finger along my jaw. "Let's go."

"Now?" I looked around, thrown off guard.

"Yeah, now. Changed your mind, luv?"

There was a challenge in his eyes and a gleam I couldn't
decipher. Not wanting to risk losing him again, I grabbed my
purse and gestured to the door.

"Lead the way."

Lord of Scoundrels
Loretta Chase
December 2007

*Jessica Trent wants only to free her nitwit brother
from the destructive influence of Sebastian Ballister,
the notorious Marquess of Dain—she never expects to desire
the arrogant cad. But when they are caught in a scandal-
ously compromising position, will Jessica submit to her passion or will she have no choice but to seek satisfaction?*

*L*ord Dain did not look up when the shop bell tinkled.
He did not care who the new customer might be, and
Champtois, purveyor of antiques and artistic curiosities,
could not possibly care, because the most important customer in Paris had already entered his shop. Being the most
important, Dain expected and received the shopkeeper's exclusive attention. Champtois not only did not glance toward
the door, but gave no sign of seeing, hearing, or thinking
anything unrelated to the Marquess of Dain.

Indifference, unfortunately, is not the same as deafness.
The bell had no sooner ceased tinkling than Dain heard a
familiar male voice muttering in English accents, and an unfamiliar, feminine one murmuring in response. He could not
make out the words. For once, Bertie Trent managed to keep
his voice below the alleged "whisper" that could be heard
across a football field.

Still, it was Bertie Trent, the greatest nitwit in the Northern Hemisphere, which meant that Lord Dain must postpone
his own transaction. He had no intention of conducting a
bargaining session while Trent was by, saying, doing, and
looking everything calculated to drive the price up while un-

der the delirious delusion he was shrewdly helping to drive it down.

"I say," came the rugby-field voice. "Isn't that—Well, by Jupiter, it is."

Thud. Thud. Thud. Heavy approaching footsteps.

Lord Dain suppressed a sigh, turned, and directed a hard stare at his accoster.

Trent stopped short. "That is to say, don't mean to interrupt, I'm sure, especially when a chap's dickering with Champtois," he said, jerking his head in the proprietor's direction. "Like I was telling Jess a moment ago, a cove's got to keep his wits about him and mind he don't offer more than half what he's willing to pay. Not to mention keeping track of what's 'half' and what's 'twice' when it's all in confounded francs and sous and what you call 'em other gibberishy coins and multiplying and dividing again to tally it up in proper pounds, shillings, and pence—which I don't know why they don't do it proper in the first place except maybe to aggravate a fellow."

"I believe I've remarked before, Trent, that you might experience less aggravation if you did not upset the balance of your delicate constitution by attempting to *count*," said Dain.

He heard a rustle of movement and a muffled sound somewhere ahead and to his left. His gaze shifted thither. The female whose murmurs he'd heard was bent over a display case of jewelry. The shop was exceedngly ill lit—on purpose, to increase customers' difficulty in properly evaluating what they were looking at. All Dain could ascertain was that the female wore a blue overgarment of some sort and one of the hideously overdecorated bonnets currently in fashion.

"I particularly recommed," he went on, his eyes upon the female, "that you resist the temptation to count if you are contemplating a gift for your *chère amie*. Women deal in a higher mathematical realm than men, expecially when it comes to gifts."

"That, Bertie, is a consequence of the feminine brain having reached a more advanced state of development," said the female without looking up. "She recognizes that the selection of a gift requires the balancing of a profoundly complicated moral, psychological, aesthetic, and sentimental equation. I should not recommend that a mere male attempt to involve himself in the delicate process of balancing it, especially by the primitive method of *counting*."

For one unsettling moment, it seemed to Lord Dain that someone had just shoved his head into a privy. His heart began to pound, and his skin broke out in clammy gooseflesh, much as it had on one unforgettable day at Eton five and twenty years ago.

He told himself that his breakfast had not agreed with him. The butter must have been rancid.

It was utterly unthinkable that the contemptuous feminine retort had overset him. He could not possibly be disconcerted by the discovery that this sharp-tongued female was not, as he'd assumed, a trollop Bertie had attached himself to the previous night.

Her accents proclaimed her a *lady*. Worse—if there could be a worse species of humanity—she was, by the sounds of it, a bluestocking. Lord Dain had never before in his life met a female who'd even heard of an equation, let alone was aware that one balanced them.

Bertie approached, and in his playing-field confidential whisper asked, "Any idea what she said, Dain?"

"Yes."

"What was it?"

"Men are ignorant brutes."

"You sure?"

"Quite."

Bertie let out a sigh and turned to the female, who still appeared fascinated with the contents of the display case. "You promised you wouldn't insult my friends, Jess."

"I don't see how I could, when I haven't met any."

She seemed to be fixed on something. The beribboned and beflowered bonnet tilted this way and that as she studied the object of her interest from various angles.

"Well, do you want to meet one?" Trent asked impatiently. "Or do you mean to stand there gaping at that rubbish all day?"

She straightened, but did not turn around.

Bertie cleared his throat. "Jessica," he said determinedly, "Dain. Dain—Drat you, Jess, can't you take your eyes off that trash for one minute?"

She turned.

"Dain—m' sister."

She looked up.

And a swift, fierce heat swept Lord Dain from the crown of his head to the toes in his champagne-buffed boots. The heat was immediately succeeded by a cold sweat.

"My Lord," she said with a curt nod.

"Miss Trent," he said. Then he could not for the life of him produce another syllable.

Under the monstrous bonnet was a perfect oval of a porcelain white, flawless countenance. Thick, sooty lashes framed silver-grey eyes with an upward slant that neatly harmonized with the slant of her high cheekbones. Her nose was straight and delicately slender, her mouth soft and pink and just a fraction overfull.

She was not classic English perfection, but she was some sort of perfection and, being neither blind nor ignorant, Lord Dain generally recognized quality when he saw it.

If she had been a piece of Sevres china or an oil painting or a tapestry, he would have bought her on the spot and not quibbled about the price.

For one deranged instant, while he contemplated licking her from the top of her alabaster brow to the tips of her dainty toes, he wondered what her price was.

But out of the corner of his eye, he glimpsed his reflection in the glass.

His dark face was harsh and hard, the face of Beelzebub himself. In Dain's case, the book could be judged accurately by the cover, for he was dark and hard inside as well. His was a Dartmoor soul, where the wind blew fierce and the rain beat down upon grim, grey rocks, and where the pretty green patches of ground turned out to be mires that could suck down an ox.

Anyone with half a brain could see the signs posted: "ABANDON ALL HOPE, YE WHO ENTER HERE" or, more to the point, "DANGER. QUICKSAND."

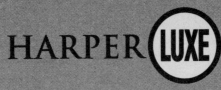